PRAISE FOR

WHERE
THE
DEAD
WAIT

"Haunting . . . ominous."

—*The New York Times Book Review*

"Spectacular . . . a breathtaking achievement."

—*Publishers Weekly* (starred review)

"Beautiful, brilliant writing about good men (and bad) facing the unimaginable. I was swallowed whole by Ally Wilkes's terrifying story of Arctic survival. Dare I say it's better than Dan Simmons's *The Terror*?"

—Alma Katsu, author of *The Fervor* and *The Hunger*

"Ally Wilkes weaves polar adventure and gothic horror together with wonderfully chilling results. The pages are full of creeping dread and malevolence that will linger with you long after you close the book."

—Christopher Golden, *New York Times* bestselling author of
The House of Last Resort

"An ice-cold brew of cannibalism and ghoulish horror served up by an author with a visceral feel for the extremes of polar exploration. Powerful stuff indeed!"

—Michelle Paver, critically acclaimed author of *Dark Matter*

"Harrowing and clawing with the iciest fingernails. The only thing harder to escape than the bloodthirsty sea is the longing and regret. *Where the Dead Wait* proves that the frozen nightmare is the domain of Ally Wilkes; we're just left to survive it."

—Hailey Piper, Bram Stoker Award–winning author of *Queen of Teeth*

"Chillingly, thrillingly existential, packed with heartache and dread. *Where the Dead Wait* is a Conradian trek into an Arctic heart of darkness, where the past is (literally) present, and the present marches us inch by inch toward our shared, unspeakable fate."

—Nat Cassidy, author of *Mary: An Awakening of Terror* and *Nestlings*

"*Where the Dead Wait* is a full-body plunge into nineteenth-century seafaring, Arctic survival, and the frigid darkness of the human psyche, in a setting as frostbitten and dread-inducing as the ghosts that haunt it. I was moved by Captain Day's inner war of longing and regret, and rewarded by the beautiful, immersive prose. With her second polar outing, Wilkes stakes her claim as the new ice-master of horror fiction."

—Luke Dumas, author of *The Paleontologist*

"An astonishing achievement. The writing is raw, bloody, and powerful, and makes me wonder if Ally Wilkes has fire and ice flowing in her veins. This is a book not so much to be described as experienced, so most definitely don't miss it!"

—Alison Littlewood, author of *The Hidden People*

"With *All the White Spaces*, Ally Wilkes chilled readers to the bone, and now with *Where the Dead Wait*, she sucks the very marrow out from them. Hallucinatory, haunting, and hunger-panged, this frostbitten novel gnawed away at my very sanity and I loved every nibble of it."

—Clay McLeod Chapman, author of *Ghost Eaters*

"Suffused with dread—and longing—from page one. A haunting read, in every sense of the word. I couldn't put it down!"

—S. A. Barnes, author of *Dead Silence*

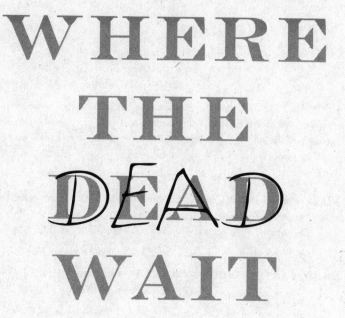

WHERE THE DEAD WAIT

ALLY WILKES

EMILY BESTLER BOOKS

—

ATRIA

NEW YORK   LONDON   TORONTO   SYDNEY   NEW DELHI

For all our past selves

An Imprint of Simon & Schuster, LLC
1230 Avenue of the Americas
New York, NY 10020

First Emily Bestler Books/Atria Paperback edition November 2024

EMILY BESTLER BOOKS / ATRIA PAPERBACK and colophon are trademarks of Simon & Schuster, LLC

Simon & Schuster: Celebrating 100 Years of Publishing in 2024

For information about special discounts for bulk purchases, please contact Simon & Schuster Special Sales at 1-866-506-1949 or business@simonandschuster.com.

The Simon & Schuster Speakers Bureau can bring authors to your live event. For more information or to book an event, contact the Simon & Schuster Speakers Bureau at 1-866-248-3049 or visit our website at www.simonspeakers.com.

Interior design by Erika R. Genova

Manufactured in the United States of America

1   3   5   7   9   10   8   6   4   2

Library of Congress Control Number: 2023940684

ISBN 978-1-9821-8282-3
ISBN 978-1-9821-8283-0 (pbk)
ISBN 978-1-9821-8284-7 (ebook)

Although this story's particular Arctic setting is fictional, the effects of European expeditions and colonial expansion are real and felt to this day. I acknowledge the Arctic as the ancestral homelands of the Inuit Peoples; I pay my respect to the lessons of resilience of these lands and Peoples, both past and present.

I desire the company of a man who could sympathize with me; whose eyes would reply to mine.

—MARY SHELLEY, *FRANKENSTEIN*

THEN

WHO CAN BRING A CLEAN THING OUT
OF AN UNCLEAN? NO ONE.

The smell hits Day in the face.

Crouching in the hut's narrow entrance, he tries not to heave. He can't afford to bring anything up: his last meal was boiled boots and lichen, supplementing the last of their rations. He presses a hand against his mouth. Grimy, his skin shriveled and yellowed, it looks more like a claw. All the fat has melted off him; even kneeling hurts. He's only twenty-four, but might as well be four-and-seventy. He knows he won't see another summer.

Day takes a deep breath. With his mouth covered, the smell is stronger, separates out into its component parts. Blubber, clinging to his nostrils. Urine, from the rusting can next to him—a latrine for those men too weak to make it outside. Sweat, layered deeper and deeper until it's something meaty. He pinches his nose, but now the smell comes in over his dry tongue and swollen gums, and he can almost taste it, like chewing on a week-old piece of liver.

It's cold, he thinks dully, *it shouldn't smell.*

Late summer in the Arctic, the temperature hovering around freezing, today's noonday sun staring down at them like a hole cut out of the sky.

This is a terrible place.

He squints. His eyes adjust to the gloom as his knees continue screaming. They all crawl around in here; there isn't enough space to stand. Nine faces look at him, pale and ghostly, eyes too large, huddled in their sleeping bags. The stillness is awful.

"What is it, Captain?"

William Day, now leader of the *Reckoning* expedition—not that he wanted it—crouches in the entrance to Camp Hope, and surveys his meager kingdom. The ceiling is the overturned hull of an eighteen-foot whaleboat, greenish and damp with condensation, and the walls are oars packed tight with boulders, moss, anything they could pry from the frozen ground with fingers and nails. Their sleeping bags are stacked in two lines facing each other, like galley slaves. A quiet sucking sound as someone wriggles their feet, disturbing the muddy surface, and their neighbor curses as the cold soup trickles slowly down the incline towards him.

It almost makes Day long for a good hard frost.

Almost.

"Captain?"

The speaker is young Tom Sheppard, and his concern sounds perfectly genuine. When Day finds him in the dark, Sheppard's got his journal clutched to his chest; he'd nursed it under his clothing all the way from the ship, taking it out each evening to cross the pages with a dense tight hand. There's a stubby pencil tucked behind his ear: Sheppard sometimes licks the tip with a pink tongue, not particularly caring where it's been. He's younger even than Day, barely into his twenties, all long lean legs, and had begged by post for a place on this expedition. Day can imagine him on the deck of an ironclad warship, the air redolent with gunpowder, sun on his face. Scribbling his appeal, touchingly expressing his faith in *the Open Polar C.*

Day stares at him. Wonders how he could have been so wrong: about a man, about the Open Polar Sea. About everything.

There's a shuffling in the entrance tunnel. Bent double, like a bear rooting out its prey, First Lieutenant Jesse Stevens pushes his way into the stinking warmth. Day can smell the cold on him, the unrelenting dark chill of the ice, and the men in the nearest sleeping bag sniff the air like bloodhounds. They're all animals here.

"You have to tell them," Stevens says. He has a very pointed nose, and the Cupid's bow of his lips has never been disturbed by swelling gums. Scurvy tore through their party back on the ship: now starvation is the nearest cause of death, though it's truthfully hard to distinguish the two. But Stevens's mouth has never bled, and in the dim light of the single blubber lamp he still looks handsome: golden hair and thick red-tinged beard. The angel on Day's shoulder.

Day finds himself shaking his head.

There's a murmur from the men; a small sound of interest, at the two of them in disagreement, and Stevens gives him a look. He doesn't say it out loud, but Day can hear as clearly as if he'd shouted. They don't need words, the two of them.

If you won't do it, I will.

"What is it?" Sheppard says again, in his lilting southern accent. His eyes are wide and apparently guileless, but then, they all have wide eyes now. Skin retreats, hollows out, as their bodies consume themselves. Sheppard looks between Day and Stevens, then back again. A mute expression of horror as he appreciates the danger he's in.

Day puts down the bundle he carries. He notices, with some interest, that he's trembling. "Second Lieutenant Tom Sheppard. You're under arrest."

A sharp intake of breath.

"What?"

"You heard him," Stevens says softly, from his position just behind Day.

Day's hands shake as he pulls back the cloth, displaying the contents of the bundle they'd found concealed by the creek. A few pieces of hardtack, dried to the texture of a raisin and the hardness of a cannonball; Day estimates—as dispassionately as possible, trying to swallow down the rush of saliva—that this represents the daily ration for four or five men, depending on how carefully it's broken up. A Virginia tobacco tin, filled with fuel alcohol. The sealskin cloth itself, when they've been chewing anything they can get their hands on, anything that will keep mouth and teeth busy, when the rations are so meager as not to be worth the name.

Men crane their necks to look at these treasures, because that's what they are: treasures. It's nearly a year since they left the ship.

If Sheppard were merely *hoarding*, Day might have been able to find a way to show mercy. He could maybe have confined him to his sleeping bag, like poor Blackman near his end, lashed in tight as the delirium of scurvy made him babble, sing snatches of hymns, and bend his wrists back at the joints, crab-like and pained.

But that kindly narrative is no longer possible. In the dim light of Camp Hope, the gleaming copper handful of rifle cartridges tells all. They make a chinking sound in Day's shaking hands.

"You're under arrest for theft and attempted desertion—"

"You dirty bastard—" one of the men bellows, and tries to crawl from his sleeping bag to launch himself at Sheppard. Kicking and thrashing, the struggling man has to climb over several others, and there's a shriek of pain, a horrible stink, as he crosses Campbell, whose feet are badly frostbitten. A hubbub of raised voices. Coughs and splutters. Shadows dancing around the walls.

Sheppard doesn't move, his mouth hanging open in a perfect circle of surprise, making him look almost unbearably young.

His attacker bares his remaining teeth, clenches his fist laboriously. Day doubts he has the strength to do any real damage, but it's the principle of the thing. Now, more than ever—*today*, more than ever, with what Day knows is up on that grave-ridge—discipline is important.

There's a sharp taste in his throat when he thinks of the grave-ridge, and once again he has to fight the urge to heave.

"Have Sheppard separated," Day says to Stevens.

His second-in-command nods.

They go out to execute young Tom Sheppard later in the evening, well before civil twilight falls. It's nearly all the same in the Arctic summer, where daylight never truly relents, but Day wanted to give Sheppard time to make peace with his god.

He doesn't see how such a thing would be possible, himself: there's no god at Cape Verdant. Ewing, sensitive Ewing, sometimes leads them in bleating prayer, but they have only one Bible left. All the others have long since been torn up for kindling. Nearly every single verse in that lonely Bible has been underlined, pages thumbed translucent with greasy fingers, and someone has ripped out the book of Job, so beloved by their dead Captain Talbot. Sheppard leaves the Bible behind when Day and the other officers come to fetch him; places his hand flat on its cover for a moment, as if trying to absorb some—comfort? Absolution? Day doesn't know.

The grave-ridge looms, watchful, above their camp: the overturned boat and red tent sit in its long horseshoe shadow, protected from the gales blowing in across the frozen water. The signal flag flaps in the hollow breeze.

They haven't bothered to tie up their prisoner—there's nowhere to go from this rocky little semicircle of land. Miles of featureless gravel cliffs to the west; ice to the north, east, and south, shining like a shattered mirror. It seems to rotate like a puzzle whenever you turn your back. Look, to the east: a berg shaped like a bear. Now it's turned to face south. Now it's crept back on itself. Now it's sunk out of existence. You can make it into anything, anything the mind can conjure.

Visibility in the channel ends after a few hundred yards, and the haze never seems to lift entirely, not for pounding sun nor howling winds. Day thinks there's never been anywhere more cut off, more profoundly distant from all human civilization, than Cape Verdant. Even the name is a lie. The ground is hard black rock, sharp enough to cut their hands.

This land is savage. Here all savagery dwells.

Perhaps Sheppard hasn't run because he hopes Day will relent; hopes his inexperienced acting commander will stumble over the limits of his own authority (*can* he have a man executed?) or, more likely, can't bring himself to bury yet another body. Day isn't a hard man, after all.

But *hope*—the word has become something they spit, sneer, imbue with all the irony of dying men.

Day swallows. The exertion of climbing the shallow ridge has him bent nearly double. Up here, the peaceless wind tugs at his tattered clothing, scours the dirt and shrapnel away from the row of graves. He steers the party until they're out of sight. He feels, rather than sees, Penn's brass buttons winking through their thin covering of gravel. The dead are always watching; reminding him of their presence. As if he could forget.

He didn't want this. He didn't want any of this.

"I will—" He coughs. "I will read the order." He pulls it out. His own handwriting looks like a swarm of ants, barely recognizable.

"Second Lieutenant Thomas Sheppard, trusted with our only firearm, has been found stealing food and ammunition. Those taken together show he intends to abandon his colleagues to their deaths . . ." Day moistens his wind-chapped lips. "Abandon his colleagues to their deaths by starvation. These actions display a wickedness"—his voice drops—"and treachery that cannot be tolerated. Sheppard is therefore to be shot today, as we have no sure means to confine him."

Sheppard continues to stare up at him, trusting. Day wishes he'd look away. Sees, in his mind's eye, Sheppard's hand lingering on that Bible, fingertips pressed lightly on the cover.

"This is necessary for the expedition to survive. After the death of Captain Nicholas Talbot, I, William Day, give this order."

It's the day after their rations finally ran out. He'd consulted with the doctor, with their scratched-off calendar, to get the date as accurate as possible. Keeping a record is the bread and butter of any officer; this scrap of paper will explain what happened here, whether or not it will ever be read by another living being. It shows he had good reason, legitimate reason, to execute Sheppard. The paper feels commensurately heavy. It's precious.

Day looks around. They have only one working rifle, the one Sheppard usually wears. Normally there'd be some anonymity for executions: several guns, one loaded, allowing each man to comfort himself with the thought that the fatal bullet came from another. But what are they going to do—get out knives, up here in the open air, and take him to ground like prey?

"Stand still," Stevens says, gently. Stevens is a good shot, good at everything to which he turns his hand. He'd volunteered. Day had noted, with leaden humor, that it wasn't as if there were any chance of missing. Stevens had shrugged, pale eyes narrowing.

Day realizes now that Stevens thinks Sheppard might run. The sun shines down on them, makes Day's skin itch.

"I didn't do it," Sheppard says suddenly. He seems to come to his senses, recognize where he is: out on the grave-ridge, surrounded by the emaciated officers who'd survived the *Reckoning*.

They shouldn't have left the ship, Day thinks, with a clarity that startles him.

Sheppard must be freezing, because he hadn't put his mittens on after relinquishing that Bible, but it hardly matters now. He turns around, looks Day in the eye. "Please! I didn't. You have to believe me!"

Day won't look away. He won't. Sheppard deserves this much.

"Did *you* find it, Captain?" Sheppard says urgently. "Captain—the things they're saying I stole—it wasn't you, was it? I've been set up—*Stevens*—"

Stevens steps forward, rifle raised. The expression on his face is almost unreadable.

But Day knows him better than anyone.

———

Their grim duty complete, the execution party crawls back inside the overturned boat of Camp Hope. They'll have to bury Sheppard in the morning; he's been left to freeze, up where the clouds are starting to blow out sleet. He's just a body now.

"Camp No-Hope," Campbell mutters, his gaze feverish. "I'm going to die in here."

Campbell hasn't been out of his sleeping bag in nearly a week, not even to use the latrine tin, his system torpid on their diet of mostly inedible things. The smell from his bag tells them his legs are likely lost; the doctor says operating in these conditions will kill him from lockjaw.

"They're gonna murder me," Campbell mutters. "Kill me and eat me. Dead weight, I've heard them saying it. I've *heard* 'em."

He doesn't specify who—but conversations are broken off as the execution party returns. Sheppard had been very popular amongst the men, sometimes conducting careful "interviews" that seemed to consist largely of noting down their favorite songs, meals, girls. Any distraction was welcome. He'd also trained with their Native hunters, now long gone and much missed, along with all the larger game. He'd brought in an Arctic fox here, a hare there: Day had joined the others in insisting Sheppard must have the largest portions, their chewy little hearts. Still barely a mouthful. But they had to keep his strength up.

"I won't let you down," Sheppard had said quietly to Day, with all the earnestness of youth. Day feels ancient by comparison, warped and stretched like refractions in ice. "I won't let us starve."

But now James, who used to share Sheppard's sleeping bag, is bartering his way out of that sodden sheepskin and into the relative comfort of buffalo. Sheppard's possessions have become the camp's new currency. Every man for himself.

Stevens nudges Day. He doesn't need to speak.

Day knows he should insist Sheppard's diary is located and turned over. It's expedition property and should be surrendered. But Sheppard lies unburied, and Day's heart squeezes. He can't bring himself to do it.

Stevens gives him a look that's a whisker from insubordination, and sighs. Day's thought of sharing his sleeping bag, yearned for it— curling in beside him for the heat, their bodies together making a semicolon, two separate but closely connected ideas. They'd done so back on the *Reckoning*, when it was so cold belowdecks that the thermometers froze, but he doesn't know how it would look to the men.

"Captain," the doctor says urgently, emerging from the canvas flap at the rear of the hut. The horrible ruin of his face, crisscrossed with scars, makes him look like a gargoyle half-eaten by weather.

Day crawls down the small gangway. Behind the flap, beside their stove, Paver lies dying, his eyelids sometimes fluttering as if struggling to wake from a dream. Day hopes he's somewhere else entirely. He's been given the liquid from the soup they made yesterday, lichen and the last of the crumbled biscuit, the consistency of thin snot.

It's the day after their rations finally ran out.

"How long?"

"Tomorrow, maybe," Doctor Nye says, taking off his broken glasses to polish them. It would be humorous—an affectation, they're all so grubby—if it weren't so pitiful. "His organs are shutting down."

Paver feels boiling hot to the touch when Day loosens his collar, presses a hand to his throat. It's probably an illusion.

"The others will die," Nye says, and Day reads accusation in his tone. "We will all *die*."

There's still no sign of night, and the sky crowds in on them.

Day sends Stevens up onto the grave-ridge with Jackson; now, he supposes, Second Lieutenant Jackson. Normally no one leaves the hut after dinner—which tonight is just tea dust; they can hardly spare the fuel to boil water—and they settle down to discuss food, maddeningly, right down to the drinks and desserts, conjuring five-course meals from the air. Raisin pudding with condensed milk. Hot rum and lemon punch. There's a hallucinatory realness to it.

But this evening, trying not to listen, trying not to let it gnaw at him, Day had caught snatches of whispered conversation.

"Someone will be held responsible—"

"Another few weeks, and then, and then, if no one comes—"

They suspect that this is a closed season: Lancaster Sound is blocked to the whaling fleets by the same ice they can see off Cape Verdant. And so rescue is unlikely to come, and they will continue to dwindle, far from civilization, in a state of pure savagery. Not even the Bible can save them now.

When Stevens returns from the grave-ridge, he has a glint to his sharp eyes. Jackson, on the other hand, looks sick; pale, greenish. Day meets them outside, where he's been pacing and looking up at that teeming sky, whispering curses.

"Is it done?"

Stevens gives a single nod. Day would rather have Stevens by his side than a thousand other men. He's golden, from his hair to his hard-edged glitter; his value. Day couldn't have done this without him.

"It wasn't hard to cut," Stevens says quietly.

Sheppard hadn't yet grown cold.

Someone will be held responsible.

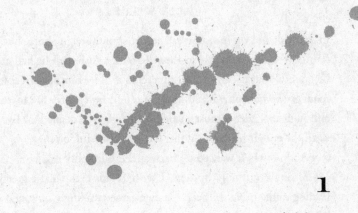

1

NOW

I: LOST
LONDON, JANUARY 5, 1882

The relentless symmetry of the Admiralty building had always given Day a headache. Columns rose regularly, disappeared in orderly and predictable lines like soldiers, and square ceilings pressed down on him, a stone sky, like being buried under the earth. Looking to his right, he saw a set of mirrors marching off into the distance, reflecting him into eternity—unbroken, undistorted. A hundred perfect William Days, as if he'd come back from the Arctic shining and whole. He looked away quickly. He almost preferred the spitting, hissing rain outside, although this wasn't proper weather, merely the suggestion of it.

They'd been expecting him. He didn't dare hope this was a good thing. Some Admiralty man might have guffawed, slapped his thigh with mean glee: "Do you know who's come forwards about the Stevens rescue? Do you *know*? Who does he think he is?"

Day rubbed his forehead, surreptitiously tried to get some of the rain out of his hat. Water pooled around his uncomfortable chair, his coat dripping like a shipwrecked mariner. Fitting, because—on his return from America all those years before—he had indeed been marooned; not on a distant island, or some foreign shore, but in his family's three-story house in Russell Square. Although he had cause to be grateful that his father and supercilious older brother had somehow managed to pass on without him, and he'd never *want* for anything—although that idea almost made him laugh—it meant he'd live alone until the end of his days. Alone, but not quite forgotten.

And now he'd washed up back at the Admiralty again.

Sitting even more upright, Day fixed his eyes on the green door leading to the private offices. Change came creakingly slow, and everything was still as he remembered it from that rather cursory "investigation" years ago. The *Reckoning* expedition had never quite been under conventional Admiralty command, hence no court-martial, and no one had wanted indecent things to be made public; he supposed he was one of those indecent things.

Turning his hands over, he inspected them for cleanliness. Neat fingernails. His hands were soft. He would be forty in a few years, and his mid-brown hair was streaked firmly with licks of gray at his temples. His face was an honest one, people said, when they wanted to be kind. An ugly scar on the back of his left hand made him self-conscious; there were only so many situations in which one could wear gloves indoors. People always assumed it was something dramatic. He was quick to disabuse them: said it was an accident in the rigging as a midshipman, and they looked disappointed.

He wasn't—quite—the monster people said he was.

But he'd always known, even back then, that William Day could never be fully exonerated. Not in the eyes of the public, or the press, or God. It would be madness to try. He could see them now, just as clearly as before: all those whisperers in uniform, elbowing one another when they saw him, falling silent as he passed through these echoing halls.

Murderer. Cannibal.

The green door opened, and a man left in high temper; he was very pale, with high well-bred cheekbones, a swoop of mahogany hair, and a face like curdled milk. Another, older, followed him by walking stick and determination, upper lip and chin covered with badgery whiskers.

"It's hardly to be borne," the younger hissed. "*Him?* Hopkins has over-stepped himself this time, the Arctic Council will—"

"Oh, the council will, will it?" the old man said with coolness. "The council has nothing to do with it. Let them sort this new disaster out themselves."

They broke off, abruptly, when they saw Day sitting there, back pressed against the wall as if he were trying to disappear. "Excuse me," he said.

The pale man made a strangled noise and grabbed his companion by the arm, ushering him quickly and roughly around the corner, out of sight. Day heard them speaking to each other in hushed voices, and swallowed. He'd seen the widening eyes, the flicker of contemptuous recognition: the moment he was judged instantly on the basis of the worst things he might ever have done.

Lieutenant Day of the *Reckoning*.

Or, as the papers insisted on calling it, *the* Reckoning *disaster*. His likeness had been passed around the illustrated news, a monster with beard and wild hair. *Desperate and emaciated*, they said, and it was utterly true: desperation was the natural state of Cape Verdant.

Day sighed. Who did he think he was? Stevens, his former second-in-command, had left civilization and disappeared once again into the frozen north. He, at least, still believed in the Open Polar Sea. But only two years of provisions, for an expedition three years lost— despite Stevens's winking insistence that they could fend for them-selves, Day knew the idea of such a large party surviving on hunting was ludicrous. The crew of the *Arctic Fox* would by now be on short rations, shortening rations, maybe no rations at all.

Day, more than anyone, knew what that was like.

"Mr. Day." A face appeared. "Captain William Hopkins." The stranger offered his hand. He had eyes set close together, like some small carnivorous animal, all sleek fur and pointed nose. "Won't you come in? I'm sorry to have kept you waiting."

The room beyond the green door was dimly lit, a fire in the grate, rain tap-tapping half-heartedly against the windowpanes. By the fireplace, twin high-backed armchairs in olive velvet, and a low table covered with correspondence and newspaper cuttings. The room looked disordered, but Day immediately had the impression that its occupant knew where to lay his hands on every single scrap of paper.

"Sit, please," Hopkins said. Although the sky outside was too lazy to snow, the room was warm; Day could feel the heat start to suffocate him. A large chart table displayed the official map of the Northwest Passage, and Hopkins bumped into it, with an air of annoyance, on his way to the liquor cabinet.

Day accepted a whisky. Hopkins sat opposite. Up close, he was even younger than Day had first appreciated. But something about him appealed. He seemed like the rare kind of person who got things done.

"I had hoped to speak with the First Lord," Day said delicately.

Hopkins frowned. "But he's busy, busy. You know. Resources. Egypt."

Day took a sip of whisky. He rarely drank, and it sat like acid inside him, in the tight hard knot of disappointment that had been building since he'd reached the Admiralty. Of *course* there were resource issues. Of course he'd come for nothing, and Stevens would be abandoned to his fate. Just another lost Arctic expedition, an American one at that.

Another act of vast indifference by the machine of British bureaucracy.

"If there's another time, perhaps—"

"Not at all. I'm the one who answered you, Mr. Day. Needs must."

Needs must—and the other half of the saying, *when the devil drives.* It reminded Day so strongly of Jesse Stevens that he found a prickling sensation running down his spine.

"The Stevens business is a concern of mine. Here—take a look." Hopkins leaned forwards, perched on one bony buttock, and plucked something from the pile of papers between them. With a creeping sense of humiliation, one that made sweat gather under his arms, Day recognized some of those newspaper cuttings.

They came back in iron caskets! shrieked the headlines. Just six caskets, sealed for repatriation, to hide decomposition and—the rest. The separation of spirit and body, played out in ruthless and gruesome detail. All those other lives extinguished in the Arctic, left behind without a trace.

Hopkins, like everyone else, had heard the very worst about him.

The velvet cushions exhaled as Hopkins handed something to Day, with arched eyebrow, and sat back again. But it wasn't what he'd expected: letters, addressed in a feminine hand to the First Lord. It felt wrong to be handling someone else's correspondence.

For the sake of the debt which at least one *of your countrymen owes my husband*—

Day's wrists prickled. He tried to put it down to the heat of the room, but there was something about that scrawling hand, and its vehement message. A debt.

Shame.

"I don't suppose you ever met Mrs. Stevens?"

Day shook his head, swallowing the sour taste in his mouth. "They married after I'd left America."

After he'd fled back to England to escape the reporters and the rumors and that horrible nickname, the one that followed him everywhere. He hadn't even been invited to the wedding; there was no place for William Day at the feast. He found it hard to imagine Stevens married. Hard to imagine him anywhere but at Day's own side.

"People say, don't they, that he's a great man. But you can imagine how indifferent the council has been, after that . . . Passage business."

He wouldn't say the name of Sir John Franklin out loud, and Day supposed he knew why: two ships lost, hundreds of men, nearly as many search parties, and all the Admiralty had got out of it was that line on the map, showing a wavering ice-filled strait, never seen passable. Quite useless to the plans of empire.

Hopkins refilled Day's glass. "Mrs. Stevens"—a small snort at the name, as if the title were reserved for those of a loftier character—"is determined that her husband is still alive. Tell me, Mr. Day—do you believe the same?"

That was, after all, why he was here, in the third winter of Stevens's expedition. Day couldn't believe—refused to believe—that Stevens was dead. The man would have found a way to survive. He might be chewing on frozen blubber with the Natives. He might be manning the darkness of an ice-locked ship, hunting rats in the hold, *small deer*. He might even be eating his own boots. But he was alive. The north couldn't kill that ceaseless, searching ambition.

And Day would know when Stevens died.

How could he not?

"Yes, absolutely," Day said without hesitation.

"Good." Hopkins unfolded his arms. "Good. Because you're going to find him."

Day stared at him, a small, uncomfortable flame of hope sparking into life.

"You've saved us the bother of asking." Hopkins leaned forwards. "Myself—I'd have expected you to come begging before now." It stung, and Day took a swallow of whisky to cover it. "You have no supporters, no—let's be candid—no prospect of ever returning to service." He drummed his fingers on the table. "I've located a ship. On behalf of backers who wish to keep their interest in Stevens . . . confidential. The council disapproves? Well, I'm not a member of that council. And the Admiralty has no more appetite for the north—not after the Passage, and then *you*."

Day flinched at the callous economy of it. Two unconscionable disasters, one after another. Franklin and his one hundred and thirty-four men. William Day and his *Reckoning*. They'd both ended up gnawing on human bones, the *last desperate resource*.

A polite euphemism for cannibalism.

"Not an Admiralty ship," Hopkins was saying. "A small expedition, crewed by whalers, and the Navy will loan you a handful of officers. But it hasn't come cheap. If something were to happen, I would expect every effort to be made for the ship's preservation. That should be paramount." He paused, scowling. "Not abandoned, or sunk, or *lost*—hmm?"

The rain rapped on the windowpane.

"You were lucky you escaped court-martial the last time—but, I suppose, what was there to say? It must have been damned hard to watch." Hopkins said this last with an air of grudging sympathy, captain to captain, as if inviting confidences. "No wonder the others never spoke of it."

Losing one's ship was always thought to be the worst disaster.

Day found his gaze going to the painting behind Hopkins's head. It showed a storm-tossed sea of ice, lit with unforgiving slashes of gray and white. A ship's splintered masts reached to the sky, and the mouth of the deep was opening. As the light shimmered, and the rain beat down outside, he could suddenly hear the waves crashing; the ice gnawing, crunching; the creak of her timbers. A dying ship, singing her death song, as loud as the silence following her end.

"I've read your statement," Hopkins was saying, a glint in his eye. "*Lost?* As if she was yours to lose." He steepled his fingers. "She took a nip. She went down."

Day swallowed. Nodded his queasy agreement.

"You'll *lose* no more ships. I've put a great deal of my influence behind this."

The mask of genial, conversational diligence slid off. The eyes of the creature sitting in the chair were the half-glimpsed flares of distant cannon, and sweat trickled down Day's back. Hopkins's gaze was the simultaneous indifference and greed of empire. He might sit here beside his fire and receive a butcher's bill featuring scurvy, frostbite, debility, pneumonia, or any one of the horrible ways to die in the Arctic. He'd receive it without blinking. He cared about his reputation, which was all.

"Do you understand?"

Day swallowed. "Yes." *Vividly*, he thought.

"I've turned down the rest of the contenders, you'll be pleased to hear," Hopkins said, easy again. "You know the man, after all. You know how he thinks."

Day looked away quickly. *Did anyone really know Jesse Stevens*, he wanted to say.

But this—a new command. A new purpose. It was like being dragged back from beyond the veil; like having new life beaten, painfully, into him. The rain knocked on the windowpanes, and the grandfather clock in the waiting room started to chime. The answering thud in Day's chest, the tightness around his ribs, make him press a fist to his sternum. His body, at least, knew that failure would be synonymous with death.

"To the details." Hopkins stood. "You'll sail via Greenland this coming season. Investigate those reports from the whaling ships. Look for cairns—wreckage. We might as well assume Stevens is retreading your own disastrous route—"

"Not mine." His mouth was dry.

"I'm sorry?"

"It wasn't my route. Captain Talbot commanded the *Reckoning*, until his death at God-Saves Harbor. I was his fourth lieutenant. Nothing more."

"Of course, I forget." Hopkins obviously hadn't. He looked amused.

On the chart table, there was Baffin Bay, the once-fertile whaling grounds off west Greenland. Lancaster Sound opened to the west, and through that sound, bobbing about in a treacherous expanse of ice, was Beechey Island: the site of the Franklin relics. Then Talbot's Channel, named for their own doomed expedition, headed north and west towards—what?

Talbot had thought he'd known. He'd been wrong.

"I did my best!" Day said. "When scurvy took all the other officers, the ship was . . . she was lost." He twisted his hands together, his heart pounding.

A pause.

"I took command, and led the men overland and through the ice, for nearly three hundred miles, to—"

Shame squeezed his throat.

"To somewhere you couldn't cross forty miles of water," Hopkins said darkly. "While Jesse Stevens somehow made it out."

Day realized he'd been shouting. He didn't dare look at Hopkins. He picked up his whisky glass, hoping to hide the tremor in his hands. "If anyone is to be blamed for what happened—"

"Then it shouldn't be you," Hopkins said softly. "I see." He smiled slightly.

They both knew what the papers said, though.

Day took a deep breath, held it in abeyance. It had been twelve years, three months, and eleven days since he'd left Camp Hope: the overturned boat, the hideous flapping butcher's tent. The grave-ridge. He'd left his reputation on the grave-ridge.

"*They mean to eat me!*" Campbell had shrieked in those picture-post illustrations. "*They mean to kill and eat me tho' I'm very much alive!*"

A story to chill all hearts, with a sick man slaughtered like cattle by the very commander who ought to have protected him. And its conclusion: William Day, a monster.

"How you must have waited, for a chance to undo the stain," Hopkins said softly. A pause. "You *will* go, won't you."

"Yes. Yes, I—I'm very grateful." Day felt it coming up from his chest, a slow tingling warmth that burned as it rose. "Captain Hopkins. I'm very grateful."

The rain drummed on.

"Good. Your command comes with caveats, though," Hopkins said abruptly. "You won't like who you're taking with you."

Day stared. "I beg your pardon?"

Hopkins handed him a newspaper. Day's heart sank at the masthead, then sank further at the photograph, dropping right into his polished boots.

The woman in the picture was not attractive, exactly: she had thick dark hair inclined towards waves, sternly center parted, and a rounded face. *Striking*, that was the word, but Day was no connoisseur of female beauty. One hand resting on a polished and grinning skull, she stared at the camera through deep-set eyes.

Olive Emeline Stevens, one of America's most famous spirit mediums, although after marriage she'd confined her talents to more private sittings; it was even said she'd hand-picked men to watch over her husband in the Arctic. He made out an engraving on the wall behind her: "out of the animal's darkness into the angel's marvelous light."

Day had seen enough of that animal darkness to desperately wish such a thing might be possible.

Hopkins tapped the photograph. Day's thoughts went, vexingly, to their little cabin on the *Reckoning*: Jesse Stevens crammed in beside him on the horsehair mattress, boots beating out a lazy rhythm on the ship's wooden backbones. Stevens was no husband, Day thought. Whatever else he was—

"Yes, I know." Hopkins waved away his objections. "The Arctic is no place for the gentle sex, despite any custom of the whaling captains. You'd think, wouldn't you, that they'd be glad to leave their wives behind?"

That wasn't what Day had been going to say: if his face had worn horror, it had been the image of Stevens, casual in his bed, that had crowded into his mind; the accompanying warmth crawling up his spine, making his clothes too tight and too hot.

"And Mrs. Stevens says she's used to adventure. I daresay she has a cohort of invisible Native spirit guides" (another snort) "to defend her honor. You can deposit her on the depot ship at the first hint of danger. She needn't go anywhere you don't want her. She needn't necessarily see wherever you find her husband."

The Admiralty man paused, delicately. "In whatever—conditions— you eventually find him."

The waiting room was empty.

Day put his back to the green door, and exhaled. He'd been in there for hours. It had seemed like a lifetime—but then, he supposed, it had taken their Savior three days to be raised from the tomb.

He was to come back tomorrow, Hopkins had said sharply, and the day after. Things would be done *properly* this time. They'd already come to loggerheads over the naval lists, Hopkins continuously circling back to a certain Joseph Adams Lee, with his grandfather (that badger-haired gentleman) on the Arctic Council. "Given I've expended significant capital—and political goodwill—on this venture, I was hoping he'd be the natural choice for your second-in-command." Drumming his fingers. Day remembered well his encounter with Lee the younger: the pinched white face, the look of disapproval, that boiling pit of shame. He could read Hopkins's annoyance in the bounce of his neatly clad knee.

Day rubbed his jaw, hardly able to believe that he'd got away with any of it.

Outside, the rain had stopped, and a grim illumination filtered through the windows, cracked open to let in the chill air of London winter. A moth battered against the pane, attracted to the light but unable to find its way out; Day knew what it was like to be doomed to batter endlessly against something cold and hard. A boy was shouting at the gates, hawking newspapers.

Day felt his empty stomach clench. He'd been very careful not to be seen.

"Horrible end in the ice!" the boy was yelling. "The *Reckoning* lost!"

No. Had he heard that right?

His head felt full of hull-cracking pressure at the idea people might be talking about him already. Stevens was a hero, after all, and William Day just a joke to any giggling urchin who—growling, beast-like—pretended to gnaw ravenously at his own limbs. Day's neighbors in Russell Square would be sitting down to their papers, pipes in hand, glancing nervously at their flocked wallpaper. How thin and fragile, those walls separating them from a monster. Civilization from desperation.

He stared up at the portraits, trying to work up the courage to step out; he gave Jane, Lady Franklin, a look of sympathy. She didn't belong here, either—who had she been, before her husband was lost? Then she'd turned up at every meeting of the Arctic Council, been politely laughed out of countless rooms of white-haired explorers. Launched increasingly frantic appeals for Lord Franklin's rescue. She must have suffered greatly.

He knew how she felt.

A breath of sharp air made him glance behind himself. The mirrors reflected the window, and in the dim light of late afternoon, the hundred perfect Days had vanished. The room was shadowy. A grandfather clock beat the time, perfect and unrelenting, malicious, every second taking the Stevens expedition further from his reach.

Lady Jane's eyes were a kind of warning.

The painting on the opposite wall was a romantic view of a group of fur-clad Arctic Highlanders—Natives from the far north of Greenland, past Cape York. The light from their fire flickered on ruddy faces, picked an opening in the ice out of darkness. But sidling into the corner of the painting, insinuating himself into the scene, peering over their shoulders—

Stevens was back.

He never walked through walls, or rattled chains, or did anything Day associated with ghosts. Stevens was still alive, after all; their connection unsevered. This Stevens was hazy and indistinct, appearing only in glimpses: in paintings, in photographs, in mirrors. Anywhere you might find a reflection. Ghostly, *yes*, but not a ghost. Which was fitting, because Stevens had never—to Day's knowledge, and despite his spirit-medium wife—believed the slightest bit in ghosts, or an afterlife, or anything of the kind.

The light of that campfire picked out his bright hair, though, a thousand miles from foggy London, and Day hugged his own elbows, a yawning in the pit of his stomach. Stevens was holding up a limp body: an Arctic fox. Its tongue lolled, its eyes glassy, a shocking amount of blood smeared over its muzzle and up Stevens's outstretched arm. His gray eyes were gleaming, pink dots in his cheeks, a wide smile of triumph splitting his face. He looked healthy and whole, utterly at home; of course he did, in his north. He was carrying Sheppard's rifle on his back.

———————

It was the first time Stevens had gone hunting. A few days before he'd been sent into the ice-crammed channel to fetch help. Day had thought—no, he'd *known*—he'd been sending Stevens out to his death. He'd wrestled with it. He'd begged Fate itself to do something, do anything, to save him from having to make that choice. To prevent him from sacrificing Stevens, the thing he loved most, to the vanishing chance of rescue.

Stevens had lived, though, and brought the whalers. In making that choice, Day had succeeded only in creating his own shining double. The burnished side of the Cape Verdant coin. Maybe that was why some part of Stevens had stalked Day the last twelve years.

"Come home," it seemed to say, as the ice glittered deadly and the blood crawled down. "Will. Come home."

———

Pain sometimes helped. Day pressed his nails hard into his palms, making little half-moons. Stevens winked at him, and Day's heart pounded in his chest. He was getting older now, but this version of Stevens never did. He was handsome and in the prime of his youth forever. The public loved Stevens, as they hated Day, and he obliged by doing the same himself.

With a rush of blood in his ears, Day realized he couldn't do it—he couldn't go back. He couldn't fail again, whether or not it would mean death.

There were other sorts of death, after all, more bitter to the soul.

Hang Stevens. He couldn't compare.

From outside, the shouts still came. "Deliverer of Cape Verdant— now lost hisself!" Laughter. This would be a good place to sell newspapers today.

Deliverer of Cape Verdant. Day ground his teeth.

After his journey through the ice, First Lieutenant Jesse Stevens had been the only survivor of a relief party that had originally numbered three. Recovered alone, he'd fallen to his knees in front of Jeremiah Nathaniel—an otherwise cautious whaling captain, who'd taken a very great gamble by being in Lancaster Sound so late in the season— and begged him to save his wretched comrades back on land.

"I cannot tell to what desperate measures they may now have sunk! Or what wickedness! Those poor souls!"

Deliverer of Cape Verdant.

It stung more than expected. Day had lost everything up there. His reputation. His self-respect. The only home he'd ever really known: the *Reckoning*, golden-tinted, creaking around him like a lullaby. Sometimes he thought he'd wake one day back in his cabin, and find that the years had vanished, Talbot was still in command, and Stevens was leaning in the doorway to taunt him gently for sleeping late. A gilded age.

Sometimes he felt he'd never really left.

Stubbornly, he looked back at the painting, where a shimmering and out-of-place Stevens held up his Arctic fox, bright-eyed and golden-haired. Looking like an illustration from a picture book, tempting and daring in equal measure. The discoverer, perhaps, of that Open Polar Sea, and its fabled shores; its people living in noble savagery, waiting for Stevens to come.

Day would have to walk into the throng outside, naked and defenseless as a skinned hare. His own name rang in his ears, that nickname given by the newspapers, and he sighed, feeling the weight of it in his stomach like a stone.

Eat-Em-Fresh Day.

II: SHE WHO ASKS THE SPIRITS
GREENLAND, JUNE 18, 1882

They had their first sight of Godhavn when the clouds parted during Sunday service, its tabletop mountain shimmering on the horizon under a cloth of snow.

The *Resolution* had been blessed with clean sailing on their journey across the Atlantic and up the Greenland coast. To be on deck again—seeing the scudding clouds, hearing the waves, feeling the wind against his skin—was, to Day, a blessing. No ghosts lingered; no bloodstained former lieutenant showed his face. He looked up at the sky each night, at the beautiful distant stars, and almost felt like praying.

His congregation of whalers seemed able to smell land, though, shuffling their feet and looking around surreptitiously as the service came to an end. Day caught the horrified look of his second-in-command—"Pay attention!"—then his guilty glance up at the bridge.

Twenty-three and sandy-haired, eyes hidden behind spectacles, Peters looked like he'd just stepped out of a Cheapside clerking office for a steak-and-kidney pie. Day had chosen Peters as his second over everyone else in the naval lists, although he was a perfect nobody: a perfect nobody with excellent scores on his examinations.

"*No one could be more admiring of your fortitude, the hardships you endured, than I,*" he'd promised when accepting the post, in a hand soft and persistent, little flicks like dark wings.

"*I would do anything in your service, anything at all you required—*"

Day nodded at Peters, and shut his Bible. The book had been a gift from Second Lieutenant Jackson, who'd joined a missionary order after being hauled off their little scrap of rock, and promptly perished somewhere snakes slithered and malaria beat its fevered drum. God had abandoned them, Day knew, when good-tempered, red-faced Nicholas Talbot had finally died, scurvy-riddled and delirious.

But looking around on this fresh morning, he could almost believe otherwise. Kittiwakes and skuas made their throaty cries around the *Resolution's* masts, and the thin howl of dogs carried on the wind. Sails billowed and crackled above, the sun unsetting.

The *Resolution* was a steam yacht, capable of being sailed by a skeleton crew, and to Day's eyes she looked rather skeletal herself, lacking in beauty and human characteristics. She was all staircases, low ceilings, and darkened companionways, sunlight wending down from deck then disappearing again. From her cavernous boiler, pipes ran through the main living quarters, creating little pockets of sound; exhalations; tapping. But Day had rested the back of his hand against his cabin wall, and found his lips tugged upwards by the unexpected warmth.

Their depot ship was just one amongst many dark blots on the gleaming sea ahead; the whaling fleet at harbor. The prospect of meeting that ship made Day pause, push his shoulders back, try to roll some of the tension from his neck. He wasn't sure he was quite ready. He wasn't sure he'd ever be ready.

Dr. Valle approached the bridge, and Day smiled. "Everything in place?"

Valle scowled, beaky nose seeming to become even more pointed. Then he stamped his way up the bridge stairs, uninvited, folding his arms emphatically. "It is. *Captain*."

Day gave him a sidelong look. "You don't have to—"

Henri de Valle might have been the closest thing Day had to an old friend. On the expedition or . . . anywhere.

They'd met on their first week on the *Reckoning*. A much younger Day had turned a corner belowdecks and slammed straight into the doctor, clattering specimen jars to the floor: Valle had planned to study the effects of moss and other mean vegetation on scurvy. "Ah," Valle said with a long-suffering sigh. "Well, I suppose you'll come with me tomorrow to fetch more, young—"

"Day. Fourth Lieutenant Day."

"Savages never get it, you know," Valle told him the next day, as they clanked fully laden across the shore. "Scurvy. It's a disease of exploration."

One of the young Americans, also nominally assisting the doctor, had laughed at Day's packhorse countenance. "You look—I'm sorry, sir," he'd said teasingly, coming right up to him with a grin, so close that the sunlight had prickled at his long fine eyelashes.

Tom, he said his name was, not Thomas. Tom Sheppard.

"Fourth Lieutenant Day," he'd stuttered in return. He'd wondered what it would feel like to be so utterly sure of your own charm.

He looked. He couldn't stop looking.

Valle had been peeved. "If the two of you have *quite* finished . . ."

"Oh, no," Valle said to him now, interrupting his queasy recollection. "Captain Day. My captain tells me I must give up my cabin for *her*, and so I do. My captain tells me to sleep in my own sick bay, as if I were some—sawbones."

Valle sniffed, wiping his nose on the back of his hand. He hadn't gone all the way on the *Reckoning*: invalided off ship, in all probability Valle's influenza had saved his life. His assistant, Nye, had taken his place, and lived to regret it. The papers said that Valle had been *Reprieved from the Cannibal Crew.*

Day folded his arms, feeling unreasonable. "She needs to sleep somewhere."

Valle's letter of complaint about the lodging situation had already been inserted in the official log. His objections were a matter of record—along with his weekly inspections of their health. No weakness, no *nervous debility*, would go undetected on this ship. Everything would be clean.

"It's appalling," the doctor said with feeling. "Some—woman! Meddling with things she doesn't understand . . ."

Day made a noncommittal sound.

". . . they say there's no death!" Valle snorted. "No such thing! When any man who's seen it, seen it up close, could tell you—"

Day looked at the deck.

"—and she claims to consort with *spirits*," Valle finished, imbuing the word with more disgust than skepticism. As if the idea was personally offensive.

Day felt himself flush; he was glad the doctor didn't yet have a stethoscope pressed to his chest. Even as captain, he wouldn't be exempt from examination, and he tried not to feel the sense of intrusion—of unease.

"I didn't exactly have a choice."

Valle snorted, and gave Day a glance in which anger and sympathy were equally mingled, his eyebrows two unruly slashes of gray.

Peters stumbled on deck below them, and that look of sympathy deepened. Peters had none of the verve one needed in a really good second-in-command, despite those fervent protestations in his letters. Stevens, Day thought, would have eaten him alive.

"She'd be far more comfortable there," Valle said, nodding to the growing shape of the depot ship. "I have my doubts—"

"Shh!" Day lowered his voice. "They're good men. Their master assured me of that."

Day lacked sailing experience. Although captain in name, he'd be relying on his crew more than most. Their old whaling ship had gone down in the eastern Greenland Sea; Hopkins had found them, and their odd-eyed master—now Day's ice-master—land-sick in Dundee. They were desperate to work in anything but whaling: in such a super-stitious industry, they were deemed unlucky.

Day, though, had liked the idea of a crew who'd been touched by the ice.

He found himself looking at the Bible, Jackson's Bible, discarded on the chart table. *Whatsoever passes through the paths of the seas.* Hopkins had his theories, of course, like all armchair explorers: based on currents and warm waters, isothermic gateways, miraculous polynyas. The world had launched countless expeditions based on the hope that they, too, could pass through into the Open Polar Sea: balmy and trop-ical and utterly mythical, encircled by its annulus of ice. And on its shores, perhaps, Stevens's beloved race of noble savages: men living free without laws or encumbrance, the closest thing to gods.

Day shivered. It wasn't like that: no, not at all.

———————

Shouts; catcalls; as they came into harbor, men abandoned their work, climbing the rigging to get a better look at the quayside. Valle, who had barely moved from the bridge in the intervening hours, despite expressing increasing boredom, gave Day a pointed look.

"Away there!" came a voice from the shadows, and the ice-master appeared, men parting immediately to let him through. Roderick was a captain himself by right and respect; chosen by his own men as the most fitting replacement when their old captain died. He had one blue eye and one coppery, an air of perpetually squinting into the sun, and Day wouldn't have liked to be on the wrong side of that glare.

On shore, a line of girls was walking down to the jetty, solemn as a funeral procession. Girls in boldly striped trousers, tucked into their jaunty over-the-knee sealskin boots. Someone beside him made a noise; Day didn't see how the sight merited it. Some of the girls wore shawls or fur muffs over their hooded jackets, but on the whole they made for boyish silhouettes, with their hair pulled up neatly into scarf-wrapped topknots. Underneath, Day caught sight of round faces and dark eyes.

The leader of the group didn't need to look where she was going— she made her way through the scree as sure-footed as a mountain dweller. *A Native girl*, Day thought. *Half-Native, perhaps.* There might well have been intermarriages in the time this trading outpost had clung to the Greenland rocks. Perhaps something worse: Day knew how men could be, without the restraint of civilization, or when they thought no one was watching.

It made him feel oddly guilty, although no one could accuse him of that particular harm—harm to girls. He caught one of the crew about to call out, and glared. "We do *not*," he said firmly, "insult the ladies."

He caught a snatch of conversation from the forecastle—*some ladies these are*—and turned to find the speaker.

Joseph Adams Lee, arms folded, gave him an impudent look, the sun flashing off the gold bars of his lieutenant's epaulettes. His high, severe cheekbones looked as though someone had used a chisel to slice them out. He cast his eye over the women like someone inspecting goods on display.

Day swallowed. He had to choose to ignore it. In this respect, at least, Hopkins had got his revenge.

As they glided past the *Louisa* to take their place in harbor, Day gave their depot ship a sideways look. He knew her well. The old whaler was a hive of activity, riding low in the water: her oily hold was stuffed with split peas, dried cranberries, salt pork, mustard by the barrel; Day had perhaps overstocked. And there, on her fresh-scrubbed deck, was—

Nathaniel.

The *Louisa*'s captain, the only black captain Day had ever encountered, stood examining the *Resolution* as if it were bringing nothing but bad luck. In his memory, Day could see Nathaniel's deep brown eyes, hard as two arrowheads dug out of a peat bog, as he surveyed Camp Hope; as he offered Day one dark-skinned hand to lift him up from the rocky ground. His rescuer.

Day had spent weeks aboard the *Louisa* learning how to eat again, how to walk again, how to think and feel again—he'd had plenty of time to see the tenderness behind Nathaniel's flinty countenance, his ship's instruments of death. A mixed crew, too: Nathaniel wasn't exceedingly unusual for being black, and a captain, in the whalers' iron-and-blubber world. Those men were hard, and valued competence more than all else.

On their own decks, Roderick stared back in turn, rubbing his crabby hands together. Day caught the look exchanged across water: Nathaniel's eyes narrowing—then, slowly, giving the ice-master a grudging nod of the head. A look of acknowledgment between colleagues, black to white. They'd gone through the most terrible ordeal. Respect was due.

"Do you miss it?" Day found himself saying. Then, when there was no response: "Mr. Roderick. Do you miss it?"

"Whaling?" He pulled his fur cap down deeper. "Captain, I'd be happy never to see a whale again in my life. Or any other sea being."

"Ah, there she is," Valle said darkly, all but elbowing Day in the ribs. He pointed.

Over on the quayside, Mrs. Stevens carried a parasol to protect herself from the sun. It hid her face, casting her cheeks and shoulders into shade, blending them into the dark planes of her unadorned dress. She was a walking shadow. Then she looked up, her parasol moving aside like an eclipse passing. A woman with firm eyes schooled to mask her fleeting expression of—satisfaction? Or hope?

The Native girl who led them held up her hand towards Day in the parody of a salute.

Valle scowled back. "Savages," he murmured.

"*Enough*," Day snapped. "Peters—ready the launch."

————————

The cool white light melted across the mountains. This was the door to the Arctic, and although the ground seemed to lurch and tumble beneath him—he'd lost his land legs—Day was no longer marooned. He took a deep breath and looked down, so no one could see him smiling as they walked through the small town. "Come home," he said under his breath. "Come home."

Valle tugged on his collar with spidery hands, his day coat beaten but presentable. Peters was scruffy, had a pencil tucked behind his ear, and it reminded Day of something. He turned it over in his mind, worried at it like a loose tooth. But he couldn't place what so unsettled him, as if someone had walked over his grave.

The Dutch sewing school for orphans was a timber-framed house like the rest, its upper windows open, white curtains blowing out in the incessant breeze; the sound of girls laughing, chattering. Day bowed, and Valle glowered, at the matron who opened the door. He hadn't wanted to come. But Mrs. Stevens had taken lodgings in town to await Day's arrival, and they had to go to her when summoned: already the lines of authority were running backwards.

Inside the school, the parlor walls were so white they almost seemed to radiate. Mrs. Stevens was a spider in a washed-out web, mercilessly drawing the eye. Her dress was navy and her jewels were like a handful of pebbles skipped across a deep, dark lake.

"Captain Day!"

He crossed the room, boots squeaking, to take her offered hand. Her voice was surprisingly deep and throaty; he realized he'd been imagining Stevens's bride as some piping little songbird. This woman was nearly thirty, a long way from the lissome seventeen-year-old he'd seen in the wedding photograph.

"Captain Day. I can't tell you how good it is to meet you at last."

"I hope your journey went well," he said in reply. Pointedly: "Were the quarters on the *Louisa* not to your liking? I understand that cabin is normally kept for the use of the captain's wife."

And, once, Day himself; bowlegged with starvation, watching out the window as the *Louisa* bore them from Lancaster Sound like a cargo of white-faced ghosts.

Mrs. Stevens blinked, her eyes framed by long lashes. "I'm not much of a sailor . . ."

"I thought you'd traveled," Valle muttered.

She laughed. "Oh, extensively. Down the Nile and the Amazon! But the great rivers are more to my taste than open seas, ruined cities and pyramids rather than a whaling station's limited charms, and as for that tiny box of a cabin—well."

Valle was scowling from ear to ear at the prospect of tending to a seasick woman. Standing behind Mrs. Stevens's chair, motionless, was the same tall girl they'd seen earlier. Her hair was twisted up artfully into a knot on the top of her head, wrapped in a scarf: it highlighted attractive features and made her look even taller. Unmistakably Native. There was something very watchful about her, Day thought, something that commanded respect.

"This is Qila." The girl curtseyed. "My companion," Mrs. Stevens said pointedly. There was the sound of chattering, giggling, then hurried footsteps outside when the matron glared at the door. For a moment Mrs. Stevens glared too—a fierceness about her dark bulk, like a bear protecting its young.

"I trust you'll find the *Resolution* comfortable," Day said into the sudden silence. "Snug, yes, but there's little we can do about that. The ice gets bad in late September, and you won't want to be frozen in with us—you'll wait with the *Louisa*. We'll do everything we can to follow your husband's trail, I can promise you."

It felt very unreal, and uncomfortable, to call Stevens "husband" in front of her unsmiling face. He wasn't a husband, Day thought. He was—*Stevens*.

"Already you're dreaming of getting rid of me," she said, fluttering her eyelashes. His expression gave her nothing in return. "I should be staying with you. Going all the way."

"I'm sorry?"

"What about the Natives? Don't they live up there? Women, children?"

Day saw something flash across Qila's face, and her fingers curled on the back of Mrs. Stevens's chair, as though taken aback by an old pain.

"You, madam," Valle said in a characteristically French murmur, "are not a savage."

Mrs. Stevens bristled. "They are *not* savages—you might as well say we are. Can you spear a seal? Can you survive on the ice?"

"If you say so, ma'am." Peters, sounding as though he desperately wished he were not speaking. "But I daresay it's no place for a lady."

"You are searching for my *husband*." It seemed to echo around the room. Deeper, more resonant. She had turned on her stage voice, and Day could imagine her before a crowd, this rolling gold reaching every corner of a man's heart. "There's nothing to fear." She fixed him with a look that lacked gentleness. "The spirits can help you."

Day felt as if he'd fallen through the thin crust covering an abyss of icy water. *The spirits.*

He swallowed. After all he'd seen in the Arctic, he was convinced there was more to man than meat and bones. There had to be. There had to be some kind of life after death, however shadowy. But the idea that those spirits might speak . . .

Her eyes glittered. "I can be of use. You'll see."

"By speaking to the dead?" Valle asked. "Doesn't that presume . . . ?"

"Many are already dead," Qila said. Her flawless English stopped the conversation immediately.

Dead. It was as if a breeze moved through the room. A cold, fresh breath of air, down from the mountains. Day clasped his arms around himself, but everything was still: glancing over at Valle and Peters, he saw them unmoved. A small creeping sensation—tap, tap—on his spine.

He looked up at the mirror, placed opposite the window to reflect that pitiless white light. Was it his imagination, or was there—

A smudge on the glass. A crack in the frame.

It was just a reflection.

There was nothing.

Day looked back in time to see a small, fleeting expression of triumph cross Qila's face, and she bent forwards to whisper something in Mrs. Stevens's ear. He knew their game: of course some would be dead.

The women were guessing, nothing more.

"You see," the medium said into the lifeless room, with a laugh that seemed entirely out of place. "I knew as soon as I came across her— eavesdropping in the corridor. She has a gift—"

"A gift for eavesdropping," Valle said haughtily.

"They call her *little ghost girl*," Mrs. Stevens continued. "Although she's been here the longest! But no; that's not the point. Her name, Captain Day. Her name comes from her own people—the very same people who abandoned her here. It means: She Who Asks the Spirits." A pause. "They believe, those Natives, that everything has a spirit." A slightly shrill cast to her voice. "Despite what some would say in more . . . so-called civilized places. They—respect it. They don't mock it. The gift."

Qila's lips quirked upwards, but she didn't speak out of turn. Others, Day knew, might have taken English names, or Danish: for Qila to have clung to her own, in the face of giggling orphan girls, meant something. She stared at Day as if weighing him up, and he believed Mrs. Stevens was right: she was good at listening.

"*You* believe in the spirits, don't you, Captain Day?" Mrs. Stevens took two rapid steps to stand in front of him. She barely came up to his collarbone. "We'll find Jesse together, you and I."

Day's skin crawled. Pinned to her breast was a glistening brooch made from a moth encased in resin: trapped, when it might once have fluttered towards the light, and there was a touch of that cruelty in the woman, too. She placed her hand on his shoulder. He couldn't draw back, but had to bend down, allowing her to murmur in his ear. He could feel the heat coming off her, mingled with the sweet smell of lilies, and it made him nauseated.

"You still see him, don't you?" Mrs. Stevens whispered, her breath moist on his neck.

Day felt his knees nearly give out. The bright clean room was threatening. He'd thought he'd managed to outrun it, outpace it, at least for a while.

"I don't know what you're talking about," he said tightly, keeping his eyes fixed on hers. He wouldn't look back to the mirror. He wouldn't.

"Don't you." It wasn't a question.

He swallowed hard. She couldn't know. None of them could know. He'd never told anyone—anyone!—of the phantom. The secret had coiled for years around his heart.

Her gaze sharpened. "Sheppard," she whispered, close enough that only he might hear. "The boy you killed."

———

No one had said that name to him in years.

The softness of it called to mind Sheppard's warm southern drawl. When they'd been in northern ports, he'd been good with the Native women, his natural courtesy only slightly exaggerated, making the other officers both sneer and cast envious glances. There were no flowers up here; he'd folded those precious diary pages into roses, fingers quick, smiling as if—for him—the sun would never truly set. There was a man who knew how to treat a lady.

Day had defended Mrs. Stevens to Valle, or tried to. The world wasn't easy. The fickle fame of a small-town spirit medium might soon have faded, if she hadn't taken her so-called gifts to New York, to dark circles of men and women holding hands, speaking in hushed voices as the table between them moved, rapped, spun. *The thrilling of the tables*. Some might call her a fraud: since she'd married Stevens, times had moved on. But she'd kept her counsel, and the business was always the same.

The spirits might comfort. Or they might *accuse*.

She wasn't a lady. And she knew nothing about him, or Sheppard. Or Stevens.

———————

The orphanage matron brought in refreshments, and two more of her girls. Day took several deep breaths, glad of the interruption, soothing himself with the smell of coffee.

"Is it all settled," the matron said, a faint note of hope in her voice. "You're taking our Qila?"

The girls nudged each other, smirking. Day could see their touches of Danish blood: there was milk and cream about their faces. They looked at Qila—taller, darker, silent—with a distinct wariness.

"She's been head girl," the matron said, as if promoting a rather flighty racehorse. "She's served in the chief magistrate's household, as companion to his English wife—"

"Though not for long," one of the girls said under her breath, giving Qila the scowl due to someone who'd squandered a rare opportunity.

The matron continued hurriedly: "She speaks both Danish and English—"

"And my own tongue—not well," Qila said. "I've had little opportunity—*here*—to learn." She gave every word weight, and the room, with its uniform-clad men, the darkness of Mrs. Stevens, the matron, and the two disdainful girls, revolved to place her at its center. Day once again found himself admiring her utter self-assuredness.

"I'm an orphan, Captain Day." The other girls looked about to hiss. "At least, that's what I was told. I was brought to Godhavn"—a curl of her lip, a look of infinite resignation—"when still very young. I've never known my parents, or been on the boats—"

"Ships," Peters said faintly, and she glared at him.

"But some of my people were guides—were known to the English explorers. Let me come with you. I'll be useful."

Homecoming.

"And if you run off to rejoin them?" Valle said. "We're not a transport ship for wayward girls."

Qila shrugged. "Doesn't *that* presume?" An arch tone to match his own. "They live overland, to the north, past Cape York: the west of Baffin's sea is a different world for us all."

Her people had been Arctic Highlanders, Day realized. Just like those he'd seen in the painting at the Admiralty, Stevens imposing himself into the frame.

"Surely, it's out of the question," Peters said. A flash of decisiveness; Day found he liked him a little better.

Mrs. Stevens turned. "Peters, isn't it?"

"First Lieutenant Peters, ma'am."

"It's not for you to say, is it?" Her gloved hands were clenched into perfectly round little fists, like apples. "Did you hire and provision this expedition? Did you finance it? I think Captain Hopkins"—the name wielded like a weapon—"would be very disappointed indeed, to hear that I'm being denied my small requirements. It's only *proper*, isn't it? For me to travel with a chaperone."

Or a spy, Day thought, and couldn't shake the word.

"My husband wished me to be accompanied. Be grateful I've only chosen a single one!"

"Madam," Valle interjected. "Her? It's impossible."

"It might not be," Day said slowly. He was looking at those other girls, with their twin looks of twisted-lip disapproval, as though Qila were something fierce and dirty. It reminded him, he realized, of those stiff-backed high-cheekboned Admiralty officers. His own family, aloof and censorious. The class of man who'd always been so keen to ensure that Day knew his place.

He knew, then, that he'd take her. Just like he knew he'd always remember the initial effect she'd had on him—the room stopping dead, and Day giving himself away as a haunted man.

He knew, despite what he tried to hide: he wasn't quite right.

Qila smiled a slow smile, which tugged at the corners of her mouth until it was a wide grin like a fox yawning. The animals stitched into her shawl were all foxes, too—every variation of the Arctic pelt, white and blue and gray.

III: AVERY

Qila walked very fast away from the sewing school, not looking back. They followed her from the red-roofed buildings; the town, such as it was, receded into the distance, and the *Resolution* was a bobbing silhouette on the bay.

"I can take you to the reporter," Qila had said. "I know his guides." The matron had given her a tight-lipped look of disapproval. "What?" she'd said testily. "Am I a prisoner here?"

An old argument. She'd bitten her tongue, looked up at Day, and said: "Come on."

Day could almost see Hopkins's beady carnivorous eyes watching him over the hundreds of miles of sea. Keeping him on a chain, like the dogs howling in harbor. This—James Avery, of the *New York Voice*—was the next link in that chain. He felt his ears make a popping sound, and forced himself to unclench his jaw. Jumping at shadows; unnerved by a table-rapper; shepherding passengers through the Arctic. Some captain he'd turned out to be.

Day's officers were scouring the town, sniffing out old rumors, and the whalers were drinking the smallest of small beers with the crews of other ships. A couple said they had seen the *Arctic Fox* entering Lancaster Sound, a year off schedule.

The *Fox*, as they all called her, was a sleek purpose-built craft, and its golden-haired captain had been standing on the deck alone. The absence of other men, eerie and implausible, had made the whalers uneasy. But eventually a sailor seemed to break ranks, come up from below, and hail them over the bow, his bright red scarf whipping in the wind. A genial exchange ensued, though a brief one. The whalers had started to quiz the sailor about the expedition's plans, but before he could start to answer, Stevens—that gilded captain—had taken him abruptly to ground. The whalers didn't see him again after that.

"They think they saw a ghost ship, Captain," Peters had said apologetically. "A *Flying Dutchman*, like in the sailors' legends. Cursed to sail the seas forever."

"There are enough mirages up here."

"For sure, Captain. Some even say they've seen . . ." He'd hesitated. "The *Reckoning*. Ringing her bells in the distance."

Another ghost ship.

"People say a lot of things," Day said sharply, and kept his thoughts to himself.

———————

Rocks poked through mossy grass, interrupted by a tent and a rough stone shelter: gouges showed where a kayak had been dragged down to the water. Beside the smoking fire stood a man almost spherical in furs. When he saw them, he waved energetically, bouncing up and down on the balls of his feet.

"We should just leave him here," Day muttered, and to his surprise Peters gave a small tight nod of agreement.

The smell of cooking meat reached him: Day felt his stomach turn over.

The reporter came tramping up to meet them. Under his tufty hood, he had bright eyes, a spill of freckles across his wide nose. Day's mouth opened, sending a stab of pain through his aching jaw. He was old, he felt it. But it didn't look as though James Avery had aged a single *week*.

"Captain Day! Good to see you again!"

An American accent, instantly familiar—too familiar. Avery grabbed his hand and pumped it vigorously, one-two, clasping his other hand over it so Day couldn't pull back.

"Mr. Avery."

The silence went on a little too long. "Oh, come, come." Avery scrambled away towards the fire pit. They had no choice but to follow. "And you! Run off again?" he said cheerfully to Qila. The glance she gave the town, the shore, and the mountains made Godhavn look small.

Avery pressed coffee on them, explaining that his guides, Karl and Lars, never touched the stuff. ("Those aren't their real names," Qila murmured, catching Day's eye, and he rather liked her for that.) The rise and fall of Avery's voice was exhausting. Day rummaged through his memories, tried to find in that cheerful face the man he had once, full of operatic ruin, blamed for his downfall.

"Have you heard anything?" To have to ask was humiliating.

Avery smiled. "No. I suppose we've heard the same rumors—but that whaling crew heard nothing more from the red-scarf man after Captain Stevens took him off deck. But they entered Lancaster Sound, we know that for sure. We should start looking at Beechey."

Day's heart thudded in his chest. Beechey Island sat at the entrance to the Arctic maze—its dead ends, and all its tragedies—like the knocker hanging on a large locked door. And if Stevens had entered the sound, then Day knew there was only one way he'd have gone: north, to the fabled Open Polar Sea.

I'm ill-made for civilization. Stevens believed it to be its own kind of dead end.

"Can't say I'm not dying to see it," Avery added, a touch breathless. "Maybe find some relics of my own." *Relics*: that was what the papers called the detritus of doomed expeditions—as if suffering made them holy.

Day coughed. The orders had been crystal clear: the Americans would put a reporter on this expedition if they pleased. The fact that it was the same reporter who'd dogged the aftermath of the *Reckoning*—well, Day could almost hear those invisible chains clinking. He remembered seeing a narwhal coming to surface in the Davis Strait, and feeling, briefly, as if he could feel the gaze of God. But no: like a specter in a penny dreadful, he was dragging something half-seen and half-remembered behind him.

Avery poured another round of terrible coffee, and Qila looked at her cup like a condemned man eyeing the noose.

"Excuse me." Day stood. "Can I have a moment."

Breathing out, his fists curled. The little camp was aureate in the midnight sun, the tent red as blood blooming on snow. He felt the ghost of a smile on his lips to hear Qila answering questions behind him in monosyllables, conveniently drawing Avery's attention, as if her English had suddenly become much worse.

Day took a few steps closer to Avery's tent, lashed shut against the chill breeze. His skin prickled; the fine hairs lifted on the back of his arms. There was a sharp smell in the air. Metallic, like biting down on the sixpence in a Christmas pudding. It sent a warning down his spine, as if those chains were *tugging*, and he hesitated.

The smell of an open fire wafted over, peaty and dark. But the smell coming from the tent was also familiar; he was opening the flaps before the horror caught up with his fingers.

It was blood. Freshly spilled blood.

———————

Red. *Red.* Fabric, floor, and all contents. The crimson shouted at Day, beat like a hammer on his skull, a hollow *rap-a-tap* directly on his temples. The sun through the tent walls was like arterial spray, full force and pounding. There were dead things everywhere, and he clapped his hand to his mouth.

They were just animals, he told himself numbly. Just animals. The cook and crew would be delighted—carcasses dangling, swaying from the movement of Day's entrance. Frozen seals hung slovenly, the meat blackish. Birds were strung up by their feet, fury captured in the brittle curve of their bodies. Everywhere he looked, dead things lolled. The air was full of it.

Red was going off behind his eyes like fireworks. He'd seen a tent like this before—

And, with the sensation of sliding, slipping, slithering—

He's there again.

No, he thinks, *no. Not this.*

He's kneeling on damp rocks, miles from Godhavn, miles into the north. Nearby, a small stream babbles. He can hear a muffled snorting. Deep throaty animal noises, satisfaction and intent.

The air reeks of old gore and fresh blood. He clenches his fists.

Not here.

The tent before him is red. The tent is moving, shaking back and forth, and he can't hear his men, he can't hear them anymore, not even a scream or a sob. Silence bears down on him, a horrible pressure, like the bottom has dropped out of the glass. A storm approaching in this perpetual and humiliating present.

The present Day has never—really—left.

The polar bear pulls her muzzle from the tent, streaked red like poppies. She looks at him. A slow huff of amusement or derision.

The screaming starts.

He'll see it forever: the worst thing he's ever done.

"Captain Day?"

He was back at Godhavn, kneeling outside another red tent, and Avery's voice was concerned. His eyes were sharp, though, and his little freckles had winked out of existence, like stars at the end of the night. Those eyes missed nothing. His fingers were doubtless itching to find pencil and paper, scribble, *scribble.* Get it all down.

Another one who'd keep records.

"Are you well? Should I fetch a doctor?"

Day shook his head. The tent swam in his vision. He felt a muscle twitch in the corner of his mouth, and tasted blood where he'd bitten into his cheek. He thought he might faint, or scream a sudden and pointless scream, like an animal.

As the ship headed into the ice, they took dinner at seven, despite the absence of sundown. A battery of skylights let grayish daylight into the small cheerless box of the wardroom. It sat at the back of the officers' quarters; the ice-master had volunteered to mess with his own men, down in the forecastle, where laughter sometimes spilled out. Another invisible line drawn between them.

Day hated being watched while he ate, but Avery's eyes never left him. So he kept his head down, picked at his white meat, as the officers chewed over Stevens's possible route.

Fish was all Day's wardroom would serve. No bones.

Avery passed his knife and fork from hand to hand, but he was otherwise an acceptable guest, until he silenced the conversation entirely.

"What I'm getting at," he was saying, "is that we're far more fortunate than all those other expeditions, search parties—"

Day looked up sharply. "And what do you mean by that, Mr. Avery?"

The reporter's eyes darted across the table towards Mrs. Stevens, black-veiled, who seemed to prefer to endure dinner in silence, listening to them passing their boring conversation around and around like a ball. An uneasy laugh. "The spirits. And a spirit medium. They could *tell* us where he is. Couldn't they, madam?"

A hitch of her breath. "What—now?"

Day thought he saw the smallest fraction of a shake to her head. Qila preferred to eat in their cabin, so the medium was entirely unchaperoned. Another way in which the ship had departed, rapidly, from propriety.

Lee, who had so far indulged Avery in his short time abroad— entertained him over brandy, saying loudly: "Write that down! You write that down!"—pressed his napkin against his mouth. "And you believe all that nonsense? Table-rapping, and so forth?"

Their navigator, Holt—who believed in nothing at all, except what could be measured and observed—put down a forkful of turbot and sighed, sharing a glance across the table with Carter, Lee's no-less-aristocratic number two.

God, these men.

Avery seemed to appreciate that everyone was looking at him. "Yes, I do," he said. "In any event, isn't that what the Good Book says? That something of us persists after death? Well, the spiritualists believe the same. They say there's no death. Only a different state of being, one we can contact—"

"When Paradise is dripping with milk and honey?" Lee drawled. "You'd think they'd have better things to do. What could possibly motivate the spirits to *stay*?"

"Aren't most mediums frauds," Valle muttered.

"Hardly means all of them are," Carter said. His enthusiasm earned him a look of censure from across the table—and possibly a kick, from the way he flinched.

"*Quite*," Avery retorted. Day caught another quick glance passing between him and Mrs. Stevens. Of course she'd put him up to this; Day almost admired her skill in doing so—and how oddly disconcerted she managed to seem.

"We have a tool in our hands, Captain," Avery said, as if attempting to lighten the mood. "Why not use it?"

Lee snickered.

"I'm only saying—" Avery was flushing now. "The spirits are meant to see all. Know all. That includes where Captain Stevens is . . . so why would we *not*?"

The reporter stared at him like a starving man.

Day pushed back his chair. "Don't get up," he said hastily, seeing Peters struggle to stand—Day had almost forgotten he was there—and Lee making a small grimace of inconvenience. There'd be hundreds more awkward dinners to come.

Day made his way down the companionway and out onto the deck, picking over ropes and buckets, tarpaulins hanging to dry from the whaleboats overhead. It looked like a Whitechapel slum; his crew was accustomed to scraping by. But they were good men. They might, he told himself—more optimistically than he really felt—come to know one another yet.

Catching his breath in the galley, Day was acknowledged with the smallest of nods, because this was not his kingdom: the cook was pounding and pummeling dough, every flat surface suffused with white, as if it had snowed indoors. There was enough for a hundred flour days: they wouldn't run out. But then there were footsteps, loud footsteps, thudding on deck, and Day pinched the bridge of his nose as he turned to meet them, shutting the door on that indoor drift.

"I think I've offended you somehow."

It was Avery. Of course it was Avery, underfoot everywhere.

"Back at camp. You looked like you'd seen—"

"It's nothing," Day said stiffly. "I'd be grateful if you'd keep your own counsel. That's all. You're a passenger here."

"Well. I'd hoped to speak to you about the *Reckoning*—"

A pause. The ship's name hung in the air. Hearing it made Day's heart ache; every inch of her had once been polished and glowing. Antique wood, beautiful shapes, the sinuous lines of her dreadful drowned-man figurehead. The *Reckoning* had been Day's first love.

And she was lost.

"You've done that already," Day snapped. "More than once. There must have been other disasters. Other gruesome tales, Mr. Avery. Don't you think it's time to—move on?"

Avery glared at him. "It's my life's work."

A laugh, bitter. "I'm aware."

"I can't leave it so unsettled."

"Get used to it."

"I've still no clear idea of what happened. This could be your chance to speak out, Captain." Avery paused. "To speak frankly, for once."

Day took two quick steps across the deck. Avery shrank back. "What makes you think I haven't been frank?"

"The *Reckoning*. Lost, despite her fortifications, her position at anchor. And that death toll—long before you even reached Cape Verdant," Avery said, his words falling over themselves. He was breathing hard. "There's more to it, isn't there?"

Thump. It sounded like the cook was battering flesh, turning it into pulp.

"And the execution—"

He knew what Avery thought—that the execution order was a fiction, Sheppard dead and gone for Day's own greedy reasons. A desperate man trying to justify wicked decisions.

Or so the story went.

Day turned his face away. "Sheppard was a good man. I regret what happened."

There had been cartoons of Day—*Eat-Em-Fresh Day*—dragging Sheppard out into the snow, the young hero saying *"Oh! Please, sir!"* and wringing his hands. Never mind that there'd been no snow on the ground that summer. Never mind that Sheppard had walked himself up onto the grave-ridge, as if he hadn't quite been able to believe what was happening. The same cartoons also showed Campbell, who would have survived his wounds if Day hadn't ordered him dragged out to the killing tent. This was Day's story; it was the only story he'd ever have.

A good man, gone bad.

"Men died. We ate them." Day's stomach threatened to upend his dinner, although he'd chewed the turbot to mush, and the potatoes had slipped down pale and waxy. "There's no more to it."

"You sure?" Avery said, very softly.

Day drew in a shuddering breath, pressed his fingers to the bridge of his nose. He could smell the pomade Avery used to slick back his tide pool of brown curls. Day wasn't a vain man, but he couldn't understand how James Avery, who'd been in his twenties when they first met, didn't look a single year older.

A hand clutched at his shoulder. "Are you—"

Round fingers, little crescent-moon nails, and Day stared at them, at first unable to grasp the sheer magnitude of what was happening.

Then he grabbed Avery by the collar, shoved him up against the galley door; hard enough to make the cook pause in his kneading, hard enough to make perfectly audible the sound of air leaving Avery's lungs.

"You do not touch me," he hissed. "Do you hear? As long as you're on this ship—I'm your captain, not some *spectacle*. Do it again, and I'll have you confined."

He let go. They stared at each other. "I mean it," Day said. "If you ever—"

It would be so easy. Avery could be put in his place. Whatever Hopkins would make of it afterwards—Day just needed a reason, an excuse, something that would hold up to scrutiny.

"Come on, then," Day murmured.

He took a step forwards, and Avery flinched. A mean satisfaction: not so confident now.

Day had once learned to be hard. He needed an *unquestionable* reason to turn on Avery, and then the problem would solve itself. He wouldn't think of it. He wouldn't think of any of it! The starvation, the disaster. The execution. They were well stocked: hundreds of flour days. History wouldn't repeat itself.

"Don't ask me about the *Reckoning*. You've done enough damage." He breathed out through his nostrils, a stray whiff of flour eddying like mist, like frost-smoke on the horizon. "There's no more to it."

———

It took them five weeks to make their crossing of Baffin Bay. The Middle Ice was a risky course: many and better ships had been swallowed up by it. But Day pressed doggedly on, despite the reservations of the whalers, forcing them to make the most of the long daylight.

"We need to find him before winter," he kept saying, shielding his eyes and looking up at Roderick in the crow's nest; they would make it to Stevens by luck, and the competence of men who worked the Arctic as slaughterhouse and factory floor. Whenever Day went below to rest his eyes, his cabin shuddered and rattled with a hostile ring, reminding him that his proper place was up on the bridge, where Lee paced with a proprietorial air.

But in the last week of that long, exhausting July, he could bear it no longer. Couldn't bear the thought of waking to see something behind him, flickering and unclear, like a ghost ship hovering on the horizon.

He knew the waters he was about to enter. Knew what they held.

Day rubbed his eyes, feeling his way belowdecks. *A ghost ship*; a transgression leading to terrible, undying life. Wasn't that how those stories went?

If Avery was going to dig up the past, then—

Ah, but Day barely knew how. He'd flattened the dirt. Poured trickling pebbles from a grimy palm. He didn't know if he could wield that shovel again.

"Where are you?" he whispered into his own doorway. "Where are you?"

The ship creaked under him. A ship that felt as different from the *Reckoning* as it was possible to be.

"I'm coming to find you. I'm coming home."

He waited for Stevens to unpeel himself, glimmering, from the corners of the mirror. To stand behind him, eyes silvery as moonlight through cloud. But nothing came. The sunlight slanted in through the skylights, illuminating dust motes, tiny puffs of smoke from a faraway fire.

Nothing came until he was lying in bed that night, listening to the pipes knocking. From across the room—the sense of air stirring. A movement.

And a footstep, as though something had entered, but not by the door.

THEN

IV

GOD-SAVES HARBOR,
SEPTEMBER 17, 1867

*HE HATH DESCRIBED A BOUNDARY
UPON THE FACE OF THE WATERS.*

I t's the fifteenth month of the *Reckoning* expedition. William Day is still twenty-three, a fourth lieutenant. Captain Nicholas Talbot still commands.

Scurvy has begun to stalk them like an invisible and terrible beast. They still have enough food—the men are eating their "salt horse" without complaint, hardtack with all the weevils ground in, and there are enough tins to feed an army. No, the problem is the scurvy, and no one knows where it comes from. It sneaks up on a man. Day inspects himself in the mirror every morning, asking if this will be the day he feels his calves start to tighten in their stockings, the flesh of his arm turn doughy; a finger pressed into it leaving an indentation that bounces back slowly and reluctantly, like a child who's been whipped too often.

Dr. Nye believes light to be the best cure. But they've passed a second endless summer in the Arctic, and now they're waiting for darkness to return; everyone who can walk drags themselves out once a day to stare at the bony fingers of light reaching over the cliffs, picking out the *Reckoning*'s denuded masts. The jagged rocks make a trap for the shadows, and the daylight is eerie rather than hopeful: the sun is telling them not to count on it.

This will be their third burial at God-Saves Harbor.

"I can't complain, sir," little hop-along John had said cheerfully. "If we can move the ship this year, I do think I'll see home again." It came from a mouth so black it looked like he'd been sucking on charcoal, gums swelling and putrid with dark blood. By then the boundary between his stump and wooden peg leg had started to bleed copiously enough to need a bucket beside his sickbed. He'd worn that peg leg for three years without complaint or difficulty, but at God-Saves Harbor his scar tissue had come unknitted, wounds opened up, and it had all gone bad in less than a week.

His coffin was so small that Day had slipped a few coins to the ship's carpenter, forced him to add an extra ten inches, so he isn't obliged to appreciate the paucity of the wooden box, imagine John rattling around in it. Day squeezes his temples, tries to hold off the throbbing headache from the unearthly daylight.

God-Saves Harbor has become a graveyard.

"This is the kingdom of ice," their Native guide Bill had said, nearly a year ago, when they'd first arrived at the top of the channel and looked out on the frozen sea above. They haven't seen another living being since; on the way up the coast they'd found long-abandoned stone circles, unimaginably old and mournful, signs this—once—was part of the domain of man. But the expedition's first acts had been to claim the land around them, as if theirs to do so. The great ice barrier across the harbor bars them from the Queen Victoria Sea: the Open Polar Sea is surely beyond, or else why would the drift lead so inexorably *up* the channel, and why else would they see great expanses of open water, tantalizingly out of their reach?

"There's only one queen up here," Talbot had said. "The kingdom of ice? Pshaw."

It'll be called Talbot's Channel in years to come, but he won't live to appreciate it.

Over that first winter, they'd removed the *Reckoning*'s figurehead and lashed it onto the mainmast, like a hostage. Open-mouthed and waterlogged, the wooden carving of a drowned man screams defiance at the sky. It's a peculiarly gruesome motif for a ship, and might be taken as a bad omen: but Death, Talbot's family had believed, is the final reckoning.

"Come on, now," Day says. The men are leaning on their pickaxes, and hewing out a grave in the frozen gravel will take hours. "You'll keep warmer if you carry on."

In his greatcoat of heavy worsted, Day knows he is woefully unprepared for the Arctic, and is grateful for the sun. But soon the dark will come again, and he feels a superstitious dread. He won't question the captain, though. He won't.

Talbot, after all, is God on his own ship.

Day swallows, massaging his cheek. Feeling for the start of scurvy—the doctor insists on calling it *nervous debility*—but the muscles are strung tight, make crackling noises inside his ears. His wisdom teeth are still in their rightful places.

"You're doing well," he says awkwardly. "Don't stint now." He thinks he hears a snort. He's expected to give orders to men who are twenty years his senior. He knows they mock his accent, his eagerness to be welcome, the way he flinches at real or imagined cuts.

A flash of blond hair catches his eye, and he turns.

Improbably bare-headed, escorting that still-too-small coffin across the ice: his bunkmate, Jesse Stevens. He's taller than Day, more muscular. Under his clothes, Day knows that fine golden hairs line his forearms and thighs. Stevens breathes out a monstrous plume of hot breath, and snaps at the men to work faster.

The cliffs above them cast a long shadow; light plays tricks out here. It becomes impossible to gauge distances. Figures appear hundreds of miles away, tiny flies crawling over an iced and marzipanned cake, then immediately loom over you, human and alive. A vast pinnacle of rock can be chased for hours, only to become its true self—a small boulder, knee-high. The ice-filled air refracts and distorts, and when the light catches him, Stevens looks like he'll burst open, reveal his burnished potential.

He gives Day a brief once-over. "Are you sick?"

"Am I sick," Day says slowly, rubbing his jaw. Something wild and terrible beats in his chest. A fear—not of death, but an absolute dread of one more day in this place, where the ice makes its unearthly cries. There's no game, only a whining lament that sounds more like human voices the more you listen.

They are occupiers here. An invading force.

Day wants to leave, wants nothing more in the whole wide world. He knows, though—in the hidden place he keeps his most honest reflections, including thoughts on Jesse Stevens he'll share with no man—he wouldn't last two days away from the ship. Others have already tried: stolen equipment and attempted to walk home; come back as skeletons months later, throwing themselves on Talbot's essential benevolence.

Day wants to leave. He wants to live.

There are pins and needles in his extremities, and he kicks his feet to restart the blood. "Of course I'm sick!" he hisses, trying to keep his voice down. "*Everyone* is sick."

Stevens glares at the men with their pickaxes, digging slower now Day's attention is elsewhere. That's the thing about *debility*: you want to lie down, lie facedown on deck and be absorbed. The melancholy and lassitude come quite some time before the bleeding, and they're all starting to suffer.

But Stevens despises weakness. "Get a move on!" he snaps.

They're interrupted by someone stumbling towards them with a prayer book clasped to his chest. Arthur Ewing is their quartermaster, and a more pious man Day has yet to meet. His prayers before mealtimes go on so long his messmates dig in well before the finish line.

"Wait!" Ewing shouts at the gravediggers, who are glad of the distraction. "Wait—don't—you can't—"

He's staggering over the shore ice, picking his way over the tarry cracks where the tide yawns and gapes, up to two feet wide. Little John's coffin sits there, mute and judgmental. And the ice has been very unstable the last few days.

A cracking sound. Ewing looks around wildly. "Who's shooting at us?"

Stevens sighs. "No one is shooting, old man."

Ewing kneels down and touches the coffin with trembling hands. "John?" he says tremulously. "John, are you in there?"

Day is, very suddenly, the ranking officer on shore.

"Give him a moment."

Ewing has climbed on top of the coffin and is starting to mutter a prayer. His jaw is unshaven, white bristles making him look like something from under a rock. He'd been teaching the cabin boy his letters.

Stevens looks disgusted with this display of sentiment. "He's holding everyone up."

Day swallows. "Just let him."

"It's pathetic."

Day shrugs, torn between cringing embarrassment and cold hard despair when he thinks about John, who'd appeared before Talbot on Christmas Eve to recite, beamingly, the story of the shepherds and the magi. He doesn't think Ewing's weeping is particularly unmanly. Often he thinks of weeping himself; not everyone can be as tough as Jesse Stevens.

"This must be very hard on him," someone says in his ear, and Day jumps.

He turns to see that Tom Sheppard has arrived, carrying a pickaxe: "I thought I'd lend a hand, sir." Of course he did. Sheppard volunteers for any duty, is welcomed into any group, befriends any stray. Day doesn't have to look to see the curl of Stevens's lips.

The three of them stand and watch Ewing's furious grief. Perhaps it would be kind to put an arm around his shoulders, draw him away. But none of them does so. Stevens shifts his weight from side to side, making his hair glimmer; Day has to stop himself from subtly mirroring the movement. Sheppard is younger than both of them, but shoulders his axe with an air of authority. Day can see the work crew stealing glances at him. There's a sense of relief: now someone *proper* will take charge. Temper the brimstone that is Stevens, the lack of consequence that is Day.

He'd been expected to follow in his family's footsteps, to grow into command. But he feels out of his depth, and desperate, all the time.

"What do you think?" Sheppard asks: the wind is picking up, and the crew starting to look nervously at the ice under their feet.

"If it opens up, we press on," Day says automatically, although he knows in his heart it's far too late for that, far too late for many things. It's the expected response of all the ship's officers. Stevens just scoffs, raising one perfect eyebrow.

"He's the captain, after all," Sheppard says mildly. Nicholas Talbot has proved himself in warmer and farther theaters of trial than this. But beyond the barrier, there's nothing but an endless shifting gyre of ice. Talbot's Channel is a dead end.

High spots of color bloom on Stevens's pale cheeks. "It's a *waste*," he says, biting: he's been arguing for months that they need to leave the ship. "To have come so far, and then just—wait. Wait here like cowards."

"It's a mistake to depend on it," he says to Day privately. "To depend on anything. We can make a go of it out there. Wouldn't that be better than—" He gestures at the tilted ship, the coffin, the scurvy-ridden men. Day thinks to himself that the Arctic is miles—literally hundreds of miles—from fur-trapping territory, but he doesn't gainsay Stevens his convictions.

Talbot, though, is still the captain.

Ewing is dragged off like a drunken man. Better to weep in private, if weeping is to be done. One of the men nudges another and makes a remark about Ewing "facedown on that poor bastard." There's a throaty laugh. Suddenly those evening lessons seem tainted: Day feels his own cheeks burn; feels Stevens as a mute reproachful presence at his shoulder. He's careful not to give him a sideways glance, as if his own urges might be written there, loud as blood.

There's a sudden yawning sound, something huge turning over beneath them, drowsy and no less deadly for it. Day holds up his hand. The men pause, sniff the air. Their eyes are frightened, he realizes. They're all frightened.

"I—I don't know . . ." Day says to Sheppard suddenly ". . . about the ice." He raises his eyes to the *Reckoning*. It seems impossible they'll ever leave.

Stevens kicks his heels against the frozen shore. The movement lets Day know he's furious.

An answering crack right under their feet; something is clawing to get out. Sheppard's face is painfully hopeful. "Hear that?"

Ewing is being held back by the men, a short distance off. "I need to give it to him." His voice is slurred with grief. "His prayer book. He can't be buried without his prayer book."

Day sighs. Heads towards him. Time starts to run differently.

Here's Ewing, poised on the edge of an ice crack as he strains to reach the shore. He doesn't seem to realize his steady footing is a lot less steady these days.

Here's Day, exasperation and sympathy mingling in his screwed-up face, because if they can't mourn John, fourteen and friendly, who can they mourn?

Here's the hole in the ice, the sides slick as a con artist.

Day reaches out to steady Ewing, lead him away. There's just enough time to appreciate his mistake. He thrashes his arms: a brief moment, sadly funny, when he realizes the indignity of it in front of the men.

Stevens catches his eye—a look of mute horror, animal in its nakedness.

It scares Day more than the frozen water below.

The water is like a pit of knives. A pit of hatchets and rusty nails; the submerged ice is jagged and heavy. There's a jarring blow as Day crashes sideways into it. Then he's beneath the surface, and it closes up over his head.

The killer water.

Day kicks blindly up. He knows he has no more than a minute before his body shuts down. And this crack might close up even earlier: the jaws of the Arctic slamming shut.

His coat drags him down, his heart beating jerkily in his chest.

Forcing his eyes open, it's a blue-and-black world. Shapes blossom. The shore ice is a white wall, veined through with silver water and shafts of light. Distances are meaningless. The cracking—so loud above—is a dull drumming of fingers.

Trying to wrestle his coat off, he hangs suspended, staring out into the shimmering debris that clasps around the ship's hull, and feels a horrible, inescapable sense of the *largeness* of it all. Something infinite and vast and deadly. The ocean stretches from here to Spitzbergen, from Franz Josef Land to Alaska, and he's a tiny speck in the emptiness, frozen, human, afraid. The perspective is ghastly.

He can't feel his legs. He kicks anyway.

Reaching up, his hands scrabble to what he thinks is the surface. It's sheer, slippery, resists him. More ice. The shiver is a full-body convulsion, and he clamps his jaws together so firmly he thinks his teeth might shatter. He has to conserve air.

He reaches up again. Beats a fist on the ice.

No answer.

There's a sharp pain, and he yanks his hand back. Blood trails in the clear water.

A nip, he thinks. That's what the whalers call it. When the ice crushes a ship, drags her to the bottom. *She's taken a nip.*

The Stygian darkness of that infinite ocean presses on him, the end of all things, and Day knows he's going down. His clothes are like a lead weight. The light shimmers as he sinks, all alone, and he opens his mouth with a storm of bubbles.

But Day can't countenance giving up. His own vehemence surprises him. He wants to *live*.

In the days and years that follow, that same vehemence will continue to surprise him—

He tries for the surface again, kicking up hard, using his numb-claw fingers to feel along the jagged edge of ice.

There's an explosion. Something grabs him and *pulls*.

A hand.

When he breaks the surface, his breath sprays out salty and frozen. He chokes on it. He's dragged out by the men, shouting, crowding around him, and someone beats his chest with both fists, so hard it hurts. The sunset is awful, turning everything a peculiar blood-red-purple, as if the water is on fire and bleeding at once. God-Saves Harbor looks like another country, stark and alien, on the shores of some endless sea.

"Will!"

He shudders. Stevens is bending over him, looking ready to lash out. "Will," he's saying, then turning to bellow at the men.

Stevens's clothes and hair are dry.

"Quickly, damn you—"

The next few hours will be critical.

"I thought I'd lost you."

Day has never seen him so distraught, he thinks dimly, has never seen this depth of emotion in him at all. Fear is out of Jesse Stevens's repertoire: it's one of the many reasons Day admires him, with a heat that warms and frightens.

Stevens pulls off his own coat, sleeve by sleeve, forcing Day's limbs into submission. "Get him back to the ship! You useless pieces of—"

Day can't make his voice work.

Sheppard, shivering, ashen, dripping like a seal, meets Day's gaze. He nods, once, and gives him the faintest suggestion of a smile. Day intends to recommend him for promotion, as soon as there's an opening. It'll be popular with the men, as Sheppard is. Day can still feel the hand pulling him out to safety, sure and strong.

He can feel his own face burning.

"What are you looking at?" Stevens says. Something dark passes over his expression as he looks at Sheppard—then at Day looking at Sheppard.

He drags Day up to standing. "You can walk? Come on, then." His arm is around Day's neck, a little like a noose, but it's warm. Day thinks, dizzily, he doesn't mind being manhandled by Stevens, even this version of him.

The coffin has been abandoned on the edge of the ice, seemingly the only thing that hasn't gone into the bloody water that day, and Stevens puts him down—Day is shivering and shivering, the cold starting to set in—to give it a final shove.

It tips into the hole and sinks like a stone, without any ceremony whatsoever. Ewing *keens*.

"What?" Stevens says, to the astonished looks of the men. "What?"

NOW

V: A DOOR LEFT AJAR
LANCASTER SOUND, AUGUST 1, 1882

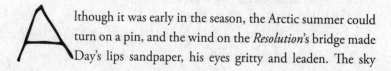

Although it was early in the season, the Arctic summer could turn on a pin, and the wind on the *Resolution*'s bridge made Day's lips sandpaper, his eyes gritty and leaden. The sky above him was bruised with clouds, somber along the coastline like the inky corners of an etching. He gripped the railings and shivered. He knew the ice of Lancaster Sound: he'd once spent nearly a year staring out at it. But now the open water taunted him, as if the door had never slammed shut on Cape Verdant.

He sighed. He needed to be seen on the bridge; to be seen commanding his ship. Only Valle dared come up the steps from time to time, his collar turned up against the wind, his nose beaky and reddened.

"You're not becoming ill, are you?"

"A summer cold," Valle said haughtily. He'd said the same on the *Reckoning*—until he'd convulsed with fever, long limbs thrashing, and had to be held down by several men to prevent him champing off his own tongue.

"Are you sure?"

"Quite sure." With bite. But without Valle, Day would be left with Peters and the Admiralty men.

The struggle through the Middle Ice hadn't made them any less alien. Over at the prow, Holt and Third Lieutenant Carter were ducking the spray; both were smartly dressed, boots shining and greatcoats immaculate. Holt said something, shaking damp hair away from his face—it was too warm for a hat—and Carter laughed at him with clear affection.

A pang. On other ships, the captain and his officers would be bound together by birth and privilege. But none of this would happen for William Day. He turned away, clenched his fists behind his back, squared his shoulders.

What if they were talking about him?

The thought crept in like a shadow. Holt's remark—it could well be about this year's openness. Carter's laugh—hadn't Hopkins said it? *Somewhere you couldn't cross forty miles of water.*

He looked sideways at his officers. They were well-fed, bright, determined. A million miles from the bedraggled, mistrustful men who'd crouched underneath the boat at Camp Hope.

"Captain?"

He jumped. Raindrops had started to spatter. Roderick, in his whalebone-colored jacket, peered at the horizon, scrubbing his palms together as if to wash them. "Summer rain. Storm's coming."

Good, Day nearly said. *Good*. Let them see how it could be. Let them stop judging him, these men who'd never had to—

Then a stab of guilt, because he shouldn't wish that on anyone.

Hands clasped behind his back, the cold was making his scar throb. The scar from the ice, the one he always lied about, because he didn't want even a hint of that rapt fascination on a listener's face. He didn't want to remember standing under the bloody skies of God-Saves Harbor with Stevens and Sheppard, three points to a triangle.

The rain chose that moment to begin in earnest, drumming insistent knuckles against the deck. From down below came an answering thud. It reminded him of whaling ships, passing through the Davis Strait, and how they would bang on the ship's side to signal how many whales—*leviathans*, to those in the business—they'd caught. A deep, resounding boom, like a bell. Each carcass rendered into grease and bones, a fortune for the ship's owners and a wage for the ship's men; perhaps those same whalers had crossed paths with the *Fox*, steering into the wind, Stevens hard-eyed at the wheel.

The thought made him shiver. Something about it was wild and lonely.

"Are *you* well, Captain?"

Valle, again, too close. Day sighed. "It's nothing."

"What's all this commotion—"

"Herridge was in the women's cabin!" Peters shouted up to the bridge, raising his voice over the worsening rain: the storm Roderick had promised was just beginning, and the daylight sky was inhospitable.

Day felt a plunging, plummeting sensation. His mouth opened: the women's cabin, where even he didn't dare enter. He thought of

Mrs. Stevens at the sewing school, surrounded by schoolgirls; that clean white room, where she'd been safe. Hopkins had said, archly: "I daresay she'll be perfectly safe on any ship *you* command."

The insinuation was perfectly obvious—daring Day to make something of it.

He swallowed. Another way in which he'd failed. He couldn't stand the thought of facing Stevens again and meeting disappointment. Or accusation. This was his wife; Stevens was always so fussy about his things.

"He was going through her possessions," Peters said darkly. "Like a common thief—"

Oh, Day thought.

"What sort of crew is this? And that girl carries a *knife*."

Day exhaled. Struggling bodies crowded the door to passenger quarters, and Lee—of course it was Lee, he thought meanly—started to drag someone through. The contrast was absolute: Lee with his pale face, spotless blue coat, brass buttons; the whaler in his beaten jacket and striped waistcoat, his skin tanned and weathered. Behind him, Qila thrashed against another man, looking very dangerous. Frustration and anger and pride screwed up her face, but she couldn't get free.

Day felt a lump in his chest.

"Let her go!" he called.

Lee gave him a split-second look of great condescension. "She could have killed him!" He was playing to the crowd in the rigging. Every one of the whalers was highly skilled, indispensable: from the sailmaker to the stokers, from the carpenter to the boatmen. Qila, on the other hand—

"Lee . . ."

Lee's mouth twitched; Qila was released, and the knife skittered across the deck. Bone-handled, it flashed in the occluded light like a pearl.

The man in Lee's grasp spat on the timber.

"He had the medium's skull." A faint curl of Lee's aristocratic lips. "The one she uses in her sittings."

A skull, a knife: Day could taste Valle's disapproval.

"That's enough." Day gestured, and Lee released the whaler, throwing him down so hard he nearly bounced. "What do you have to say for yourself?"

The man—Herridge—raised his eyes, but not his face. Crouching on his hands and knees, chin jutting out, he didn't look in the least repentant. "I wasn't *stealing*, sir. I want for nothing, as long as my brothers have faith in me." A swallow, convulsive, of his skinny throat.

"Oh, really?" Lee gave him a nudge with the toe of his boot. "What were you doing, then?"

The ship rolled. "I was going to throw it overboard. It's bad luck. We know it. It's bad luck, fatal bad luck, to keep the dead with you. Bad things *come*."

Murmurs from his fellow whalers.

"That's enough!"

The shout came from up top. Roderick was hanging in the ropes, mouth set hard as the horny baleen of a whale, rain streaming off his brimmed hat. He didn't look the sort to believe in luck; but Day knew how superstitious sailors could get.

Peters broke the silence: "What'll be done with him?"

Again, that stillness and anticipation; Lee's little half-smile. They were waiting to see what Day would do. This could make or break their expectations of him. The first major infraction.

First blood.

The rain found its way under Day's coat, dripping down his back, pooling at the base of his spine. *No.* He could well remember being held down; stripped; birched. It wasn't the pain—it was the humiliation of being utterly at another's mercy. By seventeen, Day had been accustomed to those hot tears. Talbot had forbidden it on the *Reckoning*, though, saying it was the mark of a weak captain. The boys on that golden ship had no fear of the birch.

Day thought of Stevens, laughing, running across deck naked when the heavens opened, whooping and holding his arms out wide, wide, wide. *Don't you sometimes feel as if you could eat the world?*

The lump in Day's chest threatened to become larger.

He wasn't Talbot. He wasn't anyone. He was alone on the bridge, and needed to set an example. The drizzle made things wink in and out of existence. He looked around, as if something could help him, prompt him—

"Wait," Day said, desperately. "Wait—"

And there he was. Stevens, pacing the deck with measured stride.

Every hair on Day's body prickled, like iron filings towards a magnet. Although Stevens shone, the rain didn't touch him, and his boots left no print on the wet timber. He wasn't really there.

He couldn't be.

But now he'd come out of the mirrors, out of the paintings, and into the human world.

Day looked away, blinking. The rain was hissing down on the water, refusing to freeze. It was summer, and Lancaster Sound was open. Perhaps, after all, he could have sent someone out there—someone else. Someone earlier. But he'd been afraid, so afraid. Those men under Camp Hope were desperate and sharp-teethed. Maybe it was all his fault.

Stevens looked up at Day, a smile on those perfect lips, and it paralyzed him. The small, low feeling that he wasn't good enough.

Will.

A shout—an explosion of movement caught his eye. Herridge had dived towards Qila, or perhaps it was the other way around, and he was being held back by Lee, that bone-handled knife pressed to his throat.

"*Captain.*"

Day watched as the whaler turned his chin against the blade, deliberately, making a crimson bootlace bloom against his scraggy skin. "My brothers," Herridge muttered to those on deck. "See how I love you." But no, that couldn't be right. These men were hard, hard.

Day couldn't move. Not while Stevens was just an arm's length away.

The silence had gone on too long. Everyone was looking at him, and he shook his head. He wasn't Talbot, he wasn't—*Stevens*—

A snort. "What's wrong with him."

"Lee—that's enough!"

It burst out of Peters. His face looked hot and furious behind those little clerk's glasses, and it appeared he'd surprised himself. Lee, too, was caught open-mouthed, looking at Peters like a beaten dog who had suddenly threatened to bite. The rain drummed its ceaseless rhythm on deck, but Day had stopped noticing the *Resolution*, her peaks and troughs, her crew in the rigging. He only had eyes for Stevens, who'd now stopped his pacing.

Who reached out as if he could see Peters—see something, for once, that wasn't Day—reached out a thin finger, as if to *point*—

Day thought he would be violently sick.

A murmur. "Get the doctor, the captain—"

"He's not well."

The words sent a stab through him. This was what he'd dreaded. He wouldn't look at Stevens. He wouldn't look, and confirm his strangeness. All the things that were wrong with him.

Somewhere below, Mrs. Stevens said shrilly: "I demand that man be punished!" her tone making clear that she was used to getting her own way—or fighting, sharp-elbowed, for her place in the world.

Not so different from Stevens.

"Take him below!" Day shouted, turning on his heel, because otherwise he would scream. Or laugh. Or cry. Had the whalers thought he was contemplating a flogging? Something worse?

Anything was possible, after all, for William Day.

———

That afternoon saw the first séance aboard the *Resolution*.

Mrs. Stevens shamelessly pressed the issue, clearly thinking the men could do with being put in awe of her gifts. Her authority from Hopkins surely didn't extend to this, Day thought, remembering the secretary's little nose-wrinkle of disbelief. But there were wheels within wheels, and unseen figures had put James Avery on board: the same

James Avery who'd been trying to get into her private sittings for some time.

"Oh, you won't regret it," she'd said, gripping Day's arm in delight. "You'll see!"

"I hope I won't," he'd said, pulling away. On a long journey, the men needed diversions. The belowdecks of a ship over winter bore witness to the most unlikely crazes: shell collecting, scrimshaw carving, Punch and Judy. He hoped it wouldn't turn to fortune-telling, not with Herridge's pay already docked, given Valle's untender administrations. But in any case, it was better for the captain to be aware of it.

That was all, he told himself. That was all.

"What should we expect?" he overheard Carter saying breathlessly to Avery.

"Well, that's the hundred-dollar question!" Avery lowered his voice, glancing across deck. "She's best known for raps and knocks, table-spinning and turning . . . any messages she receives, from the spirits, are repeated in her own voice. She's not a trance medium— that's when the spirits speak through the sitter. And no one has seen her produce apparitions."

"What?" Day said, despite himself.

"Apparitions—that's when the spirits are visible in the room. Normally they're spirit guides, someone connected to the medium, who act as a sort of intermediary to the world of the dead. Recently, *manifestations* have been all the rage—which is when those apparitions can be touched, or they touch *you*. I've heard of men dandling the spirits on their laps!"

Carter looked scandalized.

"And for some mediums, they bring gifts."

"Like . . . what?"

"Flowers, sometimes. Or snow. Or fruit. We call them apports."

"Why would there be fruit where the spirits are?" Carter said, fascinated, making Day's heart skip—then beat too fast.

He moistened his dry lips. "And you've seen all that?"

"Well." Avery gave Day a penetrating look. "It's normally dim in the room. To create the most conducive atmosphere. Although not the best, it must be said, for the observers."

This was quite enough for Day. He knew, then, exactly the stage he'd choose for her.

Three hours later, they gathered in the galley. The cook was off-duty, but the air was still stuffy with smoked fish, hanging to thaw above the great iron stove, which glimmered, banked, in the corner. The room had windows on both sides, and Day left them uncovered, so the afternoon sun came in at a sharp angle. "Good," Avery said, steepling his fingers like a philosopher. "It's so important to have light on the thing."

Mrs. Stevens didn't seem to share his eagerness, fussing over the table, which was built solid around the beam-and-pulley system for lowering food to the mess hall below. A faint scowl of disappointment on her rosebud lips.

I see you, Day thought. *I see you, madam.*

The sitters numbered six, with Day, Avery, and Carter joined by a couple of those curious amongst the crew. The gentle heat of the stove, the cuts scored in the table from knife-work, combined to make Mrs. Stevens and her companion a great deal less impressive—though the medium was still a black-cloaked figure, one that made him think of funerals.

"Are we ready, Captain?" she asked Day from behind her veil.

"Why not," he said without enthusiasm.

There were no hymns to be sung at the start; when Avery professed surprise, she said peevishly, "You either believe or you don't. The spirits can see into your hearts—they don't need to be appeased by a *show*." But they joined hands in the manner of newspaper illustrations, and Mrs. Stevens looked into the middle distance, veil quivering, to say: "Is there anyone there?"

Silence.

After a few moments, the stove made a ticking sound. Outside, a bird called on the wind.

"Is there someone who wishes to speak with us?"

"The Stevens expedition," Avery interrupted. "Or someone who can lead us to them . . ."

From the expression on his face, Day could only guess she'd given his hand a hard squeeze.

"Is there anyone there?" she continued stubbornly, wrestling attention back to her with an eager: "Yes! Yes, I hear you."

Day fought the urge to lean around the beam to see better.

"There's someone here," she said in a hushed voice, and behind her, Qila's eyes widened in turn. "Someone connected to—someone in this room."

Stevens, his panicked brain supplied, making his heart beat like a drum, until a more pragmatic part observed that she'd surely recognize her own husband.

"It's someone called Jack. Does that mean something to anyone?"

Another pregnant silence.

"Listen."

Clang.

Something reverberated around the room, loud as a bullet ricochet. Day found himself flinching, Carter saying faintly, "Good grief."

"Yes?" she whispered. "Yes!"

One of the sailors said, slowly, as if drawn out of him by flensing hooks: "I once knew a spectioneer—that's a harpooner—called Jack Masters." He swallowed. "But he was alive and well last time I saw him."

"Are you sure," Qila said laconically.

"Shh!" Mrs. Stevens's gaze was fixed on the beam at their center, as if she could melt it away. "Do you feel it?" she asked. "Carefully, now. Can you feel the table—"

Day pressed his hands down on the pockmarked wood. Was there a tingling in his fingers? The sensation of electricity in the air?

The thrilling of the tables.

For a second, all the dust motes seemed to hang suspended in that shaft of sunlight. "Can you feel the table moving?" she was saying. Expectant.

"I can't feel anything," the sailor said dubiously.

The bundles of hanging fish caught Day's attention. Had they moved, when there was no wind in the room? Shifted—just an inch or so—to the left?

From beneath the table came a muffled thud. Barely describable as a rap.

Yes.

Day felt the urge to look down. His knees, his calves, his lap: all felt absurdly exposed, as though there was something down there, crouching just out of sight, ready to seize its moment. A cool pocket of darkness, which could open up and swallow them whole.

"Spirit! Are you here for this man?" Mrs. Stevens asked.

Another thud, somehow wet, less clean than he'd expected. As if something was bloody. Fleshy.

He thought, incongruously, of *fruit*.

She nodded at the unfortunate sailor. "Ask a question."

"Do you—" He cleared his throat. "Jack Masters. Are you dead?"

They waited.

Clang.

Once again, that sound shot around the room, and all the hairs lifted up on the back of Day's neck. The name Jack—it was common enough. Anyone might guess a sailor would know a Jack. But this unearthly peal, echoing around the sunlit space—

Avery caught his eye from across the table, then pointed, with his chin, to something behind the medium's head. Day felt the urge to peel his fingers off the table. That hint of electricity still thrummed through them, itching, maddening.

Mrs. Stevens cleared her throat. "I'm afraid he's saying something about a shipwreck," she said breathily, apologetically, as if sorry to be the bearer of bad news.

The sound came again, this time with an air of hammers on metal. Day jumped.

"It's just the fiddle-rail."

Without breaking the circle, Avery nodded at the railing that ran around the stovetop to keep pans on the heat. The oven winked at them, the gold-limned outline of the stove door. "Cooling down on us. It's the heat."

Everyone looked back at Mrs. Stevens. Her expression behind the veil was very hard to read.

"My time is being wasted," she eventually snapped. "If you won't take it seriously. But there was something here. You felt it, didn't you? Didn't *you*?"

She pointed at Day. Pulling his fingers from the table, he flexed them. They felt hot. It was pins and needles, he told himself; he didn't quite know if he felt relieved. No messages from the other side. No voices.

No Stevens.

"You wanted something more impressive?" She laughed, as if she could guess what he was thinking. "Parlor tricks?" She looked imperiously at them. "In the presence of nonbelievers, you'll find the spirits prove very shy indeed."

She swept from the room, straight-backed, with Qila in tow, and Day went over to the stove, where Avery was testing the fiddle-rail with brow furrowed in disappointment. Metal expanded and contracted; sometimes, in the ice, a ship's rivets made the sound of distant cannons.

Day swallowed. The heat of the stove, of the concentrated daylight, was suddenly claggy and unbearable. He found himself reliving the tingling in his fingers, the moment Mrs. Stevens had said the table was *moving*, although such a thing was painfully impossible. Were they simply seeing and hearing exactly what they wanted?

The shipwreck on Cape Riley wasn't the *Fox*.

It had appeared out of the fog on the first Sunday in August, glimmering in the strange eclipse-light of the midnight sun, its masts looming taller than Nelson's Column. But Day was intimately familiar with the tricks of the ice; not far from here, it had produced the Croker Mountains, the mountains that had ruined Sir John Ross's career by being illusory. On a sledging trip, Day had once shielded his eyes to see the *Reckoning* appearing from behind a cloud like an angel.

But this ship was just a whaler blown far off course from her hunting grounds, beached in the shallow waters. If there were any justice, Day thought, she should have been lying on the seabed, mocked by her former prey. When they dropped anchor and went ashore the next morning, the detritus of her industry was all across the scree—the try-pot cauldrons for melting blubber off bone, the oily and empty smashed barrels—scattered into looping curlicues by the water. She still retained the stink of it.

Day looked across the channel towards Beechey Island. The way was still hazy, despite the pitiless sun. Roderick examined the wreck with an air of professional detachment, sucking his gapped teeth; Sinclair and Flett, his first and second mate, lurked behind.

"She must've had bloody bad luck," Flett was saying quietly.

"Or a bad captain," Sinclair interrupted. "A foolish one."

"Hush," said Roderick. "We won't speak ill of the dead. You were happy enough to take your portion. Both of you."

Sinclair's wide fleshy mouth worked. "Just think. Could've been us. They wouldn't know how fucking lucky they had it. To be on land."

"He deserved every bit of what came to him," Flett said, and shivered suddenly, like a dog shaking off water.

"I said hush. He took risks for us all—our families besides. And no one deserves *that*." Roderick's voice cracked.

Day followed his stare. The beach was nothing but a few hundred yards of frozen gravel. He couldn't imagine any man feeling lucky to get shipwrecked here. But then, Roderick's men had seen the worst depredations of the Greenland Sea in March.

Day was left grinding his teeth, staring at the skeleton wreckage. He'd been told only the barest fraction of what had happened to the whalers' last ship: greedy for spoils, straying too close to the floes, she'd gone down in minutes.

The *Reckoning*, too, had been lost—that's what he'd told the inquiry, and the phrase had since assumed a life of its own.

Over a narrow belt of ice, Beechey sat watching; he could feel its mute black cliffs at his back, its graves and relics. The weight of all its

sad history. Turning, he was struck with a sense of unutterable desolation. There was nothing up here. Even with the men crunching
around, it was silent as a grave, silent as Camp Hope's perpetually held
breath. Day realized how wrong he'd once been, to think that crossing
that channel, a different shore, might have been salvation. They'd have
starved to death under a slightly different Arctic sky. That was all.

"God," he said, and wiped his eyes. "God."

But it wasn't God he owed for his rescue from Cape Verdant.

"Captain?" Valle said cautiously, approaching with hands fluttering like a handkerchief in wind. "Am I interrupting?"

Day shook his head.

"I need to speak to you about your—examination. It's been
months."

Day shrugged. "You don't have to report to Hopkins until we
return."

Valle made a face. "It's in my contract, Captain. And I intend to
honor it. If everyone on the ship is subject to examination, so are you;
I won't risk overlooking any warning signs."

The *again* was strongly implied.

Day's stomach was hollow. He thought about saying: *I thought we
were friends,* but it was so unlike anything he would ever say. He told
himself that the phantom Stevens was invisible, some trick of his own
innermost mind: that he was buried so deep no stethoscope or ther-
mometer could ever find him out.

Day could pretend, as he always pretended. He was good at it.

"What if I tell you no."

A sigh. Too quick: "If it's personal, William, then I understand. I
will join the *Louisa*. You can have Dr. Jenkins to perform my duties for
the winter."

"You'd really go?"

"Of course." Valle sniffed, and Day felt it like a dull blow. He
thought for a moment about calling the doctor by his first name. Laying a hand on his shoulder.

"You're very worried, aren't you?" Valle said, keeping his voice low.

"And you miss him." He paused, clearly weighing something up. "But he wasn't your friend, you know. He wasn't anyone's friend."

Valle, too, had known Stevens—before he'd become a legend. Back when Stevens was just an acting lieutenant, prone to strange moods, who'd taken an inexperienced British officer under his wing. Day had thought this bound them together, somehow: the memory of Stevens, sitting boots-up in the Great Cabin, eating open-mouthed, spearing food with the point of his sharp little knife.

But Valle had hated him.

———————

Unlike Mrs. Stevens, Day had never been to the pyramids of Egypt; something about the cairn evoked them nonetheless. They'd spent the rest of the day toiling up Beechey's cliffs, counting the graves, kicking the debris, finding nothing but sad little pebbles that might have been buttons but were more probably rocks. Until a new cairn was discovered, crouching against the sky on the highest point of the island, as if it were looking out—across the ice and dark water—to Cape Verdant.

Mrs. Stevens regarded the cairn with interest, a little out of breath from the climb. Qila was holding up a parasol to protect her from the sun; the medium was turning her bear-claw pendant around and around in her gloved hands. They hadn't seen any bears yet, but the thought made Day itch. A polar bear could overpower a man in a matter of seconds—could run him down, take off his head with a single swipe. Guns were little use against those armored skulls. It would open up its bloody maw, stinking of entrails and destruction, to roar defiance at those watching—

He pressed his eyes closed, feeling the world reel. He opened them again in time to see Lee raising his eyebrows meaningfully at the other officers.

The men needed picks to remove the top layer of stones: the cairn's architects had used water to set them like cement. "They were here," Day said, even before he was handed the brass message tube, light and hollow as old bones.

A hand he knew well on the scroll inside, as if twirling a knife on a wooden table.

There it was, as he'd suspected. North, through Talbot's old channel. Where once they'd glimpsed, together, the promise of an impossible sea. He knew where Stevens's obsession had driven him, and the knowledge settled into his stomach like a body consigned to the deep.

He was going to have to go *back*.

Peters coughed, to break the silence.

"We're on the right track." Day rolled up the paper. His hands were shaking.

Mrs. Stevens exhaled loudly—"I knew it!"—but he wanted none of her dramatics. He wanted to be alone. After thirteen years apart—Stevens hadn't written, he hadn't even telegraphed. The paper smelled of peat and salt. Day knew he was clutching it to his chest a little too tightly.

The rest of the note outlined unlucky progress. Two lives lost at sea, and a third snuffed out in a brawl belowdecks, *here interred*—Stevens hadn't bothered to press his men to hew out a grave in Beechey's frozen ground. He knew the hard labor it entailed, and wouldn't have wanted to waste time. The crew member had been left under the message, as if he were—

A depot, Day's mind supplied unhelpfully. *Provisions*. His skin prickled. The wind was starting to warble over the cliffs.

"There's a grave," he said to the men. "Under the cairn."

A pregnant pause.

Someone whistled.

How many ships would come to Beechey after them, searching for Stevens? *None*, he thought, this was the very end of the earth. He couldn't imagine a more desolate resting place; maybe this man deserved to be left undisturbed, as they all did—awaiting Judgment Day, when the earth would give up its dead.

"Then it should be disinterred," Mrs. Stevens said clearly.

A muttering. Roderick, a spade propped against his bony shoulder, narrowed his unmatched eyes. "Captain?"

"What? It's just a body, after all. The spirit lives on. If the vessel might tell us more, then we should dig it up."

They'd been well matched: she was as pitiless and practical as her husband.

Day gave Roderick the nod, and the whaling captain turned to obey with the slightest twitch to his narrow lips. The men, though, seemed reluctant to take their own part in the disinterment. *Bad things come.* And although Day knew the order to be justified, it felt somehow unclean: he couldn't shake the feeling he'd put out his hand and unwittingly touched something vile.

He tried to insist that Mrs. Stevens return to the ship, expecting some sort of feminine sensitivity. But she sat on a nearby rock, shivering underneath Qila's shawl. The sky darkened and darkened until they were walled up in a cave. The picks sent sparks flying up from the stone, as if releasing tiny spirits from an eternity of imprisonment. He heard her murmured exclamation: "How lovely."

The coffin lid was warped and buckled, had to be pried off in pieces. Peters looked around apprehensively as rain started to patter down from that eye-socket sky. The light gleamed off a frozen bundle: sailcloth, lashed around a lump the size of an Alsatian dog. Day's memory supplied the image of men curled up in their sleeping bags, fetal and dank, blinking their rheumy eyes against the light.

The shape was unrecognizable as human.

"We'll need heat to remove it," Valle said quietly.

A search underneath revealed some old hymnals, handed to Avery. Their covers were greasy and stained-looking, as though the body had suppurated. Around its hidden head, a red scarf, rotting away in the freeze-thaw cycles, emitted a noxious scent. Day couldn't help imagining claw-like hands, fingers brittle as spider legs, scraping against their bindings.

It was suddenly hard to breathe.

"Just a body," Qila said.

Valle cleared his throat, caught Day's eye. Jenkins, on the *Louisa*, was a good enough doctor. A little too ready to pull teeth. But he wasn't Henri de Valle.

"We are on the right path," Mrs. Stevens proclaimed. "Follow the spirits, and all will become clear." Over lacy fingerless gloves, her wedding ring gleamed in the threatening light. Pearls and carbuncles, like a tooth spat out bloody.

THEN

VI

THE RECKONING, FEBRUARY 3, 1868

THAT MAN WAS PERFECT AND UPRIGHT, AND ONE THAT FEARED GOD, AND ESCHEWED EVIL.

I saw orange groves," Captain Talbot says with effort. "William, did you ever see such a thing?" He gestures with limp hand. "I walked amongst them. A ruined city made of pink stone, trees whispering overhead. I could smell the fruit, warm and fragrant. Ripe oranges on the ground. Split by the force of the fall. I picked one up—" He moistens his lips. "And started to peel."

Day shoots a look at the ship's doctor. "You should have stopped him."

There are gouges several inches long on the captain's arms, and Day knows the skin will never grow back, the wounds will never heal. Talbot had woken up screaming, drenched in his own torpid blood. They're running low on clean linen. On clean everything.

Dr. Nye looks affronted: Day is still—officially—only the fourth lieutenant. "I can't be at his side all day."

The captain's cabin is warmer than most places on the ship. No light creeps down from the covered deck, and the air is musty with whale oil; Nye says this is unhealthy, prone to exacerbate *debility*. But it's still cold enough for a glass of water on the nightstand to freeze overnight, and if the captain should find himself passing over, Day can only hope it's less frigid on the other side.

"I was warm," Talbot says. "Bless it."

Day is holding the captain's blood-spattered Bible. Injuries never truly heal once scurvy sets in; old wounds reopen. Any kind of blow or insult—it comes back. That's the promise of the Arctic: things always come back. The sufferers bleed constantly, a slow drip-drip-drip that can never be truly stanched. By contrast, Day's lucky: the place where the ice nipped his hand has started to scar. He runs his fingers over it ceaselessly, so conscious of the fact that one day it might gush open again.

Talbot is pale as a ghost, and asks Day to read to him the trials of Job. They're being tested, the captain says. To see whether they're worthy to pass through the ice. "We won't give it up," he says. "Promise me, William. *When he hath tried me, I shall come forth as gold.*"

Day doesn't know whether he believes in the Open Polar Sea, or anything the captain says about their situation. What he'd seen under the ice—in that cold Stygian darkness—wasn't warm water or orchards. It was a yawning passage to the very opposite of life, and it had terrified him.

"Did you ever see orange groves?" Talbot asks haltingly, and Day shakes his head. "I was stationed in Malta. Beautiful place. The stone so warm you could bask on it. Orange and lemon trees. Tall citadels and the sound of . . . of insects at night." He narrows his bushy eyebrows with effort, as if a thought is just occurring to him. "I daresay I won't see it again."

Day's heart aches. Nicholas Talbot has always been so kind. A father, in place of his own disapproving one; Day had dared to hope that this ship might furnish him with a family. He's only twenty-three years old. "I never went to the Mediterranean," Day says carefully. "Maybe when we get back."

"I need to talk to you outside," Nye says quietly.

Day nods, and presses the small leather-bound book into Talbot's veined hands. The captain's knuckles are swelling painfully, like timber warped underwater. "Rest now, sir."

———————

The *Reckoning*'s wood-paneled companionway is utterly still, a single pool of light cast by the lantern at the hatch. The ice has shifted everything to starboard, so a marble rolled across the floor is sucked into the shadows and disappears. The ship is acquiring its own dark gravity.

The doctor is just a blurry shape, then joined by another, taller— one that Day would know anywhere. Well made. In the gloom, Day can only imagine the blond hair, the heavy-knit sweater. No overcoat, no uniform, no badges of rank; a true savage in every way.

Day exhales, feeling like a weight has been lifted from him.

"No better?"

"Worse," Nye answers. "He tried to peel off his own skin."

"Orange groves." Day can't put into words the way his flesh had crept to hear Talbot speaking of warmth, and light, and all the things gone from them.

Stevens sucks his teeth. The Open Polar Sea: tropical fruit, sheeting waterfalls. They all know the theory. But what truly holds Stevens's imagination is that *ascended race of men*, cut off from civilization, living like gods. He's ravenous to meet them: men unsullied by war and cities and cash and laws, all the grubbiness that's taken the sheen off his promised golden age. "Imagine," he sometimes says to Day, "what it would be like to live without cages. Without being judged. A truly new world."

But they're manifestly still on Earth, stuck fast as they have been for sixteen months. Before the sun went down on their expedition, they'd thought they saw the dark black skies of open water somewhere ahead. Hubris; now the *Reckoning* won't move again.

"He doesn't have long left, if he's seeing marvels," Stevens says. "And the others—"

"The other *lieutenants* are still alive and conscious." There's an arch tone to Nye's voice. Stevens doesn't react, although it's clearly intended as a slight—putting him in his place as a mere acting lieutenant. Day shivers, remembering the stumbling parade on deck: fresh air; cleanliness; exercise. The senior officers had been led on a slow hobble; someone had proposed they be leashed together, and Day had tried to root out who'd say such a thing. Someone else had proposed they be put off the ship, to scream themselves hoarse when the delirium came, and Day hadn't looked too closely to see who made that proposal.

"The best cure for general debility," Nye elaborates, "is sunlight. And we've got none of that."

"Oh, *debility*," Stevens says bitingly. "Call it scurvy, won't you? We all know what's happening. Seven of the men, three of the officers, now the captain—it's going to take us all, unless we get out of here."

"There's nowhere to go." It rolls over Day, the sheer oppression of it. They might as well be stranded on the surface of the moon.

Stevens's eyes glint. "That'll be up to you, soon, won't it?"

The doctor makes a small *tsk* sound, as if it's in poor taste to discuss the captain's death while he's separated from them merely by a bit of wood; dreaming of orange groves, agonizing over why his god is testing him so. But Talbot's legs have started to swell, and he can't walk. His mind is becoming fragmented. "She'll answer to me!" he'd raged. "Put me to the wheel! She needs her captain."

Talbot won't last much longer. And out of the officers aboard, the only two still healthy, teeth in their right place, are Fourth Lieutenant Day and the acting lieutenant. They are rammed together in the dark, in a small two-bunk cabin, where the ice claws at the hull and Stevens washes bare-chested in front of the basin each morning.

Day swallows. "Perhaps," he says miserably.

"Good Lord," Nye scowls. "Excuse me, gentlemen, I'll leave you to your *plans*."

Stevens shrugs as the doctor departs. When the swish of his coat blocks out the light, all Day can see is the after-image of the corridor, like a tunnel into the vast mountain range of night surrounding them.

"It's only the truth," Stevens says. Day watches his lips move. "There's no harm in acknowledging it. Being prepared."

"I don't know how."

Stevens looks at him sidelong. "How does it feel? Knowing you're a few deaths from commanding your first ship?"

"It makes me feel sick."

"It must," Stevens sighs. "But you're a good man, Will."

It's the only hope Day has left—the only real hope, that he'll be good at the inevitable end.

The companionway is so narrow their feet are touching. Coming on board, Day had been intimidated by these tall Americans with their sunlight hair and easy ways, but now he knows Stevens better than he knows anyone. Could find him in the darkness by the glint of his smile, by the way he exhales. By his wild and sometimes irrational moods.

"If we could get our hands on some fresh meat—"

"Those savages are useless," Stevens says.

It's said with such utter self-assurance that Day laughs out loud. "They're trying," he says. "Their usual hunting grounds are so much farther south, and this coast is—"

"Terrible. We should call it Terrible Coast, not whatever ridiculous tribute to the queen—oh, I'm sorry, long live her—Talbot has in mind."

Day can't stop himself smiling. Stevens has firm antimonarchist views. He believes men are accountable only to themselves, exist in a state of nature, as essentially blameless as wild animals. Up north, he says, he knows that to be doubly true.

It's like sharing a cabin with a dangerous lunatic, or a Darwinist. Stevens sometimes likes to measure the width of Day's skull, a tiny pink corner of tongue sticking out in concentration as he loops the tape around Day's head. He speculates on the men he'll find on the shores of that shining sea, his new men, and what their particular dimensions will be. "Don't squirm," Stevens says peevishly. "It's so hard to get this right."

"Come," Stevens says now. "You need to make sure the men take their lemon juice." They have half-rations of it, quarter-rations, grown in its casks thick and pungent as horse urine, and it doesn't seem to do much good. "They should listen to you," Stevens says, his hand lingering warm on Day's shoulder. "You'll be in charge, soon enough."

Day watches Stevens climb the ladder and disappear through the mouth of the sky.

"I don't want it," he says quietly.

He examines—briefly, with terror—how he feels about Talbot dying. He's relieved to find nothing but grief. Talbot is a good man, fond of the Bible and Shakespeare. Day isn't grasping, or ambitious. The thought that the men will soon depend on him, depend on him utterly, fills him with horror.

———

"Sir," someone says, lowering himself down the hatch in Stevens's place, like an automaton in which two figures move in tandem but never quite meet. The interruption makes Day jump, but it's just Tom Sheppard. Day's scrambling eyes light on a book sticking out of his front pocket, and he thinks he recognizes Sheppard's famous diary. Sheppard is always scribbling—means to publish his account of the expedition one day.

Day forces himself to smile.

"I'm come to read to the captain," Sheppard says. "Found this in the library. Thought he'd like it." He shows Day the book's cover, nibbled at the corners—rats again, because they scratch and breed in the hold, their squeaks echoing belowdecks; it sometimes feels as though the rats are running the ship, simply waiting out the men. *Tales of the Alhambra*. There's a sudden clutch to Day's heart. He thinks of Talbot wandering through his orange groves, his swollen and contorted limbs dragging, straining. Bending to take a bite from a rotten fruit, blood pouring from his hair follicles, his gums, his nose. The fruit is split in two, something crawling within. Talbot is crawling.

They should split him open, Day thinks for a fleeting second. *Put him out of his misery.*

He blinks. Where had that come from?

"He will. Thank you, Sheppard. I haven't forgotten—"

"Of course, sir. I don't expect anything." A lesser man would try to impress on Day that the captain is dying, and if Day means to get Sheppard promoted, he should hurry up and do so. But there's no guile or malice in Sheppard's lilting voice. A genuine gratitude.

No wonder the men like him.

Day nods. He touches his mouth reflexively. The skin around his gums feels firm. He is still, somehow, whole and healthy, while those above him rot.

―――――――

"You should eat this," Stevens had said to him, sometime in the first year of bleary darkness. It was cold enough that Day could hear, down the corridor, men sobbing in their sleep. Day was using a candle to read *The Paths of the Seas*, trying to derive comfort from its talk of open-water currents and whales passing through, it was all connected, or how else might a cetacean speared in the Atlantic display that harpoon in the Pacific? But there was no comfort to be had, the ice relentless, and his bunkmate a madman, who'd come into their cabin to present Day with a scrap of meat on a silver platter from the officers' mess.

"It's rat, isn't it?" Day said, as a joke. "Small deer."

Stevens didn't laugh. "Needs must."

"Rat? Seriously, Jesse?"

"Come now," Stevens said, and favored him with a wide grin. "Eat and be grateful, and you'll die last."

Day had stared at him in the swinging lantern-light. They sometimes slept together in the same scratchy bunk, to preserve body heat. The *Reckoning* hadn't yet settled into her icy coffin, and she would roll slightly, creak back and forth, Stevens's weight pressing into Day then releasing. A door down the companionway was opening and shutting.

Day shivered. Of course Stevens would have no compunction about any source of food. "Why would I want to die last?"

VII: THE MAN IN THE RED SCARF
LANCASTER SOUND, AUGUST 8, 1882

*T*he weather had given them credit; the very next morning, it came to collect. Day stared up at the jagged bergs crowding ahead. The channel had become a narrowing gullet, hard to judge. "An hour or so," Roderick said. "Then it'll get rough." He looked sidelong at Day with one blue eye and one tawny brown. "No time to get back to the *Louisa*."

Their depot ship had been lagging behind, two or three days late to each scheduled rendezvous. "So be it." Day clasped his hands behind his back; even a day might count, in the short sailing season, although being separated this early would be a dangerous gamble.

Roderick nodded, didn't make any further suggestion; he probably supposed it wasn't his place. Looking out at the melancholy waters ahead, though, Day wished he would. The ice-master had spent twenty years in the Arctic, and if he advised them to make anchor, surely that would be enough.

Day had been unable to stop thinking about that horribly suggestive body in the cairn—about its warped dimensions and grasping claw hands. It had become a symbol of disaster to him, and he found his shameful heart waiting for some corresponding disaster to come.

He couldn't turn back without one.

Holding the rail as the *Resolution* pitched, Day looked uneasily at the water, the way it was pulling and sucking around the hull. He glanced about the deck for anyone who shouldn't be out—although, he realized, that description no longer applied to one of the passengers. As they'd approached Cape Riley two days previously, Qila had sidled out to watch the ice crashing, her dark eyes wide with excitement— although she'd kept peeping behind herself at Roderick and at Day, up on the bridge, unhappily surveying that same ice. He could almost see her chest expanding, her shoulders widening, with each gulping breath of fresh air.

After a few minutes, he could watch no longer. "You know—you can come on deck whenever you want," he'd called to her. "You don't have to stay in passenger quarters. You're welcome out here."

She'd nodded, her shawl whipping in the wind.

Even so, it would be dangerous for anyone inexperienced to be on deck now. Day went too fast through the door into officer country, was flung down the companionway like a drunkard. Outside, the sun still shone behind the clouds, half-light; but down here it was dark. He could hear a door opening and closing somewhere in the distance. *Slam.*

As he came around the bend by the wardroom, a crouching shape in the gloom made him stop short, heart in his throat. Then the light flickered as unseen somebodies walked over the illuminators above, making it glint off Qila's hair; aboard ship, she'd dispensed with the scarf, and her topknot was sheeny and black. She was sitting across the corridor in front of Mrs. Stevens's cabin.

"You should be inside," he said gently.

"Olive is sleeping." She shrugged. "So I am watching."

Day flushed.

"Don't worry, Captain Day. I can take care of anything." Qila took hold of her sealskin trouser leg and raised it away from her boot; he was a little surprised, distantly, to see that these were short trousers, and against a sliver of bare leg, the knife handle stuck out pearly. Her brown eyes looked like she'd already lived a lifetime. He knew the feeling.

"No one here would—"

"The men are frightened." She pulled the knife out as punctuation. "Men are dangerous when they are frightened."

Day didn't know where to look. Above her boot, he could still see the tight smooth skin of her thigh. "Things aren't like that here," he said.

It felt like he owed her an apology, although he wasn't sure what for.

"Men are like that everywhere, Captain Day."

A pause, and she looked at him expectantly, guardedly, drumming her knuckles on the floor. He could have said something about that knife, which he was sure Lee hadn't given back. "Keep it," he said instead, and was rewarded with a half-smile, gone as quickly as the Arctic summer.

"It'll get rough soon. You should go inside." A sudden crash from the deck above. Men shouting, the rumble of the rain coming closer. Qila nodded, folding up her legs to allow him past.

The next cabin along belonged to Peters—the women were sandwiched between the captain and his second, for decorum's sake—and Day had to dismiss the impulse to look within, to see what quiet Peters was like behind closed doors. Instead, he knocked for Avery. No reply. Inside the reporter's cabin, the sheets were rumpled, the tray shoved under the bunk an invitation to rats.

Slam.

The storm could throw Avery overboard for all he cared. Down the unlit stair to the belowdecks, the sick-bay door was already creaking open ahead of him. Day caught it mid-swing.

The room beyond was just one bed, a table, some shelving; if things went badly wrong for them, Valle would have to use the mess hall. It was very warm, the cot neatly made, Valle's long fingers evident in the tidy creases. But the figure bending over the microscope in the half-light was far too short and stocky to be the doctor.

"Captain—"

It wasn't like Avery to be lost for words. No—he usually had a mouthful. He was holding the pamphlets they'd fished out from the corpse's keeping. They smelled vile.

"What's this?"

"Nothing," Avery said too quickly. "You said I could examine the artifacts—"

Day had handed them over willingly, far too preoccupied with Stevens's disappointingly clinical progress report. He'd expected, ridiculously, the inclusion of a message just for him.

Day grabbed at the pamphlet, Avery shrieking: "No, no, you'll tear it!"

He held the paper up to the light—much less light than the moment before—and braced himself against the desk. The *Resolution* was starting to buck; they should both be at their assigned places. But on that peeling hymnal, small copperplate handwriting was scrawled in the margins, spiraling around the page like a puzzle.

"What's this?"

Avery flushed so pink he looked like a midshipman.

"A message from under the body. I was going to bring it to you, I swear—"

Biting his lip so hard he could taste salt, Day tried to decipher the handwriting. The sick-bay door had started up again: open and shut, open and shut, like booming footsteps.

The words danced in front of him. He was suddenly exhausted. He'd spent the night sleepless, corpse-haunted, since their discovery. He should ask Mrs. Stevens how she dealt with mummies. It was the age of inquiry, she'd probably tell him—grave robbing was only to be expected.

"It was left by Gregory Patch."

"Who?"

"The *Fox*'s helmsman. He was a sort of—crew representative. He wanted us to know what happened to the man in the cairn."

"Killed in a brawl belowdecks?"

"Not quite." Avery's voice hitched. "The dead man was the same man seen on deck—with the red scarf—who called out to the whalers. Stevens was seen striking him, and he disappeared, remember?"

Day pressed his lips together.

"Patch, here, says that the red-scarf man was beaten. Badly beaten, by—by the officers, and Stevens, too. Beaten to within an inch of his life. Put in irons. Then thrown into the hold."

The bowels of the ship would be a stinking darkness, sloshing with freezing water, teeming with rats. "It's not unusual," Day said tightly. "As punishment."

The hold part, at least. And Stevens was a man of action, of quick decisions followed through. He didn't suffer Day's agonies; Day had admired him very much for that.

Beaten to within an inch of his life.

These things happened at sea, he told himself. But Day was familiar with Stevens's face when he lashed out: the wild intemperate glee, as if something proper inside him had come undone, and he was reveling in it.

"His ribs were broken," Avery said quietly. "Badly broken. When they opened up the hatch again, he'd suffocated."

Day thought of that hunched shape in the coffin. An eternity of coughing, ceaseless coughing, lying on those stabbing ribs, every moment a little more torturous. Perhaps he'd crawled about in the Stygian gloom. Perhaps he'd shouted for help. Perhaps he'd been able to feel the wheezing deflation as his lungs ceased to hold air.

A horrible way to die, down in the darkness.

Day thought of him trying to work his hands free. Lifting them up to his chest, claw-like and cramped.

The door slammed, and they both jumped.

"It must have been an accident," Day said.

"Patch says—*he* fell to his knees, screaming and sobbing."

Day swallowed. "Well, then."

He tried to imagine Stevens weeping over the death of one of his men. It wasn't easy—Stevens so rarely regretted his actions—but it wasn't too hard, either. Those mercurial tempers: his fury, his love, his anger. Day could see Stevens gnashing his teeth, weeping with rage.

For Stevens, of course, it would be rage: for Day it would be fear, because rage wasn't open to him.

"He couldn't have known," Day said. "Sometimes you have to make a decision. The best decision you can. Under the circumstances."

Slam.

A red scarf. A red tent. Day pressed his hand to his forehead, remembering—

The trickle of the stream, splashing down through the endless pass.

The silence of the men, sleeping around him, the dreamless sleep of the *Reckoning*'s exhausted refugees. The low quiet noises of the polar bear, seeking, endlessly seeking. Day's own heartbeat loud in his ears.

Someone moves beside him, readying a rifle, and Day shakes his head, pressing a finger to his lips. The daylight waits. The bear waits. A pause loaded with possibilities, waiting for Day to tell it what happens next.

Shhh—

"He must have done what was necessary," Day said, tasting blood. "So who are you to question him?"

Avery looked down. "Well," he said slowly, and Day could see the flush around his collar. "It might shed some light on the *Reckoning* expedition. His conduct . . . and that of others."

"Others?"

Day stared at him. The ship plummeted. His balance went with it, and he grabbed at the bed, destroying Valle's hospital corners.

"I'm here to gather any evidence—about what really happened. Captain Hopkins and my editor came to an agreement."

Day remembered the curl of Hopkins's lip. *Lost? Lost? What does that mean?*

It seemed the Admiralty had never had any faith in him.

"I'm sorry, Captain Day. But we both have our jobs to do." In the far-off flicker of lightning, the spray of freckles over Avery's nose looked like blood. A wide nose, round face, guileless green-grass eyes.

A horrible crunching sound came from above, a dark chewing, a shout from Roderick. A crash from beneath them, loud enough to make the floor shake. Day was moving before he had time to think.

"Captain!" Avery shouted, and Day grabbed the door frame, wheeled back around. The wind beating down the stairs was like a physical force. "If you'd just tell me what happened—"

"Write what you like, Mr. Avery!" Day shouted. "It's a long way to New York."

Outside the sick bay was a confusion of men and movement. "It's the bilge pump!" Carter called to Day. "There's something blocking it." As if to punctuate, the *Resolution* lurched to starboard, making the timbers yawn.

"Who's down there?"

Carter knelt beside the hatch to the ship's hold, an ugly-looking lattice that—particularly in the flickering secondhand light—always reminded him unpleasantly of a mortsafe. Something constructed secure and fast, bristling with locks, to prevent resurrection men from disturbing the dead.

Carter rattled off the names of the carpenter and stokers. "They say there's something *banging*." Above the gathering shriek of the storm, Carter's near drawl, a little incredulous, was almost comforting. "Something knocking."

There were a hundred possible explanations. The boiler. The ballast tanks. The water.

"Just—get it cleared," Day managed.

He didn't catch the next word drifting up from that darkness: half-shouted, half-screamed, threatening to become part of the wind entirely. The ship plunged, and the bottom dropped out of his stomach. He thought of that man drowning in Stevens's hold. He was suddenly more afraid than he'd been in a long time.

VIII: WHAT PASSES THROUGH

*T*he dark bergs swung and drove; clouds entirely blotted out the sun. The spray pelted them in blasts, and the lightning was cold and sinister as magnesium flash. Peters's face beside him was blanched, pinched. None had rested in the twenty-four hours since the storm began: Day had been roused from his cabin at the sharp, resounding twang of their first whale line breaking free.

"What about the *Louisa*?" Carter yelled through the gloom.

"Gone," Day shouted. The ship bucked, trying to shake off its second kedge anchor.

As good as. Nathaniel, they thought, had been making repairs some sixty miles behind. Day had pressed on regardless, unwilling— unable—to lose dearly earned ground. And if it hadn't been for Lars climbing out, sure-footed as a circus acrobat, onto the huge overhanging iceberg that now dominated the ship, the *Resolution* would have been swept clean out of Lancaster Sound and back into Baffin Bay.

Pinprick spray lashed at Day's face. Maybe the *Louisa* was at the bottom of the channel by now; it was impossible to tell. The berg they'd been using as breakwater and shelter was a sheer wall of ice, veined with fissures like the skin around a scurvy patient's mouth, making baleful groans.

"It seems to be holding," Peters shouted, hands cupped around Day's ear, loud enough to make him wince. They both stared at the remaining anchor, the six-inch cable tight as sinew.

They were moving. He could feel it in his bones.

Something was wrong.

It was now so dark he could barely make out the men aloft. When the lightning flashed—*lightning, in the Arctic*—he could see their ship superimposed on the sky like a ghost.

The wind roared. The berg, he realized, was starting to move with the current, dragging them along with it. And in its path—the rocks. They would be smashed against the implacable headland like an orange on stone.

"We need to do something!" he yelled.

Peters's tight white face asked no questions. But they both knew that without the berg's protection, they'd be driven north into a churning mass of floes larger than ocean liners. Both choices were equally damned: the myth of man's agency in the face of the ice.

"Captain!" Roderick staggered towards him. "She's breaking up!" Above them, a dark marbling had appeared on the surface of the berg, which was making a yawning sigh like an animal despairing.

"We should turn," Roderick bellowed. "Make for the island!"

"We'll be driven into it!" Day shouted back.

He could see the skeptical cast of Roderick's face. But the running gear had started death-rattling as if it would tear free.

"She's moving—"

Between the ice and that headland, the ship would be crushed. Day felt like laughing, wildly. Hadn't he longed for a disaster?

"Captain!"

Now Lee, too, had left his post.

Day manhandled himself down from the bridge. A crash at midships as a chunk of ice, sheared off from the berg, fell onto the deck with the thunder of heavy artillery.

"We don't stand a chance!" Lee shouted.

Day stared across the foamy waters. To the north, the pack was menacing, champing like misshapen teeth. He wiped his face. North. He'd left a part of himself up there. The ice scraped against the ship's hull, a grinding screech he could feel in his bones.

Needs must when the devil drives.

"We're getting her loose," Day yelled. "And holding course!"

The berg glimmered, furious with lightning. Roderick turned to yell orders—an unexpected lurch threw Day to the deck, palms smarting, shooting pain up his legs. He'd always had problems with his knees.

Someone belowdecks yelled, "The pumps, damn you!"

But it was suddenly Peters who was preparing to follow their anchor cable—noose tight—out over the churning water. Someone passed him a pick, and he hefted it, looking up. There was no fear on his face; for a moment he was utterly unrecognizable.

"It's bearing away," Roderick shouted. "*Captain*—"

Wide eyes in the storm-light. Day realized, looking from the ice-master to the crew: he was expected to cut loose, flee south into Lancaster Sound. To get them out of there. To prioritize the ship, and the lives of all aboard—wasn't that the first duty of a captain?

The men were shouting about the pumps, they'd lost their supply ship, they were about to lose a second anchor. The expedition hung by a thread.

They all expected him to abandon the mission. Abandon Stevens.

Day gripped the deck to stand up; opened his mouth; tasted salt spray. It was blowing the Devil himself. Suddenly, he thought of Talbot. Good Captain Talbot, a little too old to lead an Arctic expedition, who'd turned north into this channel and never come back. Day could almost see him: hat askew, cheeks flushed red, water pooling at his feet. He seemed to turn, catch Day's eye, give him a conspiratorial smile—

She needs her captain.

He hoped Mrs. Stevens's spirits were giving her comfort. She was the only person here who had expected him to succeed.

"Get that anchor!" he bellowed. "And we hold course!"

North.

Peters dropped onto the berg like a stone. Roderick was shouting to the crew, preparing for the moment the ship would be free. The gale battered at Day's face. That man belowdecks was still yelling, "The pumps, the puuuuuuuumps . . ."

The *Resolution*'s plating screamed like a knife-tip on slate; the shrill song was coming from her stern, and Day's heart was in his mouth. Losing the rudder would cripple them. The decks vibrated, and he snatched up his telescope, looked past the berg, north past the headland. The pack beyond was enormous; seething; deadly. The spray like waterfalls. *Crash.* He could feel the storm gathering itself in the cannonball sky.

And something beckoning—

He could see it now: there was a narrow crooked-finger lead into the pack. Just wide enough, though the ship's boats might be shelled off like peas from a pod.

"Remove the boats!"

A shudder. The hawser cable quivered. Peters was trying to pry out the anchor, and Day could *feel* the blows of his ice pick, feel the tension on the ship as the cable tightened, and tightened, the berg pulling away.

The choice had been made.

"Cut it!" Day yelled, and others took up the cry.

Peters had lost his glasses, was chopping away at the cable as if his life depended on it.

"No—come back!"

The cable was groaning, starting to give.

But Peters was like a man possessed. In an instant the ship would be free. The entrance into the pack ahead was narrowing—quivering. Getting ready to close.

"Jump!"

It was too late for the anchor. Too late for the ship. *This is the end*, Day thought in a daze. He'd misjudged it, misjudged it all. He'd never make it back.

But there was nothing for him in London. Up here was Stevens, golden, his hand outstretched. The *Reckoning*.

The horrendous snap of the cable, like bone splintering.

Come home.

A hundred yards to the gap between the bergs.

Men thronged the decks. Silent. Knapsacks and coats gripped tight. Awestruck, with the wind whistling about them, a deep bellow urging the ship on towards that narrowing gullet. Crouching in the doorway to passenger quarters, the two women clutched at each other, merged in distress into one blurry dark form. Neither, he knew, would be praying.

A stray thought: *She won't survive the boats.*

Thunder from the south, a long way beneath them. They were running for their lives.

"Captain—" A bedraggled Lee, shouting in Day's face. "This is madness! It's—bloody—madness!"

"Follow your orders!" Day bellowed, the full-throated roar he'd heard from Talbot in his prime. And oh, it was satisfying—made his fingers tingle.

"Are you mad—"

"We're holding course!"

Day shoved him aside, fighting his way down to the stern. One of the floes seemed sickeningly close, looming up from the wrong angle, blotting out the clouds. "Hold course!" he shouted.

Lee blocked his way again. He was very tall, and well-fed, and young, and healthy. A vision of what Day could have been—what he'd never come to be.

But dark times called for dark measures. Day knew that.

You'll be in charge, soon enough.

"Stand aside!" Day shouted. No one was watching; all eyes were on the bergs ahead, before which he and Lee were ants. He found his grip tightening on the telescope, blunt and heavy as a crowbar.

"You'll get us all killed!" Lee shrieked, the whites of his eyes horribly round. He reached out to Day with the trembling anger of a dog about to bite. "We must turn back—"

"Stand down—"

Something drew taut, and Day raised the telescope above his head, his breathing coming in fits and starts. The ship rolled. The light gleamed on Lee's hair. Day braced himself to feel the sensation—wet, familiar—of a skull smashing. Its horrible eggshell quality.

A shadow lurched.

Then, in a frenzy of motion, Peters was tackling Lee to the deck. Lee was stronger, but Peters was holding him down with strength born of anger and resentment. There was a sudden *whoosh* as the ship jerked forwards: Day was at the wheel at last. The pull was stronger than a freight train, more inevitable than a clock chiming midnight.

The men stood in silence. Lining the decks, all hands drawn out by the horrible scene. The sky felt too low. Roderick was frozen in the rigging, Lee and Peters crouching with twin expressions of disbelief.

A hitch of high-pitched breath was completely audible over all other sounds, ending as if stifled by a lace-gloved hand.

The ship slid into that opening like an oyster being tipped down a throat.

Between the bergs, it was dark, glimmering, impossible to judge distances. Their masts reached to the heavens and back, elongated and bent.

The opening held.

The opening held.

Then it collapsed behind them with a boom, spraying water over their decks, battering Day against the wheel like jetsam. Shouts, screams. They were still shouting about the pumps, he realized dazedly. But he was half-drenched, and—turning—he could see a solid wall of ice behind. There'd be no way back. Wherever the *Louisa* was, she wouldn't be following.

The storm had receded, and they'd dropped anchor in the patch of still water behind the bergs. Fog billowed towards them, as if a giant had opened his mouth to puff out pipe smoke. Frost crystals settled on exposed skin like a thousand painful needles, and the whiteness dampened the sound of ice booming farther south.

Day felt his heart shivering, an agitated animal. *Talbot was right*, he thought. About what, he didn't know.

As if in response, Roderick said softly: "A bold choice not to cut and run, Captain," and they stared off the stern together. "An uncommon bold choice." His eyes were hard, and the ice looked as firmly shut as if it had never opened at all. Day schooled his face into expressionlessness. He hadn't done this for the respect of a Dundee whaler. He was—he could be—captain of his ship.

"Two feet of water in the hold," Carter said when he reported. "The men had to dive to clear the obstruction." It didn't bear thinking about, the dark water whirling around like a maelstrom. "Terrible noises down there." But hadn't it been a long and terrible day for them all? The fog was casting strange yellowish shadows, and it was hard to see where the sky ended and the sea began. Day exhaled.

There was a body in the water.

Something had been sucked under their stern. Day looked back at Roderick, who appeared to have been examining him. Measuring him up.

There was a body in the water.

No, Day thought, rubbing his sore eyes. It was a piece of clothing, discarded overboard, attracted to their hull. *Fouling*, that was what it was called. When ships dragged something along with them. He felt a horrible stillness come over him, something that gripped his hands tight on to the railings, swollen and painful.

For a moment, the thing in the water seemed to glimmer, crimson and serpentine. Rippling in the pale gray light, undulating long and slippery as an eel swimming behind them. Then it disappeared into the fog.

2

IX: SOMETHING IS COMING THROUGH
TALBOT'S CHANNEL, AUGUST 13, 1882

A bell in the distance.

"William."

Someone was shaking him awake. A tangle of limbs and bedsheets. Sweat on his forehead. Day felt like he was clawing his way up through dark water. On cracking open an eyelid, though, he could see that the skylights were still light; night—true night—wouldn't fall until October.

"William, wake up!"

"I was asleep," Day said automatically, pulling the sheets around himself like a shield. His voice sounded hoarse. Had he been shouting?

"My word. Don't you look terrible." For a moment the light caught Valle's face, and it was cadaverous—then blinked into his familiar features, long nose, sharp eyes. He sniffed, looking suspicious. "Are you sure you're—"

"I'm well." Day raised himself up on his elbows. "What—" He cleared his throat. "What's the matter?" If there was an emergency on board, it wouldn't be Valle coming to wake him.

There was a boom from the depths. Day held up his hand, listening, as the *Resolution* creaked around them. For days they'd drifted around in that thick fog, until it felt like the world was unreal: they were recognizably in Talbot's Channel, chivvied by the ice, but that was all. "Nathaniel will follow," Day had said, unconvincing, remembering how miraculous their passage through the ice barrier had seemed. "Or carry out his orders as a depot ship—lay caches in case of our retreat. He knows what to do."

If he trusted any man with his life—

But Valle had written a long letter about *reckless endangerment*, to be entered into the official record. No more than Day expected.

He blinked at the floor, half-expecting to see a little medical bag, crammed with gleaming instruments. When it didn't materialize, he shook himself out of bed; shrugged on his overcoat and jammed his hands into his pockets, as business-like as possible.

"Captain," Valle was saying. "What were you dreaming?"

Day tried to force a smile. "A man's dreams . . ."

Valle shook his head.

"Nothing." Then, more vehemently: "Nothing." His voice cracked.

A pause. "I need to examine you. As per orders."

Day looked at him, almost too tired to feel betrayed. "Valle. It's the middle of the night." And the idea that Valle had been standing over his bed, eavesdropping on his dreams, made his skin prickle.

"I'm as sane as I ever was. Can't this wait?"

Valle wrung his hands. "After that business with the crewman, and the skull . . ." A faint note of triumph. "I told you no good would come of it. She's in the mess hall—"

Day felt a cold finger of unease. Down in the forecastle with the crew was no place for a woman: even less so, with the men inexplicably on edge.

"—she's holding spirit circles," Valle finished.

Day clutched his coat around his shoulders, as he clutched at this diversion. Not a welcome one. "Then someone should—chaperone." Trying to make it seem normal; he was surprised, actually, that Qila hadn't dissuaded Mrs. Stevens from this course of action. His voice was still thick from sleep, thick from lichen. It always took a while to get it out, after the starvation dreams.

He looked in his mirror as he passed it. Nothing.

The twin branches of the companionway were two dark mouths, and all the doors shuddered as he went, as if something was drawing a titillated breath. Down on the lower deck, the coal bunkers loomed, and the clanking boiler made the air acrid. Such a temperamental thing for their lives to depend on.

Day felt an unpleasant tingling sensation, a pricking, as he passed over the hatch to the hold. They still hadn't found what had fouled the pumps off Beechey, and it was impossible that red scarf in the water, sinuous in the dying light, had been anything other than his own overwrought imagination. Patterns in the water. Shapes in the clouds. Nevertheless, he was grateful when he could pass into the damp heat of the mess hall, Valle sidling in behind.

He surveyed the scene. The sliding doors were open, hammocks and berths empty, and no one was sitting at the long trestle table, with its treacly veneer of grease and soot. One of the whalers—Herridge, again, the man who'd tried to throw that skull overboard—was on the bottom step of the galley staircase, staring at the table as though it would come to life and bite him. Mrs. Stevens sat clenching and loosening her clasped hands, her rings winking at him in the candlelight. The motion seemed reflexive, as if she had no sense of what she was doing.

"Captain." She didn't look up. "I knew you'd come."

He'd always heard that séances were parlor tricks—or a malicious undermining of authority, of *male* authority, by this very type of woman: a lone traveler, childless, quick to argument. He'd always expected her to be indiscreet. But there seemed nothing at all seditious about the look on her face. All sorts of possible reactions ran through his head. Alarm; fury; outrage. When he opened his mouth, he found only sadness. "What have you done?"

"They asked for it, you know." Her deep voice was almost slurred. "You don't speak for the crew."

Herridge shook his head violently. Graying hair, white eyebrows. There was something thin and desperate about his expression, making

Day think of a prey animal at the end of a chase. "It wasn't what we expected. No, not at all."

Qila moved to stand behind Mrs. Stevens's chair. Her shadow spilled across the table, too tall—she'd put her headscarf back on for the occasion, and it gave her an odd silhouette. Mrs. Stevens flinched, but her hands stayed clasped, as if she were determined to keep them in sight. Old habits, Day supposed.

Herridge said: "There's something on the ship with us."

The door to the cable locker squeaked. Where the mess hall gave way to stowage, the hanging provisions swayed. The creaking sound of rope being tested. A sense of restlessness.

The ship was settling, that was all. It was nothing more than the fiddle-rail clanging.

Valle sniffed.

"I mean it!" Herridge clenched his fists. "Cold. Big." Day followed his gaze to those overturned chairs; the abandoned mug, moisture still beading on the side. He could easily see someone stumbling, panicked, to stand.

"It asked us—horrible questions."

Day cleared his throat in the silence that followed. "Madam?"

Mrs. Stevens shook her head.

Footsteps came from the galley, where a low hum of voices showed that this was where the crew had retreated, and Avery appeared. "They're still angry," he said. "You shouldn't have stirred it all up!"

"It wasn't *me*," she hissed, and gripped the table as if holding herself down. "Someone should have intervened."

"When it was speaking, whatever it was?" Avery said with an air of challenge, his eyes sharp. "I thought you didn't believe in channeling the spirits."

"I don't!" she said shrilly.

Beneath her veil, Day caught a twist to her mouth, an angle of expression that spoke of—fear?—before she shook her head again, composed her blunt features. Day remembered the progression Avery had set out. Knocks. Then voices. A true trance medium would lend the spirits her body. Her lips. Her tongue. Giving herself over entirely.

"What questions?" Day interrupted. "What did it ask?"

A thump came from the hold below.

Again, Day thought of *bodies*.

"It sounds like she didn't give them the usual comforting nonsense," Valle said. "Captain—this man has had a shock. I can give him something to help him sleep."

Herridge flinched. "I won't sleep." His eyes seemed drawn back to the table. "I told you. Not when there are dead things aboard."

Day knew enough about shipwrecks to guess the condition of the water around the whalers' lifeboats: scavengers were always drawn to carnage, noise, effluence. Mrs. Stevens's pet skull sat between the candlesticks, gleaming toothily, seeming a little too large for the space it occupied. The mess-hall ceiling was low, barely six feet of headroom, the air thick. Washing lines dangled. Stearin wax and drying socks, and the thin sharp smell of snuffed wicks. Nothing should make him feel suddenly cold.

He had an idea about how mediumship was done; under certain circumstances, it was easy to suggest things. It was easy to make something out of what was already in the room; the accumulation of hopes, fears, secrets. But this lingering atmosphere of terror reminded him of the electricity he'd felt in his own hands, that afternoon in the galley. The *thrilling*.

The fascination of a child turning over a rock, to see what squirmed in the shadows beneath.

There was an echoing boom from the ice outside, and the table vibrated—Day saw the skull wobble. Its jaw was slightly open, a half-inch or so, from which something might worm its way out.

A prop, his unquiet mind supplied. *Just a prop*.

There's nothing wrong with you.

Another creak. The skull fell on its side and rolled towards him, making a sound like a door being opened. He thought, for a moment, it would fall at his feet.

Tap.

He exhaled shakily. "That's enough."

Avery was tapping his pencil against the table.

Looking up, Mrs. Stevens was shivering—he could almost hear her teeth chattering. Qila suddenly seemed younger, less self-possessed. They should have been aboard the supply ship, he realized, with sensible Captain Nathaniel. They should have been safe, following the demands of propriety. But Mrs. Stevens had been granted her wish; the ice had swung shut behind them like a cemetery gate. And though Day had awoken to the sound of a ship's bell—there had been no sign of the *Louisa* since.

―――――――

Tap tap. The motion of Avery's pencil took Day back to an airless room in Louisiana. The air was heavy and wet, the scent of pink-and-purple bougainvillea. He'd traveled to meet Sheppard's family in person; he hadn't been required to do so, it wasn't expected, and the journey had been exhausting for a man still recovering from starvation. Clothes hung off his frame, the weight of his coat hurt his arms, and sitting was painful. Day walked with a stick, very slowly, like an old man, and had no idea how long it would take to recover, or whether he'd ever eat meat again.

You killed him to eat him. He knew what Avery thought, what they all thought, that polite but damning southern family. That Day was a desperate man trying to justify his wicked decisions, the execution order a sham; others, perhaps, also murdered for the cook pot.

Tap tap went Avery's pencil. The smell of rot lingered in the air. The press had trailed Day to Louisiana as if hounding a sick and injured animal.

Tap tap.

Sheppard—young and popular, handsome in the pre-expedition photographs, blessed with a good but brief military record—was said to have been slaughtered like livestock.

And Day couldn't explain it.

―――――――

"It's all nonsense."

Valle's peevish voice startled Day back to the present, and the relative stability of the wardroom, where they'd repaired for drinks, leaving the creaking mess hall to its own emptiness. Mrs. Stevens stared into her hands as if trying to divine the future, and Qila draped a herringbone blanket over her lap.

Day poured brandy; it seemed like the thing to do. But Valle wouldn't drink. He bent down so his long nose was inches from the medium's face. "Madam, you must stop this."

Mrs. Stevens exhaled, rubbing distractedly at her throat. The room was cold as the grave, and Day didn't need to look outside to know that mist still shrouded the decks. "Something came through," she said, in a thin harsh whisper that made his flesh creep. Her voice sounded . . . used.

"What?" Day asked despite himself.

She shook her head. "Something big. I've never seen or heard anything like it. There's something on this ship already."

"Madam, I can examine you—if you've somehow come to harm. But it's not safe to be playing around. The men—"

"I thought you were an experienced medium," Day said, sharp. "Haven't you had something like this happen before?"

He meant: *Haven't you ever been taken over?*

A drum of her fingers on the table, and she scowled at him. "Well. I suppose it's no surprise it's happening here—"

"What," he said, "do you mean."

She seemed breathless. "It's no surprise there's something on *this* ship, given its . . . occupants."

He stared at her.

"And you must dread that sort of scrutiny, Captain Day! To be asked about the worst thing you've ever done."

She lowered her voice, insinuating: "Is that why you still see him?"

"That's enough," Day snapped. A pain shot up his right arm, and he realized he'd slammed his fist down on the table. But young Tom Sheppard was gone, sent no messages from the beyond. *Men died. We ate them. That's all.*

There's something on this ship already.

The medium gave a low, rich laugh, and Day's skin crawled.

"Are you so foolish." Valle didn't make it into a question. This time he did take a sip of his brandy, giving the two women a calculating look. "The men are already on edge, and we can't send you back now."

"I'm not afraid," Mrs. Stevens said hotly. "You think I should be? I came out here to find my husband—find him by any means necessary."

"You've seen how superstitious they are. I've examined them . . ." Valle trailed off, uncharacteristically. "Rescued after weeks in water-logged boats, at the very end of their resources." He paused. "They're lucky so many of them survived."

"What happened?"

Valle shook his head. "It's not for me to say. But the idea—your idea—that there is no death—"

"Just another mode of being," she interrupted.

"You don't know what you're talking about. What you're dealing with." Valle's hands were veined like chilly running water, and must have ushered countless souls into the afterlife. The ship's doctor was a kind of confessional. Goodness knew, Day thought, what those men might have confessed to.

"I can protect her." Qila put one foot up on a chair, making it creak gently on its castors, and drew up her striped shorts to reveal, once more, the hilt of her knife. Day looked away, flushing. He looked back, and for a moment their gazes met. A look of confidence; of conspiracy. He felt a shade warmer.

"You, too, *mademoiselle*. I know how your kind can be—"

"Valle!"

The doctor gave an expressive shrug with his narrow shoulders, and it wasn't clear whether he meant women or Natives: both broadly contemptible. "You shouldn't be running around the ship, armed or unsupervised."

Day opened his mouth.

"Is that why you were dismissed by your former master?" Qila's eyes flashed as the doctor bore down on her. "Give me the knife."

"No. I need it. I *need* it."

"Enough, both of you."

"Come, now—"

There was something startled on Qila's face; a too-wide look in her eyes. Valle cast a long shadow twice her size. He lunged, bony hands going to her wrists—

A hiss. It seemed to happen both slowly and quickly. Day found himself pulling the doctor away, hands fisted in his ragged day-coat. Valle was lighter than he'd imagined, and brittle as an insect. "That's enough!"

Get your hands off her.

Valle's eyes were beady. "I'm trying to help you, William." Not *Captain.* "You were sadly weak as a lieutenant, and now . . ."

"Peters!" Day bellowed. "Peters!"

His second-in-command came through the door in a rush, all legs and boots. Valle gave Day a small shake of the head, as if to say: *Not him.*

"You can't put your hands on our passengers, Valle. I'll . . . overlook the rest. Peters, see the doctor out."

Pulling his mouth into a tight hard line, Valle swallowed the rest of his brandy. Pushed the glass across the table as if moving a chess piece; checkmate, or concession: it was impossible to tell which.

Day drew Peters aside, almost dizzy with anger. "Make sure this doesn't happen again. I've put a lot of faith in you. I didn't *have* to choose you, there were other candidates, better qualified . . ." The words fell over themselves. "You know what's expected!"

Peters's shoulders straightened, drawn up by an invisible thread. His glasses had gone overboard in the storm, and he'd lost that slightly owlish look with them.

Valle stalked past, looking every one of his fifty-something years. "I'll go by myself. But I'm officially protesting my treatment."

"Protest all you like, doctor," Peters muttered. "It's a long way home."

Something about this phrasing sounded familiar; Day glanced at his reflection in the wardroom mirror, as if it might hold the answers.

The dim light recalled the *Reckoning*'s Great Cabin, glimmering with candles, packed with guests in the days before they set sail. A violin being played in the corner. The wink of jewels, female voices, and polished brass buttons.

But there was nothing to help him now: the surface was dull, and he was blurred at the edges. He wasn't Talbot, perfect and upright.

Day braced his hands on the table, took a deep breath. Allowed Peters to pour him another brandy. "Leave us. Both of you."

"But—" Mrs. Stevens met his eyes with such naked defiance—a look he knew from Stevens himself—that he nearly bit his tongue off. "You still haven't answered the question, have you?"

"That's an order," Peters said, his eyes gleaming. "Madam."

He knew the question the spirits had put into her living mouth: *What's the worst thing you've ever done?*

"I've always been that man," Day replied. "Eat-Em-Fresh Day— that's what you meant, isn't it? Fine. I've been him for years and years."

It was who he was. Who he *had* to be, to survive intact up here.

Hadn't the storm taught him that?

X: LEVIATHAN
TALBOT'S CHANNEL, AUGUST 15, 1882

The color had been sucked out of the world. As Day stood watching the drift of their ship, two days since the abortive séance, he felt a disturbance in the torpid air: someone had come up onto the bridge behind him. Whoever it was stayed silent—Day was grateful for that. He didn't think he was up to speaking.

No birds wheeled where their masts reached up to incongruously blue sky. In the misty morning below, everything was pearlescent, the texture of discarded bones. The cheerless frostbitten cliffs of Cape Verdant hovered out of the fog on their port side, and he longed to put them firmly behind.

Day wrapped his arms around himself. The person beside him still hadn't spoken, seemed similarly content to engage in silent communion.

He watched his breath disappear into the mist. If you observed it long enough, you could try to pick out shapes. There, off the starboard bow: a polar bear reaching out her paw to swipe at the ship. She vanished with a single shrug of her humped shoulder. And then the swish of a coat—the sunlit glimmer of blond hair, or a knife.

The human mind abhorred a vacuum.

Day shook his head. Exhaled. He'd fallen into this trap before. And it was odd that he hadn't heard anyone on the bridge stairs, not a creak. Not a groan.

Never had he heard such ominous silence.

A shifting; something was standing directly behind him.

Slowly, very slowly, Day steeled himself to turn.

The ghost of Jesse Stevens.

That was how he'd first thought of it. Day had been aboard the steamer *Beauregard*; the powers-that-be had paid to hurry him away from America as fast as possible, trying to escape all the rumors and name-calling and bad luck. Word of his presence aboard, though, had spread through the ship like wildfire, and he'd spent most of the journey contemplating the unchanging view from his cabin's porthole. Like those bodies, he was going home in pieces. It was only a few months since Cape Verdant.

One morning he'd felt inexplicably better—the sun was shining, and things seemed possible again. He'd decided to go down for breakfast, and was trying to make himself look presentable. The skin around his chin was still hanging off the bone, his stubble growing back in clumps, as if too weak and etiolated to push itself through the skin.

Day was looking into the basin to rinse his razor, captivated with the way the foam swirled, frothy and inoffensive. Little things, these ordinary elements of civilization. Water. Warmth. Cleanliness.

Sheppard popped into his head.

Sheppard had used a razor to sharpen his pencil, and now he'd never shave again. Some of him might have been repatriated, but Cape Verdant had been a frightful jumble of bones and debris by the end. Nothing remained intact. Nothing remained unspoiled, and part of Tom Sheppard might still be up there, even now. A lump in Day's skinny throat. He looked up into the mirror, taking a deep unsteady breath, and nearly cut off his own finger.

Stevens was standing behind him.

Day turned—but Stevens was absent from the room. Only visible in the glass, just over his shoulder. Day could see the slight upturn to Stevens's lips. Cruel lips, someone had once said: Day had always found them particularly fine, generous and pink-hued, looking liable to yield to a thumb. Stevens vanished the moment Day looked at him, as if this little glimpse, lasting no more than a second, were all he could muster.

On arrival in London, Day had been sure the death would be well reported. But Stevens was alive and at a gala in New York, and William Day had looked up from the paper—in his breakfast room, where the clock beat a measured tick, the seconds and minutes of his life marooned—and into a world in which he was haunted by something far less straightforward than a ghost.

It stood beside him now.

Stevens's arms were folded. He was wearing a cream knitted jumper, dirty and ragged about the sleeves. He looked like a *voyageur*, one of the Frenchmen who plied their trade on the fur routes: it was always hard to tell what had given birth to Jesse Stevens, as if he'd walked out of the north one day complete and whole.

There was nothing ghost-like about him.

Day gripped the railings until the veins stood out on the backs of his hands. He squeezed his eyes shut. Sometimes this was enough to make him—*it*—go away.

Because he feared—in the place where he kept his worst secrets—the day that the apparition might change. He could just about bear it, as long as nothing changed. But he feared the day that Stevens would smile and his handsome face would stretch and stretch, pulling back from his bones until it had the hard, leathery skin, the lipless teeth, of their dead. Day had seen Stevens wet, and bloody, and grimy. He knew all aspects of him, and it wasn't that. No: it was the *change* he feared, being able to see it happening. Moving through the in-between states. Transforming in front of his eyes.

Somehow that would be worse, worse than anything.

In the newspaper illustrations, Day was battered and haggard, a desperate castaway, and Stevens the noble torchbearer. It was always so clear which one was the monster.

Those eyes were a weight on the base of his skull.

It's not real, he said to himself. It wasn't even a ghost. It was a memory. Or a feeling. Something had decided Day was incapable of living without him.

He wouldn't look.

The hairs were lifting on the nape of his neck. It was right behind him, close enough to touch. It wasn't breathing.

Silence.

Stevens's voice was pleasant: he had a way of making melodramatic statements, his words tumbling over themselves when angry or enthused. A showman's turn of phrase. Day thought he could spend days listening to Jesse Stevens. But this version was always silent.

It was no use. He had to look.

"Captain!"

Avery, coming up the stairs and wafting the fog away. Day let out his breath. Surely it would leave him now.

"Have you thought about my request? To join the shore parties, I mean." Once the fog cleared, the officers would be leading small boats to comb the inlets, looking for debris, cairns, a camp. Any passing clue. "The ice seems relatively free, doesn't it? I've heard a lot about how impassable it can get."

Avery gave him a sideways look, and Day remembered something he'd decided early on: this man was cleverer than he appeared.

"It's out of the question," Day said with bite. Cape Verdant felt close enough to touch. He couldn't stand the thought of Avery tramping through the cavernous recesses of the past. Only a few fragments might remain—and the chopping block, washed clean over time. The bodies were buried on home soil. Most of them.

Most of them.

"It's not far, though—as the crow flies—"

"No." It came out strangled. No birds flew at Cape Verdant. They'd have been brought to earth immediately, their bones chewed and sucked.

He was sure the apparition was smiling.

Day knew, rationally, that no one else could see Stevens—not this Stevens. But the fear lingered nonetheless: the horrible fear that one day someone might look at him, eyes wide, voice shrill, and say, "Who's that behind you—"

And Avery, of course, would recognize Stevens instantly.

"Very well," the reporter sighed. "Hope Captain Nathaniel fares better." Avery took out his notebook, and Day found himself fixating on his pencil-scribble handwriting, trying to read what was written. "The job of laying caches falls to him, doesn't it? Assuming he can penetrate the channel. It's some time, isn't it, since single ships were sent out—since the *Reckoning*, in fact. To prevent the risk of a lone vessel being lost."

Day worried at his lip with his teeth. Didn't answer.

"And Nathaniel only ever went as far as Beechey because he came across . . ."

Stevens appeared more solid and worldly than ever: Nathaniel had come across him making his fateful way south, minus his two companions. *The Deliverer of Cape Verdant.* This time, though, their depot ship, their asylum, was under strict instructions not to imperil itself in the ice. They were alone up here.

"Are you . . . well? Captain?"

Day realized some long moments had passed, and he was clenching his jaw. "I—"

There were procedures, of course, for having a captain removed from duty; that was the point of Valle's regime. It would leave Peters in charge, trying to navigate the same maze for which Day had proved himself so unfit. Day remembered the moment Stevens had appeared to point at his second-in-command. A mute blessing?

It rankled, for him to acknowledge anyone but Day.

"I—"

Think.

The apparition leaned towards Avery, holding its little knife, the one Day had seen the real Stevens sharpen a hundred times. "You know," he had remarked, "a man with a knife can make his own fortune."

That knife was very close to Avery's neck.

Day couldn't speak.

Stevens was smiling, wide and intemperate as a fox. Sharp teeth. Day didn't know if he could yet be touched. *What a waste*, he thought wildly. What a waste of all the days and years, if he hadn't taken the time to learn whether Stevens's lips would indeed yield to his thumb.

Manifestation.

A flash of sunlight, and Day wondered what would happen if Stevens wielded that knife. If he was to plunge it straight into Avery's throat, just above that moving Adam's apple, stop the voice pouring out, the nagging, the questions, that were still running on like babbling water—

"Captain! Is he disturbing you?"

For a confused instant, both Day and Stevens turned towards the voice. But then the apparition glimmered, disappeared like a thunderclap. Peters was coming up the stairs. "You shouldn't be on the bridge without permission!"

"I thought I had it—"

"You're a passenger," Peters hissed. "It's not your place." His face illustrated quite how sick Day must have been looking.

"Well." There was no longer any sign of Stevens, just a cold feeling eddying around them like a mist. "Well, Captain, if you think any more on it—"

Then Avery was gone. Day grasped the railings and exhaled a long, slow breath, telling himself Peters would understand it as relief at being released from a nosy passenger. Nothing more. But the image of the knife glimmered behind his eyes, and he pressed his knuckles into them, feeling his head pound.

The danger had seemed so *real*.

"Always questions," Peters said darkly. "And rumors. He talks about you, constantly." He rocked on his heels, watching the departing Avery with an expression of righteous anger, something Day had never been able to find within himself. "You did well. May I?"

"I'm sorry?"

"I said—if I might—you did well, Captain. Back then."

They both stared out at the fog. If a crow flew, Day knew, over the brash ice and leads, it would reach a jagged cape. A grave-ridge, dark rocks falling away pitilessly to the sea. A sense of crushing desolation. He'd stood by the signal flag and cursed it all at the top of his voice, screamed until his voice was hoarse.

"Whatever that man says—whatever he wrote." Peters's ears were pink, his voice vehement; Day remembered that letter, Peters's expressions of admiration, the pen scoring through the paper until the words were embossed like hieroglyphs. A fervor that had unsettled him. "And whatever they say about you . . . you did well. You and Stevens. No other man could have done the same, I'm sure. He has no *right*."

―――――――

That night, Day found himself staring into his mirror, kneading his face, pulling back his lips and inspecting his gums, making a death's-head mask. He caught himself—flushed. Looked down. Although he was entirely alone, he still felt observed.

The companionway outside creaked like stealthy footsteps, and Day exhaled. He was starting to get used to the ship's sounds and moods. Their figurehead was a torchbearer, breasts bare, her muscles—some had said—distinctly unladylike. *Resolution*: to make a decision one way or another; to convert something abstract into another form. He swallowed, throat tight. He'd have to speak to Peters, in the morning, about how they could keep better order. Start to redraw those blurred lines of command.

A door groaned open, and Day extinguished the lamp. In the shaft of bluish civil twilight, his reflected face looked all bones. Stevens had always collected skulls on his travels; he would later pose surrounded by the open sockets and gleaming teeth of his *specimens*. And if Stevens found that ascended race of men, Day asked himself how long it would be before he looted their burial sites—or whether the bubbling try-pots would be pressed into service to render down something fresh.

He gave himself one last doubtful look in the darkened mirror before turning in.

The simultaneous sounds of a door slamming—a guttural cry—footsteps scuffling.

He was up and at his cabin door before he had time to relight the lamp. "Stop!" Avery was shouting, his sliding door gaping open, and Day shielded his eyes as light flickered across the corridor, revealing a dark shape at the stairs. Taller than a man.

It was cloaked. Folds of fabric around its head, pooling on the floor, the impression of running water. A face that wasn't human—dark, shiny, like a beetle's carapace, its nose impossibly long. Light flashed off a knife.

Day froze. "Jesse," he said stupidly.

Then it bolted down the stairs, and Avery staggered out of his cabin. Bleeding.

The deck had become a confusion of bobbing lights. The gloomy footprint of the ship was claustrophobic against the glittering water. Day drew his coat around himself. All present.

"Did anyone . . . see anything?"

Carter shook his head. "No, Captain."

Even Valle was up on deck, leaning over the side as if Avery's assail-ant had dived overboard. Day swallowed. He'd imagined it, he told himself firmly. He'd imagined Jesse Stevens, and no one else could see him, no one at all.

Qila led Mrs. Stevens delicately out into the light, wrapped in a dressing gown and shawl. The girl broke away for a moment to exchange a few murmured words with Lars, then returned hurriedly, like a silent watchful shadow.

"What happened?"

Day nodded at Avery. "There was someone in his cabin."

"Not someone," Avery said wildly. "Something. It wore a mask." His voice was high. "A terrible mask, black and—and snouted. Like a porpoise, or something. Sharp teeth."

Day rubbed his eyes hard enough to bruise. *There's something on the ship with us.*

The idea caused a slow sick dread to unfurl in his stomach. But if Avery had seen it—had fought it—then surely it couldn't be what he feared.

Could it?

Tiny black eyes. Slick leathery skin. Something not like a human face. Or a human face warped and distorted, exactly as Day had once feared seeing Stevens.

Let me keep him perfect, Day had begged the sky. *Perfect to me.*

"This is all her fault," someone said.

"What do you mean," Mrs. Stevens hissed; Day had the impres-sion she was fighting to keep the expression of outrage pasted on her face. Without her veil, she was in danger of showing fear.

Up on the stern deck, Lee was shining a light into Roderick's face, making his single tawny eye gleam. One of the men crossed himself, and another broke away to stagger against the gunwales, staring down at the ice as if something was coming for him.

"Anything?"

Roderick shook his head. "No, Captain. I've gone through them. No one saw anything." Lowering his voice: "Talk of someone in a guise—some sort of sea creature—it's the last thing they need, Captain, if you don't mind my saying."

"Hand it over—the mask." Flett took Herridge aside by the scruff of his coat. "Wherever you've been hiding it. Now!"

"I was on watch." Herridge set his jaw, crossing his arms defensively. "It wasn't me."

"Then *who*?" The man by the railings, his voice croaky and parched.

"Nonetheless," Roderick said, wheeling around, staring fiercely. "I won't have it. You chose me as your master. I'll burn that thing if I see it." Lower, directed at Herridge: "You shouldn't've brought it on board. We made it through. *You* made it through."

It sounded like a warning. Day eyed Roderick, protective and righteous, as he hustled his men towards the railings. Something had happened in those boats.

But Day wouldn't ask. He wouldn't dig it up.

He could do Roderick that courtesy, at least.

"Yes, thank you," Lee said briskly. Even in the middle of the night, his boots still gleamed blackly, his uniform immaculate—Day couldn't help but feel a pang of admiration at the way he'd taken charge. "The man has a point. How sure are we that the—American—saw anything at all?"

"I'm sure," Day said.

It sounded hollow. Lee gave him a penetrating look. Then Peters was coming towards them, panting, and leaving damp footprints on the timber.

Back at the group of passengers, Avery's broken finger was being tended, and Day could see cuts scored into the reporter's palm. "Are those—" His voice cracked.

Avery bit his lip, nodded. He'd been lucky not to lose a digit.

The dread rose up Day's gorge, burning. He thought of Stevens standing behind Avery, smiling, menacing him with that too-sharp knife. Day had dismissed the idea that it could touch anyone, the apparition, perhaps because he couldn't face the alternative—that it could, and it never would.

That expression of interest on its face. Had he somehow . . . *sent* it after Avery?

And if so—what had he sent?

Mrs. Stevens tugged the shawl around herself; glanced down at her own hands, then up at Day, as if she were about to say something. He walked away quickly. The deck was too small. The *ship* was too small. For him, and her, and her husband.

Day felt as though his stomach were full of worms—as though he'd eaten rotten meat. He couldn't tell anyone what he'd seen.

Avery grabbed Mrs. Stevens by the arm, towed her away from the group, their heads together. Day flattened himself against the chart table, trying to make himself as small as possible. They appeared too intent to notice.

"We need to talk about the séances."

"What?" She sounded defensive. "Why?"

"You've been carrying on—trying to make contact—haven't you." It wasn't a question. "And it would be easy to figure out what ails the crew." Avery nodded at Qila. "When you have your eyes and ears everywhere. It would be easy to make something of it . . ."

"I can assure you," she hissed, "that's not what happened. You heard it! You felt it! When it came through . . . when it used *my voice.*"

"I felt it," Avery said, low.

"But—you don't think it's the same thing, do you?" She clutched at her throat, looked around with a furtive air. "The thing you saw tonight?"

"I don't know." He cracked the knuckles on his good hand. "Too— solid. I've been to other séances, where the medium produces spirit matter, or the spirit guide moves around in the dark. No doubt . . . you're aware. But the spirit is normally a very young girl, dressed in cheesecloth. A slip of a thing, whether she's corporeal or not. This was something very different. Heavy. Real."

Manifestation, Day thought.

"Then," she said, hushed, "it's stronger than in—those séances. Better. I'm—"

"Careful," Avery said darkly. "Madam. Be careful what you let through."

Day ducked around the corner, his heart hammering.

He ran headfirst into Qila, who was lingering by the whaleboat davits, watching the crew at a distance. "Captain Day," she said quietly, "what do you think happened?"

Day shook his head. "I don't know. Avery said it was—"

"Some sort of monster." Her eyes were very serious, and flicked over towards Mrs. Stevens, black-clad in the shadows.

"Some sort of mask. But we're safe," he said, and she snorted. None of their cabins were safe, it seemed, and he could see how that shook her. He wouldn't say that monsters weren't real.

In a rush, he asked: "Do you think you could . . . maybe . . . find out what it was?"

The pause went on so long he became aware of the tightness of his jaw, the way his heart was slowing in leaps and starts, boom, *boom*.

She nodded thoughtfully, and sidled back to the group as if she'd never left.

"Captain. They've searched the ship. I think you'd better come and see." Lee came up with a click of those smart boots.

Over his shoulder, the crew were starting to mutter, suck their teeth. The light made everything harshly delineated and unreal all at once. Day tried to feel hope for their onward progress, out of the fog, towards Stevens. *Where are you*, he asked the shivering night.

What are you?

———

The hatch was a bite taken out of the real world. It was so dark below, Day couldn't make out how far the ladder went. The echo of his boots, as he scrambled down hand over hand, made the space sound impossibly large.

He landed on one of the braces between the pits of stinking water; the hold was where condensation dripped and grew fetid, where things collected and festered. It was cold enough to make his nostrils tingle. "Come on, man!" he hissed at Lee, to cover his own unease.

They'd come down between the two freshwater ballast tanks; behind them was a cavernous warren of "spares and wares," anything that wouldn't be harmed by freezing. "This way," Lee said, clipped and disapproving, tapping away into the distance. Shadows leaped out at them. The timber was slippery underfoot, and in the extremities of the light, Day could hear the scurrying of rats. *Small deer.*

He stopped, sucking in a breath.

There it—that *thing*—was again, at the darkest part of the long tunnel. That masked creature.

This time, its spindly arms were held up at impossible angles, as if reaching to embrace him. The lantern swung, horribly suggesting movement.

Day swallowed. It stared back at him.

The head was protruding and pointed, nearly two feet long, jutting obscenely into the darkness. Two rows of teeth. A blunt cetacean nose. Hard shiny skin. The tanned hide of a killer whale grinned at him, sideways and sly, sawn and stuffed and beaten into something that would fit over a human face. The eye sockets were small, two elongated pinpricks of darkness. A sense of recognition. He'd seen this thing before . . .

But it was static now. Perfectly still.

In the light of Lee's lantern, he could see it was just a mask hung up on the door to the chain locker. The white arms merely timbers.

Lee gave him a sideways look. "*Captain*—"

Day knew he'd been staring, mouth open, a little too long.

"Leviathan." Peters's voice echoed from behind them, although it sounded—for a moment—as if it were coming from that lengthy jaw.

XI: THE WORLD OF THE DEAD
LANCASTER SOUND, AUGUST 21, 1882

Day put his hand on Mrs. Stevens's door, steeling himself. But he'd put this off as long as possible. It had been nearly a week since they'd found Avery bleeding, and impatience was making everyone jumpy; they'd drifted up and down and all around, but visibility was poor, and the sailing season would be over in September. The mission felt to him like a bolting horse, about to pull away. And sometimes he turned his hands over and over, inspecting that scar from the ice; remembering, with a pang, the feeling of electricity running through the séance table. Being connected to something—no matter what.

Qila was out on deck, leaning over the railings, naming the things they passed. Lars beside her, carefully sounding out the words. Birds. Seals. Ice. Things that belonged in her world. She was smiling as she pointed, as if she'd started recognizing her surroundings.

Day wished she were down here.

He sighed and pushed the door aside. Valle's former cabin was changed. The walls were draped in trailing shawls of crimson and navy; it felt like being inside a chocolate box. Mrs. Stevens's jewelry dangled gaudily, swaying, from a hook. Day heard the faint tap of a bear claw on timber, and suppressed a shudder. What might she know?

She knows nothing, he told himself.

"Good day, Captain."

He glanced around. Books were crammed onto the shelves: she looked to be a prodigious reader. But then, Jesse Stevens had once lolled in Day's bunk by candlelight, reading out passages from Maury's *Physical Geography of the Sea*. He'd so loved the idea of a secret race of men, governed by no one, ungovernable. It was blasphemy, or mad fantasy. But Stevens had never cared about that; and it looked, from cursory inspection, as though his wife might also have her wild beliefs. A new world. Equality between the sexes, between the races.

All the things that dreamers dreamed.

"I've been expecting you."

Mrs. Stevens's hair was loose, unbraided, heavy. As she sat there on her bunk, Day was seized with the sudden terror that she was trying to be attractive to him. She might have succeeded with another man, he supposed; she must have been attractive to Stevens, all the more so in her youth, wide-eyed on his lecture tour. Day tried not to look at her rumpled blankets, her flattened pillow. She might have slept side by side with him, in a fine bed in a fine house. Far from the ice, and far from William Day.

"Madam—" he said, and didn't know where to go from there. He cleared his throat. "Herridge has been placed back on duty."

"Ah." She put aside her book. "No longer unwell, then." She looked as though she wanted to say something else. Something about hysteria, perhaps.

He heard Valle's sneering voice: *weak.*

All Day knew about Herridge's debility was that he'd made that dreadful whale-faced mask, made it out of the sea creatures who'd come to investigate the wreckage around their lifeboats. Even the doctor had heard little more, the whalers closing ranks as silently and decisively as the waters had come together over their ship's masts. Peters knew nothing, and the mask had disappeared too.

There was something about that whaler's air of devotion that made Day uncomfortable.

See how I love you.

"After the séance, did he confide in you?"

She shook her head.

Day hesitated, thinking of the knife marks on Avery's hand. In life, Stevens's favorite tool had been capable of slicing sinew. There'd been stories that he'd won it in a card game with a backwoods cannibal, or traded it for furs with the Native tribes. There was as much mystery about that knife as about Stevens.

"Well?" she said defensively. "I assume you're here for a reason?"

"Herridge seemed to think that whatever . . . came through, in the séance . . . meant him mischief. Meant all of us mischief."

"Ah," she said again.

Moments ticked by.

"He was afraid."

You said there was something on the ship with us.

Day swallowed. He found his hands against the sides of his jaw, where the muscles were tense as the mainmast rigging. In a rush: "And what about the thing that attacked Avery? Was that a spirit, too?"

She examined his face. "So you *do* believe," she said, her eyes sharp and beady with satisfaction. The sense that she was exhaling, settling herself down amongst plump drawing-room cushions, rather than in a spartan bunk, on his ship. "I knew you couldn't possibly think we die—that all parts of us die—with our earthly bodies. The end of all flesh."

Day hadn't seen the soul on the chopping block. And he knew they'd have found it. His memory conjured a picture of Campbell's armless and legless torso, sternum cracked open to get at the ribs. Later, the organs would be pulled out. No soul in there. Campbell was—elsewhere. The body was just a body. That's what he'd had to tell himself.

They came home in pieces.

"Good, Captain. Good. If we work together, I know we'll find my husband. Just let me ask, and they'll lead us to him."

He swallowed. ". . . Who will lead us, exactly?"

"The spirits."

"Who are they?"

She sighed. "Those that have passed over."

"And you think, after death, that we go . . ."

"To the world of the dead. The spirit plane."

"Not Heaven or Hell? Or . . . somewhere else?"

"I don't quite follow."

He gave her an angry look. "Can anything come through from somewhere . . . else?"

"Whatever do you mean."

Day didn't quite know himself. But he had the sense that a doorway opened, a hand extended, was a dangerous thing. He knew enough to be frightened of what the human mind could do. Of what his mind might do.

Before him, her writing desk was crammed with curiosities. A box of moths, pinned mid-flutter, neat as though they'd never taken flight. The effigy of a Native American in a feathered headdress. That skull, its teeth still slightly parted. He thought of the whale-skull Leviathan in the hold.

Day had kept Sunday service each week; had picked up Jackson's Bible as if there'd never been a time he'd hesitated to hold it. He'd returned from Cape Verdant. Maybe in pieces. Good enough.

But it was all slipping away, whatever goodness he'd managed to retain. And the thought of Jesse Stevens walking the ship with a knife—

"Can you banish them?"

He tried to make it sound offhand. As if the problem were smaller, much smaller: something that had merely disconcerted the men. As if he hadn't wished, even for a moment, to be rid of Avery. The guilt sat bitter and fibrous in his mouth.

"What?" She regarded him accusingly with those deep-set eyes, looking up so the curves of her cheeks caught the light. "Whatever for?"

He might have asked more. But suddenly, face-to-face with this woman, he remembered her conviction that he saw Sheppard, sad-eyed, noble Tom Sheppard. Day thought he would rather die than admit that her husband, instead, appeared in his cabin at night. There was no way to get there from here. Not without digging, elbow-deep, for things Day had tried hard to hide from the light.

He turned away, collecting himself, and picked up the skull. It was the color of the clouded-over eyes of their Camp Hope dead, frozen then thawed, irises like weak tea. His hands let go, and it hit the floor with a muted thud, like a hammer taken, dull, to a rib cage. "That night at the séance," he said. "When you said there was something on the ship with us."

She stayed silent.

"You said it asked—"

Her lips turned upwards. "What's the worst thing you've ever done?"

"Are you asking me—"

"*Telling*, Captain Day. That was the question it asked." A pause. "It must mean something to you?"

They looked at each other warily.

Yes, it meant something to him. Something that made him both flinch away and lean forwards in horrid fascination. Because he could easily imagine Stevens asking the very same question, boots up on that grimy table—as he'd once lounged, insouciant, boots up on Talbot's polished oaken table. Twirling his knife. Grinning a little, because he knew the answer. The real answer.

It led to a red tent, somewhere on a rocky pass. A polar bear.

Sheppard, crouched beside him—because Sheppard was alive, up there, as alive and real as he'd ever been—waiting for the screams.

A tap of the bear claw against the wall made Day jump. It made him want to grab Mrs. Stevens by both shoulders and shake her; made him want to reach through the veil of life and death, and take whatever was there by the hand. To clutch at it.

Maybe it was Stevens, after so long.

With effort, he fixed his eyes on hers. "Well, can you? Banish them? If they might be . . ."

"Capricious?"

"Dangerous."

She narrowed her eyes, made a noise of disagreement.

"Well, you must."

"I *won't*," she said fiercely, suddenly looking much younger. "I won't give them up. We need them. I need them."

But what if something had slunk up on Avery in his bed: something tall, handsome.

"It's dangerous," Day said. "I need to keep order. For your sake, too."

A small pursing of her rosebud lips; then Jesse Stevens's wife smiled a disingenuous smile, patting the bunk beside her in invitation, and turned the conversation easily on. "Captain Day—we're the only ones who really know him, aren't we?"

Day couldn't tell whether he was seeing behind her constructed image, or through to another, no less constructed one. Before she'd married, she'd simply been a curiosity, the child spirit-medium of a rural town. She might have looked at Jesse Stevens, golden as a flame, been drawn to him in the manner of moths everywhere. Or she might have seen something she could use.

Perhaps longed to be used by in turn.

"What was he to you, Captain Day?"

"He must have spoken about me." Day kept his voice level.

"Oh. He *barely* spoke of you."

It was like a plunge into icy water. "The other men—yes, he told me stories. I know about John—he was the one-legged cabin boy, wasn't he? I even know about Sheppard—how he got his men to sing, to drown out the sounds of weeping. But William Day, the fourth lieutenant who became captain because everyone around him died, because Jesse was beneath him in the chain of command—no. He never spoke of you. So I have wondered."

The room felt ready to spin; a kaleidoscope of shawls and colors and books.

"He didn't have to, though, did he? Because here you are . . ."

A small smile.

"No, I suppose not," Day said. Everyone knew what he was.

"Here you are, with your secrets." She picked up her book again. "You must let me help. We need to hold another séance. Some things work best for an audience."

Day thought of his niece, Amelia, and how carefully she arranged her hair, her lips, and her dresses. She'd been a tweeting songbird, and Mrs. Stevens was some big dark carrion creature, her barely suppressed cruelty unveiled under threat. The necklaces swung, the bear claw tapping, and Day remembered all the gifts he'd tried to send Amelia, in the years after Cape Verdant. The telescopes and compasses, beautiful and delicate as they were practical. All returned. The whole family had wanted nothing to do with him. Sometimes he felt that his ability to feel love, even basic fellowship, had atrophied. Like muscle wasting on a starving man.

"And as for the spirits, well . . . they'll leave at the end, you know. When they've been heard."

The gifts he'd sent Amelia had been practical; perhaps not meant for a lady. But a woman, he thought, could use a tool as well as any man.

———————

"Now we join hands."

Her veil, that afternoon, was deep purple lace. Qila's hair was once more neatly spun into a scarf, a dark nub of it peeking out the top. The wardroom's polished table reflected the formality of the scene, making Mrs. Stevens and the waiting circle into a host of murky expressionless shapes.

Day glanced around. Peters found his hand at once, getting on with it unquestioningly. On his right: "This is abominable," Valle whispered, clasping Day's hand in a death grip. "We don't need to pander."

Day shrugged, trying to make this seem commonplace. "It might help."

"Help *who*? You surely can't believe this will find out where he is."

"Help . . . restore order."

Because he wouldn't get a straight answer out of Mrs. Stevens, spinning her invisible web, playing her inscrutable games. He had to see for himself what was on his ship, stalking her companionways. Otherwise he was sailing them blindly into a storm.

"Parlor tricks," Valle muttered, but a prickly truce was better than none at all.

A snort of agreement from Lee. "She won't move the table on my account."

Peters glared back, and for a moment Day was startled by the naked dislike on his face. But perhaps it was just the gloom. The skylights had been covered with sacking, to create the proper candlelit atmosphere; this time, she'd had longer to prepare, and the room made Day feel a ghastly nostalgia—so reminiscent of the last days of the *Reckoning*, all crammed with absences.

Although it didn't yet get dark worth the name, save a few milky hours around midnight, they would still have to ration the lamp fuel, and the ship would get much darker over winter. To say nothing of the cold. Better to do this now; if it was Stevens—any aspect of him—that was stalking the ship, toying with them, Day would rather know.

Then what?

He shoved it down.

"Gentlemen," Qila interrupted. The men stilled. She rarely spoke directly to them.

"Is there anyone there?" Mrs. Stevens asked.

The circle strained to hear a reply. There was a shuffle as someone moved their feet under the table. Nothing.

"Spirits . . . make yourselves known."

Day felt the pressing need to glance behind him. But he knew there was only his familiar wardroom, pressed flower arrangements hanging over the prickly horsehair couches. He'd thought they would provide a welcome glimpse of life in winter; with the dark room and veiled celebrant, they looked like they belonged over a coffin.

It was quiet.

Peters looked very uncertain: this was probably all beyond him. Day thought, with a pang, of youth long gone, of Stevens taking his hand, dragging him onwards with all his contagious enthusiasm.

Come and see—there are such marvels!

What he'd give, to see that particular version of Stevens again.

It was so very quiet. Day realized that sounds from the deck had slipped away, and the ship seemed to have stopped moving. Even the ice was silent, holding its breath. The quiet deepened and deepened until it lay over the room like snowfall. No one coughed. No one fidgeted.

Mrs. Stevens asked again: "Is there anyone there?"

This time, there was a perceptible change in the atmosphere, as if some-one had just wandered into the room. Day felt goose pimples bloom under his clothing. This was what he'd been waiting for. Craving. The *connection*.

The sense that he was . . . joined to something. Something larger than himself.

A knock.

It seemed to come from under the table. Loud. Impossible to ignore. There was a gasp, and a nervous laugh from Lee. Nothing in the mirror. Nothing in the corner of the room.

Valle squeezed his hand hard enough to hurt. "This is a waste of time."

"Don't break the circle!" Avery hissed.

Mrs. Stevens kept both hands visible. Her eyes behind the veil were wide, her lips pressed tightly shut, as if she refused to permit the slightest word—the tiniest fingertip—to enter her mouth uninvited.

Stubbornly, she refused to give herself over.

"Ask it," Day snapped. "Now!"

His heart was pounding deliciously. It was the same impulse that had led him to storm into his cabin and demand that Stevens show himself: he was sick of half-life. He'd had enough whispering. What he'd give—

But she hesitated, and he hesitated with her. A cold hand seemed to clutch at his throat. The composure she'd shown in her cabin was faltering, although Day had supposed she'd held hundreds of séances, maybe thousands.

"What do you want?" she asked, low. "What do you want from me?"

He could feel it even more clearly now: something vast and dark. Oppressive. In the mirror—in the room he couldn't stop thinking of as the Great Cabin—their seated group looked like a large many-headed beast, made up of multitudes.

Something is on the ship with us.

The room seemed to tremble. Day wished it wasn't so dark: bring a thing into the light, and it would lose its power to terrify. Or so he'd heard. But they'd just created a slavish copy of one of those drawing-room séances, and he didn't want—and *wanted* so hard it made his fingers prickle—to see what was in the shadows.

He sniffed. Someone was cooking. But the galley was at the other end of the ship.

Day caught Peters's eye. "Who's doing that?"

"Doing what?"

"Cooking on deck."

"Captain?"

Qila was wrinkling her nose, looking around. The candlelight made the wardroom recede into the darkness, until it was hard to tell where this ship ended and the Great Cabin began.

"If you can hear us," Mrs. Stevens was saying, appearing to rally, drawing their eyes back to her, "knock once for yes."

She would use her knees, he told himself distractedly. If she refused to give in, produce a voice. But the table just seemed to tremble, slightly, like something breathing.

"Did it move?"

A sharp thud from under the table, as if something agreed, and Mrs. Stevens let out a small, kittenish noise.

But all Day could think about was the smell. It was getting stronger, and he could recognize bacon. His stomach turned over. He wouldn't have it on his ship. The smell made his skin crawl, made him want to scrub it off.

"Peters!" he hissed. "Go and tell that man—"

"No." Qila stared at him, sizing him up. Her voice seemed to come from very far away. "Don't break the circle."

Mrs. Stevens lifted her head. Fixed her wide eyes on Day. "Don't you feel it?"

As if she was sure he could.

The air shifted, and still the smell grew stronger. Day's mouth watered involuntarily. It was burnt, acrid, with a greasy hint about it, as if fat had been left to blacken in the pan.

Valle squeezed his hand. "William . . ."

"Can you . . ."

The smell was almost tangible. Mrs. Stevens's gaze pinned him in place.

"Well, I think this hasn't . . ." Lee said.

It crawled into him at last. A nauseating sweet smell, coppery and rich, worming its way between Day's lips. There was too much blood in it, that was the thing. When animals were slaughtered—butchered correctly—they'd have the blood drained.

This was the stink of something still fat with blood. Being cooked hastily, for starving men.

Something was in the room with them.

Day heaved, and the circle was broken. Peters jumped to his feet. "Captain?"

All the candles flickered. When Day stood, the solid oak table finally moved, a full five feet. There was something wrong about its motion: too light, as if skating over a pond. A delicate, uncanny glide.

Day bent double and retched, trying to get the taste out of his mouth. Copper. The inside of his cheek was chewed and raw. Something bloody was being roasted over an open fire.

"Captain . . . William—"

"He's having a seizure," Lee shouted, and grabbed Valle. "I told you he was unfit—Carter, damn it! Hold him down!"

"Give the captain some air!" Peters yanked open the door. But the smell grew no stronger when he did. No; it was coming from inside.

What's the worst thing you've ever done?

But it was almost a relief, as Day crouched on his hands and knees, staring at the oiled grooves where the table had been, Valle tugging at his collar. "William!" Starvation—human flesh—knowing that what you were eating had been a crewmate, had lived and breathed and laughed with you. Had trusted you. That wasn't the worst thing he'd ever done.

Of course they'd eaten their dead: they'd been starving.

He'd kept them alive, had Eat-Em-Fresh Day. Who could blame them.

Who could blame them?

He doubted Valle would need the stethoscope. Sitting in the cloying warmth of the sick bay, where he'd been all but dragged, Day could feel his own heartbeat in his wrists, throat, and temples. "Stay still," the doctor said. "I don't know how I could have missed it." He didn't mention that they'd barely spoken since the first séance. "I should have seen—"

"I'm well." Day dug his fingers into the side of the bed, ill at ease, feeling like something trapped. "I should get back—"

"What did you see?" Valle asked for the hundredth time, and Day blew out an exasperated breath.

"Nothing," he said truthfully. And gladly.

"At night," Valle said. "Do you still have bad dreams?"

Day shook his head.

"But if it returns . . ." Valle knuckled his eyes.

"It wasn't an apoplexy," Day said again. Bleeding on the brain—something small rupturing inside the delicate cathedral of his skull, causing strange sounds, smells, the sense of a presence. Surely, if so, he wouldn't feel so alive: as if he'd seen a giant predator stalk towards him, turn its terrible head, and pass on by.

"The smell . . ."

"You're going to tell me it wasn't real," Day said. "Don't say I wouldn't recognize it." He heard the anger thickening his voice. "I'd know it, wouldn't I?"

Whatever had come through, it had given him a salutary reminder: where he'd come from. *Who he was.*

Valle shook his head, his lips thinning. "You don't have to be like that."

"Don't I?"

The Butcher of Cape Verdant. It was a familiar skin, worn until almost comfortable. And Day knew the alternative was much worse. There was another story, so unthinkable he'd shoved it away—inside himself—and slid fast the bolt.

"I should have done better." Valle's voice lacked its usual sarcasm. "I should have done better by you. And while you're here . . ."

Day swung his legs off the bed, found his boots. He hated being treated as fragile. He shook his head when Valle asked, insistently, whether he could still smell anything. "Hear anything? See anything?"

"Valle." He exhaled. "It wasn't *real*—"

"Real enough to you." Valle stood in the glare of the lamp, making himself into a spider-like shadow. "Have you been seeing anything, William?" A pause. "Anyone? You must tell me. I can help you."

"How?" A pause. "Exactly." It would be impossible to explain thirteen years of seeing Stevens to Valle's expectant silhouette.

He wasn't your friend.

Day turned over, sometimes, what it would have been like if Valle hadn't been invalided off the *Reckoning*, if he'd gone through the hell of Amelia's Pass and Cape Verdant. Whether he'd have survived, as that other doctor had survived. It would certainly have come to blows along the way; Valle had known Jesse Stevens only for a few weeks' sail, and that had been enough.

<hr />

The hatch to the hold yawned open. Peters held the irons, a crude pair of cuffs linked by chain; the shape holding a lantern proved to be Avery. A cool faint breeze came from below, then a creak. Then a thud. The whole ship was moving again, trying the ice, and the sound of the engine was like a belabored heartbeat. After a difficult day and night since the séance, it seemed as though their stalemate had been broken. But the *Resolution* bore its own scars; their master carpenter swore that the rudder had been nipped, was unstable on her post. He had halted work in consequence, to regroup, and the ensuing argument with Roderick had been heard all over the ship.

Now Ward—that carpenter—stood at the hatch. The muscles bunched in his neck as he stared down, a small scar curving around his ear like a lick of silver.

"Wait," Day said.

He hadn't thought to get involved in this punishment. But something had drawn him off deck, away from the unsettled morning, like a fish on a hook. He had to see this for himself.

"What are you looking at?" Day asked. Ward was a bruiser. Someone who could hold his own, command respect.

"The knocking, down there. He keeps saying it's bad luck." Ward made a gesture that left it very clear who he was talking about: *Herridge*. "When you sleep in the forecastle it's like something rapping on the inside of your skull."

He looked at Day. "We've heard that knocking before."

"How bad did it get . . . on the boats?" Day found himself asking, with a small tight knot of shame—because he knew he wouldn't ask Roderick to his face.

The man shrugged. "That was a long time ago. We've forgiven him—he was off his head, seawater mad."

"You could have cut him off."

"Aye. Well. There's no point in losing a good man."

A good man.

Day tried to imagine who would dare to wear that terrible black-skinned mask, molded into the shape of a long, dripping snout. A man? Or something else? . . . something with curled claw-like hands, fingers worn thin from scraping, nails sloughed off, suffocating on the frothy fluids in his own lungs, red scarf wrapped around his neck like a noose. Although they'd reburied the body, left it in their wake at Beechey, it might—somehow—be waiting down there still. Listening for the first shuffling steps on the ladder.

"If she leaks, now, it's on you," Peters said grimly, and shoved Ward in the chest. "Hold out your wrists."

Ward's sleeves were short enough to ride up over his bony protruding ulna. The light dipped as Avery leaned forwards, holding the lantern over the blackness of the hold, trying to see the bottom. The crunch of ice. The drip of water. The patter of tiny feet. Avery drew back in a hurry.

"That's enough," Day said sharply to Peters. "I won't have him chained." He knew that Avery was listening, knew that everything said in this moment would be scribbled away for posterity. "A man should be able to fight off the rats."

Silence. If he expected thanks, he didn't get it.

Peters gave Ward a push down the ladder, and he disappeared into the darkness of eyes squeezed shut. Capable of hiding anything.

"Do you want to close it, Captain?"

No.

"Close it up," Day said. "Go on."

A twitch of Avery's face, round and speckled as the moon. Day swallowed. He knew how this looked. He was struck with the sudden terror that Avery would say something, would draw the comparison. The obvious comparison.

"He needs me," Mrs. Stevens had said, grabbing his arm, as if Day could part the ice and make the search go faster, as if he wasn't looking hard enough. "I made a promise, Captain Day, and I intend to keep it. We *must* go on. Do you understand?"

Day set his jaw. He wouldn't look away.

THEN

XII
GOD-SAVES HARBOR, MAY 15, 1868

THE LORD GAVE, AND THE LORD HATH TAKEN AWAY.

*P*ale gray-white light illuminates the Great Cabin. The ornate stern windows open onto nothingness, a blank page—Day had once thought the Arctic similarly full of possibility. He's trying to teach Stevens how to play chess: it's a ruse to explain why they're sitting on top of the hatch to the orlop deck, where the ship's provisions are stored in darkness just a few degrees warmer than her cavernous hold below.

"This is pointless." Stevens's breath plumes over the board. The rows of leather-bound books offer scant insulation against the yawning cold outside. One day they'll probably burn them, but for now, they're both bundled up in greatcoats, hats, and scarves.

"Chess is a civilized game." Day makes his move. "A test of wits."

"Give me a pistol, and give the other man one, too, and I'll show you wits." Stevens scowls. "Surely he's done by now."

Day listens. The constant lament of the ice. But nothing from below, where they'd posted the doctor through the hatch into the spirit room, to sneak from there into the provender store, where canned goods freeze and casks of the crew's "salt horse," dried into one solid mass, stink out the darkness. They'd hoped the groaning of the hull, the ice trying to squeeze the life out of it, would cover any sounds.

Everyone aboard is on a knife-edge. The scurvy—and its accompanying delirium—is thought by some to be contagious, and their sick are shunned like medieval lepers. Men drive other men from their hammocks. Arguments over rations turn violent. Friendships dissolve like the last of their sugar.

A faint rapping. Stevens uses the distraction to move a few chess pieces around, seemingly at random, not caring if Day notices. Then together they lift the hatch, release Nye from his well of shadows.

"How bad is it?"

"It's bad." Nye doesn't elaborate, looks about to polish his glasses, then relents. "The seams have burst on the canned stuff. It's going rotten fast."

Day and Stevens share looks of mutual horror. The *Reckoning* is down to its last supplies. The banquets of the first few months, the lavish Thanksgiving dinner, are a distant memory. They hadn't meant to be out here this long. But the ice holds fast, and no one really believes this summer will bring a thaw.

"At least we don't have to worry about *debility*," Stevens says tartly. "We'll starve first. Or freeze." They can heat the ship only a couple of hours a day, and the men carry flasks of ice under their clothes, warming them with their bodies, to get more drinking water than the meager allowance provides.

"It's scurvy," Day adds. "Anyone can see that."

Stevens shoots him a look of profound approval.

Nye does polish his glasses, then. "First Lieutenant, Acting Lieutenant, we need to do—something."

"What would you have us do?" Stevens is twirling his knife on the table, rotating it on the tip of its blade. It's the captain's table, carved with the swooping plumes of his family crest, and Stevens is ruining it, lazily, an inch at a time. Day wants to say something, but can't bring himself to do so.

"We redouble our hunting efforts."

Stevens scowls. He knows, more than most, how hard it is to scrape an existence above the frost line. "They're doing their best. There's just not enough." As if he doesn't himself call the Native hunters every name under the sun. As if he hasn't, more than once, pulled a rifle from the armory and stamped down onto the ice to prove he could do better. "There are—let's see—three quarters of us left. At least, if we keep dying at this rate—"

"Then we send them farther afield—keep looking for other Natives, larger game . . ."

"There aren't any," Day says. "Not that we've found—"

"Three months," Stevens interrupts. "August. Then what?"

Nye starts to say something, perhaps some comforting lie. Day is suddenly sick of it, sick of all the pretense, all the attempts to put on a brave face. Trying to maintain morale. For what?

"There are just too many of us."

When Day acknowledges this dark truth, the room falls deathly silent. His voice seems to echo, as if it's the very first time these words have been spoken by man, and in the weak daylight of the Great Cabin, the empty velvet armchairs, the silver candlesticks, the shine of the gilt mirror—the veneer of civilization—are all judging him.

They turn to look at the bulkhead. On the other side, Talbot lies sweating through his blankets. Both legs lumpen and swollen, white socks of skin stuffed with water, like a sausage badly made. "I'll die." Talbot had clutched at him with clawed hands. "I'll die with my tongue chewed out, my fingers in my mouth. Don't let me eat myself, William."

The three other officers are dead—Day refuses to think about their dark fates—and command is about to pass, extraordinarily, to an undistinguished British officer who's never before been north of the Shetlands. He'll make Stevens his first lieutenant. But there are too many of them aboard this icebound ship, too many of them sick, for any plans he makes to last.

Man proposes. God disposes.

"Another year." They all know what that would mean.

"We try to refloat the ship, break through—"

"We'll never do it," Day says. "Not with seven men too sick to leave their beds."

And they all know that no one will leave the ship while Talbot still lives.

"If we wait, we'll have nothing left," Day says, and is surprised how hollow his own voice sounds. Stevens looks at him, and is it Day's imagination, or does the light flicker as he does so? Like something large and dark beating its wings.

"You two. Plot elsewhere," the doctor says with an air of disgust.

Day follows Stevens down the companionway, where paneling has been chopped away for fuel; the *Reckoning* is down to her bones. Condensation drips from the beams above, stalactites forming and falling with the crackle of broken glass. They climb to the upper deck, where the ship is still shrouded in canvas, masts gutted of their rigging: there's no point fitting her for sail, and she looks like a half-made model in a collector's bottle. It's the middle of the night, but it makes no difference to the misty gray. Two blurry shapes tell them the hunters are sitting by a seal hole. The void around them is absolute, cold and still as the bottom of the ocean.

Day follows Stevens up to the bridge, to look out over this little kingdom.

"Yours, soon," Stevens says quietly.

Day squeezes the railing. He'd loved this ship from the moment he saw her. She looked nothing like the other gunboats he'd seen: she was ornate and stately, all curlicue and filigree, as if her designers couldn't make her useful without making her beautiful, too. He wants her, more powerfully than he'd ever *wanted* anything . . . before Stevens.

But oh, what he wouldn't give for a tiny sliver of open water. A night without the chew of the ice. Rosy-perfumed English sunlight.

"I don't want it!"

It bursts out of him like a sob. Not if it means Talbot's death, and the responsibility for all left alive. Stevens sighs, puts his hand on Day's shoulder.

It no longer matters what any of them want.

"You're right, though. They won't all make it." Stevens pauses—it's not like him—and looks at Day sideways. "*We* might, though."

"Who?"

"You, me." Stevens stares into the distance, gray eyes gleaming. He keeps his voice very calm, as if judging how to appeal to Day's reasonable nature. "Jackson. The guides. We're still strong. We could take a boat into the channel, make it to Lancaster Sound before the whaling season is over, find a ship. Talbot wouldn't even know we've gone."

It sends a shiver down Day's spine. He's calling him *Talbot* already. Stripping him of his rank. And this is . . . desertion. Mutiny. The end of everything Day knows.

"No," he says desperately. "No, we can't."

"What," Stevens says with a strange high tinge to his voice, "is the alternative?"

Silence.

Stevens doesn't press it. Day curls his fists into tight balls, and turns to look off their bow. Some say the ship might be got free with dynamite: but Day knows, instinctively and with a touch of belligerence, that this just isn't true. They're doomed. Men sleeping in the forecastle have dreams of being devoured by the ice. Perhaps it's a good way to die: quietly, in your sleep, simply swallowed up into something bigger.

Day fears, more than anything, the pain and anguish before death. He knows how man's animal nature reveals itself, has seen it in rolling eyes and thrashing limbs, blood-flecked spittle.

He can't stand it. The scurvy patients are gagged before the end.

"What about the others?" he says, breaking the silence.

"What about them?"

"James. Ewing." Day walks through the sick bay in his mind, with all its shivering patients. James had joined them as a newlywed, but with his swollen black mouth he looks like a septuagenarian. His teeth are coming out in twos and threes. And it's as if Ewing—not Day— had been dunked under the ice.

"The others," Day says. "If we leave them here, they can't hunt. Or fetch ice for water." And without water, without fuel, they won't last long. The *Reckoning* will be as cold and dark as the grave. Even in spring, the temperature sometimes drops suddenly to twenty below, making the frozen hardtack tear up their mouths. One man had managed to rip off his entire soft palate, blood fountaining out like a fish-mouthed statue in one of London's royal parks.

"We leave them the rest of the tinned food," Stevens says. "They can use the ship for firewood. Poor souls." He glances away, as if he can't quite bring himself to lie: to say that the men left behind need only wait for their return. Because Day understands—understands perfectly—they wouldn't be returning.

Their drowned-man figurehead gleams in the frost. It feels like a portent: the *Reckoning*, his once-golden home, is fast becoming a ship of the dead. Day realizes that he's rubbing at the scar on his hand, a compulsive motion, and places both hands behind his back.

"How—" He catches Stevens's eye, because he feels this is important. He trusts Stevens to keep this between them, because they're inching closer to something that might be described as a *plot*. "How much could we spare?"

Stevens exhales slightly, as if in profound relief, giving him a slow blink. Long blond eyelashes, more or less the only part of his face visible in the pressing cold. Although the misty haze surrounding the ship is warmer than the alternative, their winter clothing is so wholly inadequate that Talbot intends—intended—to write a strongly worded letter on their return. *Man proposes.*

"The lemon juice. The salt meat. We wouldn't be able to carry most of it anyway. I'll teach you how to hunt."

Day thinks about the doctor's report. Whatever's down in the hold is a feast for the rats. He thinks he should say something, but he doesn't; he doesn't want to poke too carefully at the miracle that he hasn't got scurvy. Man cannot live by rat alone: if there's no fresh game, he too will eventually die. With Stevens's hand on his shoulder, he finds the notion almost picturesque.

"Do you really think we could?"

"At least some of us will make it out to find the fleet."

Day feels his mouth twitching, and knows the expression he's wearing—that of the unhappiest man alive. But that man might be down in the makeshift sick bay even now, the privacy sheets spattered with bodily fluids. In Day's imagination, the sick man raises himself up on his elbows as he hears the telltale creak of the davits—the sound of Day and Stevens making off with a boat. Others hear it too: a low moaning communicates itself amongst the sick and dying men. A threnody of pain and abandonment. The unhappy man stumbles from his bed and onto hands and knees, crawls across the still and frozen galley to the ladderway, claws his way up towards the hatch, and the men *leaving.*

But he sinks back defeated, stick-fingers quivering, and his sob is small and snotty and woebegone, because the hatch is closed and someone has shut them in . . .

Day can feel his hair standing on end. This is wrong, he tells himself. This is not what a good captain does.

This is not what a good *man* does.

But there's something of a tonic in making plans; even if they're hopeless, even if they're reprehensible. He leans into Stevens. There's no harm in discussing it. Let him dream! Let him dream that the two of them will head south together, tumble out of the Arctic with fearful beards and the nightmare of the *Reckoning* firmly behind them.

"We should leave Nye behind, too," Stevens says. "Otherwise they won't live to eat those supplies."

Day swallows. He's grown to like their replacement doctor. There's something about the way Nye challenges them at every turn that he finds oddly reassuring. He knows his own limitations, does William Day; he wants, more than anything, for someone to tell him what to do.

He nods.

"But we can only take a few," Stevens says quickly. "We can't support any more. Who else?"

He means: *Who shall we leave?* Whoever is left will surely die. Day runs through the list of candidates, and can't bring himself to say a name out loud.

"Your friend Sheppard, perhaps?" There's a way Stevens says it, as if offering up a sacrificial lamb. "An officer. To command those left with the ship."

"Perhaps," Day says reluctantly, knowing he would be dead if it weren't for Tom Sheppard. He deserved his belated promotion to acting lieutenant, putting him on a rank with Stevens: a fact very much resented.

Stevens is close, complicit. "Soon it'll be up to you," he says.

———

A creak on deck breaks the spell. Long, hesitant. As if someone has been waiting under the bridge, just out of sight, and is only now deciding to make his move.

Day's heart thuds. He'll soon be a captain. He's meant to go down with the ship: Day knows if he says this Stevens will laugh, like it's the most ridiculous thing he's ever heard.

A shape steps forwards and clears its throat.

It's Sheppard.

Day doesn't meet his eye, thinks frantically whether he'd heard a hatch or door slam. Neither. There's no way of telling how long he's been hidden there.

Stevens seems to realize this, too, and arranges himself: he's a master at it. He leans a little farther back, his shoulder pressed against Day, and fixes Sheppard with an icy look of indifference. *Nothing*, he's saying. *You heard nothing.*

NOW

XIII: REVENANT

TALBOT'S CHANNEL, SEPTEMBER 5, 1882

Looks rather small, doesn't it?" Carter remarked.

Day didn't answer. From the hunched gray bluff, the *Resolution* was framed against the sky, looking like a figurine made to commemorate battles at sea. The ice was glittering like diamonds, and they'd found no trace of Stevens in three weeks scouring both sides of the channel as far as conditions permitted. Three fruitless weeks. "I know it," Mrs. Stevens kept saying fiercely, whenever he couldn't avoid her. "We'll find something. Anything! Those men would have fought to the last."

They wouldn't have given up—and the unspoken message: *Neither should you.*

He gritted his teeth.

"Permission to speak freely, sir?" Carter was passing his telescope from hand to hand as if he were about to bowl for England.

Day nodded curtly.

"We might be quite alone out here."

The sun glimmered over the ice, turning it orange then peaches-and-cream. Day looked at him. Carter had come highly recommended by three different captains. He had connections, but seemed cheerfully aware of his shortcomings, which explained how he hugged the edges of Lee's limelight.

"We're not alone." It came out harsher than he intended. "Captain Stevens and his men are out there. Waiting for us. Depending on us."

"All we know is that he didn't return via Beechey," Holt pointed out, as if Carter's permission to speak naturally extended to him. "He might have passed into the sea beyond . . . he might be anywhere." Day could discern the regulation skepticism: Holt was Admiralty, and the idea of an open sea at the pole had long fallen out of favor, let alone the idea that it could be reached through Lancaster Sound. Talbot's Channel was accepted to be something like a dead end.

He might be anywhere. Wasn't that what Stevens had always dreamed of? Discovering an Arctic homeland, going amongst its inhabitants, not needing to be found. But Day knew how hard it was to sustain an expedition by hunting, even with the best men alive. He stayed silent, and thought he saw a knowing glance pass between the two officers. He was tired, so tired, of being on the outside.

"It only takes one good freeze, and we'll be stuck," Carter continued.

"What are you suggesting?"

"We ought to be able to find the *Louisa*," Holt said. "While the season's open. Wait for her to catch up. Or rendezvous back at Beechey."

Day spun around. "And lose all our progress? These next few weeks are critical. Do you have something to say?"

"Nothing, Captain. Nothing." Day could almost see it melt its way across Carter's face, his wide jaw, his aquiline nose—none of them even knew if the *Louisa* had survived the storm. The suggestion that they turn around hovered on Carter's lips. Abandon Stevens to the great unknown.

Day thought, quite frankly, he'd rather die.

"We're still making progress. I won't turn back while that's true." He took the telescope with a tug.

Carter swallowed again and glanced at Holt, but the older man just gave a small shrug of his shoulders. "The ship seems very unsettled, that's all. The men say they've never heard anything like it."

Day exhaled, watching his breath freeze. "You'd do well not to encourage those men."

He turned his gaze to the ship; noticed he was clenching his jaw. Carter was right: if he stretched out his hand, he could cover her entirely. Only a third visible, the rest below the waterline, where every sound echoed like something hammering on the hull. The pumps plagued them still—something was clogging it all up—and dark figures swarmed on the ice, attempting to use this pause to find the trouble with their rudder. The carpenter swore it wasn't quite right.

The—*apparition*—would naturally be more vivid up here. That was all. That was all. Whatever had troubled the ship was troubling them no more; just the usual dangers of ice and water. And the *real* Stevens was up there, waiting to be found—along with Day's reputation.

If he could just reach out a hand and pluck it back.

—————

"Captain—come and see!"

Avery, shouting up from below. Carter let out a small snort; although a self-proclaimed adventurer, the reporter's outdoor gear was clearly newly purchased. The officers had needled him at dinner, like schoolboys, about whether he'd fit into it much longer. Day had pushed his own food around the plate, not saying anything; the men were cruel. He supposed it was in the nature of men to be cruel.

"Found—something," Avery panted, placing his hands on his knees. Lars was with him, and Day realized, awkwardly, that he would never have thought to ask their guide to . . . well, guide. Day lacked those easy ways. He had no idea how to approach Lars, skinning his catch on deck, perfectly competent and perfectly alone.

He had no idea if Lars missed his cousin, Karl, on the *Louisa*; if he feared for his safety, so far from home. But he must, mustn't he?

"Come and see!" Avery urged.

That *something*, when they reached it, looked like a hump of snow, and Carter made a dismissive sound. But the round structure couldn't be anything other than man-made—albeit heavily covered with drift. Lars nodded at Day grimly, clearly of the same mind.

Someone had learned to live up here without supply ships and Admiralty gear.

Then the guide jerked his chin: just below, tucked into the curve of the channel, were the remnants of a jolly boat. Not a kayak. Unmistakable in its Western style.

Dread crept its fingers over Day.

There was no apparent reason; except that there was something desperate and incongruous about the scene. There should have been flags, messages in stones, a signal fire. It made him think of the deserters who'd sloped back to the *Reckoning* after several months on the ice. If this camp had shoulders, they would be hunched and furtive.

It belonged to someone who didn't want to be found.

Avery, rooting inside, shouted something muffled. It took Day a moment to make out the words.

A body.

He sucked in a deep breath.

"Captain." Avery poked his head out. "He's—a white man."

Day's blood froze. A slow nod as he acknowledged the meaning of it, and Lars went down the slope to lend a hand dragging the body free.

Stiff as a lump of firewood, but unmistakably human, bit by bit it came into the daylight world, like a burial in reverse. Day put his boot in the thing's waist, pulled it over to see its face—

He made a harsh noise of surprise.

The cheek was dark, almost black, on one side. The eyes were shut, the lids translucent. There were no signs of scurvy, but the man was thin, desperately so. His clothing was threadbare and grimy, the black of seal-blubber smoke. A coat and hat, a muffler—the sort of clothes that might be issued from a ship's stores.

Avery crowded in on him. "He's one of them, isn't he? From the *Fox*—"

Day held up a hand.

"What does that mean?"

Day wheeled around, scanning the whiteness, the shore stretching away. The blood was pumping loudly in his veins. The high sun cast stark shadows, making rocks into shapes crowding at the corners of his vision; crouching figures. The body was relatively fresh, not yet despoiled by animals. It should have been good news. But he felt as though he'd stumbled upon something repellent.

"Stevens!"

It exploded out of him unbidden; Day barely recognized his own voice.

This man had been alone on the ice, separated from his party. No one should be left like this. No one should be abandoned—

All the hairs were prickling on the back of his neck.

———————

The man was gone—whoever he was. In the warm light of the sick bay, Lars's eyebrows were two decisive slashes of ink. He'd taken the man's hand in his own, cupped it against his chest, as if trying to share some vital spark, as if this stranger were family. Valle was uncharacteristically quiet as he tried the jaw with a speculum. It was pity, Day thought. Hanging in the air.

"Can you tell how long he's been dead?" Avery murmured.

"I'm not a coroner." Valle turned his attention to the man's left hand, frozen into a claw. "And someone seems to have cut off his fingers."

"What the—" Avery grabbed the lantern and held it up.

The door was closed; Day knew the men were listening outside, Roderick picking his teeth. "Keep your voices down," he hissed.

"They've been sawn off," Avery screwed up his face. "Deliberately."

"You can't know for sure—"

Avery gave Day an angry look. Day cleared his throat, tasted something thick and bitter. He resisted the urge to defend himself from whatever this was, from whatever it seemed would—inevitably—be laid at his door. He hadn't done it at the Admiralty; he wouldn't do it now.

He shook his head. "We can't know what it means. Frostbite, maybe." He looked to Valle for support.

Two fingers wouldn't make a meal, after all.

"Really, William," Valle hissed. He took the man's right arm gently.

It was frozen under his jacket, disclosing a bulky shape the size of another forearm. Day had never seen Valle use such care on a living patient.

They watched in silence. The man's leathery skin had turned deep brown from the relentless Arctic sun, although he'd been a white man once; on one side of his face, a livid handprint covered his eye socket and the side of his nose, as if someone had used a burning palm to push him down. Valle worked to free his remaining arm. Whatever was under there, it had been well protected.

"I'd expect slashes on the palms," he said quietly to Avery. "If there was a fight . . ." He paused. "If he was permitted to struggle."

Something large and cold walked over Day's grave.

They might never know where this man had come from. At the very most, he told them of a possibility that some on the Stevens expedition were still alive; but he'd clearly parted from it—and it from him. It left Day with a knot in his chest. He couldn't help remembering how the little camp had appeared to be an attempt to *hide*.

"Ah," Valle said faintly. Bony fingers trembling, he held something up to the light. But it wasn't the man's arm. It was rigid, a piece of timber as long as a humeral bone. The gleam of polished wood. Coming from that grimy camp in the middle of nowhere, it looked impossible. But it was smooth, sinuous, dripping.

Day took in a sharp breath. Valle's hand wobbled, and their eyes met.

A wet lock of hair. One lidless staring eye. The curve of a neck. And the water, water, carved in slashing lines all over, unique as a fingerprint. Ship's figureheads were meant to calm the storms. He'd heard that to sink without one was one of the many ways you could be condemned to haunt the seas forever.

———

"Hey!"

Footsteps in the companionway. A grasping hand caught at his arm, and all the breath left Day's body before he saw who it was.

"Don't lay your hands on me, Mr. Avery. I've warned you!"

"Oh, really?" Avery hissed. They were barely inches apart. Day wasn't sure he'd ever seen such a look of anger on the reporter's wide face. "It's from the *Reckoning*, isn't it?"

An icy hand clawed at Day's throat.

He'd told himself it couldn't be—it couldn't be. Because that would mean he was wrong, in the worst way possible.

All those times he'd told himself—

"You and the doctor knew it at once. You *recognized* it." Avery looked like he was about to shove him. "Tell me how that's possible."

Everyone knew the Arctic iconography: proud ships keeled, broken spars, wreckage, the ice taking back what man had made. A national fairy tale to make those at home quiver in frightened delight.

But they wouldn't have a formal inquiry, would they, to redeem him in the eyes of the public? Well then, Day would tell them his ship had been *lost*. Let that be the end of it. The newspaper illustrations had shown Day kneeling on the ice, watching his ship disappear into the deep, her drowned-man figurehead gasping for air.

But they'd taken that figurehead off the bow over the first winter, to protect it from the ravages of the weather, the weight of hoarfrost. Day had been part of the work party himself. He'd become intimately familiar with the half-bust carving, some four feet high—had run his fingers through the water etched on its screaming brow.

The man from the ice had taken an axe to it clumsily, chopped off just enough to make Talbot's family device identifiable.

Day drew a breath, shallow, through his fingers. He hadn't realized he'd raised them to his face.

In his mind's eye, men laboriously dragged sledges and boats away from the dark ship. A row of tiny crosses on the shore were in perpetual shadow, under the cliffs of God-Saves Harbor: somewhere the sun would never break and summon the dead to their dawn.

The *Reckoning* waited. She would never go down.

"So that's it, is it?" Avery was breathing heavily. "All lies."

She could still have gone down, Day's panicked mind tried to supply. Her figurehead thrown free by the action of the ice. He wished he could believe it.

"And someone carved that man up, didn't they? As punishment, as—who knows what." Avery stared at the hissing boiler pipes as though something were building up inside, liable to explode.

"Stevens did that, didn't he?"

Day opened his mouth to deny it, the sudden change of subject making him reel. No, it couldn't be Stevens, the man he'd shared a bunk with. The man he'd shared so much of *himself* with.

Stevens had kept him alive, when he'd been ready to give up. Had told him what to do. *Stick with me, William.*

He wanted to say no, Stevens wouldn't—

"Yes," Avery said. "I thought so." He shoved past into his cabin, slamming the door on the man who'd abandoned the *Reckoning*—on Eat-Em-Fresh Day.

———————

That night, the ship was quiet. But Day was awake.

He was curled in a ball of sweat-damp blankets, lying there listening; something had shocked him awake from a dream of bare limbs, golden hair; hauling rope, the lines slapping through their palms, slippery and sinuous and intent, taut as muscle, flexible as an eel. He didn't feel able to move his arms and legs: he had the horrible suspicion it would alert something in the dark to his presence.

After a few moments, he felt the weight shift on his bunk. That was . . . wrong, wasn't it? But the sensation was unmistakable: someone had sat down beside him.

Paralyzed, Day counted his breaths. The ship appeared to inhale, too, contracting and squeezing, until the air was thick with malice.

He couldn't look.

He couldn't *move*.

A small hissing sound came from the darkness: a wheeze of sorts, getting louder. It made Day feel dizzy. Someone was injured, laboring to draw breath.

He thought of the sound he'd once heard coming from his mirror at night. Something entering the room, through a door he hadn't realized he'd left ajar.

Too late to close it now.

Eventually, inch by inch, he rolled over. Pulled the blanket back. There was a shape in the darkness at the end of his bed. And the strange thin noise, the wheeze, was getting louder; it was no longer trying to be quiet. It was learning to breathe.

Manifestation.

He struck a light.

Stevens swam into view. He was bloody, his bare arms—very white and very strong; Day could trace the gleam of muscle all the way from sharp elbow to delicate wrist—covered with a dusting of golden hair and clotted blood. He turned to look at Day, and his face, too, was smeared with gore from the nose down, as if he'd put his head in a bucket of entrails and shaken it.

Day's heart was pounding.

Stevens held up the tongue cradled in his hands, still sluggishly pumping blood at the root, offering Day a ghastly, lazy, almost *erotic* smile. Stevens's tongue was usually so pink and dainty, sometimes seen when concentrating hard, or stuck out at the medical inspection with an air of insolence.

Day had thought long and hard on that tongue, and how it would taste—wintergreen, he thought, but warm. The sort of warmth that would make everything else bearable.

"The human mouth is filthy," Valle had once said to him, tightly, but how could that be possible? Why was everything Day wanted disgusting and unclean?

Someone shouted. Stevens looked up, an animal scenting prey. Day lurched to standing, eyes half-shut, and grabbed his coat, holding it in front of him like a shield. He could still hear the blood dripping, *pat-pat-pat*, on the floor. The horrible wet, ghastly sound of Stevens breathing past the root of his own tongue.

Day would have given him everything, everything. He didn't know what Stevens gave him in return.

The sick bay. The sound had come from the sick bay.

————————

Stevens and Valle must finally have come to blows. Day stumbled on the steps, fell heavily; he wasn't thinking straight. Could *it* be in two places at once? Did it have weight, or not? He had no idea of the rules anymore. At the bottom of the stair, Valle was holding up a lantern, the *Resolution*'s chilly depths like dark water around him.

"Captain," he said. "His tongue—"

Day barreled into the sick bay, the door ricocheting like a gunshot. Bottles clanked, chinked. Another lantern cast sickly light over the scene. But Stevens wasn't there. Just the man from the shore, his head in a vise, his jaw finally pried open. It was wide, too wide, and empty as a scream. Standing over the bed—Mrs. Stevens, dressed in black. A mourner. A grave robber, peering into that open maw, as if looking for gold. A ghoul.

"What did you see?" Day whirled around. "Valle, what did you see?"

Stevens could be anywhere. He was, Day thought wildly, surely capable of anything.

Valle's face was gaunt. "She shouldn't be here." Mrs. Stevens was lit in chiaroscuro, her bear-claw pendant catching the light. "I just—she startled me," Valle sniffed.

Henri de Valle had never, in his entire life, been startled by anything.

"He's missing his tongue," Mrs. Stevens said faintly. "Is that normal?"

Valle appeared to collect himself. "It could have been chewed off by bears. Or in the last paroxysms of death."

Day pressed his knuckles into his eyes. "You should go back to your cabin."

"But this is—this is one of Jesse's men! You should have come to fetch me."

The air seemed to be sucked out of the room. He could smell her perfume, like moldering flowers.

Jesse.

"I knew them in America. All his men. I—" She gulped. Composed herself. "I was involved in the selection process. He needed men with the right sort of ideas. Men who'd think like him. Men who wouldn't . . . falter."

Her eyes said, flickering: *you know.*

"Well?" Valle snapped.

"This was Gregory Patch," she said. "The helmsman. I liked him." She looked as though she was struggling with something too overbearing to put into words. "I—had to convince him to sign on. He was reluctant. He needed persuasion, the sort of reassurance only I could give." Low: "And now look at him."

"We don't know exactly what happened," Day managed.

"I didn't know he'd end up like this." She looked up, furious. "I didn't!"

Valle said, very quietly: "Trust not every spirit, hmm?"

The crew, alerted by the commotion, were starting to gather in the forecastle. "Captain." Roderick wore a long sleeping robe that puddled at his bare calloused feet. "We can't have that on board any longer!" He was wringing his hands. "Death calls to death. It's unlucky, weighs on the men. Attracts—bad things."

There was something ugly about the gleam in the men's eyes.

Boom.

"Did you hear that?"

An uglier gleam still. The muttering ended so precisely it might have been cut by a knife, and Day crept out into the dark of the belowdecks. Mrs. Stevens followed.

"You should get back to your cabin," he whispered.

She shook her head, mouth set into a small tight rosebud. "I am not afraid." She took his hand. "Come with me, Captain Day. We could *ask* Patch—"

"No!"

The reverberating sound came again.

"It was nothing," Day insisted, his heart hammering. "Rats."

There was a scrabbling beneath their feet, sometimes on one side of the ship, sometimes on the other. He tried to get rid of the image that presented itself: the claw-fingered dead, all down in the stinking hold.

The ship is restless.

"Monstrous big rats," someone said. "With hands an' all."

"Hush!" Roderick hissed.

"'S come," another man said. "It's followed us here."

Day thought about Stevens, offering his tongue to eat, a grotesque parody of the man he'd known. Stevens was always so golden, so clean, so—noble-looking.

Someday, Day had heard, his sins would find him out.

The noise below continued to make its presence known, always sounding like it was on the verge of tipping over into something else.

"Is there anyone there?" Mrs. Stevens asked.

Silence, all at once.

The darkness down in the hold was absolute, not the sort that suggested shapes. Day found that his hands were covered in soot, grimy, as if they'd opened the hatch of their own accord. The group of silhouetted men looked ready to take up pitchforks and torches, a mob from a fairy-tale etching. And their sick bay held Gregory Patch, the tongueless helmsman. Someone—or something—had made very sure he couldn't lead anyone to Stevens.

XIV: JOSEPH ADAMS LEE
TALBOT'S CHANNEL, SEPTEMBER 7, 1882

When Day first encountered the mutiny, it was a cool, clear September day, as if the sailing season would never end. The day after Patch had been committed to the ice, like feeding time at London Zoo: sewn into a blanket with scrap iron, he had knocked once—*boom*—against their hull, making the men cross themselves, and Avery glower at his loss. A rare relic indeed.

Day knelt with Qila at the foremast hatch, feeling his joints complain. Dust motes sparkled in the narrow shaft of light, and he could hear voices filtering up from a secret place in stowage, the brittle air trapping sounds like a bell jar. Poised beside him, like a hunter beside a seal's breathing hole, Qila pressed a finger to her lips. Day wondered if she'd spied on her previous master—the one who'd inspired that wary disdain. Had taught her to carry a knife. To mistrust what *men were like.*

She'd come to get him in secret, drawing him down from the bridge at the precise moment when everyone on deck seemed to be looking the other way. "Captain Day. You need to hear this. It's connected to the . . . mask. The thing that attacked Mr. Avery."

As they walked around to hide themselves in the spiderweb of lines behind the foremast, she'd added: "You're going to hear this at inspection: Herridge has gone. No one can find him on the ship."

Now, she gave him a withering look, directing his attention downwards.

The voices continued below.

"I'm telling you, Herridge was onto something." A cough. "We've all heard the knocking down there. It gives me the creeps."

"We're unlucky." Day struggled to place the speaker. He dredged up a name: Flett, who had long white hair, and had looked at the Cape Riley shipwreck like it was all his nightmares come at once. "Damned to go down. He knew. Any day now, we'll take a nip—get swallowed up. Then it's the boats again, naked on the face of the water. I tell you, I won't do it again. I won't do it, not for no one!"

"Aye, he put himself into the water," someone else said. Low, pugnacious. Sinclair, Roderick's other mate. "For our sake, as well as his own."

There was a shuffling, scraping sound. "Gentlemen," someone else said, and the whalers paused, as if the person who'd entered the festering room, with its stink of ropes going rotten, had sucked all the air from it. "So we're of the same mind?"

Day opened his mouth, and Qila squeezed his arm. Her hands were very strong. They locked eyes. Day would have recognized that well-bred drawl anywhere.

Joseph Adams Lee.

"We all know what happened," Lee said smoothly. "It's perfectly obvious. Stevens's expedition went up and never came back down: probably ended up eating each other." A small sound of mirth. "There's no sane reason why the same should happen to us."

"What about the captain? We'd face the consequences. Maybe not you."

Day closed his eyes briefly, the image of the Admiralty spinning around him: the warm room and the rainy London morning. Lee, marching out with his venerable grandfather, all those portraits staring. The *contempt*. A man couldn't escape it. Could sail for miles and miles, and never escape it.

Qila nudged him back to attention.

"Leave the captain to me," Lee said. "I'll make sure everything's aboveboard. The doctor's got to have his own misgivings. Compulsory examinations: they know he isn't right." A pause. "We need to get things under control while we can."

"Your time to shine, eh?"

"I won't help you with this." It was Roderick's voice that spoke quietly, making Day jump. "But once it's done, and you have the ship, we'll be heading back to the *Louisa*. Or at any rate, going no farther. There'll be no boats, I promise you that." The familiar sound of the ice-master sucking his uneven teeth.

"We shouldn't've come back out," Flett said bitterly. "Or shouldn't've brought *him* with us, with all his ranting and raving about sea creatures and sacrifice."

"How would Herridge's wife and family have eaten," Roderick said calmly. "A whale man who wouldn't sail. We took him back. And now you disagree?"

Flett hissed in response, "I went *into the water*, if you've forgotten, in all that . . ."

Day felt cold fingers on his heart, the pitiless glare of the Arctic sun. "What about the officers?"

Lee laughed, a supercilious sound that made Day press a fist to his mouth. "Oh, I'm sure I can make them see reason. A man wants to live, doesn't he? You don't have to be superstitious to see it's madness to continue with no supply ship, and our own ship leaky." His voice dropped. "A fool's errand. Where we'll all get scurvy or starve or just go plain *mad*—"

"Shh. Someone's coming!"

Footsteps in the mess hall. Day stumbled back on his tailbone at the glimpse of a shadow with sandy hair passing directly beneath the hatch. Another rasping slide of the locker door, and Day could hear his heartbeat in his chest. *Boom. Boom.*

"What's this?" A quiet voice, laden with unmistakable menace.

Someone laughed nervously.

"Ah," Lee said. "Peters Peters." The drawl of a bully; *Peters Peters*, as if Day's chosen second-in-command had no Christian name, or perhaps no last name, was utterly unremarkable. But Peters's spectacles were now on the ocean floor in Lancaster Sound, a curiosity for sea creatures. And this voice no longer fit that man.

"You shouldn't be down here."

"Why, I'm just passing time with the men. The heart of this ship. Salt of the earth. Am I not permitted?"

"You'd be better off elsewhere." A pause. A hiss: "Don't think I don't know what you're doing. Having a grandfather on the council won't spare you—"

"Am I supposed," Lee drawled, "to be afraid of you, Peters? You . . . you *nobody*?"

An exhalation. "The captain—"

"Oh, Peters. Peters. Always so loyal, like a dog. His days are over, old Eat-Em-Fresh: haven't you seen him jump at shadows? You could be the young officer who saw reason, helped us turn it all around, make it back to the depot ship in one piece. Stick with him, and if you come back *at all*, you'll be the disgraced second to a disgraced captain. Is that what you want?"

Low: "I know you begged and scraped your way on board. Some, in fact, would say you were *hungry* for it." A short laugh, as if Lee had nudged one of the men. "Eat-Em-Fresh. Do you really think he'll let you share in the feast?"

Day didn't want to hear any more. Lifting his head, the lemon light of early afternoon hurt his eyes. He was glad, immeasurably glad, he'd chosen Peters over Lee. A nobody.

He pulled himself up, refusing to meet Qila's gaze.

"And the mask?" he asked, because he couldn't tolerate the silence. The shame.

"It's not clear," she said quietly. "Their captain was a little too uncareful. Their ship went down, and he died. They were in the boats too long, drinking seawater and . . . other things. Less wholesome."

Day swallowed, tasting lichen.

"And in the chaos, one of them—you know which one—killed a sea creature. Kept its head and fashioned it into a mask. Started saying things no one wanted to hear."

"Like what?"

"Oh, I think you can guess," she said. "What do men do, when they think they're cursed?"

Day shivered.

"And now he's gone." Day looked around uneasily. There was nowhere to go, on a sailing ship. "Vanished."

She nodded. "But they're right, aren't they?" It sent spiders crawling through his veins. "And Olive. There's something aboard this ship already." Qila studied him. "I think there's something haunting *you*."

He felt his mouth fall open.

She shook her head, a hint of a smile playing on her lips. "No. I'm not an angakkoq, though I do respect them. My name might have meant something when it was given, but I came south too young. Or was taken—I don't really know how it happened, how I ended up there, and no one will tell me." Bitter. "I've seen the way you look around yourself, that's all. How wary you are. Starting at shadows. I'm not stupid."

"No, of course not." She spoke three tongues by seventeen. What might look like wariness was actually a keen intelligence.

"I've seen," she added, "what a . . . guilty conscience looks like."

Day thought of the wardroom table moving in their séance, lissome and light as a lie.

"But you're a good man," she said, as if that explained everything and nothing. She'd touched him, he recalled, several times, without the slightest fear of any consequence. "And you asked for my help. I saw many ships come and go into Baffin's Sea. This—" she nodded at the bright day, the clear, close air, the ice jagged like a thousand teeth. She paused. "It's not my home. But you were the first who'd take me north."

They were eye to eye. "Be careful, Captain Day."

He remembered her earlier warning: *men are like that everywhere.* And now he'd seen their quality for himself.

Laughter, from the deck.

It drove a stab of impotent rage through Day's heart, a feeling that he knew well, and he jammed his hands into the pockets of his greatcoat to conceal their shaking. He wouldn't let them see. If he was angry, well, that would make him the monster they all thought he was.

He wouldn't let them see it. There were so many men in the rigging; Carter and Holt were at the stern, and their faces seemed to blur together into one composite Admiralty officer. For a moment, the ship was crewed by faceless strangers, and anyone could be a foe.

Soon the knock started coming to his cabin door.

At midnight, the nautical twilight was royal blue, a harbinger sort of light. Day could hear the ice grinding, the creaking timbers separating them from the endless depths below. He was thinking about the whalers' boats. Salt water. Things less wholesome. The salty taste of blood. What you'd do to survive. The boiler pumped its inky water through the pipes as if the ship itself had a heartbeat.

The *thud* of knuckles on wood, though, was distinct. It made the walls of his cabin seem to billow, expand around him.

Stevens was waiting outside. At least, something that still looked a lot like Stevens; Day could see the long pale line of its throat, disappearing towards a collarbone sharp and precise. It didn't look at Day.

What do you want?

He didn't know whether it still had a tongue to answer, or whether its mouth contained nothing but a bloody stump, the muscle lying flaccid on Day's cabin floor. Whether Day had forever lost his chance to hear that tongue speak, to swallow around its lissome shape.

Day shivered. He felt he could see inside the cabins around them, as if the *Resolution* were dissolving. Peters might be reading, or sleeping the sleep of the righteous: Day had no idea of his private habits. Holt and Carter would be sitting together on a bunk, feet under the blankets, laughing softly in the light of a single candle. Day tried not to see himself and Stevens in their quiet complicity: tried not to long for it. Stevens alive, and smiling, rather than—

Was this, he thought, the only crumb available to him now?

The tiniest *morsel*.

Stevens unbent himself from the wall, as if Day had seen enough. He was barefoot, leaving blurry footprints. One hand dragged behind him, fingers splayed, fingernails catching.

Day followed.

Stevens kept at the limits of the lantern-light. Day realized he was barefoot himself, and the decks were achingly cold. He could smell the sickly sweet smell of rendering fat. A fire burning outdoors, black-smoked and harrowing.

You're just in my head.

The stairs creaked. Stevens's teasingly outstretched hand disappeared, and Day increased his pace. The—*manifestation?*—had stopped at the foot of the stairs. Day paused, trying not to breathe. It felt as if catching up with Stevens—really catching up with him—would cause him to disappear. A bubble bursting. A mirage dissolving.

He noticed an oily-looking trail on the wall.

Looking back at Stevens, Day saw that his face and neck and shoulders were all in shadow, as if dipped in tar. His face was almost unrecognizable under a thick coating of grime, the blackness clinging to him, thick like blood rendered down for drinking.

And that was why he had to follow.

Day knew Gregory Patch had left them a warning, if they'd chosen to listen. A man in a red scarf, beaten and murdered. And the proof of Patch's own body, fingers missing, figurehead clutched.

Day felt as if he'd been asleep, and was just about to wake.

He held the lantern high. With a profound, ice-water horror, he felt sure that he was back on the *Reckoning*, down in the pitchy rat's-nest black of the orlop deck. Damp. Rot. A ship slowly accumulating foul matter.

A good man gone bad.

Stevens knelt at the hatch. In the bobbing light, Day thought he saw a bundle of sticks, discarded on the precipice, thin and warped. But as he watched, one of them stirred.

A hand was clinging to the deck.

The fingers had been worn down to the bone, stumps, defleshed, one single nail hanging by a single thread of skin, and Day covered his mouth to stop himself making a sound. There was blood on the open underside of the hatch. Something had been scratching away down there for a very long time. It had ceased to be a man, ceased to be anything except the desire to be *let out*.

And in the shadows, Patch stood with his face turned away, pointing with one accusing remaining finger.

What are you trying to tell me?

The ice responded with a crunch, as if the ship was caught in the jaws of a giant animal. The *Reckoning*'s supposed death knell. He looked around himself wildly. Her hull was screaming, the scream of a hull that would never break, and he covered his ears.

You're just in my head, he told Stevens.

But no, that wasn't right.

I made you.

Better.

Because it was his shames and doubts taken form, wasn't it? He'd thought, once, that it had come to help him. And now it was getting darker, bigger, louder.

Patch still pointed. The hand from the hold still scraped.

They're your ghosts, he said. *Not mine.*

Stevens gave him a look. *Are you so sure?*

It would only get darker and colder, and those in the cable locker had been right: they might be past the point of no return. He had to continue chasing Stevens. With a sudden rush of blood to the head, he found himself back on the *Resolution*, the boiler hissing away. He blinked.

A shadow peeled itself off the wall, and Day nearly screamed.

"Captain," it said with a low sound of delight. Lee.

"Don't look," Day managed, trying to block his path. "Don't look."

Because he wasn't in control, was he? And if Lee met Stevens's silvery eyes . . .

Who's that behind you—

He couldn't be responsible for what might happen.

"My great-aunt, too, was prone to sleepwalking," Lee said with a sly smile. "They had to dose her up on laudanum and lock her into her room. What a pity."

Day had been followed, that much was clear. He grasped the bulkhead, breathing like a man hauled out of the water. His struggle was met with a supercilious look: any chance of dealing openly with Lee's ambitions was now gone.

"Heave!" Peters yelled to the men at the capstan. "Come on!"

He'd rolled up his sleeves so his bony elbows were exposed, even though frost-smoke billowed in the still September air, and the dark lead of open water remained tantalizingly out of reach.

"It's too thick," Lee shouted from off-ship. "This is pointless!"

Lee's face spoke of how ill-prepared the *Resolution* was to break ice; they hadn't been meant to take these sorts of risks. His coat was sooty from two days in the coal bunkers overseeing the shoveling. Without the *Louisa*, they might soon find themselves in a tight spot—for coal, and much else besides. Lee had barely seen sunlight since that night he and Day had found themselves on the brink of the hold: "If he's so comfortable down there," Peters had said, when Day had told him a version of what had happened—his voice like steel cables—"I'll take care of it." Like a good second should.

Lee tried to brush off the clinging dust, looking so angry and ashamed that Day found it hard to tear his eyes away. It kindled an unfamiliar sensation in Day's chest, like a beating of wings. Some wild satisfaction rising.

Even clearing the bunkers hadn't revealed Herridge. His hammock still swung in the mess hall, a pair of socks pegged to the line above. This far from port, there was only one place he could have gone: into the water, hopefully taking that dreadful mask with him. Day didn't want to interrogate too closely the *how* or the *why*.

The reign of Leviathan, he thought, had been brutal and short.

He shaded his eyes; the ship was silhouetted against pure white, a short distance from the banks of a great icy river. If they could just break through, follow it past the little chain of islands and islets, to somewhere they couldn't make a run south before winter, whatever might happen . . .

Devil take the hindmost.

"Heave!" Peters shouted.

They were tracking: planting the anchor and winching the ship along with it, yard by yard through weak spots in the ice, and the sound of the machinery was sharp enough to set Day's teeth on edge. Best to keep the crew busy: this labor had marked the last three days, and had taken the focus off their other troubles.

He could do this.

"The men are exhausted, Captain." Roderick's quiet voice startled him. Wearing a battered and shapeless hat, goggles pushed around his neck, he looked very ordinary all of a sudden: just someone looking out for the welfare of his men.

Day shook his head. "He's up there. I know it."

Stevens, with his grimy face and hands. Ahead, the ice was beautiful as a lady's jewelry box, flashing with bloody rubies and glinting amber, polished to deadliness.

"Did you ever hear the theories of Captain Symmes?" Day asked, to draw the whaler's attention from the capstan.

Roderick's lips twisted. "Aye. At the eighty-fifth parallel you start sliding down a hole into the middle of the globe. The seas make a waterfall, and the sunlight comes through strong. A land where fruit is ripe for the picking."

"I used to be sure I'd find something marvelous."

"If you don't mind me saying, sir, it's nonsense." Roderick's hat cut a slash of darkness across his face. "It's no new world up there. No place for men like us. Get in and get out. That's our business."

"I know," Day said. "My business, now, too." He'd never again command an expedition to the great wild unknown. Everyone knew that.

Roderick weighed it up. Quietly: "Mmm." A look of common feeling, and for a moment Day felt almost warm towards him. "We drifted in circles for weeks, Captain. Saw no sign of your Hollow Earth or Open Polar Sea. Nothing more uncommon than ice, and all the squalor of the seas."

Day looked at him sidelong. He didn't want to broach, not directly, the weird and slanted idea that had come to him—that Herridge had put himself overboard deliberately, to try to *draw something off.*

"But the men," he said instead, "got superstitious."

The rasp of Roderick rubbing a hand on his chin. "It's a hard life, out on the water. There's normally little time for superstition. We get our catch, and we get paid, same as any other men. But if you're out long enough, you need to be careful you stay right.

"It was like that in the boats. Herridge was desperate. Thirstier than the rest. A man who was inclined to get attached—to his own particular understanding of things. When the killers showed up, the killer whales, it was a bad time, a very bad time indeed. But it also allowed us to eat. To drink. Removed some of our troubles." Roderick shuddered a little. "The mask was fashioned as a sign of respect."

That wasn't all, Day thought.

A very bad time indeed.

"I stopped it before it got out of hand, the—mania." Roderick's gaze rested on the youngest member of the crew: a slender fellow called Tulloch, barely old enough to grow a beard. He looked paternal. "It was a close thing."

"So you're glad he's gone?" Day said, sharply.

Roderick shook his head. "As if you could ask me that. No. Herridge was seawater mad, and a brother. We were glad to get him back. And we're not glad he's gone now."

Day realized he was twisting his telescope in his hands. "We'll find him—Stevens," he said. "We have to find him. I made a promise."

Knowing you'd be taken back, welcomed back into the fold, whatever you'd done: did it curb the worst of your excesses, Day pondered—prevent you from ever finding yourself outcast, with nothing to lose, no way to go but down?

Or did it encourage the *worst* in you?

Roderick, who'd never met Stevens, didn't reply.

On the ice, Lee had made some sort of supervisory role for himself; no one questioned his God-given right to delegate. He belonged to that class of men Day had been cut out of entirely, the moment England learned how Talbot had coughed his last. Day's whole life had been spent trying to find a place. First at school, then in the Navy, and then losing it again. Having it ripped away with both hands, leaving them bloody.

"Hey!" Lee shouted up to them now. "The men won't go any farther!"

Day gripped the railings. Here it was, at last.

"What did you say?"

"I said it's impossible to go any farther."

Roderick shook his head minutely, and Day feared that he, too, had transparently looked to the ice-master for support.

Lee made a sound of frustration, flinging down the axe he'd been using to hack away at the ice barring their passage to that teasing stretch of water. His efforts were perfectly useless. It was thick enough for him to stand on.

"Pick that up!" Peters bellowed. "Lee!"

But the men at the capstan had come to a halt.

Talbot would know what to do, Day thought. When his deserters had limped back over the ice, they'd been taken into the Great Cabin, then later welcomed into the crew again with open arms.

He wasn't Talbot. No, any chance of that was long gone.

Day climbed over the side; Peters followed. Lee picked up his axe, swung it again, making a show of it. The cable beside him was taut as a bowstring; he was more likely to sever it in his carelessness, and lose them another anchor. Day ground his teeth, the old headache gripping at him like a pair of jaws. They couldn't keep losing things.

It took the two of them a few crunching, sliding minutes to get to the banks of the channel. Lee was still hacking away at it, showing them all how little he cared. The shudder of each blow made Day uneasy; the varying textures and thicknesses of the ice—from the ship, a flat uniform nullity—were far more visible here.

"*He'll* have to wait another winter." Lee kicked at the crack he'd created, looked sideways at Day. "If he's even alive—Captain."

Day's gaze was drawn north like a compass needle.

Alive—was that what Stevens was?

"I won't tell you again," Peters growled. "Get back to work." He raised his voice to the men at the capstan. "All of you!"

Day felt the ice gathering itself, raising up on its haunches, a hunting dog crouching for the spring. It had grown darker, and the reflected sunset made it look as if everything were on fire. But Lee was still engaged in his little drama, one arm stretched out to keep Peters at bay.

It wasn't a straight fall to the water, Day realized; no, they were standing on an overhang.

And it was moving.

"Lee!" Peters shouted. "You're—"

A crack.

Peters began to back away, slowly, while Lee stamped back towards the waterline, axe slung over his shoulder, his footsteps unsteady. Refusing to acknowledge what was happening, that his efforts hadn't, after all, been useless, that the ice was moving restlessly beneath them.

"Lee!" Day bellowed. "Get over here!"

Not a chance.

He moved forwards almost without thinking. "Lee!"

With a resounding bang, the ice started to crumple into the channel, like paper fed into a fire. A wide-eyed look as Lee saw his horizon vanishing. Day reached out his hand, wasn't going to reach him—

Peters lunged. Grabbed Lee with two wide and grasping arms.

The momentum took them over the side together, with a crash like a plate-glass window shattering.

And then the overhang went, too, thundering down into the inky-black water.

Day's feet didn't seem to work, and he stumbled, breathless, stubbed his toe—a little thing—but it made him bite his lip with the effort of not howling. The "river" was now a series of bobbing bergs hurrying on a silent tide, the dark water grainy as powder suspended in a glass.

Shouting—crashing—all other sounds receded, until it was just him and the ice, sharp and indifferent as a set of hungry claws. There was no sign of Lee and Peters.

It was cold enough to kill down there.

Day thought, distantly, that he mustn't weep. In the amber light his reflection had the face of a devil, tortured and twisted and utterly lacking in the possibility of salvation. *A good man*, he thought wildly, and made a sound not far removed from laughter. His heart felt as if it would explode.

That explosion came from the surface of the water.

Peters came up gasping, pallid hair matted to his face. It sharpened his features, showed the pointed shape of the skull beneath. For a moment he was a different man.

He drew in a deep, shuddering breath, keeping himself afloat with little cycling motions of his legs, churning up the slush. His arms were trembling. His lips blue.

"Lee?"

Peters met his eye, very calm. Then shook his head.

As the twilight darkened, lanterns bobbed on shore like tiny amber fruits. Some called out "Lee! Lee!" even though there was no possible way he could hear them.

Day stood on the bridge, utterly divorced from it all. He felt outside his own body, as if someone could untether a string and let him float away.

"He's dead, isn't he?" Qila appeared at his side.

"Yes." Day tried to unclench his fingers, grateful to be brought back to earth. "He was under the water for far too long."

She gave him a grave, pointed look as she turned away.

Day had been too numb to consider the implications, but they came to him regardless. Without Lee, any plan to take the ship would result in a stalemate. *Don't think about it*, he told himself. *Don't think.* He turned his hands over and over. Clean. A bit scraped.

Clean.

He wanted to explain that it wasn't his fault.

I know what a guilty conscience looks like.

His scar throbbed in sympathy.

Under the ice, Lee would be weighed down by his clothing, thrashing around, hopelessly disoriented, striking out desperately for the gleam of daylight. He'd raise his head for air—find none, just the implacable coffin lid of the ice. Day clamped his own jaw shut, refusing to allow the slightest possibility of a gasping breath. Lee's fists would smash against the surface, beating at the knowledge that there was no way out, and he'd sink to the bottom to be buried forever. Day thought it was one of the worst ways to die.

He exhaled. Asked himself whether he was glad.

You'd have been glad, wouldn't you?

Something about the dwindling light implied Stevens's feral smile.

Boom.

Men looked up.

The sound came again—*boom*. Under the ice, against their hull. As if the ship were fragile as an eggshell.

"The ice," someone said.

"Bollocks." Day saw one of the crew cross himself, hands shaking. Silence. Above them, the aurora meandered.

Can't say it's rats, either.

The next knock came from the side of the ship, just above the waterline. The men stood frozen—then a scramble of boots as they ran to peer over the side.

"There's nothing there!"

Roderick was paralyzed in mid-step, like a man seeing a fuse lit.

The knocking sped up.

Boom—there it was against the midships. Moving upwards. Louder. More determined.

"Be quiet," Roderick bellowed. "Whoever's doing that—"

Day's heartbeat lurched. He was somehow reminded of that killer-whale mask, the rictus grin. Leviathan.

In the boats they obeyed the rule of monsters. It came to him as a thought whole and entire.

The men waited, hushed. It had reached the railings.

Roderick held up a hand, tugged off his hat as though it would help him hear better. He looked . . . afraid.

"It's not what you think," he said.

"Death calls to death," someone else said, clear as a bell.

Day knew how you could get attached to your own understanding of things—he was a master of it. They'd called out to Lee, and now something was answering. He stared at the railings, thinking of the man with the red scarf. *Fouled.*

The things a ship, or a man, might attract—might trail in its wake.

Qila was right: there was something haunting him. *He* was what was on the ship already; his iron chains, and all his ghosts.

But through the vents and illuminators, very faintly—*tap, tap, tap*—the knocking died away completely. Nothing appeared.

Perhaps, he thought, ice in his veins: not yet.

———————

The awful death of Joseph Adams Lee would sell papers: a career officer, with a grandfather on the Arctic Council, it would make righteous men bay for consequences. Day hadn't felt able to leave the bridge, had stood motionless as a faint squally wind sent fine snow across the decks. The approaching night was watchful.

After a time, he'd started shaking.

"Come," Avery said quietly. "You've been here all night, Captain."

And that had finally broken the spell.

Staggering off with legs all pins and needles, Day crossed paths with Roderick on the stairs. They eyed each other uncertainly—each reluctant to broach the subject of the *knocking* they couldn't deny having heard.

"He'll live," Roderick said dourly. "What was he thinking?"

Day felt himself flushing. Down in the sick bay, Peters was being swaddled in hot towels and grease; he knew how they sometimes rewarmed freezing sailors. Naked men clasped together in a bed. The only time such a thing would be pardonable.

He swallowed.

Peters was, indeed, past the worst. But he cried out to see Day, still hazy with shock. "I tried to—"

"He's been rambling," Valle said quickly, pinching the bridge of his nose.

"You tried to save him." Day took Peters's hand. "Anyone could see that."

Peters burst into tears, noisily, and Day tried not to look away. There was no shame in tears, no shame at all.

"Carter will be better," Day said. "As your second lieutenant. Lee . . . well. I knew what he was planning. Hard to have secrets on a ship."

Especially the *Reckoning*. But he and Stevens had kept their plans secret, hadn't they?

Peters stopped crying; arrested it so abruptly, Day misjudged whether he'd dreamed the earlier, distraught Peters, who'd clutched his hand in a vise-like grip. "I was dealing with it," Peters said faintly. "I won't ever let you down."

Valle gave them a confusing look of—disdain? Disgust? Fear, maybe. He looked at Peters like he shouldn't have made it.

Day seemed to feel the cold hand of Stevens on his shoulder.

XV: CANNIBAL COVE
TALBOT'S CHANNEL, SEPTEMBER 16, 1882

They took their search to the islands at the top of the channel, chasing the vanishing midnight sun. Chasing Stevens, but he was nowhere to be found.

On a low, rocky shore, search parties prepared to return to the ship: even the birds had left. There was something eerie and oppressive about the lack of visible life. More than once, Day found himself turning around to speak to Carter, only to find that he'd veered away. There was something about the surroundings that made Day expect someone walking beside him.

He took one last look at the coal-dark shores, the looming cliffs veined with ice. Mrs. Stevens had crouched there wearing black, like Lady Franklin never did, looking around numbly. Her faith appeared

to waver—as Lady Franklin's never did—in the face of these sulfurous barrens. No men could live here. Not without considerable other
resources.

"Jesse . . ." she'd said, and Day had felt, despite himself, very sorry
for her. They'd both been drawn to that flickering and deceptive flame.

"Boats," Avery insisted about some groove marks in the scree.
"Boats were here. Look, where they were dragged." Day had to admit
Avery's investigative skills were becoming valuable. Stomping across the
rocks in his many layers, he was round and puffy as a Native woman
carrying a child in her hood. Just as determined.

"It's enough." The *Resolution* sat in silhouette against a dull sky.
They needed to go farther while they still could.

Avery pulled down his hood. Underneath, his wide eyes looked
naked. "Over there."

"It's getting dark," Day said, although in truth the stars were barely
out, the new moon waxing like a rind on cheese. "I won't have us firing
rockets for you, too." He found his voice unexpectedly gruff. They'd
fired rockets, guns, flares. Lit up the skies for miles around. If Stevens
or his men were out here, they were in no position to respond.

Avery just blinked. It nagged at him.

Boats were here.

"All right." Day hoisted his rifle onto his back. As they walked
along the narrow spit, pebbles rattled away from them, with a sound
disconcertingly like footsteps through running water. Quietly: "Do
you know how to use that rifle?"

"What do you think I've been doing to prepare for this, Captain?"

Day laughed, more in shock than mirth.

"Do *you*?"

"I was never a good hunter, it's true," Day replied, focused on
keeping his balance. "Barely handled the rifle. Stevens, now he could
shame us all. Except Sheppard."

Avery stared at him, and Day realized he'd said something he
hadn't intended.

"What?" he snapped, but it lacked heat. Some small crevice of his heart must be tired of concealment. He thought of Avery telling him to stand down after Lee's death: *You've been here all night.* A hand placed next to his own. No hint of suspicion on his face.

"I've never even heard you say his name, Captain . . ."

"William."

"Pardon?"

Day shielded his eyes. "You're not one of the men, or an officer. You can call me William, when it's appropriate."

Avery snorted.

"You don't like it?"

"Just—of course you think I'll know when it's appropriate," Avery said, that southern accent coming strongly to the fore. His eyes narrowed into the very slightest of crow's-feet. But the resemblance to young Tom Sheppard, who'd never lived to call Day *William*—who might have done, in another lifetime—was still strong.

It clawed at Day's heart. Avery was larger, but Sheppard had been starving near the end, hadn't he, so it wasn't a fair comparison.

He'd met James Avery for the first time in New York Harbor, the Cape Verdant survivors leaving the *Louisa* as a tight group. Paver was incapable of speech, and Ewing had to be rolled down the ramp to the dockside; they'd scrounged up a wheelchair, battered and creaking, when the *Louisa* had off-loaded her catch at the St. John's fishery. Day had expected to be thrown off there, too, to be picked up like an unwanted parcel by the Royal Navy. But Captain Nathaniel had bigger ambitions. He'd insisted on taking them "home."

On the quayside, police held back the well-wishers, and Day's group didn't exchange words; he had no way of knowing he'd never see any of them again. But the crowd was turbulent, turning like a weathervane in the wind, shifting from cheers to long, expectant silences.

No one knew how to react—that's what Day remembered most. The chilling silences.

And in the throng of the press, a younger and thinner James Avery. "Mr. Day!" he'd called. "Mr. Day!" he'd called again, and something that might have been *Eat-Em-Fresh*, that might have been where it came from, though in truth Day could never quite remember. He'd barred Day's path. The shouts and screams paused for the space of an intaken breath. Day had long since departed from what was proper, what was expected; thousands of miles from civilization and dignity, he'd become a half-wild animal.

———————

That broken nose had healed rather handsomely, Day thought. He kept Avery in the corner of his eye, in case he'd find him gone, too.

"What is it?"

Day shook his head. "Nothing."

"You know, I've never seen a bear up close." Avery kicked at the pebbles, which chattered like a handful of loose teeth. "You must have."

But the look he gave Day was merely curious, a swivel of his fur-trimmed hood. Not an accusation.

Avery suddenly held up his hand. "Someone's here."

The shadows were gathering. Day unshouldered his rifle, motioned to Avery to do the same, but he was already there, easily and competently, as if he'd been doing it all his life. As if there'd never been a time he'd worn a suit and waited on a quayside. As if once they might have been shipmates.

———————

At last, Day thought, and the shock of it sent all the blood rushing from his heart to his fingertips.

A man knelt inside a semicircle of boulders: they'd obviously been placed to fortify a camp, but any tents had been whipped away by the restless wind, and the shape at the center was alone. All in furs, like Stevens on the hunt—white and sleek and leonine, his high arched eyebrows giving his face an expression of perpetual judgment. The other men said he was stuck up, thought himself too good. Only Day knew the truth: Stevens was different from all of them, in a way that sometimes knocked cold fingers against his heart.

The figure in the circle was muttering to itself.

"It's just Lars," Avery whispered.

"*He* was here, though," Day said slowly, looking around at the remains of the encampment. "He's not . . . dead."

The conviction was utter. That unbreakable chain, the golden thread that bound him and Stevens: it hadn't been severed. He could feel Stevens like a sailor might feel a phantom limb, like a landlady might be aware of an upstairs lodger.

Avery looked at him. A solemn nod acknowledged this to be true.

It felt, though, like entering a burial ground.

Lars turned reluctantly. "I was coming to find you, Captain. I wanted to be sure."

Avery made a small sound, as if he found the air suddenly foul. Around the blackened remnants of a fire, small eggshell fragments glinted up at them. "Bones," he said. "They're bones."

Day knelt suddenly, his jaw tightening, that terrible throb of tension making him want to scream, pull his head apart, drill it open.

"Animals?" Avery said, hushed. But anyone could see there were no animals here.

Day picked up the largest piece of bone. Light in his hand, and with the telltale curve of a temple, it had been defleshed, turned white with the perpetual sunlight of Arctic summer.

Phrenology, the study of human temperaments by the shapes of their skulls: Stevens wouldn't be able to tell anything from this one, though, left in pieces. Left out in the open, as if it were nothing. As if someone had determined it meant nothing.

The dawning horror sent a tremor down Day's spine.

The survivors of the *Fox*—survivors, he supposed that was what they were—had once crouched on this shore, where game was scarce, stacked on top of one another like bodies in a plague pit. Looking around so desperately, in the midnight sun, that their eyes swelled, became gritty and dry, then unbearable to open.

Some of them had died.

And this skull fragment lay out in the open. Unburied. Tossed aside from the fire.

Day could see where it had broken—a spot two fingers' breadth from the ear, the site of Day's own terrible headaches. The light was falling away faster than he'd thought possible.

"William?" Avery said quietly. There was a look on his face that put years on him. They stared at the skull together. The relic.

Is there anyone there?

A burst of anger, hot and sickly as bile. Because there wasn't, not anymore. The owner of the skull was gone: would no longer relish the animal pleasures of lying down, being warm. He'd never laugh, or cry, or hold a child.

And Day knew who was responsible.

The sound of sawing. Rasping, shuddering, shaking, making it seem as though the *Resolution* were being eaten by some relentless creature, chewed slowly and deliberately until it could spit her out in pieces. The men were sawing the ice, trying to relieve the pressure on her workings. She was ill-suited for this degree of cold—deceptively flimsy against the ten thousand horsepower of the floes—and they couldn't retract her rudder to safety. They were worried. They were all worried.

Day set his mouth into a thin tight line and stared at the sick-bay floor. The empty eyes of a pelvis gazed up at him, the largest piece of bone they'd recovered intact. The rest were broken, capable of being pieced together only in a sort of puzzle, buried in a shallow, shallow grave.

"Geological specimens," they'd told the crew, in the hope of keeping some secrecy. *It weighs on the men.*

This morning, though, was uncomfortably close, as if summer was putting on a final show. Mrs. Stevens sat on the corner of the desk, her round face flickering in and out of existence behind beats of an ivory-handled fan, making it impossible to read.

Peters elbowed himself upright on the bed he'd occupied for the last six days: Valle seemed reluctant to let him resume duties. "Someone's taken the hands and feet," he said abruptly. "Haven't they?"

It was as if a chill wind blew down from deck, although Peters was only saying what was plain to see: the skeleton, even reassembled, would have tottered, crawled. Held out beseechingly its broken-off arms.

"It could be animals," Day said, the excuse like ash in his mouth.

"There aren't any goddamn animals on that shore," Avery said, looking at him with pity.

Day sighed. It felt like he was seeing himself from a long way off. A young fourth lieutenant again, perhaps. Too young to have anything but loyalty, too young to think or believe the worst.

"No teeth marks, either," Avery continued. "If they'd been attacked by animals, they'd have been—mauled. Or dragged back to their dens."

"You *can* see marks, can't you?" Peters's voice was hushed. "Where knives hit bone."

Day pressed his hand to his mouth. There wasn't enough air in the room. The sawing echoed, ceaseless and raw, sounding like it was coming from all directions at once. He remembered an argument at Camp Hope about blunting their good knives on the tough carapace of the leg bones. They'd first used the saw from the doctor's kit, then broken its teeth, and howled with pain and frustration as it slipped and slid. Who'd have thought bones could be so greasy?

"It doesn't smell like you'd expect, does it?" Peters said, fascinated.

"*Really*," Valle hissed at him.

Day couldn't stop staring. Bodies decayed slowly, unpredictably, in the Arctic. After a few days, Sheppard had just become stiff, his skin darkening as it shrank. It was a welcome change, making him less recognizable. They'd taken the good cuts first.

And then, with almost unimaginable hubris, they'd buried what was left.

Things didn't stay buried, though. Each time, the flesh had become darker and redder, the fat waxier and greener, and it was harder and harder to get into the bones. Again, almost a relief: because the greasy yellow marbling of the marrow had been one of the hardest things for Day to accept, repellent and unclean.

And eating the hands had been by far the worst. Too human. Fingers. *Human.*

They'd never even bothered burying Campbell.

Bodies decayed slowly in the Arctic, and that was why their grave robber at Cape Verdant—their *ghoul*—had been so successful. It was quite obvious, when the bodies were brought back home, that they'd been desecrated after burial.

Day tried never to think of it. But whenever it slid into his mind's eye, he saw a furtive gray stranger. Indistinct, lacking form. Not quite in the shape of a man.

Mrs. Stevens composed an expression of inscrutability. She was good at that, Day felt bitterly. He wondered whether Mr. and Mrs. Stevens ever took off their masks in front of each other; if there had ever been a true moment of unveiling. The veil pinned into her hair that day was silver, accentuating how her scraped-back waves were shot through with white. She was plain, nearly in her thirties, and had no children. A lost husband.

A great man. But an unlucky one, they'd say, with two disasters like this.

Very few men would be that unlucky.

And when Day thought of Jesse Stevens, that word didn't apply.

Who knew his true purpose?

"It might have been a year." Day forced himself to shrug, but the convulsive motion of his shoulders was more like a shudder. "We don't know if this is the main party. If the *Fox* went down before this point. Or whether these are more deserters trying to flee south."

Mrs. Stevens bristled. Gregory Patch had been good and loyal, she'd said, and would never—never!—have met circumstances prompting him to desert. She knew the quality of the man; she would have examined him just as minutely as if she'd wielded calipers. Worked out to a nicety what particular encouragement he needed; words ventriloquized by a dark-clad visionary, capable of edging a man over the precipice.

A newspaper image came to mind: two figures disembarking from a steamer, black and white and hand-in-hand, their luggage crammed with dead things. Where did they get them all? Whose bones were no longer resting peacefully?

She didn't care.

"But he's alive," she said coolly. "It's possible, isn't it—that Jesse is still alive, and this is what he did to stay that way." Her eyes shone. She was certain.

"It must have been necessary," she added.

The last desperate resource. That was what they called it.

Public attitudes had changed a little since Day had staggered home, although what he'd really done was still unspeakable anywhere men considered themselves civilized. He supposed that America was a frontier land acquainted with hardship; Mrs. Stevens had clawed herself up from dirt poverty, had journeyed to visit the cannibal tribes of the Amazon. And sailors sometimes spoke about the *custom of the sea*: casting lots, the short straw, as an acceptable way to mark someone out for death.

The whalers understood: it was built on willing sacrifice. It had to be.

Still Mrs. Stevens was unmoved by disgust or revulsion, despite Valle's misgivings about the weakness of women. And, looking around the room at their faces, Day noticed the lack of what he'd become so accustomed to seeing. It sent a shiver down his spine—

It wasn't the cannibalism, he thought. They might have pardoned that.

It was everything else.

And something distant in him said, *yes*, you have every right to be angry.

She turned back to Day, her eyes flickering, belligerent. "My husband is an idealist. A visionary of sorts. But even idealists have to appreciate certain—realities. You know, don't you, that we're more than the body? Only the flesh was consumed, and I'm not ashamed that Jesse did what he had to. And I shouldn't think—on *this* ship—that anyone could condemn it."

There was a creak from the door, and Peters's eyes narrowed. He held up his hand for silence: soon the presence of so many of them in the sick bay would invite suspicion. Outside, Qila was poised to give the signal if anyone came their way. "Be careful," Day had told her, unnecessarily, and she'd rolled her eyes at him. He'd thought of their first meeting, which felt like more than months ago: a coffee set, prim whitewashed walls, a hired companion for a lady. Felt the corners of his lips tugged upwards.

"I promised I wouldn't give up on him," Mrs. Stevens said.

You were a child, he didn't say. Little more than a child.

Day wouldn't condemn Stevens, nor defend him. There was something . . . very wrong with that man.

A horrid idea was whispering in his ear.

He swallowed it down for now. Just caught Avery's eye, and gave a single nod, trusting him to interpret. *Write what you like.*

3

THEN

*PUT FORTH THINE HAND NOW, AND
TOUCH HIS BONE AND HIS FLESH—AND
HE WILL RENOUNCE THEE TO THY FACE.*

Do you have anything to say for yourself?"

Day has put forward Dr. Nye as prosecutor—there's a widespread assumption that a medical man must be impartial. Suffering, too, is currency at Camp Hope: after what happened on Amelia's Pass, the doctor has earned their additional respect. Lit from above, his awfully disfigured face makes him into a crouched raven. He has trouble swallowing, one of his facial muscles painfully seized in the area of torn flesh, where the polar bear had placed its jaws around his head and shaken him roughly—before being distracted.

But although Day has watched him carefully in the months since, he hasn't been able to detect the least trace of bitterness. Nye's not a pleasant man. But he doesn't seem to hold a grudge for the choices Day has made to get them here.

The doctor casts long avian shadows on the walls of the overturned boat, softened and warped with damp, scored with unmistakable marks: someone has been gnawing at the wood, scraping at the fibers to load them into a hungry mouth. They've started eating anything, to supplement the little actual food they have.

It's the day after their rations finally ran out.

And this is Sheppard's trial, after a fashion.

"I've never seen those things," Sheppard says. Hunched over in the mess of sleeping bags and rotting clothing, he's a knot of limbs—but still broader and stronger than the rest. While they've been trying to conserve energy, he's been out hunting, and his face is browned. The light reflects mercilessly off the ice, and in June he'd been part-blinded when the insides of his eyelids burned. Day remembers the small hissing noise he'd made as the doctor applied grease. His boots are comically large, would give several days' worth of leather.

There's a youthful openness to Sheppard's face that makes Day's heart clench. Although he's the one making it, he can barely believe the accusation to be true.

"Second Lieutenant—"

"I've never seen them!" Sheppard says desperately. No one wants to meet his eye.

Nye clears his throat. "They were found hidden by the creek." That little handful of ammunition; the hardtack bread; the paltry supply of fuel alcohol. Though anyone could get down to the mean trickle of a creek, Day has forbidden most of the men to leave the safety of Camp Hope. The pool of suspects is small. Confined to officers.

"Who found them?" Sheppard asks.

"They were found by the creek," Day says, not answering his question; not seeing whether it matters one way or another. He'd brought the items in, had hugged the bundle to his own chest like a cold hard cannonball of betrayal.

"Then it could be anyone," Sheppard says obstinately. "If they were going to steal ammunition—they could steal the rifle, too." He wears it across his chest, their only rifle, protective as a Native mother. The doctor sighs, heavily, and all eyes turn back to the objects. Day supposes this is the most entertainment they've had in weeks.

"No one could get it off you," Stevens says, voice sharp like spruce needles. "Not without a fight."

It's a surprise to hear him speaking up. Stevens, in particular, had loudly protested at the idea of putting Sheppard on trial. "No!" He'd run the stolen cartridges through his fist, making them glimmer in the faint light like salmon swimming upstream. The sound of running water. "Not Sheppard. Surely not *Sheppard*—"

But now Stevens sits beside Day and accuses him.

"I'm not the only hunter," Sheppard adds.

There's an intake of breath. A shifting in the darkness, where the condensation drips down the walls and makes misery for them all.

"Oh, Tom." Stevens glances at his fingernails. "I saw you lingering by the creek a few days ago." His tone is regretful. His face says clearly, clear as daylight, that he's sorry it's come to this. But if Sheppard insists on wielding the knife, then Stevens will meet him halfway.

"Where were you, then?"

"I was—"

"Gentlemen—" Nye tries to interject.

"You must've been up on the grave-ridge," Sheppard says slowly, as if it's just coming to him. "To see me across there, when it was so dark out."

Day feels cold fingers wrap themselves around his heart. *When it was so dark out.* They'd had a string of bad days, where the freezing rain and slate-gray clouds had made it dark at noon, walling them up alive.

"I've also seen him," Christiansen says unexpectedly. He raises his head—juts out his jaw in defiance—looks at Day. "I've seen him up near the graves. First Lieutenant Stevens." He's obviously been waiting for this opportunity: Christiansen is half-Native, and denouncing an officer—well. He's no fool, must be able to tell this could go wrong for him.

The grave-ridge is strictly off-limits. Day can feel his pulse in his throat.

"The first lieutenant's conduct is not under question here," Nye snaps. He takes off his glasses, polishes them on his shirt. One of the lenses is missing, scraped clean out by bear teeth. It could very well have been his eye.

Stevens gives Christiansen a disparaging look. "Maybe I didn't," Christiansen mumbles. He doesn't look at Day. He just looks at his own grubby hands.

"You don't deny it, then?" Nye says, glad to be back on track; it's clearly addressed to Sheppard.

But, maybe because Stevens is angry at Christiansen, he mistakes himself. "No, why should I?" Stevens says sharply.

An admission.

In the muttering that follows, the degree of anger makes Day wary. This court is made up of resentful, desperate men, some confined to their sleeping bags. All hungry, all tired, all staring death in the face. Their anger could just as easily turn anywhere: from Sheppard to Stevens. To Day himself.

Stevens, though, doesn't show a flicker of concern. His lips are slightly parted, his face fox-like and handsome.

But there's a *look* in Sheppard's tawny eyes. A cautious relief.

"The Bible," Day says out loud, almost without thinking, as if his lips and tongue and vocal cords are working of their own volition. "You borrowed it."

Stevens looks down. Smiles.

"Yes."

The doctor makes a small "ah" sound. This has clearly been settled to his satisfaction, and there's no more grumbling from the darkness. The four men buried on that grave-ridge had been given proper funerals. It's an easy assumption that Stevens borrowed the Bible to read over the dead, although it's a burst of piety more befitting Ewing.

The air seems to grow thicker, and Day swallows.

He knows that Stevens is utterly faithless, it's one of the most shocking and thrilling things about him. Where most men have an ordered faith in the universe, in God and the devil and salvation or perdition, Stevens's belief systems are patched together wholesale with him at the center, making himself into one of those godlike men he'd been so eager to find. And more and more he acts like it—like nothing in this godless place is capable of holding him back.

It makes Day uneasy. There's a difference between freedom and chaos.

Stevens had been talking about making some sort of signal fire. The Bible would have been intended for kindling, nothing more. He'd stamped back down when the sleet started, sharp and resentful, and thrust it, soggy, back into Day's hands.

Stevens, alone up on the grave-ridge. A prickling in Day's spine.

He quashes it down. Swallows bile. Not *now*.

Nye, their prosecutor, tries to reassert control. "You'd only need these if you were planning to leave us, live off the land."

Someone spits, in the gloom. Day thinks with resignation how that spit will run down the slope, become part of the horrible soupy ground that squelches and freezes and thaws under them.

"Without the rifle, we'd be left with no way to hunt. Even if the game returns."

The doctor doesn't have to spell it out. Game hasn't been sighted in weeks, and there's just a scraping of tea dust, and they've eaten all the leather uppers from their boots. Day had particularly dreaded eating his boots, with all its grim connotations.

"A death sentence," someone says. Whether about Sheppard, or about themselves—it doesn't matter. The mood in Camp Hope has shifted, the anger found its proper course. There's now only one way this can go. "And if one of those goddamned bears finds us—"

A collective shiver. They've all seen what bears can do.

"Can anyone speak to what you were doing?" Ewing asks, his voice soft. Tender-hearted Ewing. He so badly wants Sheppard to have a fair hearing; had asked Day if he intended to appoint defense counsel. "Can anyone say you're not responsible?"

Sheppard looks over at Stevens, wretched. He's being asked to prove the negative.

"No."

The verdict follows inexorably: Sheppard is guilty of theft and attempted desertion. Nye had wanted to add attempted murder, one count for each man who'd have been abandoned at Cape Verdant. They'd chosen their prosecutor wisely.

Day thrashes at the knowledge that the men might care more about the doctor's views than his own. William Day, age twenty-four, acting commander of the *Reckoning*, has got them this far. They're alive, at least. Are they not grateful?

But he knows that's not how it works.

Day walks back and forth outside the hut, watching the shadows as Stevens secures Sheppard in the red tent pitched some distance away. They've taken him outside straight after that "guilty": they don't want any communication between him and the rest of the men. Day's legs feel weak and tottering as stilts, and he's sure his muscles are wearing away. His knees are huge and bony.

In the daylight he can see all the way to the shore, where the ice hovers immense and inhospitable, where the water had swallowed up both their guides with barely a splash. At the time, he'd managed to be glad, selfishly glad, they wouldn't be put to the effort of digging graves, scraping out fifteen inches of gravel with tin plates and bare hands. Now, sometimes, in the dark of Camp Hope, he doubts how such skillful and shrewd ice-masters—

Enough. This isn't the time.

Stevens crawls out of the tent, made especially for their expedition— a shrieking shade of aniline red, intended to promote visibility— and walks swiftly and quietly back towards camp. He's borne their privations nobly. His eyes are shiny like burnished tin, and the golden hair that once had women swooning has been scraped and tied back, Chinese-style. He doesn't sway or stumble as he walks through the rocky ground—he's still as utterly *himself* as it's possible to be.

Stevens puts a hand on Day's shoulder, and Day's heart thumps at his touch. They'd disagreed on the issue of restraints—a small disagreement, but the slightest thing can fester out here, take on a life of its own, and he's glad he won't lose Stevens over it.

"You did the right thing," Stevens says, as if he realizes the degree of horror that's started to trickle down Day's spine.

The rifle, Sheppard's rifle, is slung across Stevens's back.

"We'll have to execute him," Day says, to cover the *rat-tat-tat* of his heart.

"You write the order," Stevens offers, "and I'll read it." He has a pleasant speaking voice; not an accent anyone has been able to place, although he's fluent in Russian and French, claims knowledge of a number of indigenous languages. Day considers this surprising, given he'd barely spoken two words to their Native guides, right up to the point of their sudden deaths. Stevens eyes Day, seeing his reluctance. "Or—I can write it if you like."

Day shakes his head. "I should do it." This burden has fallen to him alone.

Stevens lets go of him, and it's like a cloud passing over the sun.

"Have you given any thought to what comes next?"

Stevens is always one step ahead of Day.

Their gazes turn back to the tent. There's a long, cold moment in which a sob makes its way to them, carried on the ceaseless breeze. Sheppard is crying, and it makes Day feel so deeply uneasy he looks away, but only finds his attention drawn, like a magnet, to the grave-ridge.

"We bury him," Day says, trying not to think about those desecrated graves. The mute reproach of the dead, uncovered, their tattered clothing unwrapped. He doesn't ask Stevens about his trip up there with the Bible. He doesn't mention Stevens feeding him rats—no doubt how they both survived the scurvy.

But, with a chill, he realizes they'll need to bury Sheppard deep.

"We're starving," Stevens says, unnecessarily. "Paver—the others—none of us will make it." He looks at Day through slate-colored eyes. "We haven't even got scraps left, and it'll get colder soon, dark again. We can make it maybe a few weeks from this point. Those of us who are strongest. But that's it. You've seen the others, they don't have the strength. Our window of opportunity to seek rescue"—he gestures at the channel—"has shut."

Day feels his heart clench.

"I'm not criticizing," Stevens says.

The time has never been right to leave. The ice is too mobile for sledging or boating, even if the men weren't so weak. If they consign themselves to the floes, there's every chance they'll get swept from Lancaster Sound into Baffin Bay, drown in an autumn squall before encountering another human being.

"We're going to die here." A bite comes into Stevens's voice. "So what are we going to do with Sheppard?"

The sky stops its scudding of mackerel clouds.

"What are we going to do with his body?"

The ice pauses its ceaseless rapping at the doors of the shore.

"Will."

They're going to starve to death. All of them, from handsome Stevens to pale milksop Ewing. They'll sit under the overturned boat and wait for their bodies to eat themselves. Day has become familiar with hunger, but he understands the sufferings of the next few weeks will be more intense than he could possibly imagine.

"Of course, you've thought about it," Stevens says, looking sideways at him.

"Of course," Day says slowly.

Has he? He honestly doesn't know.

Always one step ahead, Stevens gives voice to things Day won't dare to articulate. As if he speaks directly to Day's heart, his blackest and most awful heart.

Because they have a source of food now. Maybe not enough to save them—but enough to alleviate their sufferings. Sheppard, sitting in that tent, is young and healthy. Six feet tall, with broad capable hands, long legs, and Day thinks of the muscle in those legs, toned from exercise.

Horribly, his mouth starts to water.

Day claps a hand over it, eyes widening. The air is so dry and cold it stings his eyeballs. He swallows, tasting acid. His breath stinks, he knows; like fruit left too long to rot. He tries not to think about Sheppard in those terms. But his body is betraying him, hunger starting to take command of his reason.

Savage.

He has to spit. Does so, on the rocky black ground. Stevens just watches, his expression unsurprised. *Of course he's the first to bring it up*, Day thinks with a hostility that surprises him, and turns away. The sky is everywhere at once, so colorless he can see shapes swimming in it. The wind is whistling quietly, tugging at his clothing. Day covers his face with his hands, wanting to shut it all out.

"We should vote," he blurts. "Put it to a vote."

Stevens laughs: a single *ha*, precisely expressed. "You think the men won't all vote for a hot meal? It's a foregone conclusion."

He's right, of course. It's called *the custom of the sea*: there's a ghastly kind of precedent for all this. Perhaps Day should have thrown the bodies into the dark water; removed the temptation.

"The officers, then." He turns. "Jackson, the doctor—"

"No." Stevens's face darkens. "Not if you want to lead them afterwards. Trust me on this, Will. It needs to come from you, and you alone."

Day doesn't want this. He doesn't want any of it. He wishes, powerfully, that command had fallen to Stevens instead; that Fourth Lieutenant William Day had died on the *Reckoning*, and the man in command at Cape Verdant is tall and blond, scandalously atheist, with his well-honed knife and utter shamelessness.

"And there's nothing wrong with it," Stevens adds fiercely. "Don't you see? We're being given the means to regain control of our destinies."

Again, Day draws a hand across his face. Everything aches. Glancing over at the tent, he appreciates that they haven't been lowering their voices, and Sheppard is under canvas only thirty feet away. Sound plays tricks up here. He might have heard them. His pencil might, even now, be moving feverishly across the page.

"No." Day shakes his head. He glances up at the terrible sky, the rings emanating from the sun. He's lived his whole life in the certain knowledge of Judgment Day. And if the dead are called from their graves, to march towards the light—let it not be said that William Day mutilated his men. Denied them eternal salvation.

But it's a weak *no*.

Sheppard isn't yet dead, and Stevens knows better than to press him.

––––––––––––––

Later, it's four degrees above freezing, the inside of the hut damp and clammy. The oars supporting the roof are mossy, and he knows that if they dismantle Camp Hope it'll prove rotten to the core.

The men are sitting outside, trying to protect their skeletons with blankets and coats. Even those who haven't moved in days—weeks— have fled. The only people left inside are Day; the doctor; poor Campbell; and the cook.

"It's best to do it while the others can't see," Nye had said briskly, because Day has given in, and the cook is now preparing *Sheppard*.

"There are morbid thoughts going around," he adds, and Day almost laughs.

"I don't want to be told how bad it is," Campbell says feebly. "D'you hear me? Don't let me know." He has his face pressed into his elbow, trying to avoid the urge to look, and moans horribly as Day and Dr. Nye work him out of the tattered sleeping bag. They've all been carving off scraps of the bag's tanned leather waterproof fabric, chewing them until saliva creates an unsatisfactory mush of hairy hide, the buffalo skin beneath.

The doctor's mouth opens, and he pushes up his glasses. Finally exposed to the air, the dressings on Campbell's bony calves and feet are soaked through. Day covers his nose at the smell.

"We're going to need hot water," Nye says to Miller, who drew the short straw and is their cook for the evening's proceedings: he's crouched at the back of the hut, where the stove hisses away, and Day can't bear to look at the waiting parcel of meat. Normally, drawing straws allows the coveted role of cook to be rotated, so no one can be accused of sequestering food.

Tonight, it's because they're seeking to divide the responsibility.

The doctor starts to unwrap the dressings. Campbell had gone through ice on an early attempt to leave, both legs submerged up to the knee. Frostbite had set in before he'd made it back to camp, and it had never healed: nothing heals, up here. Not really. His legs are leaking fluid, the flesh soft and spongy.

"Oh—my," Nye says, and that's enough to make Campbell start sobbing.

Day leans in. The horrors of this day are more than any man should hope to stand. The skin and muscle have started to slough away from Campbell's feet, like the flesh off an apple in a damp root cellar.

Nothing clean will ever come out of this place.

"How bad is it?" Campbell says, forgetting his earlier request. "Doctor? Captain?"

Dr. Nye puts one finger to his lips, gives Day a meaningful look.

"I'll need to operate," he says in a reassuring voice. "I know I've said the risks are too great. But I can't leave your legs like this."

"When?" Day asks.

"Once he's eaten," the doctor says. "Once he's regained some of his strength. We'll feed him tonight. Let him sleep—"

"Lockjaw." Campbell's voice is high and terrified. "Please, I've seen it—"

Day's heart is thudding, because he's seen it too. A man in spasms, back arching, toes curling, as if summoned for the Rapture. Lockjaw is a horrible, superstitious way to die in the latter half of the nineteenth century.

"Am I gonna die?"

Campbell seizes his sleeve, and Day lets out a sound that isn't quite a whimper at his horrible claw-like fingers, disproportionate knuckles, yellowing nails. He stares at it until the image is burned into his mind's eye. It's the hand of something that has ceased to be human.

He thinks what Stevens would say.

"Probably," he says harshly. Tells himself there's no point in lying— this can only be a short reprieve. "Yes, Campbell, yes."

"You should go outside," Nye says. Day strains to find judgment in it, in the doctor's fastidious little glasses, his round balding head, the skull deformed on one side. He's right, though—the cooking smell is rich and deep, like a physical presence, and must be seeping out to where starving men are waiting.

When Day leaves, the cooler night air makes sweat trickle down the back of his shirt. He tries not to think of the same condensation doing its ghastly work on Campbell's feet.

Day has timed it poorly, as always, because now he can see the expression on his men's faces as the smell reaches them.

How to describe cooking human meat? Day knows he'll never forget it. He'll never again eat bacon, or beef, or pork. The scent is nauseating and sweet; Day tries to take shallow breaths through his mouth. And although he tries to fight it, to shout at his senses that this is not food, this is not meat, this is not—*delicious*—

His mouth waters nonetheless.

He swallows down the saliva. *Pears*, he thinks. His spit tastes like pears. When Miller had suggested thickening the stew with foraged lichen, someone had threatened to knock him out. "First meat we've had in months. Don't ruin it."

That's what Sheppard is now: meat.

Paver groans. Unmercifully, he seems to be awake for this. Day privately doubts whether a meal, even this meal, will save him. "Imagine you're somewhere else," Ewing says. Such a soft voice. An educated man. Earlier that month, he'd broken down and cried like a baby to find that his copy of *Walden* had rotted away.

Day crawls over to Stevens, who moves aside to allow Day to share a tiny handkerchief square of flat ground. They sit back-to-back, propped against each other. Day can feel the steady in-and-out of his breathing.

"Well?" Stevens says very quietly, but Day just shivers. He knows if he opens his mouth, the smell will get in, his mouth will start watering again.

Someone will be held responsible.

"Will he live? Campbell?"

Day shakes his head.

Around him, the men are avoiding one another's eyes, and he wishes desperately for the concealment of true night. The moon hovers overhead, and the cerulean nautical twilight is heartbreakingly beautiful.

"Sheppard would have wanted this," Stevens says clearly, his voice carrying. "Before he lost his senses. Before he tried to kill us all. He was a good man. Loyal and kind. He would have wanted us to live."

They listen to him, with their gaunt faces and wild matted hair: Ewing crawls a bit closer, a child wanting to be told a bedtime story, tucked in and told there are no horrors under the bed, nor tapping at the window. "Sheppard would have asked us to do this," Stevens says. "If he knew. And Campbell and Paver won't survive without it."

Stevens's voice echoes around camp, vibrates through Day's body. The men are nodding. He nudges Day in the side with one bony elbow.

"You hear that?"

Day listens. He can hear someone smacking his lips. He can hear the wind playing coyly with the flaps of the empty tent. Somewhere a bird sings, very faint and far off, and they're all silent while they wait for it to stop.

Day notices that the ice has fallen quiet. He can hear the sound of open water somewhere in the distance.

"It's stopped moving," Stevens says. "I've been keeping an eye on it. If it stays like this—opens, and stays open—the conditions might be right to get to the whaling fleet before it leaves. It's worth a shot."

"We should have held a funeral," James says suddenly. He'd been Sheppard's friend; Sheppard had nursed him out of scurvy on the ship, when the summer's game had returned scant and stringy. "We should have waited for that, at least."

"We needed the meat," Day says. "There's no time."

He knows this is a pitiful excuse, but he feels Stevens looking at him approvingly. Finally, he's done something right. The men nod, heads bobbing on scrawny bearded necks. Their eyes are wide, so wide. The smell sidles around them, a physical presence, and Day fights the urge to wave it away.

It's meat, he tells himself. Just that. Just a body.

His bones are sharp against the rocks. He's made this thing his own, and has to see it through. There's a certain relief in acquiescing to the course that has been chosen for him.

"We should skim the fat off the top," Stevens says. "For cooking." The captivated men recoil, as if they'd put their feet too close to the fire, suddenly remembered it could burn.

Stevens turns his head until it's nearly resting on Day's shoulder, a groove he slots into as naturally as if it's made for him. He says, very low: "We need to get to that diary. Find out what he wrote about us."

But Day is looking at his hands. They're trembling again. He can't stop seeing young Tom Sheppard, who'd raised his own hands at the final moment. Bare hands, clean hands, making Day think of stigmata, a red bloom of blood in all that grayness. Martyrdom. Day wraps his arms around his wasted frame, tries not to think like that. Sheppard was a thief, a murderer—perhaps worse. They'd stood surrounded by graves picked clean, all the things Day can't afford to let the men discover. Stevens had grouped the two bullets neatly, as if he'd already known what Day would decide.

Day thinks of those Native guides, lost without a trace, and speculates—

NOW

XVII: THE NUCLEUS OF AN ICEBERG
TALBOT'S CHANNEL, SEPTEMBER 18, 1882

Arctic expeditions were designed to cling to the ship, a life raft in the unrelenting hostility of the landscape. The sad tent circle at Cannibal Cove told a story of desperation.

Peters paused on his oars. He was rowing Day through leads of glimmering dawn water: while the rest of the ship was sleeping, they'd crept away. Peters's time under the ice seemed to have given him strength; there was a strong curve to his bruised cheekbone that had been invisible behind those spectacles, and a new sharpness about his gaze. He'd become more attractive, Day realized, by degrees.

Hidden behind the islands, a long ledge of land rose up like a barrow. It made Day's heart squeeze. Stevens would remember this anchorage, the best one between here and God-Saves Harbor.

"What do you think it all means," Peters said. "What we found?"

"There are always deaths." An exaggeration. "And someone would have had to decide what to do with the bodies."

It always came down to bodies.

"Will you tell me what he was like?"

Day didn't need to ask who: Peters had asked about Stevens so often it was like a catechism. He stared towards the curve of dark land, trying to will the *Fox* into existence by sheer force of wanting. Even if they'd have to wait out winter together, those survivors thin and desperate. The very sight of it would remake William Day.

"No one really knew where he came from. They said he'd been a guide in the far north. The story I heard most often had four of them going into the pinewoods in September, to scout railway routes, and only two coming back in spring. There were whispers.

"The sort of rumors no one would dare spread now.

"When I asked him, he always told it the same way: there was the officer, the liar, the lamb, and the victim. An early snowfall. The officer saw there wasn't enough food. He left the other three in the cabin, so he wouldn't be a burden, and struck out for a frozen lake, hunting to survive. But when he returned for more ammunition, things had . . . changed.

"The cabin had a smell to it.

"And the *victim* was nowhere to be seen.

"The *liar* said that he'd gone to fetch firewood and never come back. But there was . . . something in the kettle that didn't look right. An ash heap that had teeth in it, too small and dainty to be wolf or deer. The officer left them again."

Day swallowed. *Though they begged him not to.*

"He was the best hunter, and was taking the ammunition, and they had . . . skins and roots, and whatever was left in that kettle. They were too weak to leave their beds. Too weak to cry out."

New ice dusted the sea in their path, like a handful of bones outside a tent circle.

"He came back when the snow started to melt. On the front step, he found the *lamb*, sobbing, saying it wasn't his fault, hunger does things to you. They'd fed floorboards into the fire. Eaten all the skins used for bedding. Squeezed out the grubs that were breeding in those skins, and eaten those, too, before they'd turned on each other."

Day glanced at Peters, who'd paused, rapt, in his oar strokes.

"Stevens said: *Needs must.* And he never told me whether he was the officer or the lamb." Whether it was a creation myth or a tragedy.

"He must have been a great man," Peters said at length. "A very great man indeed."

Day nodded. Looked away. Unclenched his fists, trying to get the blood flowing again.

"But he followed you—Captain—didn't he."

Silence fell. Day refused to think about what might have been if Jesse Stevens had been in charge of their retreat from God-Saves Harbor. It was a thought for the darkest reaches of the night.

The ship's silhouette loomed into the sky before them.

No lanterns bobbed on her decks; no stove glowed, red-tinged, from the windows of her Great Cabin. Her masts were three bare fingers reaching for the sky. The fog swirled around her ominous bulk, gleaming off her coppered hull, emphasizing her dark emptiness.

Day realized his mouth was open, and shut it so hard he bit his own cheek. The rusty-nail taste of blood. *I knew it.*

A short step off a precipice. From seeing Stevens to seeing—

"I'll be damned," Peters said softly, and sounded like he meant it. As if all his dreams were coming true at once. "Captain—"

Day felt his knees buckle. He knew that figurehead lashed halfway up the mainmast: a drowned man, missing a wide chunk of cheek, his mouth open in a silent scream. Ravenous. Revenant.

Reckoning.

Day returned to his Dutchman alone.

She shouldn't be intact. She shouldn't be here.

Reckoning: the punishment of past misdeeds.

Day wondered whether she would even take his weight. Whether the whole ghost ship would disappear under his hands and feet, casting him off like a piece of jetsam. But she looked exactly as he'd left her, and as he climbed over the side, he was met by a sense of presence. The same presence he'd felt in the séance: something hanging over him, as she'd hung over his entire life.

He was unable to escape it.

"Hello, old girl," he said quietly.

Her deck was a dark maze of oiled canvas, yawning caverns formed by drifted snow, and Day knew that darkness well. It might have been any one of a hundred ice watches, with Day counting down the chill hours, hands clenched into his armpits, until he could report to Talbot in the Great Cabin below. The captain would be sitting in his oversized chair, wig jammed firmly onto the crown of his head, a well-thumbed Bible by his right hand. Rubbing his eyes, because he'd spent too long staring out the stern windows, until they'd become an endless mirror. "Ah," he'd say, knowing him by his hesitant footsteps: Talbot had *known* him, and that was hard. "William Day. I hope you're keeping good company."

Swallowing down a muffled, agonized sound, Day fumbled for a light. Under the canvas, the deck shimmered into existence, rimmed with icicles sharp and fat as the teeth of a killer whale. The frosted brass reflected his lantern back at him, and he was suddenly aware of the loudness of his own breathing.

In a pool of darkness as profound and still as deep water, he could see the mouth of the mainmast hatch. It stood open, inviting.

Come home.

He'd shut it. Day racked his memories. Of course he'd shut it: he'd been the last man out, had checked the belowdecks, echoing and bare; had given the order to batten down the hatchway, desperately schooling himself not to look back.

Now it was open again.

He took a step and slipped, going to hands and knees. His heart thumping, he looked around desperately, as if the sound would wake the sleeping ship; pulled himself up by the goose-neck structure of the empty davits, their whaleboats now rotting into the landscape of Cape Verdant.

At the bottom of the hatch was a perfectly square patch of snow-drift, and Day stared at it, a cold, hard pit of uneasiness in his stomach. There was an indent to one side—about the size of a boot. The horrible suggestion of someone disappearing into the bowels of the ship. Someone who could still be there now.

The darkness below seemed to flicker.

He thought of someone down there, waiting just out of sight, waiting to step forwards—

"*No.*"

Everything seemed to press in on him. Clouded illuminators stared up from belowdecks like a line of eyes put out.

At the stern, the ship's wheel was frozen in place. Day kicked cautiously at its base. Her rudder must be warped and buckled, he told himself, her propeller sheared off. Her hull must be damaged in a hundred ways. It was only the drift that brought her here, the currents and ice that had pried her out of God-Saves Harbor and given her the illusion of agency.

The illusion that she'd come looking for him.

It wasn't possible that they could have refloated her. It wasn't possible that they could have sailed her out through that impenetrable ice barrier. Other men said their prayers before going to sleep: Day said this. *She was as good as lost.*

It sounded hollow, even to him.

Letting out a single harsh breath, he put all his strength against the wheel. For a moment nothing happened, the mechanism frozen fast, and relief flooded through him like a drug. He was safe. Of course she was a wreck. He'd been right to check. To put it all to rest.

Then it turned.

Barely a fraction of a degree. But that was enough—the implication was there.

Impossibly, damningly, she still *answered*.

He was shaking, as though he'd fallen from a great height. It could mean nothing, he told himself; they could have waited another season on the *Reckoning*, tried to hack her out, and failed. They could have waited in vain. Slipped away. Died. It was impossible to know.

But the choices he had made—to take them overland, where their story ended with a bear, red of claw—and Cape Verdant, and *Stevens*—

He found himself doubting whether Coleridge's Ancient Mariner had really killed an albatross. If it was just that single decision, to take down a bird, that had condemned him and his crew to wander the Polar seas. Or whether it was far more complicated than that.

Day could see his own face reflected, distorted, in the curves of the ship's bell.

"God," he whispered. "God."

But God had abandoned him all those years ago.

And he couldn't shake the feeling, panicky and furious, that he was about to grab an axe and climb down that hatch to the hold, allowing the darkness to eat him up. Hacking away at the ship's backbone, sinking her for good. *Lost*. His hands were trembling with rage and fear.

He pressed his mittens to his eyes, holding them tightly shut, feeling the ice scraping against his face. No one was here. Of course no one was here.

He had failed. This was where he belonged.

I am the captain of a ghost ship, he thought numbly. Doomed to sail the ice forever.

For whose crimes?

———

He opened his eyes, then let out a strangled laugh.

Stevens's hair was brighter than the ship's dulled brass-work. It was the Jesse Stevens he'd met on the quayside in Philadelphia: thirty, or thereabouts, burnished with mystery and excitement. No doubt the same Jesse Stevens that his bride-to-be had met years later. Handsome and healthy, as if he'd never squatted under an overturned whaleboat at Cape Verdant, never carved human flesh at Cannibal Cove. There was something obscene, vaguely repellent, about the curve of his unblemished lips.

Will. You've come home.

Stevens smiled like he belonged there: this thing that Day had dragged from the Arctic to London and back again. The decks seemed to brighten in turn, like clouds burning away from the sun, like a benediction. An uncanny kind of light. Day wondered if this was what a religious vision felt like—or an apoplexy. He could hear the blood rushing in his ears, loud and fatal.

"I should have listened to Valle," he whispered. "I should have known there was something wrong with me."

Because standing there, insubstantial, he could see—

A man of middling height and middling build, uniform neatly pressed. Face turned up towards Stevens, as if that were the north of his own particular compass. No wonder he'd become so lost.

They were laughing together, a bright, clear sound. Stevens steadied that younger man with a hand on his shoulder: holding him close, because there was something infinitely intimate about that gesture. Holding him at a distance, because Stevens kept no one close, perhaps not even him.

Fourth Lieutenant William Day.

This was before they'd left Newfoundland, long before Stevens had ever been promoted. Day was holding a rifle; Stevens was a crack shot, and he was sure, so sure, that Day could be taught.

They would never get those days back, Day realized: that easy trust in Stevens, those untainted times before everything turned sour.

And under the canvas, thronging the darkness . . .

The other officers, their half-remembered faces smudgy: Jonny Greenstreet and his cronies, straight and clean-shaven, reminding him of Holt and Carter with their neatly pressed appearance, a lifetime of orders and camaraderie. They were giving Stevens unmistakable looks of disdain. Stevens smiled, appearing not to mind, though the curl of his lips spoke volumes—a darkening horizon, like storm clouds hidden by the curvature of the Earth. He'd make them pay, whether it took weeks or months or years.

And farther back, behind the mast: the familiar shuffle of young John the cabin boy.

Thud. Thud. *Thud.*

Day found himself shrinking away, a clot of dread stopping his throat. But he'd sat beside John's sickbed, held his small, calloused hand. He'd paid the carpenter. William Day had done nothing to John.

The cabin boy had died far too early for that.

"No," he said. "No—"

Stevens was approaching the stern, his footsteps shattering the ice like a shell being smashed open. Footsteps with weight and texture.

Manifestation.

Day had always known it wasn't real, that there was something wrong—terribly wrong—with him. But now he'd brought it home. Of course it would be strongest here. Stevens was all black polished boots and long greatcoat, ice clinging to its hem, working its way up towards Stevens's nonexistent heart.

The . . . *manifestation* knelt to look him in the eye.

Together again.

Day could see the tiny flecks of green in his gray eyes, the faint pockmarks on the underside of his chin. No steam came from Stevens's parted lips. Day's own breath filled the gap between them, hung crystalline in the still air. It was the closest they'd ever come to an embrace.

Maybe, Day thought. *Maybe.*

But Stevens just stood, crisply, as if receiving instructions. He reached up his hand to the ship's bell, fastened his long, bare fingers around the stalactite of ice.

"No—"

They'll hear you.

The thought came into Day's head so sudden and complete that he flinched.

Stevens rang the dead ship's bell.

The wind whipped suddenly into Day's face, smelling of deprivation and desperation, thin green algae, and the smell of frostbitten wounds gone bad. He stumbled back.

Another gust of wind brought the faint sound of hooting in the distance, something articulating, wordless and garbled, like a child making meaningless sounds for the desperate need to be heard. Day craned his neck, trying to work out where it was coming from, but the next sound made him freeze in terror.

On the ice, something was scratching. Slow, steady.

Both near and far away at once: the crunching, shuffling sounds of something approaching the ship, slow and deliberate.

And, closer, a tap-tap-tapping. As if the ship were sitting on a glass sea, and someone was rapping at the pane insistently with long bent fingernails. Claws.

Reaching through from the other side of . . . what?

Day wouldn't look. He couldn't look.

He'd done nothing to John. He wished he could say the same of the others.

The crawling, scraping sound took on a ghastly significance, one that made him want to scream, press his hands to his eyes, so he wouldn't have to see—

He'd once comforted himself, hadn't he, with the idea that the body and spirit separated at death. That whatever was done to the body was immaterial, unhallowed. He'd told himself that, hugged it tight to his chest. Sheppard was *gone*. It was the only way he could live with himself.

But nonetheless, something was crawling beneath him.

Oh, he could imagine them, those revenants. Called back to the ship after all this time. Making their way to him on stump legs, hollow defleshed thighs. Clawing across the ice with severed fingers. Pained, crab-like. Agonies.

The bell was still echoing, throbbing in the misty gray air. Dis-

tances in the Arctic were all wrong, infinitely fluid, and it didn't matter that Cape Verdant was eighty miles south, Amelia's Pass some
way north above them. They had all the time in the world, those
crawlers.

And Stevens had shown them exactly where to find him.

Day saw, as if standing outside himself, the tent, the bone saw,
its teeth serrated and gummy with frozen blood. If there was life after
death—it was more brutal and sadder than he'd ever contemplated.
He thought, dizzyingly, that one look from those ruined faces would
cause his own mind to rip away from his body. The madness he'd felt
chewing at his heels for years.

Stevens smiled at him, and Day knew that the ship's ghostly company were back, their eyes burning. *We warned you about him*, they
seemed to say.

He spun around.

They were all staring, the crew of the lost *Reckoning*, teeming the
decks, mute and pitiless. Trapped. It was unfair that he'd escaped when
so many had died.

Come home.

Day was breathing so hard that white spots spun behind his eyes.
He'd never really escaped the *Reckoning*, none of them had. His sins
had found him out.

Stevens turned.

And *oh*, Stevens was turning in front of him at last. His princely
face was distorting, skin stretching and rippling, mouth slitting to
become wide and rapacious, nose and chin lengthening into impossible points, eyes growing dark and beady and coal-black.

A predator's face.

A splintering in Day's chest. Whatever Day had created, whatever
he'd given form, it belonged here—in this company of the damned.

His coat billowing, Stevens disappeared down the hatch as if he had an errand to complete. He left an impression, confused and terri-fying, of teeth, the smell of blood, eyes like iron.

Day was alone.

And as the deck wheeled away from him—

He saw the belowdecks, alive with candlelight. The creak of a cabin door. Day knew every inch of her: it was Talbot's door, and a dark shape unfolded itself, dread and deliberate as the masked Leviathan. Inside, Talbot had stopped coughing. He'd forgotten, hadn't he, the moment that Talbot had fallen silent—and who'd been the first to know.

"Go and get the doctor, Will," the shape said quietly. "I think his heart's given out."

———————

"Captain!"

Someone was shaking him. Peters.

Little flakes of snow were falling. When Day tried to stand, he found that the freezing meltwater had penetrated his coat. A chill against his heart, like the memory of Stevens leaving Talbot's cabin.

"I must have slipped."

He knew Peters wouldn't contradict him.

"I heard the bell . . ." Peters was staring around himself like a man watching a glacier progress into the sea. Awed by the presence of majesty.

She'd never been *lost*. Day had never crouched on the rocky shore, cold seeping through his boots, and watched her disappear. No: he'd chosen to leave. And she might have escaped the ice the next season, or the next. She might have. He couldn't deny it.

"Just tell them she was lost," Stevens said, very softly, and Day turned with a shiver. The disappearing hint of his smile in the gloom under the hatch. His teeth, white and sharp.

But whatever was out on the ice, clawing its way to muster—

It was worse by far.

"Captain?"

"It's nothing."

Peters tried the frozen wheel. Seemed to reach the same conclusion as Day: *she moves.* And Day knew, suddenly and completely, that he'd come alone—with Peters—because he'd wanted to buy himself time.

What would happen if they simply turned around, said nothing? Left her to rot?

"I can't quite believe it."

"Believe," Day said grimly, clawing himself upright. He thought about asking Peters to go belowdecks and wield that axe. Destroy her.

Talbot had known full well that he was dying. The book of Job had been meant to prepare Day for the burden of command. "Some men are too stupid," the captain had said. "Or too cowardly. Incapable of making decisions. Some are too greedy, too ambitious, too cruel. It's no accident you'll be taking charge, William. You're a good man."

This good man had killed sixteen men.

And Talbot had given Day another instruction: "*That* man, though—don't give him a command."

XVIII: APPORT

TALBOT'S CHANNEL, SEPTEMBER 19, 1882

They crept closer.

Their progress towards the *Reckoning*'s new anchorage seemed infinite, but inevitable. The men on deck crossed themselves, sucked their teeth, as she shimmered into view through the hazy mist, pregnant with the possibility of snow. The Arctic summer was ending, and true night, true darkness, was just two weeks away. The search for Stevens—stalled.

Down below, the pumps creaked out their dying man's heartbeat.

"The ice around her must be stable," Roderick said. "If she's survived this long. And she must be—uncommon sound." He didn't mention the fact that she was hundreds of miles from where she was meant to be. Day could see the journey in his mind's eye: skimming up north over the ice, rocky headlands, the barren desolation of Amelia's Pass, all the way to God-Saves Harbor, with its row of little graves. Countless unmarked upon the way.

This approach, by contrast, was agonizingly slow. Feet and inches. A crawl, stop-start.

This is it, Day thought. A nervous, horrible laugh bubbled up inside him as the Great Cabin windows winked. *I've come home. We'll all come home. One by one—*

"Oh, is this funny, Captain?" Valle said tightly. He was unshaven, uninvited on the bridge, but Day hadn't said a word when he'd stalked up the rickety stairs. "Is this funny? Is it a *joke?*"

The first snowflakes started to patter on Day's sleeves, melting on contact. He stared at them, numb.

"Are you listening to me?"

Everyone had turned out to see their approach to the *Reckoning*— or her approach to them. Mrs. Stevens leaned heavily on Qila, and Day was grateful when the snow started to obscure them both. "We must search her," Mrs. Stevens had insisted. "Every inch of her, for clues. He might have been here—"

And Qila, he could tell, was narrowing her eyes at him in that way she had, her face all stern angles. She'd gone off-ship with Lars earlier that morning; hadn't come to find Day on her return.

"Are you *listening?*" Valle shouted. His nostrils were quivering, his eyebrows drawn together like shutters, and Day could see the bitten indentations on his lips. The doctor looked about to shove him. Spit in his face.

Let him, Day thought numbly. *Let him.*

"I defended you," Valle hissed, as the wind blew colder and colder. "And for what? I said you wouldn't have left a single man behind. He wouldn't have abandoned his ship without good reason—"

Her solidity was a reproach. Who'd have thought a ghost ship could be so awful?

Valle clamped his jaw shut. He looked at Day with a wrinkle of his nose, and the snow whispered around them. Something was dawning behind his eyes. A look of fastidious disgust. As if he could guess exactly what that *good reason* was, and it appalled him.

Day had known that it would come back to haunt him. He'd argued with Stevens on the *Reckoning*'s stern deck, the wind smacking him in the face just like this, the clouds hiding the sun just like this, and the snow like tiny reproachful needles.

"Lie," Stevens said flatly. "Who will contradict you?" And put a hand on his shoulder blades, as if to steady him. But Day could feel his anger burning, and behind that, something else, something harder to place. Unthinkable. Was it fear?

"Who will lead them?"

Silence.

"I can't. I *can't*."

"You're the rightful captain now. And who will live to contradict you?" A deep sigh. Impossible for Stevens to contemplate waiting, on the ship, for another winter. For the Arctic to carry them off one by one.

We can't wait to die in our beds!

It's almost a scream.

"Will. I can't help you if we stay here. You have to do something."

That footprint at the bottom of the *Reckoning*'s main hatch had been smudged and blurred by several pairs of boots. Day stared at the slush. It was no longer possible to tell whether anyone had been on the ship in the long years since her abandonment.

Lost. A pointless lie: he might have said they were forced by circumstance to leave the ship, as so many other captains had been before. Shouldered the burden of the choice entirely. Owned it. But that felt shiveringly close to another course of action, one he'd turned over in the dankness of the belowdecks night: who to leave behind, and who to save.

He'd simply overcompensated. And the lie had taken on a life of its own.

"Search the cabins," Peters told Carter. "Force them if you have to!" His lantern illuminated the corridor sideways: the ship still had a touch of that strange old gravity about it. Day stood frozen at the fork in the passage, which led one way to officers' country and the other to the mess hall. Queen Victoria gave him a long cool look from her oil painting: no one had dared chop it up for firewood.

Around him, darkness yawned. So many empty places. The ship wasn't quite as he remembered her: there had been crates and boxes stored here, narrowing the passageway even further. Day had once sat with his back against them and wept, burying his face in his hands so Talbot wouldn't hear. He'd carried on weeping until Stevens had come looking for him, and pulled him up impatiently.

Will. What on earth are you doing.

"Has anything changed?" Peters asked, a smile on his face, and Day found himself shaking his aching head. Perhaps he'd remembered it wrong.

"We could put it to use immediately," Peters was saying, blind to Day's discomfort, as he strode through the ruined mess hall, sharp eyes darting around, seeming to draw animation from it: this place where two men's histories had been made. "Additional quarters. Spares. Before we make her fit."

"No," Day said, and it echoed. "I won't have people traipsing over her. Wait—"

Peters lowered himself down the hatch to the orlop deck. Day followed. "Wait—what did you say?"

"Before we fit her for sail," Peters repeated. "We'll be taking her back, won't we?"

His second-in-command looked at the ship the same way Day once had: a process not dissimilar to falling in love. Dewy-eyed and unreasonable. But there was a great difference between the *Reckoning* then and now.

"No," Day said, as Peters disappeared again into the dark. "We won't."

Winding his way through the orlop deck as if he hadn't heard, Peters stopped at the hatch to the ship's vast and frigid hold. "Well," he said softly. "That's disappointing, isn't it?"

Because the final hatch was sealed, the grating bolted shut, frozen in place by layer upon layer of hoarfrost, as if the coldness itself was blossoming.

"What?" Peters said.

Day was shaking his head.

He couldn't remember sealing the hold when they'd abandoned ship. Why would he, when they'd picked it over so many times. He couldn't remember sealing it: just like he couldn't remember leaving the main hatch open. But then, his memories of leaving the ship were all sideways, crammed with shame: the polar bear lurking, Stevens beating the men. Their desperate eyes fixed on their captain.

"Pity," Peters noted.

"There's nothing left down there," Day managed. After three years in the Arctic, anything edible had long since been dragged up to be consumed. Anything flammable to be burned.

Peters shrugged. "We might get an axe."

"No."

They both jumped—Day with a shiver, Peters with something harder to quantify—as Avery lowered himself, boots first, through the hatch from the Great Cabin above, landing with a puff of dust. "I thought I heard you," he said warily. "Is there anything down there?"

He looked Day squarely in the face.

Anything.

"No," Day said, squeezing and uncurling his fists, feeling the answering pressure in his skull. "No. There's nothing."

"We should move the bones over." Avery looked around. He'd insisted that the relics from Cannibal Cove couldn't be buried. Not yet. He couldn't return from their mission empty-handed. "There are plenty of hiding places. It'll placate the men."

"No," Day said again, fighting the rising, irrational horror. *A ship of the dead.*

The ice on the hatch winked in the gloom.

"The bones tell a story about him—not you," Avery said patiently. "You can't feel responsible forever."

Peters, in the darkness, said: "He was a *great man*."

Day had once thought they'd be entwined forever: now the thought that he and Stevens might part ways gave him a—kind of hope. What might it be like, to be someone whole?

But men were picking through the *Reckoning*, through the rib cage of his past. And from time to time he could hear it, if he paused to listen: the sound of something hooting—crawling—over the ice to find him. Something brought low and bestial. Being drawn back to her, and him, like iron filings to a magnet.

And the time for movement had ended. If they were going to spend the winter frozen-in off her side . . .

Will. You have to do something.

———————

"The other ship is . . . haunted."

Day swallowed, clutching the door frame as if it were the only still point in the world. Mrs. Stevens's cabin was too hot, too crowded, and she looked at him over tiny reading glasses, her hair scraped primly back.

You forbade me to hold séances. Why should I help you?

He didn't apologize.

"Haunted?" she said aloud, her mouth twisting. But there was no mistaking the gleam in her eyes. "By who?"

Day didn't answer. "We're going to be spending the winter beside her, that much is plain. I need you to help me. Communicate with—whatever's there. Find out what it wants."

Find out if it can harm us.

A pause. The whale lamp flickered, sending a shadow licking around the edges of the room. For a moment Mrs. Stevens looked as though she would go back to her reading. Day cleared his throat. "We can't find *him* if we're in danger ourselves."

She looked at him sharply. "Jesse? He's close, then?"

Day didn't answer.

"It could be dangerous, Captain," Qila said, where she was leaning against the wall, arms folded like a bodyguard. It was too warm for her usual sealskin jacket, and her sleeves were pushed up. "Dangerous for you," she added.

Mrs. Stevens gave her an impatient look, and Qila rolled her eyes. So utterly self-assured. She brought it to hunting, to speaking: to everything she did. Day knew she was thinking about their earlier conversation—

There's something haunting you.

The ship wasn't haunted—not really. The *Reckoning* was simply where it had all collected; dank condensation pooling, dark wings come home to roost.

"Well?" he said. "Now's the time. I thought you were willing to do anything—"

"Very well," Mrs. Stevens said briskly, and started gathering up her paraphernalia with a shake of her head, a drawing-in of her spine. "If my husband can be brave, then so can I."

The *Resolution* was now firm in the ice, and those gathered at her hatch were bundled up in winter clothing. It was a horrible place for a séance. The hold, though, was where Stevens belonged. Out of sight; beneath the surface. You might watch him retreat to that darkness, and think him gone. But he always crawled back out again.

Day bent down. This hold, at least, showed signs of human activity: scrapes where bellows and piping had been dragged down to fumigate. But the concoction used, brimstone and cayenne, just created billows of crimson smoke that stung like the fires of Hades. "'S hell down there," one of the men had coughed into his muffler. And the rats scurried on.

Mrs. Stevens crouched, her dress gathered around her, making a face at the soot. The decks were scrubbed regularly: Day didn't know why the route down always appeared grimy.

"Are you sure about this?"

Day swallowed. Nodded. "Yes. Please."

"If you think the spirits—"

"The haunting," Qila interjected.

"—might mean you harm . . ."

"You said they just wanted to be heard," he replied. "So we'll hear them."

He tried to sound more sure than he was. Because the idea of one word from those scornful officers—who'd seen right to the core of Day—made him shrivel up with shame. He felt like a schoolboy, begging not to have his embarrassing failings disclosed.

"Captain Day." Mrs. Stevens twisted her wedding ring on her finger. "I'm not a priest. I don't *really* know how to . . . put them down." She lowered her voice to a whisper. "A medium who can call the spirits reliably is a rare thing."

Day thought that Stevens would have killed to get his hands on such a prize: the ability to cloak himself in borrowed, unimpeachable authority. Who would dare question the dead?

So. Whatever came through, Greenstreet, poor John, or any one of the other, lesser unfortunates—anyone in that large, many-headed, amorphous beast—Day would let them speak. He felt that fascination, glimmering again, of someone bending to examine a baby bird fallen from the nest; back broken, beak open. Chirping into silence.

He'd done nothing, after all, to those who'd been taken off by scurvy or bad luck. Nothing!

So—what could they say?

The wind made a low hollow sound, like something moaning in the distance, steadily getting louder, and the hair stood up on the nape of his neck. Things were . . . coming back.

Things he knew, instinctively, he might not survive.

He had to do *something*.

Day descended. Long tails scampered away into the shadows: rats, after all, had once been key to their survival. The hold was awash with stinking water, steam from the boilers. Dark pools were bisected with planks, like the ribs of a long-dead whale, and the boiler wheezed away behind the bulkheads. The heat it produced was immediately sucked up through the pipes, leaving a sense of desolate absence, worse than if there had never been any heat at all.

Mrs. Stevens followed in a cloud of fabric, like a squid expelling its ink. Day placed his hands on her waist to steady her. He'd never had the art of making things look gallant.

"*Oh.*" She looked around, rubbing her arms. "I didn't know. It's horrible. You put men down here." The faintest air of accusation. "Don't you?"

Day's stomach knotted. He remembered how grateful he'd been to Peters for taking that decision. For being the one to do what was necessary. Day could stand back and watch it happen, didn't need to dirty his own hands—

That had always been the problem.

"I know." She took a deep breath. "*He* did too." As if the mention of her husband would give her the strength to take on these ghastly surroundings.

And Day couldn't be remade, he knew that now. Not by finding Stevens, not by anything else. *Who can bring a clean thing out of an unclean?* He was always going to be the man who abandoned his ship. Condemned his crew to death. The sum of his choices.

"Carter," he called, "keep watch at the ladder. Make sure no one disturbs us."

Avery, coming down last, carried a Mackintosh sheet and a fistful of candles. "They won't stay alight," Qila murmured, and sniffed pointedly. The air reeked of paraffin and the decaying bodies of vermin. *Fouled.*

"Well." Day looked around. "Let's get this over with."

"Yes. Let us join hands." Avery's accent made the words light.

Mrs. Stevens set her mouth in a tight line, and nodded. "But I won't let it speak through me," she said presently, in a small whisper. "Not this time."

Raising her voice: "Is there—is there anyone there?"

A low, harsh screech made them jump, and the shadows seemed to shudder.

"Concentrate."

Day fixed his gaze on their candlelit circle, refusing to look at the ship's buckling beams and cofferdams. The *Resolution* was starting to feel the pressure. The air was cold and greasy; he fought the urge to cough. It was a familiar smell. Almost tangible.

With a start—which he kept entirely inside himself—he realized it was the smell of Camp Hope, the blubber stove under the whaleboat, clinging to him as if he'd never left.

The past had its claws around his heart.

"Is there anyone there?" Mrs. Stevens asked again.

The ice grew louder, a high-pitched whine, pained and discordant and ululating. Behind them, in the shadows, Day heard the patter of tiny paws.

"Rats," he said. "Ignore it."

But there was something deliberate about the way the scratching moved, as if something light and fleet of foot was stalking them. Yellow light played across the dark water. The nearest candle puffed out.

The air seemed to thicken.

Beyond the puddle of light, the darkness was so total that the eye tried to conjure shape and movement. The soft splash of water. The muffled clank of the boiler. Down in the *Reckoning* hold, Day felt sure, there was water too—deep and dark and poisonous. Never mind that it was impossible: she hadn't been breached, and all water would have frozen, along with the *small deer.*

Rats had been why he hadn't got scurvy like the rest of them; he had Stevens to thank for that. So why didn't he feel grateful?

He swallowed.

"Make yourself known," Avery said.

"Only the medium should speak," Mrs. Stevens admonished.

Qila glanced at Day, and he read in her eyes her conviction that whatever was there was linked—inextricably—to him. As if in agreement, there was the sound of someone placing their weight, behind him, on one of those whale-rib crossbeams.

The shiver came from the base of Day's spine and traveled down his arms. *Transmission.* Someone made a small sound of fear. They could hear it, he understood.

They could all hear that footfall.

"Come *on*." Avery was impatient. "What's it saying?"

"I can't—do it," Mrs. Stevens whispered, like a scream. "I can't channel it. I won't produce the voices. You can't expect me to let it take me over!"

Her eyes were terrified. Day thought what it would be like, to give himself up entirely. To abdicate all responsibility. All reins. All control.

An intoxicating prospect.

She addressed the darkness. "You need to leave us alone, whoever . . . whatever you are. You need to leave this ship alone."

Day chewed his lip, and tasted soot: the acrid stink of day-to-day existence at Camp Hope, marinating him like a piece of meat. The blubber stove, burning grimy and plaintive, while Stevens walked outside in the fresh cold air. Stevens had been almost inhuman in those last miserable weeks: the ice had sanded away any remnants of softness, revealing the deep, harsh lines of his soul; perhaps the same harsh lines he'd shown to the dead. Chewed-off tongues and broken ribs and clawed hands. Missing fingers. Although Day had done nothing to the red-scarf man, or Patch, and hadn't been at Cannibal Cove—they were trailing him nonetheless, as if they couldn't distinguish between the two of them.

As if there was no telling where Stevens ended and Day began.

Creak.

"Something's here," Avery murmured.

"You need to leave us," Mrs. Stevens repeated. "Leave us alone."

Another candle wavered out, and the darkness seemed to advance by inches.

Avery coughed.

"Do you smell it?" Day whispered.

"What—"

"The smoke."

Avery shook his head wildly.

The boiler whistled.

"What is it?" Qila asked in the dark. "What can you smell?"

The ice outside hooted.

"Shh!" Avery looked up. "*Listen.*"

The sound was muffled by the gloom: the sound of a child rolling an india-rubber ball.

"Rats?" Carter said. His voice from the ladder made them all jump.

"No." Day knew where the sound was coming from—

Just behind Mrs. Stevens's left shoulder, where Jesse Stevens crouched.

His watch chain gleamed, describing a perfect parabola towards the wide cuff of his pressed trousers. The blood-red necktie, loose around his throat, emphasized the slimness and paleness of his neck: an alabaster saint. Day had never seen Stevens on his wedding day, his hair slicked and groomed to show the shape of his skull. He could imagine Stevens at the altar, though, waiting to take possession of his bride. A promise of loyalty, sanctioned by state and god. No William Day in the crowd. Nothing to spoil it.

Day would have given him everything, *everything*, and Stevens had taken it all.

Stevens looked young, full of wild delight. Again, the sound of a ball rolling, as if he were playing with a child. Day shuddered at the thought.

"What can you see?" Qila murmured, following his gaze. "You can see it, can't you?"

Day paused. Stevens was very close to touching them. Madness be damned: Qila's eyes glimmered in the dim light, like the mahogany of the *Reckoning*'s wardroom, once polished and warm. Everything about her suggested a terrible pity. An understanding.

He nodded. "It's here."

Mrs. Stevens raised her eyes, and he could see every inch of the whites. "Where?"

She wasn't blinking, so utterly still she might have been a doll. Refusing to show fear. He respected her for that.

"Don't look." His voice was hoarse. "Madam. Don't turn around."

He'd always been so sure no one else would ever see it; after all, who could see inside another man's head?

But now it had joined the *Reckoning*'s crew.

And he didn't know how she'd react. With horror or with love. A wedding day. *One flesh.* The exchange of promises, binding two people together. Or, he'd sometimes thought, swapping one cage for another.

She turned slowly all the same, jewels winking in the light. Stevens was only a few inches from her face, staring at her like a carnivore.

"What is it?" Avery asked, avid. "What can you see?"

"Nothing," she whispered. "Nothing."

It was tinged with longing.

Something bobbed towards the lantern-light. It appeared to roll downhill, although there wasn't a slope, as if bowled with a deft flick of the wrist. Into the center of the circle, gleaming: a single orange. Glowing in the candlelight like a tiny sun.

Mrs. Stevens screamed.

"Did you see it?" Avery was frantic. Day shook a hand free of his grasp. "Don't break the circle!"

But it was too late.

It was an ordinary orange. Shiny pitted skin, little green star at its apex. It held a faint, uncomfortable warmth; not the dry heat of the boiler, or the clamminess of the crew deck. It felt as if it had been in the sun very recently. As if someone had been walking in orange groves, and simply reached up his hand to pluck it.

"We don't have any on board," Carter was saying. "Captain? *Captain?*"

"Get rid of it!" Mrs. Stevens's voice was harsh.

Avery scrambled to his feet. "Was it you?" he demanded.

"No!" She tore off her veil, as if she couldn't endure it a moment longer. She looked . . . betrayed. Betrayed by everything. Her hand shook.

Qila was staring at her with flint-like intent, as if this was a revelation she'd waited for. "*Olive.*"

"It came from your direction."

"It wasn't me, I swear—"

"And the knocking? The table moving—that was you, wasn't it?" Avery grabbed her by the arm. "I said *nothing*. Fake mediums produce things," he said to the others. "Hidden in their clothes, or worse—"

"Yes!" She breathed raggedly. "I—yes, I've faked it before. I've even smuggled in fruit, we call it—we call them *apports*. But this wasn't me.

I swear." She was tearing at her veil, kneading at it, as if she wanted to rend it in two.

And she'd have no reason to know about Talbot, walking in his orange groves; Stevens slipping out of his cabin, giving Day a look, and disappearing into the darkness.

Stevens met Day's eye, now, holding up an orange of his own. Then he *squeezed.*

The orange split in his hand, the juice pattering onto the deck. Then the pulp was exposed, the gemmy interior. Bursting like a scorbutic abscess, or—like a windpipe. Hands around a man's throat. A pillow over the face.

I've taken care of it, William.

Because no one would leave the ship while Talbot was alive. And Stevens wouldn't wait.

"You'll be a better leader," Stevens had said, his eyes sincere, full of terrible hope—hope that Day would keep his word, keep his promises, and now they'd be leaving, the two of them together. And the darkness under the hatch, in the hold, was the essential darkness of Jesse Stevens. Attractive in its way. Possessing gravity in its way.

Day had done anything, anything, to avoid facing that darkness.

He dug his thumb into the peel of his own orange. It stung the tender skin of his nail bed. The white pith was the marbling of fat on meat, deep under the skin, the reserves living in the organs and marrow, like the nourishment from the summer hunting, but Talbot had died too soon.

Shouting. Avery was calling Mrs. Stevens a fraud. Qila wasn't defending her.

Hands from outside the circle fastened around Day's neck. Thumb to windpipe. Fingers to carotid. The candle beside him flickered.

"What's doing that?" Avery's voice was anguished. "Why can't I *see*—"

The candle went out. Then the next. The next. It was the foul air belowdecks, things wouldn't stay lit—

Darkness, and Stevens *dragged* him away, his hands like a vise.

Day scrabbled against the boards, splashed in the filthy water, fighting for air. His nails tore. Someone was screaming. Could the others see it now? Apparition. *Manifestation.* He couldn't breathe.

Looking up, Day saw—

Eyes like burning stars, too large and too black. Something tugging at Stevens's face, breaking bone and cartilage, his lips widening into a smile and still widening. At the corners of his mouth, teeth poked through, conical and sharp. A zigzag line of them, continuing up his jawbones, towards his ears, and his mouth was wide enough to *eat the world.*

Day's head met timber with a resounding crunch. *Crack.*

———————

When Day blinked his eyes open, he was in darkness. He was lying on a heap of misshapen, claggy things, cold and yielding and frozen all at once. There was something familiar about the sulfurous gloom, and Stevens—all eyes and teeth now, barely recognizable as human—appeared in the shimmering red and orange light.

This is hell.

He knew, suddenly and deep, that he was back on the *Reckoning.* This was her hold. The pile of things he was lying on were bodies, loose-limbed and staring-eyed.

Some of them *missing pieces . . .*

The spoilage of exploration.

Stevens was holding an ornately carved chair, with worn burgundy cushion. Talbot's chair, from the Great Cabin. And Stevens pulled it back, like a waiter or an executioner, inviting Day to take a seat. *I bought you this,* he seemed to say. *Your place at my table.*

And now you don't want it?

———————

Someone was holding Day's arms as he fought.

The rage he felt was immense and vast. It was a rage large enough to split the sky, to blow a hole in reality. He might kill the others: he might kill them one by one, and lingeringly. Hadn't Stevens always said he'd die last?

No one could possibly contain such poisonous fury, although it had always been bound up in him, beating against its prison walls. Its swells and tides keeping him an outcast, always on the very edge, clinging on to society by his fingernails. Knowing that on each side of him yawned the abyss—

Then he was kneeling in the corner of the *Resolution*'s hold, Carter helping him to his feet. The rage dampened as quickly as it had come.

"What—the dickens—was that?" Carter said raggedly, his eyes terrified.

Day coughed, holding his throat. Looked at the distance between himself and the others. Mrs. Stevens sobbed quietly, and for a moment that anger sparked again.

Qila knelt in front of him. Tilted his head up with two fingers, eyes searching his. She'd once thought him a good man, he remembered wildly. Maybe this was the moment she'd let it go. She was still young, after all. Shouldn't associate herself with monsters.

"That was it, wasn't it? The thing that's been haunting you."

". . . Stevens was here. He was here!"

She nodded. "Stevens. The dead. They have—attached themselves to you."

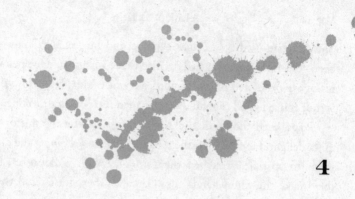

4

A whistle, high, up on deck.

Then the slam of the door into quarters. Down in the wardroom, Day ran a hand through his hair, straightened his collar. In the candlelit mirror, he looked like a reflection of a reflection, a man stretched thin, gray-faced and grave-like. Around his eyes the skin was creased, as if four bony fingers on each side were gripping his skull. Pulling it back. He scuttled at his mouth with the heel of his hand. Stared again.

It was torturous, the endless *waiting* and *watching*. Others might leave the ships, go out hunting or on search parties. A captain rarely did. But it might have to come to that soon—anything, he thought, was better than this enforced vigil.

October was weighing on him already.

The smart knock at the door was obviously Peters. "Come!"

His second-in-command was cherry-faced and wind-chapped. "Captain—they've seen a light on the ice. The search party returning."

The word *Stevens* hovered on his lips like a prayer.

Day stretched his cramped shoulders. It was now dark longer than it was light: they'd started their precipitous slide into the long night, and soon it would be too risky to send out any more search parties.

This last one—led by a bright-eyed Second Lieutenant Carter—had been gone for weeks. Day had decided to see what would happen when his newly promoted officer stepped out of Lee's shadow. This was the sort of thing a good captain did, gave men their chance to shine.

Peters eyed the candlesticks, gleaming away by the mirror, with quiet delight. He'd brought them back from the *Reckoning* and sanded them to sparkle: presented them to Day with a flourish. "Don't they make the room handsome, Captain. They must recall the old days—"

"Yes. Thank you," Day managed, although the merging of this wardroom with the Great Cabin was something that made him shiver. He felt like Talbot, he realized: past his best, ragged with contradictions. Had the old captain ever been so full of doubt?

Peters smiled. He was spending more and more time on the other ship, running his hands over her pipes, knocking on her stumpy masts, pacing her belowdecks. He was fixated on his idea—that they could crew her, sail her home.

He thought they'd be greeted with plaudits. A ghost ship returned to life.

"Anything else?"

"The crew complain, as ever."

The *Reckoning* had jealously prevented them from reaching safe anchorage. The *Resolution* was uncomfortably squeezed, her plates made popping sounds, and the rudder post screamed in agony whenever the ice moved. Cracks opened up unpredictably, crevasses appearing inches from the ship—deep enough to show black water at the bottom—then closing up again with the hiss of escaping steam. Hard pumping was required. Someone had sworn, white-eyed, that they'd heard something going at the hull with a hammer.

"They're saying—"

"I know what they're saying."

We won't go down again.

"You're the captain," Peters said.

Day followed him up on deck, jamming on a hat, wrapping a muffler around his exposed face. There was an air of expectancy everywhere he looked. Although it was past ten o'clock, two men were shoveling drift, silent save the unpleasant scrape of metal on wood. In the fortnight since they'd dropped anchor, the crew had stopped talking in front of him. Not even a whisper.

"We need to keep an eye on them," Day murmured.

Peters nodded. There was stubble on his jaw, the penny-colored suggestion of ginger hair. At the noonday inspections, too, it was clear the men were starting to change. Roderick had shaved off his beard altogether, making him look severe and old-fashioned. His two mates had tattooed their gums, bit by bit, until they were black-mouthed as scurvy victims. Day didn't understand why anyone would want to tempt fate. But he sometimes thought he'd have been better off if someone had *forced* him to hold a mirror up to himself. His torments and secret shames.

"Keep everyone here, but ready Valle. I'll go." Day looked at the shore ice as if the doors to the underworld were starting to yawn open.

Behind him, First Mate Sinclair paused in his shoveling, a cloudy breath pluming out from what looked like elongated teeth, lips still swollen from the ink. Day shuddered: the flesh gleamed black and blue, like the slick skin of a killer whale.

Out in that shipless dark, rope lines crisscrossed the shore, tapping in the wind, no definition to the world. The officer on duty at the fire hole was Holt: he simply nodded at Day's approach. With Carter away, he parceled out his words even more sparingly.

Movement in the sky; the aurora was beginning to wriggle its green fingers, and Day looked down to where the surface of the water shimmered, inky, under a sheen of new ice. He could see a black shape silhouetted against the heavens. It took him a few shallow breaths to recognize his own ghostly countenance.

Lee came to mind: floating under the ice, its serrated edges nipping and tearing at those haughty cheekbones.

Gone, he thought. *Just a body. Just another dead body.*

"Captain? Captain?"

The jolt of waking from the threshold of sleep. Day's lantern guttered, and this time he heard the whistle, faint and plaintive.

"That must be them!" Holt was scrambling to his feet, silver in his hair and hollows under his eyes. Ah, he'd missed Carter so.

The cliffs of the nearby islet sucked the perspective out of the scene, and the aurora seemed to inch along the ground rather than the sky.

"Shh!"

Day pulled Holt to a crouch, his heart pounding.

"Give me your rifle," Day whispered.

"What?" There was a stark question in Holt's narrowed eyes.

"Just—give it to me." He swallowed. "You don't know what's out there."

Two days before, Lars had returned with an apology. He couldn't reestablish communication to the south: the ice immediately below the ships was too treacherous, too mobile. He'd killed some Arctic foxes, created caches for the next trip, and—

He thought he needed to apologize? Lars was worth his weight in gold, and the only one of them with a chance of finding the *Louisa*. Day thought of dark-skinned Captain Nathaniel: in a more just world, Lars might have been an officer on his own ship. Or whatever it was he wanted.

Lars had also found a cairn—a vast triangular cairn built from discarded cans. Where the spindrift flowed down over the cliffs like a misty waterfall, like smoke from a far-distant fire, it was frozen into the landscape, this pyramid tall as a man.

Lars was heavyset, older than Day, laughter lines etched into the corner of his eyes. Native to the whaling grounds below them, the frozen shores and beaches off Baffin Bay, lands that rang to the sound of song. Day had never heard him complain or voice dissent; his English was accurate to a fault. The word he'd associated with the cairns was *territory*.

There was something in the idea that spoke of a great and familiar hubris.

———————

And two days before, Day had sat in the mirrored wardroom, turning one of those cans over and over. Its seams had been sheared open with a chisel, its base blackened, as if it had been used to cook over a fire. It smelled of cold: sterile. But there were smears—brownish smears—that he couldn't help finding horribly suggestive.

Day glanced over his shoulder. He'd taken to turning his collars up, tucking in his scarf; the bruises on his throat were coming up in purple. He looked much older than he'd ever imagined becoming.

The can spoke of the bones and charred stones of Cannibal Cove; it raised worse questions than it answered. The two weren't far separated in geography, and no one in their right mind would haul empty tins along in order to make a point. No, whoever put those cans there had enough to eat.

Perhaps there was a main party, with cans—and deserters, with bones. But the tent circle at Cannibal Cove had been far too large to speak of desertion, unless it was wholesale and utter. And who'd desert—en masse—leaving all that food?

It might have been cans first, then cannibalism after. He supposed.

Or—Day shuddered, feeling the thought creeping in like a kind of madness—the other way around. And by the glimmer of Stevens's toothy smile, Day knew with queasy certainty that he was right to ascribe to these small clues the worst possible explanation.

The cans, and the cannibalism, had been at about the same time.

It wouldn't have been about hunger—not exactly. It had never been just about hunger. He saw, in his mind's eye, the way Gregory Patch had been carved up. Tongue out, fingers off. A lesson. *Don't give that man a command.*

Whatever Stevens had become, Day had a hand in creating it.

"He left those tins—"

Avery was tapping his pencil against the table in brutal time.

"Stop."

"Piled them into a cairn which must have taken some time to construct—"

"Stop."

"While the men were *dying*—"

"Stop, stop, stop!" Day hissed, trying, for the sake of everyone else, not to raise his voice. "We have to find him."

"Yes. It hasn't changed for you, has it."

Bitter. But wrong.

A scream of wind outside made them look up; gale force, battering the ship, pushing them closer to the *Reckoning*. Her anchorage was deathly sound.

"He's gone mad, hasn't he? Captain Stevens."

Shadows. The mirror behind Avery showed a smudgy shape. Stevens must have loved James Avery, the architect of his legend: *the deliverer of Cape Verdant.* Day had tried so hard to avoid those interviews. But Stevens had reveled in them; and what he'd left out was more damning than the things he'd actually said.

Poor souls.

"Stevens is still alive, and still . . ."

The word *still* hung in the air between them like a thousand sparkling frost particles.

"We can't let her know," Day said slowly. He felt this was the right thing to do. "His wife. She shouldn't have to face that."

Avery shook his head. "I think she knows more than you realize. She picked his men, didn't she?"

Day exhaled. Somewhere Stevens might be crouched over another dead body. And there might be another young lieutenant, looking across the carnage, wishing he were more like his voracious captain.

So the search party had been gone too long, and Stevens was still out there.

Holt passed Day his rifle, and he took it, numbly. The aurora had started to swirl, great billowing sails in the sky, and Day couldn't guarantee that what came out of that darkness would be friendly.

The sky lit up, suddenly rendering their hiding place visible—brutally exposed on that sheer landscape. Day flinched.

A few hundred yards away, something was approaching.

Shapes were slouching through the gloomy haze. The horrible suggestion of something crawling, clawing its way along. They bobbed across the darkness, convulsive, swimming. Low to the ground.

Too low.

Noises crept in. The crunch of rocks. A whimpering or moaning made him suck in a single panicked breath. His fingers froze on the rifle, and he fought the urge to run. Where was there to run? There was nowhere left.

They've caught up with me already.

He could feel the blood in his veins. The moaning was tongueless, weary. An expelling of the last iota of strength.

Here they come.

A light: stuttering over the ridges, veering off course, then righting itself.

Day breathed out.

They wouldn't carry lights, he thought. *Wouldn't need lights.* The soft parts went first. Eyes. Noses. The dead would be at home in November's perpetual darkness.

The yellow light passed a vast hummock, the size of a beached and contorted whale, and Day could make out the light-bearer: blond hair, collar turned up. A sinister Pied Piper.

He hissed.

"We have to help them," Holt whispered hoarsely. "Captain!"

Day clenched his jaw. He couldn't say it. He couldn't tell Holt, forty-five and a lieutenant in Her Majesty's Navy, that he was afraid of being found by Jesse Stevens: that they should all be very afraid. *Needs must when the devil drives*—and that devil had killed Talbot, had led Day to Cape Verdant.

He wasn't ready.

He could make out the skeleton dance of other men, following that light-bearer in procession. Their footsteps were labored, their movements scuttling, and the moaning was worst of all. Holt's breathing was harsh.

Shouts from the ship. Then a red flare went up with a resounding crack.

"My God." Holt got up. "My God, Thom?"

A laugh, throaty. The search party. Carter, at the head of this madhouse procession, staggered towards them like a sleepwalker. His face was wild, as if all his features had shifted a fraction, and the resulting portrait was ghastly. Holt ran to catch him.

"Who—" Carter mumbled.

"He's freezing," Holt said desperately, rubbing Carter's bluing face. "Fourteen days!" There was a horrible undercurrent to his voice, one that Day knew well. "Fourteen days—"

Day could see, now, the rest of the search party. But no sign of the sledge. The aurora gave the men a sickly tinge, echoed in the low-slung slump of their shoulders. Their mouths were swollen, their faces puffy, like corpses that had spent too long underwater. Hesitantly, he lifted the nearest man—a boy—from his companion's shoulders. It was Tulloch, barely eighteen, and cold as metal; dragging his feet, Day couldn't carry him more than a few yards.

"Just wait here," Day said, desperately, to the crowd of ghouls.

But it was obvious too few men had returned.

"Where are the others?" Holt was asking Carter. "Thom. Please."

"We left them." Carter waved his arm vaguely, too weak to keep it up. "We were attacked."

"What do you mean?"

Day struggled with his rising panic. More men were out on the ice. More men were dying, out on the ice, where those *things* crept and gibbered.

"We left them," Carter said thickly, and placed his head against Holt's chest. "It was horrid. I think I need to lie down."

Shouts. The ship party had reached them, and Day turned to see Roderick's mismatched eyes, a sharp inhalation of breath—"Jesus!"—when their lanterns illuminated the state of the shore party. Shivering, he looked for Valle—but no, the doctor would be stoking the sick-bay stove, getting the cook to brew hot tea and rum. The faces around Day, on the ice, were blank. Blank and unhomely.

Roderick came very close, close enough for Day to see the flecks of black in his one golden eye. "Look at the men."

Day looked, but their eyes were rheumy and unfocused in turn, snow-blind, snow-stupefied. Their mouths had lost definition. They must have been eating snow. He'd seen it before: men who were desperate enough would do anything.

"Look at my men!"

Roderick walked away, silently, and the ship party touched their caps to him before bending to their stretchers. Something passed through the group: a restatement of the lines of authority. Day recognized it bitterly. The aurora flickered, like hundreds of watchful eyes winking in the darkness.

"It was something we couldn't see. The shape of a man, but it wasn't a man.

"It came into the tent, after a fashion. Ward said it must've untied the tent flaps, but I don't know they were tied in the first place. It was a mild night, not much . . . not much below freezing. Snowing a little out. We were all turning in, getting into our bags. In a good mood—we'd be back at the ship in a couple of days. And then it was dark, and there was a scraping sound outside."

Day felt a convulsive shiver pass through him, and for a moment he was inside that *other* tent, the red tent, sunlight coming through. The sound of something moving outside, stealthy and deliberate.

"It sounded like metal being dragged over stone. Like a rifle barrel scraped across rocks. Someone whispered, *Bears*—"

"It wasn't bears?" Day said sharply.

Tulloch was still shivering, short of breath. "Something reached into the tent. Grabbed Thompson by the feet, because he was nearest, he'd drawn the short straw. It might've had hands, but something was—wrong with them. Thompson opened his mouth. But he was taken out of the tent so quick he didn't have time to scream. Into the snow. It was drifting—you couldn't see your hand in front of your face. And you know how long it takes to get out of a frozen sleeping bag—by the time we were out, it was—

"There was nothing there." Tulloch swallowed, his skin ashen. "We took lanterns, but it was like walking around in a snow globe shaken up. And drag marks everywhere."

"Men?"

"Survivors?" Day said at the same moment.

"Maybe." Tulloch hesitated. "No." Then looked sharply at Roderick. "I know what I saw, though. Its head was too *big*. Not a man at all." Day felt cold fingers clutch around his heart. "It cast a strange shadow."

———————

Day found Kirkness not three hundred yards from the ships.

Despite objections, he'd gone out on the search himself, crunching over the ice with as much stealth as he could manage. Others called out, fired rockets or rifles. But Day went alone under the lingering aurora, trying to make himself unnoticed. Unable to be found.

It had taken five days for Lars to reach the search party's tent—to find it empty, the sledge untouched—and return with the grim news. No sign of Jones, who'd been too badly frostbitten to walk. Nor Kirkness, who'd been complaining of irregular heartbeat, sweating, pain in his fingertips like galvanic shocks.

It was as if something—*not a man at all*—had abducted them.

A hooting noise on the wind made Day freeze in his footsteps. It was the terrifying sound of someone screaming without a tongue.

He turned frantically, trying to work out where it was coming from. Echoes mocked, and the ice played its tricks of near and far, large and small. Visibility narrowed to a few paces in each direction, and he thought: *I'd never see them coming.*

Staring into the whiteness, the stars like gunshot wounds in the sky—unmoving, when everything around him was blowing—he barely noticed the shape in the drift until his boots stumbled over it.

A body.

It was curled up like a tadpole, face towards a hummock, as if refusing to look at something dreadful, or burrowing in for a warmth that would never come. Day bent down with horrible numb curiosity. What could those—*crawlers*—do to human flesh and bone?

Kirkness's face was frozen into a grim mask, his eyelids gray and stiff, mouth drawn open to expose his teeth and gums. Day could see that some had shattered in the extreme night cold, lodged in the jaw as if someone had taken a hammer to them.

He shuddered.

But there were no obvious signs of injury. Exposure, that was all, and Day stood still for a moment, preparing to signal the other searchers. Kirkness might have been stumbling back to the ship like a drunkard. Panicked as well as hypothermic. Perhaps not trusting that anyone would—really—be sent into the killing snow to fetch him.

Or desperately hoping to leave behind whatever had happened to his comrades. The drift suddenly seemed like it hid the world, and whatever was coming. Kirkness's frozen expression spoke of a great and terrible fear.

The *apparitions*—Patch, the red-scarf man—didn't seem to distinguish between Day and Stevens. The crawlers might not either.

Poor souls.

They'd be a danger to anyone out here, the *Fox* and the rescue mission alike. Anyone who came there, in service to—

Day put a hand to his own throat. Kirkness's body was heavy, despite its comma-curled size. It was hard to imagine dead things could have so much force. Stevens—the thing that was Stevens—had only gained his monstrous vitality after years of siphoning it off Day himself.

Surely the others, the ones on the ice, would be half-broken, missing limbs, casting those strange shadows with pried-open jaws and empty skulls. How far could you drag yourself with one arm, when the other had been fed into the maw of a polar bear? How much strength would be left if you'd been slit open, gorge to pelvis, to get at your entrails? And how much damage could be done with toothless gums? In those last days at Cape Verdant, they'd been weaker than kittens, those who hadn't yet succumbed.

But Day knew that whatever was out there was *angry*, angry enough to drag a full-grown man from a tent. And it was the anger that animated, the same anger he'd felt in himself.

A fury that might eat the world.

The mess-hall door opened before Day had time to announce his entrance. Roderick was sitting at the long table, flanked by his tattooed mates: Day had barely had time to come off the search, splash chilly water on his face, mumble an unconvincing prayer for Kirkness, before going to find him. "Captain," Roderick said. But he didn't stand. Day supposed he had no need to do so: this place was his, with its low ceilings and smell of candles and rope. And the crew was his, too. You only had to look at them to understand.

From the sick bay, a cry echoed through the empty spaces around the coal bunkers. The sound was too garbled, too unruly.

"Animals," that voice was saying. "Get them away!"

"That's Ward," Roderick said, steepling his fingers. "My master carpenter. Who'll fix her up now?" He nodded at the groaning timbers beneath their feet. The floor was, very subtly, bowed under pressure.

Day swallowed. A captain never apologized. "A terrible loss. You have my sympathy."

"And the others?" one of the mates said, dangerously.

The ship had been bedlam on the search party's return. Some of the men still thought they were on the ice, awaiting rescue. Crying out to their colleagues, brothers. Imploring them not to—

Roderick's mouth worked. "I knew him as a child. I knew his mother, who died young, and his father. Ward's a good man, and should've lived to become a better one. But he'll have died looking for someone . . . already dead."

No one, Day knew, came back from that kind of delirium. And Ward's jaw had begun to seize.

"We need to send another search party—"

The whalers had the temerity to laugh. A humorless laugh, one that suggested a life far wilder and harder than Day could ever imagine.

"We have to," Day insisted, his heart thudding.

Roderick shook his head. The lines on his forehead made it look as though the ice had washed and receded across his face, year by year. "I don't care what the Admiralty will say. That was the last until spring."

"You believe them?"

"I believe my men."

The tattooed sailors looked like marble statues, the darkness of their lips emphasizing the pallor of their faces. The significance of those killer-whale mouths—their silence, their unease—came suddenly into focus: they were haunted by the boats. They thought they'd attracted bad luck, so they'd made themselves into whale-faced gods. As if by imitating the omen of death, they might cheat it for a while.

Day felt something lip softly against the top of his head, and stumbled back from the table, his skin crawling. Just a swaying rope. But Roderick believed there was something on the ice. The things Day had heard. The things Tulloch had seen—

Here be monsters.

"What?" Day asked. "What do you think—"

Again, Roderick shook his head. "Men with animal faces, I suppose." His voice was hoarse. "We never found Herridge."

"He can't possibly be alive out there!"

"What, then?" Roderick rubbed a hand across his face. "We never found the mask." His mates gave each other uncertain, slant-eyed scowling glances.

Day was silent. He knew what was out there: things that *crawled*.

Oh, there was a lot to be done to a skull, if you wished to process its contents for consumption. No whaler's try-pot had ever been so voracious. Jaws snapped off. Noses broken with hooks. Scalps torn back. Who was to say the dead hadn't been frozen in those attitudes, creating—

Men with animal faces.

"And I can't see any more of them like this." Roderick looked Day square in the eyes, a pleading tinged with violence. "D'you understand?"

Day opened his mouth, and the *Resolution* chose that moment to give a long low groan, as if someone had rammed an india-rubber tube down its gullet. The reverberations ticked away through her hull, making the rivets pop and the decks grind, right the way down to the hold, where the waters might be rising. They all listened, barely daring to breathe. Those ice-cracks opening up and smacking shut had maimed her rudder, compromised her planking. They were living over a powder keg. Waiting for the explosion.

Roderick nodded, as if he could tell what Day was thinking.

Day breathed out, seeing it swirl. The ship was cold, but they'd all become accustomed to the chill. The process had been invisible.

There was no use in force nor shouting. He thought of Talbot, who'd propped himself up on his pillows and said, with great dignity: "You all have your orders. And I expect that, if I'm ever fully incapacitated—" A pause in which they acknowledged, silently, the long night of wailing and gnawing that would come. "—I expect every man to do his best to follow them."

Something was wrong with him, Day knew. And now the expedition would fail from it.

"It would be a shame," he chose his words carefully, "if on our return, it was said that the men disobeyed me."

"Who's giving orders? You needn't give any for us to disobey. I'm not your enemy, Day! My only purpose is getting us all home safe. That's what they chose me to do. They trusted me."

And his authority, Day understood, extended only as long as that was true. How different a world it would be, if everyone was led by who was *most fitting*.

No one, he knew, would ever have naturally looked to Day.

Roderick drummed his fingers on the table; mucky fingerless mittens, Day noticed, but his hands and nails were very clean, as if he scrubbed them fiercely. He bent closer, until Day could feel the breath against his cheek. "Well. If you're hell-bent on sending someone out, even now, a word to the wise: send that hellion you've got for a second. Put some distance between yourself and him."

"Peters?" Day wanted to say: *But he's loyal.*

Roderick nodded, once. The light gleamed off his mismatched eyes. "There's a lot of danger in an ambitious second." Too soft for his mates to hear. "And I'm telling you. That one's ambition should make us all afraid."

XX: OUROBOROS
At anchor, October 8, 1882

The *Reckoning*'s masts loomed over him in the darkness. The whale lamp shuddered in the ceiling as Day entered the makeshift sick bay—occupying what had once been her meteorological observation chamber—but Valle didn't look up.

Day stood to his full height, chewing the inside of his cheeks. Talbot would have gone to the doctor earlier, he thought numbly. He would have taken responsibility, would have taken every precaution to ensure his own sanity—and command. Wouldn't have waited until Roderick took it from him.

He would have swallowed his *pride*.

The room was stifling, the stove making it warmer than an abandoned ship had any right to be. Day was suddenly too hot, sweaty, itching under his greatcoat. Over on a low cot, one of the sailors sat with arms outstretched. His wrists were red welts; slow-moving blood chased the cloth as Valle washed them without much tenderness.

"You need to control your officers," Valle muttered, not looking up. "This is hardly fitting punishment." He wound a bandage around each wrist. "There. Make sure you take your lemon juice. You may go."

The door slammed.

There'd been speculation about what punishment was justified for "looters," as Peters termed anyone found belowdecks on the ghost ship; he had a possessive glint in his eyes, as if she was for him and Day alone. But in the end, he'd just attached this man to the rigging in irons, wrists too high for him to take the weight fully off. Looking at the results, Day could appreciate how ingenious the punishment had been. A slow torment.

"Will it heal?"

"You tell me." Valle's voice was biting. "Without the *Louisa*. What a waste."

Scurvy was the invisible debt collector. New wounds would fail to heal. Old scars would unknit themselves. An unsympathetic *recurrence*: a man's history would become liable to kill him. They couldn't expect sufficient hunting for the next four months, perhaps five, and with the stores they had would be lucky to stave off the wasting disease.

Day had considered sending Lars out, once again, to search for the *Louisa*, but something had stayed his hand. Perhaps it was the thought of losing him—although he knew that wasn't a calculation worthy of a captain.

You've lost your guides before, after all.

A snort. Valle knew what he was thinking; scurvy in the first winter would be an unprecedented disaster. The doctor turned away, busying himself with the pail of bloody water, and Day squeezed his hands behind his neck.

"You have all you need? Valle."

The two of them had hardly spoken since the *Reckoning* had been sighted. For three weeks, Day had relayed all orders through Peters—

including the one that had banished Valle, and his sick bay, to the other ship. All had pretended to sleep as Ward's muffled sobs thudded their way through the *Resolution*'s passageways, becoming more and more garbled as his jaw seized further. Just like Talbot: no one had wanted to gag their captain, and it had dragged on for long pitiful weeks. It had been very apparent that Ward would meet the same fate.

We'll all go the same way, Will, while we stay aboard this bloody ship. I'm doing you a favor!

Stevens had always seemed so angry—so accusatory. Looking back, though, Day thought it had been a glimpse of fear: Stevens's terror at a death he couldn't control. He'd wanted to do anything, *anything*. There had been no master plan, no overarching aim, save a hunting rifle, and one day at a time.

Ward had eventually fallen wide-eyed and silent. Day couldn't abide that silence.

"If you've come to check up on me," Valle said now with icy formality, "know that I'm doing quite well." This small room had been built on the upper deck, was cut off from the rest of the ice-bound ship and her inky underbelly.

The *Reckoning*. An accounting for past misdeeds.

Valle pursed his lips. Another sigh, in which he seemed to unstring himself a little. "I shouldn't have said those things in front of the men."

"It'll be a long winter. And if scurvy appears—better to shield them from the suffering of their shipmates." Day wrapped his arms around himself. "This is for the best."

Valle snorted. "Someone else will be the judge of that."

"You apologized," Day sighed. "Let's leave it."

"I didn't say I was wrong." Valle scrubbed at his bony hands with the cloth, making them wetter and dirtier. The silence hung between them. Day knew what he should say: *I need your help. I need you to say I'm fit for command.* That he was still able to discharge his responsibility to his passengers, officers, crew. That he was still fit to command the search after Stevens.

Tell me I'm still good.

The doctor should have been the captain's natural ally. But up here, everything was warped. Twisted. Dragged.

"I don't suppose this is a social visit. Has someone else been taken ill?"

Day shook his head.

"What, then?" A sigh. "Don't tell me you've finally decided to start following standing orders."

Day unbuttoned his greatcoat. "I intend to lead a search party myself," he said. "With the officers. They're preparing now. I'd like you to confirm—for the record—that I'm fit for command."

There was a horrible pity in Valle's eyes, like a wash of icy water. Day held up a single warning finger. "Don't say anything yet. Just listen. I need to know whether things over here have been quiet." He nodded towards the locked door, the ship beyond.

"What?"

"If I'm to go—I'll need to show my judgment is sound. And I want to know you'll be safe in my absence. I can leave tomorrow, if we make haste—"

"Oh. Oh, William. So this is why you've come."

Valle looked every one of his fifty-something years, and Day could hear the disappointment in his voice. That Day had come to him now, finally, and only when he thought the doctor could be of use.

But wasn't that what a captain did?

"I'll tell you anything you want to know." Day swallowed past the knot in his bruised throat, speaking so fast the words tumbled over each other. "You have to examine me. I just want you to answer something in return. You know this ship: tell me if you've seen or heard anything strange. Any knocking. Any footsteps. If she's compromised."

"You want me to tell you if she's *haunted*?" A snort.

"Valle, please." He exhaled. "Not your pride. We're—past that now."

He struggled to put into words the horrible watchful presence he'd felt, the sense that the ship contained a vast something that wished him ill.

"Just listen. Something bad happened on this ship." Valle snorted again, but there was an unhappy twist to his face. "There were so many deaths. So many bad deaths."

Talbot was big enough, to Day, that his murder had torn a hole in the world. Nature abhorred a vacuum, and maybe something had found itself capable of stepping through in return, casual as Stevens in the doorway of that trapper's cabin.

Something that would hold Day responsible.

"The ship has a sort of—gravity to it. A sort of magnetism. Things get trapped here, or drawn here. The dead. And they're angry. Dangerous."

Day tried to put it into words of science, and for an instant, in the softening to his sharp features, it seemed as though Valle understood. But then he sighed, looked burdened. Something had landed heavily on his shoulders, and he drew back with a twist of his thin lips.

"Do you know what I think, William? I think that this place—this place in particular—is bad for you. In particular."

Day exhaled.

"You're unwell. There's a mental or spiritual *confusion*."

Day shook his head automatically, like a dog cringing before a blow. "It'll be better . . . I'll be better. Once I find him."

"You've been unwell for a long time; I think I saw the start of it," Valle said. "When you first came onto the ship, and met Stevens. The way you'd look at him, it just wasn't right."

His voice held a mingled pity and accusation Day knew well. Shame: men pressed into a bunk together, the fine golden hairs on Stevens's arms. The nights he'd thought he'd die, happily die, if he could only possess Jesse Stevens—whatever hazy meaning of the word his young self was able to conjure up—just once.

One flesh.

"It wasn't like that! It was never like that!"

Valle shrugged, unconvincingly. "I don't care how it might have been between you. But William, please. I can help you now." He reached out and took Day's hands in his bony ones. "You're still seeing things, aren't you?"

Day flinched. His shoulders were prickling, burning, a hundred tiny insects burrowing through the flesh. He snatched his hands back. He'd thought he'd scoured it *away*.

"Consider this my prescription for what ails you." Valle bent in closer. "He wasn't your friend. He wasn't anyone's friend. You should let him go. Don't go running after him—you won't make it back!"

Day was startled to find a hot red feeling behind his eyes, as if he were on the verge of some horrible unraveling. He'd navigated by Stevens his whole life.

Stevens was dreadful. But he was *his*.

All those nights—didn't they mean anything, anything?

"What are you saying?"

Valle shrugged. "There's no need to make a scapegoat of yourself. For his sake, or the sake of the Admiralty. If it endangers you, or others, that man doesn't deserve to be found."

Day's heart was pounding as if he'd run a race.

Valle caught him by the shoulder. "Don't worry about him—look at me! The man with the broken ribs. Mr. Patch. All those bones! Leave him, William. He *used* you. Maybe it's time to return the favor."

"You know nothing about him—"

"Don't I?" Valle's chin was jutting out. "His influence over you has always been—"

"Enough!" Day bellowed.

He was breathing hard. Of course Valle would recognize Stevens, wherever and in whatever form he encountered him. Their sullen mutual resentment had only come to an end with Valle coughing on a pitiful northern quayside, watching the ship sail on. Valle's influenza was one thing Day couldn't lay firmly at Jesse Stevens's door.

And admitting he saw Stevens would be useless now. A one-way ticket off the bridge and to the asylum. A sign of weakness, madness. His skin tingled.

Perversion.

"Oh. *Oh.*" Valle's eyes widened. "Is that why you've put me here?"

Day stepped away, but there was nowhere to go. The chill green medicine bottles glinted in the lamplight. He imagined lifting one to his lips, Valle's bony fingers supporting his head. Sinking into a dreamless sleep. Abandoning command. Walking away.

He'd wished for it, once. Wished so powerfully.

When he turned, they were face-to-face, Valle's beaky nose inches from his. Day could see the deep scowl lines on his old-man's forehead; his oldest friend, or something like that.

Day didn't blink. He didn't move. Lee had been right, all those months ago, when perpetual sunlight still glinted through clouds. Any plan to take back the expedition would have to start with the doctor.

"I want to help you." A note of sadness, ringing false. "I want you to return to England safe and sound. But I won't say you're fit. I won't lend my authority to any search party. It's madness."

"Who will you give the expedition to? Peters?" He didn't miss the tightening of Valle's jaw. "Roderick, then."

Day swallowed, thinking of the mess hall, the table worn to a shine, a line of weathered boots arranged for blacking. It made a lump form in his throat. Because if Stevens didn't deserve to be found, what of his men? Good men, innocent men, who hadn't had a choice—hadn't had any real choice—who to follow.

Poor souls.

Valle had been a friend, once. But he was right. There were no friends out here.

"Perhaps you should be careful about crossing me."

The anger in Day's voice made Valle take a step back. It was as if something had reached down his throat and plucked the words out. The wrath in his own chest made him uneasy. What right did he have to be angry, after all?

What right had he ever had?

Valle's eyes widened. They stared at each other, and Day looked down to find that he was holding a pair of scissors. He was unable to make sense of a world in which he'd picked them up. He unbent himself, forced his shaking fingers to drop them.

Still, that rage burned on.

The bucket of bloody water glimmered. Peters had been unspar-
ing—Day had to applaud him. There were no traces left of uncertain
Peters Peters, who'd once dithered in doorways. He and Day had to
keep command at all costs. Keep up the search for Stevens.

Something inside him knew: dark times might call for dark measures.

Out on the silent deck, Day's shoulders still burned: that morning
he'd sent for hot water, scrubbed hard at his shoulders and back, sobs
squashed down into heaves, his arms shaky and heavy, muscles cramp-
ing. He'd scrubbed and scrubbed until his skin was red-raw. Trying to
scour it off, whatever influence Stevens had left behind.

The previous night, he'd had to feel his way into quarters, outstretched hand following the cold pipes into the familiar yawning
mouth of dark wood, dark illuminators, dark doors. They couldn't
afford to waste fuel. But there was something uncomfortable about
this darkness: a particular greasy quality to it.

Inside his cabin at last, Day had reached for the lamp. The darkness thickened. And all at once he knew he wasn't alone; there was
something else in the room.

Crunch.

There was something underfoot. Day stepped back, and it ground
and squeaked. A sound to set your teeth on edge.

A slow curling sense of dread.

The lamp wouldn't light. The stuff on the floor was behind him as
well—*grave-dirt*—and he didn't think he'd be allowed to make the two
paces to the door.

"Are you here?" he whispered.

Nothing responded.

But when the aurora lit up the sky, he could see a crouching shape
in the corner. A glimmer of golden hair, but Stevens was dirty up to
his elbows, as though he'd been digging. His arms were scratched, as
if from countless tiny sharp rocks, somewhere the ground was black.

The exhalation he made was the animal *huff* of a predator.

Day crawled into his bunk, fully clothed, like a child. He drew the covers up over his head, a small whimper making the sheets billow like a tent in a light breeze.

The crunch of gravel.

Day stopped breathing.

When he dared to peel back the covers, Stevens was examining the map on his desk with thin fingers, horribly bent nails, one ripped clean off. There was no more delicacy left in those hands. Day watched as Stevens left dirty prints on the map, like a spatter of spilled blood on snow.

Amelia's Pass, a location inland, a short but critical distance in the long journey between God-Saves Harbor and Cape Verdant.

Stevens offered him a wide and bloody smile.

The desk was close enough for Day to see Stevens's chest moving laboriously in and out. He was breathing. There was a faint hiss on each exhalation, as though his lungs were unfamiliar with their task. As though he were relearning how to be a person.

The manifestation was painfully thin, unlike Stevens at Cape Verdant, where he'd been strong and sleek. His teeth jutted from his lower lip, giving a hint of that killer-whale smile. And he stank; he smelled of the grave-ridge, of crisp air marred by the peat-moss stench of things rotting slowly. Bodies decaying by inches. This Stevens was a ghoul, had clawed his way out of a grave.

No. Not out.

"Come on, then," Day whispered in the wavering moonlight, baring his throat. "Come and get me."

Then he'd know it was real. He wasn't—mad. Fresh bruises would be worth it. It would all be worth it, wouldn't it?

Touch me.

Finally.

Stevens pulled back the bedcovers, a grin on that razor-sharp mouth. He didn't listen to Day's protests. And by the time Day had realized what was happening, his limbs no longer seemed to work.

"No. No—"

Because Stevens crawled into bed with him, wrapping his long arms around Day's chest. He was strong as the ice, and the aurora wavered and went out, plunging them into darkness.

Day felt breath on the back of his neck, and gulped down a scream. He tried to move his arm. Nothing. His legs. Nothing.

He was able only to squeeze his eyes shut, pretend it wasn't happening.

I've got you, Will. Isn't this what you wanted.

The ghoul was pressed against him all the way down, their limbs entangled in a lovers' embrace.

The following day, his shoulders burned and itched, as if he were growing two vast and painful wings. Mrs. Stevens might have been drawn to Jesse like a moth to a flame; but Day had been drawn to the dark.

And, after speaking to Valle, he wished that he'd scoured harder.

———

"What are you doing?"

The harsh cry carried clearly over the ice between the ships. It startled Day back to reality as he stood shivering, still smarting from his conversation with the doctor: *it wasn't like that.*

The cry had come from Qila: Day reacted instinctively, scrambling down the ship's side, then starting to run. There were bears here—if there was one thing William Day knew, it was that. The rifle slammed against his back, and the twilight had become full of crepe-like mist, stealing across the ground.

Over at the *Resolution*, he could see a struggle. "No—let go—"

Qila again, clear as a bell, lashing out as she tried to get free. Dark shapes around her. Men. Day's heart pounded: he was meant to be protecting his passengers, they were his responsibility. But that little green medicine bottle was, perhaps, what he deserved instead: the dreamless sleep, relief of command.

He'd invited Stevens into his bed, had scoured off his own skin. He'd done it to himself. He was starting to understand: he'd done so much of this to himself.

His boots went scudding past the fire hole. "Hey!" Day shouted. "You there!"

"Captain!" Qila yelled, a high quality to her voice he'd never heard before.

From behind him, something bulky stirred.

Day hit the ground face-first, knocking the wind out of himself. Rolling over, he scrabbled for his rifle. The mist was making big shadows—the thing leaning over him was all eyes and haunches. It was First Mate Sinclair; he opened his black-blue mouth in a ghastly smile.

"Captain. Best you don't get involved."

"Stand aside—"

"Leave her alone!" And oh, Mrs. Stevens was there, too—they were marching her down onto the ice. Snapping at her heels. She was unbound and so far unmolested, drawn out after Qila like a bear protecting her cub.

"Peters!" Day bellowed. "Carter!"

"No one's coming," Sinclair said. A large hand fastened around his wrist. "I wouldn't."

"Let go of her!" Day shouted. "That's an order!"

One of the men holding Qila hesitated: Day recognized young Tulloch, still weak from his time on the ice. The other continued dragging her forwards, a pistol pressed to her breast, and Day felt a sick helplessness. *The women aren't safe here.*

"What are you—"

"We're going to the other ship. Just to have a look, like." The pistol wielder was Second Mate Flett, the fog making his tattooed lips look bloody. "The women can go first." He gestured as well as he could without the use of free arms. "Then we can all follow, eh? Get her boilers up, make nice and snug for the winter. Wouldn't want your guests to freeze."

"No one is going—"

"All of us will be, sooner or later. Didn't you hear the knocking?"

Qila pressed her lips together, looked at Day with wide grim eyes.

"Ask *her*," Flett said, "The spirit medium."

"I did nothing," Mrs. Stevens hissed. "This isn't my fault!"

Someone spat on the ice, and was it Day's imagination, or did he hear it sizzle?

"Tell that to Herridge," Sinclair said. "He went to you, got touched by the old conviction. It found its way back, and look where it got him."

Day could see, now, that Flett's mouth was bleeding, his nose starting to swell. Qila must have fought. He felt a fierce burst of pride.

"Are you hurt?"

The girl raised her head just long enough to give him an accusing look: some part of her had trusted him to prevent this.

Men are like that everywhere, Captain.

"Put down your rifle," Sinclair said in his ear. "There's no reason for this to go bad. We won't hurt them. You have our word."

"You could sink her," Stevens had once whispered against his neck. "You could do anything you wanted, Will!"

"No." Day raised his voice. "This is a direct order. Anyone who disobeys me will answer for it. The women stay with me."

"She good as killed him," Sinclair rumbled.

Herridge had been asked by something unseen, *What's the worst thing you've ever done?*

And then disappeared, as if the answer had swallowed him up.

They continued coming forwards, boots crunching on snow. Mrs. Stevens's head was high, her skin deathly white, a too-big whaling coat thrown over her shoulders. She looked up at the other ship with wide and shivery eyes. She hadn't kept presssing for it to be searched—not since the séance. The orange.

Stevens, crouched possessively behind her.

Day could feel the blood rushing through his veins. He thought he heard a faint creaking sound, like sails starting to unfurl.

"Let them go," he said quietly. "There'll be no more said. I know how men can get—over winter. We'll write this up as a momentary disagreement. Or not write it up at all."

"Oh, come on," Flett said. "If it's good enough for the doctor, it's good enough for all of us." He nodded at the *Resolution*. "Have you been at her waterline? Not long left, I'd say. We'll be down by the end of the month."

"It was just a mask," Day hissed. "Made by a madman. It's not some omen of destruction." And some of that madness, he now realized, had transmitted itself through blue-black lips. Through fear.

Tingling in his wrists. The fog billowed.

"That *madman* was part of our crew."

"There are—"

A female voice cut through, and they all glanced at Mrs. Stevens, who was standing stock still, hands over her mouth. "There are—men—on the decks over there."

The whites of her eyes were the white of bones and ivory.

"Fakery," Sinclair said with emphasis.

Tulloch looked unsure—like he wanted to let go of Qila, and slink off, and pretend none of this had happened. He'd ended up on the wrong side of this, whatever it was, and Flett jabbed him with his free elbow. "Come *on*."

"Stand down, or I'll have you confined. Put you in the hold over winter, so you can listen to it up close."

"You have no idea. No idea what you're saying."

Flett came closer, then, dragging Qila along with him like a hostage. Day couldn't catch her eye, as he'd once done so easily. "Don't I?" he shouted. "Go on, then. Tell me how *bad* you are. Did you kill your bloody captain, was that it?"

"We're not murderers," Sinclair growled. "He was a blowhard and a swindler, but it was an accident. Don't you go saying—"

"Aye, it was an accident," Flett replied. "We decided early on to put him overboard, once he'd passed—we knew how it would look, otherwise. How were we to know he'd get stuck under the hull? Trapped. Knocking. Bloated. I could see his face sometimes, through the water, as he came apart. His body attracted the killer whales, and they circled, and circled . . . waiting for us to weaken. Sometimes you'd see an arm. A leg. Like we could see death following, all ragged and in pieces. You don't keep dead things with you. You don't!"

It had the air of a prayer.

"You could eat," Day found himself shouting, bitter as pith. "You could *eat*!"

"Not enough to stop us thinking—what else could we use. To draw the killers off." A gulp of laughter. "Or draw them closer."

He eyed Tulloch meaningfully.

Sinclair: "Come now. Let us go. You know you don't have the stomach for it."

They could eat, Day thought again, baffled at how it had come to this—this madhouse comparison of wounds. The last trickles of his authority slipping away, an authority he once thought he'd justified, by clawing himself to Cape Verdant and back with at least some of his men. But it meant nothing to them. Talbot had suffered, before the end. But he wasn't Talbot, a good man and upright, was he?

No. He was someone else.

"He's holding a noose," Mrs. Stevens whispered. "He's holding a noose!"

They all glanced, instinctively, towards the *Reckoning*, sitting there waiting to spring. The fog caught the sliver of moonlight, and the resulting shimmer made her look alive. Day felt covered in tiny electric shocks; he wasn't entirely in control of his limbs, as if he were struggling out of a cocoon, learning how to fly—

A dark tide approaching. He opened himself to it.

"Run."

And he shoved Flett's pistol out of reach.

Qila took off like an arrow from a bow, fast and sure-footed. "Get her!" Flett yelled, turning his attention to Mrs. Stevens. Sinclair started running, and the moon flickered, went out. The haze was dark again. "Get her—"

Qila was fast, and Day found—with a crazy kind of unfettered joy—that he was fast too. His old knees were young again, and the frigid air felt good in his lungs. He was gaining on Sinclair easily. He didn't know what he'd do when he reached him.

Somewhere, in a corner of his head, he found that unusual.

The *Reckoning* creaked. Through the obscurity came a babble of voices. Some he didn't recognize, but one he did: Jonny Greenstreet, bloody First Lieutenant Jonny Greenstreet, saying: "I just don't think I can take it any longer—"

It undid something inside Day, until he felt like his chest must be hollow, open to the night: he ran harder. Sinclair glanced back, a stunned look on his face. Then a stumble. Day grabbed him by the collar, and they both went down, the ice sharp enough to sand off skin.

For a single panicked moment, Day took in the sheer size of the man.

But wild glee was singing through him, and he punched Sinclair, hard, with a satisfying crack. This was better. It felt good to be hurting someone else for a change.

"Give me the knife," Day heard himself say. Qila was a wavering shape in the whiteness. Mist covered them all. "Come on, I know you have it. Give it to me."

Sinclair heaved himself up. Qila held the knife out in front of her, looking from Day to Sinclair and back again.

"Come on, come on." Impatient.

The gathering night held its breath.

In one smooth motion Day grabbed the knife, blade-first. The sharp pain made not the slightest indentation in that fierce, bubbling, hot joy.

He was the sum of everything he'd ever done. All he'd ever been.

Day turned—held the knife out—and Sinclair ran into it, easy as lying.

But no, that wasn't how it happened. The knife flashed in the moonlight, and Day wielded it true. A downward motion. It felt good. Martial. Righteous.

Time seemed to become ragged, full of contradictions. Day could have sworn the sudden bloom of Sinclair's blood came long syrupy seconds before the blow landed. Qila crouched with her knuckles on the snow, bent over, watching Day with wild eyes.

Sinclair went to his knees; Day looked at the wide bruise of his mouth, and was glad. An animal satisfaction. The law of the weak and strong had only one outcome.

Stevens had tried to tell him, once.

"Captain!" Carter's hoarse voice, boots, and bobbing black shape came through the snow. "Captain!"

Sinclair crumpled, and Day stared, the feeling coming back into his arms and legs. He was still holding the knife. He didn't quite know how it had ended up like this.

"You'll live," Day told Sinclair, although he didn't believe it. He bent down, jerkily, to press his hands against the man's ribs, feeling the rat-tat-tat of his heart. The blood was starting to freeze. The sharp smell of urine.

"Shh, shh, it's all right," Mrs. Stevens said to Qila, and pulled her into an embrace until all Day could see was her topknot glistening black in the dark. Neither looked at him.

Valle was suddenly there. That fierce gladness was starting to dissolve.

"Will he live?"

Valle swore, didn't answer.

"He was threatening her," Day said. "They were threatening the women—"

"Get a stretcher!" Valle yelled, waving at the other officers. Then he turned to Day with a fury that made him take a step back.

"Get away from me—get *him* away from me!"

———————

Back on the *Resolution*, Day stared numbly into the distance, examining each thought as it came into his head; weighing it up; seeing whether he claimed it as his own.

He couldn't quite believe he'd ever grabbed that knife.

Day turned to face the scene on deck. Qila, blankets wrapped around her shoulders, crouched shaken in the lantern-light, silent as if she'd forgotten how to speak English. Everyone else was talking at once, the two coaling hatches suggestive of open mouths, and Avery barred the galley door with his body.

"She did for him," Flett was yelling inside, banging on it with his fists. "She murdered him, that—savage."

"It wasn't me!" Qila shouted. Her voice was high and desperate. "I swear it!"

"Lies," Flett's voice snarled in response, and she whipped around, staring at the others, searching for support. Finding none.

With a jolt, Day realized his gloves were crackling with frozen blood. His hands smarting. He was courting frostbite, and would need to see the doctor. He was surprised again at the messiness of it all.

Sinclair. He'd killed Sinclair.

A man deserved a trial, didn't he? Day thought wildly of Ewing, milksop Ewing, asking if he intended to appoint defense counsel for Sheppard. But it had always had a foregone conclusion. He knew that now. One way or another, Sheppard had always been for the pot.

"Tell them," Mrs. Stevens said fiercely, and shook him. Her physical proximity startled him more than anything else: with the stale smell of sweat, perfume, it felt almost like an embrace. "Tell them it wasn't her!"

Avery, too, was looking at him with a curl to his soft lips.

Who knew? Qila, after all, was the only one who'd seen what happened.

"There needs to be a fucking *hanging*," Flett yelled. "Captain Roderick! Roderick!"

He could say anything, Day realized—there was a sort of wild freedom to it. He could lie. He could make up any story he wished, and damn them if they didn't believe him.

Burning hands on his shoulders.

What would Stevens do?

A shiver went all the way down to Day's tailbone. He could still feel it inside himself: something foreign and fierce, the tail end of that glee from the ice. He could do anything, say anything.

A dark kind of power.

Even if she denied it, if it came down to his word against hers—*Will, who will they believe.* Qila's eyes were wide and defiant and foreign as she looked at him. He could do it: confirm all her long-held and worst suspicions about how men might be.

But he wasn't Stevens, even though he'd once wished—

"I did it." Day's voice was croaky. He raised it. "I took the knife. She was nothing but innocent." He nodded to Avery. "Open the door."

When this was done, a hubbub of voices came from the galley stairs, where Roderick stood halfway up, arms folded, the light catching his silver hair and riming his eyebrows with frost.

"Did you hear that, down there? I landed the blow myself. He was engaged in a mutiny under *my* command."

A captain was the Word of God on his own ship. And Day wouldn't let it slip away from him. Not this time.

"If anyone thinks there should be consequences," he said softly. "They must wait. Well?"

"He was doing what he thought best," Roderick said at length. "I won't defend his choices. And I needn't tell you, Captain, that I had nothing to do with it."

Calm eyes. But Day knew him at last: someone who was losing control of his whale-mouthed men, and trying not to show it.

"I daresay," Roderick said, "this is another thing we'll have out later. You and I."

Tulloch was being guarded by his outstretched arm. In the thickly slanted light of the galley, Day could see the scar slashed into the boy's left cheek, as if a knife had once been messily deflected by bone; wielded by a monster, something animal-headed.

"One day you'll have to tell me what happened in those boats."

Roderick shrugged. *We made it back*, the gesture said. *Isn't that enough?*

Peters came up the stairs. It was Roderick who flattened himself against the wall to let the younger man pass, the flicker to his tawny eye betraying unease.

Ambition should make us all afraid.

His cheeks flushed, Peters gave Day one clear hard look, and nodded. "I knew," he said under his breath. "I knew it."

Peters had once told him that he knew the *Reckoning* story inside out; that he admired Day's fortitude, his instinct to survive. That he thought it marvelous. The triumph of the human spirit. Back in London, Day had almost decided to revoke Peters's appointment for that wrongheaded and incomprehensible letter. He could just about understand the cult of Jesse Stevens. But a man who thought William Day any kind of hero was mistaken indeed.

"We should get the women back to their cabins." Carter held out his arm for Mrs. Stevens. "Madam—"

"Oh, and what were you doing," Mrs. Stevens said fiercely. "When they were dragging us out of those cabins?" She wheeled around to confront Peters, who looked about to take her other arm, like a not-so-gallant escort—like an asylum attendant.

Peters gave her a smile.

"You're meant to be keeping order on this ship! Aren't you? *Aren't* you?"

"It's regrettable, ma'am—but the captain proved himself more than capable," Peters replied. His eyes glittered. "I have to apologize, though, for what might have inspired them: I sometimes spend my nights on the other ship. It's a wonderful thing, isn't it? That she's sound, after so long. A miracle."

Mrs. Stevens shivered. "It's not—wonderful" was all she said. Day thought of how terrified she'd been when that orange had rolled into their candlelit circle, with its message of *responsibility.*

"You'll see," Peters said reassuringly. "Captain?"

She looked at him, then at Qila, shivering and smoothing her hair off her sweat-damp forehead, twisting it, retying it—then back at Day, who'd been so close to making another indelible mistake. The fury in Mrs.

Stevens's eyes was almost a shock. It altered her face entirely, all traces of roundness and languor burned off. She clutched Qila to her side.

"You shouldn't even have been here," Day said, numb. "You should have been safe in America! Why did you have to come?"

"Because—" She shook off Carter's hand, letting out a wild choked laugh, as if some of her fury was finally turning inwards. "Because I can barely remember what life was like before him. I was . . . no one. I *struggled*. And to go back to that struggle—"

The snow was starting to come down in a whirling dervish dance. "Could you?"

"I don't know what I could go back to," Day said slowly. "I don't know anymore."

XXI: HENRI DE VALLE
AT ANCHOR, OCTOBER 14, 1882

The ice took the decision from them.

The pressure wave that passed through the pack in the second week of October lifted the *Resolution* up to the sound of gnashing teeth, howling dogs, organic gurgling, and suspended her in a fresh pool of ink-black water. The onset of the enemy had come unexpectedly, and they'd all heard the convulsive, shivering crack that came from her stern.

The sound of bones breaking.

"Don't light those," Day snapped at Peters, who was taking a taper to the wardroom candles. This was no time for *relics*. The skylights above were milky enough to see a circle of worried faces—but the sun was going down in the afternoon, and they were on a broken ship.

"It should've been retracted," Holt said, matter-of-fact, bracing himself against the table as the ship shifted around them. Little bows and dips, showing the immense pressures building up. A book fell off the shelf with a *thud*.

"We couldn't," Roderick replied. "Not without blasting the ice with dynamite."

With immense tact, both refrained from looking at Day, who'd sown the seeds of disaster when he'd pressed through into Talbot's Channel. You only had to step off the ship to see that her rudder had been pulled off, that part of her stern was mangled beyond all recognition.

Come spring, this ship wouldn't be steering out through the rat-run of the pack.

The unwanted candlelight danced over the table, glinting on Roderick's dark-shadowed eyes. He hadn't left Day's side in the past two days, ever since they'd awoken to the sound of a rumbling in the firmament, like an earthquake. He said at length: "The cofferdams will only hold as long as the ice. If she settles—"

Day thought of the axe-man, that preternatural knocking in the ship's hold. The pumps bellowing away. Work parties had been forced back, time and time again, by lanterns that refused to stay lit. Bad air.

Fouled air.

There was a sudden slow yawn, and Day felt the deck pitching, the table creaking, the heavy clunk as the candlesticks fell and rolled like a door creeping open. The noise outside was deafening, a hundred solid waves booming against cliffs—the walls seeming to distort, timber screaming—and Day clung to the table as she plummeted down again.

The lurch made the bottom drop out of his stomach. And behind the sound of the pressure, there was a voice, seeming to come from all directions at once. A distorted scream.

Another crunch, and the booming hiss of the shock waves running away. An audible tidal churn of water. Day knew, without having to look, that the *Reckoning* had been spared. The slightest difference in position mattered, up here, and she was stronger than she'd ever been.

"If the plates are sprung . . ." Holt didn't finish the thought.

"The other ship is *sound*," Peters said. "She's perfectly capable of sheltering us until spring breakup comes." In his eyes, Day could see the image of a triumphant return: the two of them, side by side, Talbot's legendary ship restored. Hang the . . . mystery of her demise.

Hang Day.

An ambitious second.

"We're too weak now. We need to start moving across," Roderick said with finality. "Sooner rather than later. Before a pressure wave hits and we go down with all stores."

This time, they did look at Day. Who was listening, hard, not quite in the room—because over the low thunderous creaking outside, he could hear a shrill voice.

"You," it seemed to say. "Youuuuuuuuuuuu—"

He blinked, with a cold hard stab of resentment.

He'd learned by now that it would all be up to him. He clamped his jaw shut. The horrible thought, one he'd hoped never to voice again—

We're going to have to leave the ship.

"All right," he said out loud, nails digging into his palms. "All right." He nodded at Peters. "We'll take the ice watch tonight. And fetch Lars."

Roderick pushed his chair back from the table—*squeak*—and beckoned Day out into the companionway. "It's our only sensible option," the old whaler said when they were out of earshot. "We need to speak as one on this."

Day sighed. Looked down the passage, its dips and curves, as if it could melt away; as if he could see the *Reckoning*, denuded and grimy, the corridor where he and Stevens had had such similar conversations.

Roderick was making a scrubbing motion with his hands, as if he wanted to peel the palms bare. "They're deathly afraid."

"I heard. About the boats."

"Aye." Roderick sighed. "I know. But—look. We stopped it before it turned to true madness, the worship of that whale-headed thing. *Leviathan*. The saltwater prophet. Herridge—in that mask—wasn't suffered to harm one hair on the cabin boy's head. But here and now?" He gave Day a very sharp look. "Men believe what it suits them to believe—so they can go on. No matter how outlandish. In desperate circumstances you'll believe *anything*. We must take the other ship."

"I've got reason to believe she's dangerous," Day said. "Unsettled."

Roderick sucked his teeth. The most temperate of that whaling crew. "She's survived this far," he said. "I'd say she's nigh-on indestructible, whatever else might be on board. I made a promise to my men—we'd see no small boats. Nor go tramping off over the ice to Nathaniel, wherever he might be. To suggest such a thing, now . . . there'd be unrest worse than you'd believe."

The image of those black gums swam into Day's mind. An attempt to propitiate. To appease.

"There are worse things than death."

"As you say." Roderick rubbed a gnarly hand at his face. "There's death, and there's *bad* death. We can only pray for the former."

———————

Tomorrow, the men would wake in astronomical twilight, the stars overhead having lost their twinkle, and start the long process of abandoning ship. Around them, the endless ice yawned. Mid-October, and the Arctic night was dead, too.

Come home, Will.

Something screamed, *ah-ah-ah*. A fox barking—perhaps.

Anything could be out there, hidden in the waves of floury snow.

Over on the *Reckoning*, to mark the quarter-hour, Avery rang the ship's bell. It echoed away in the still air, booming and reflecting back from every inch of the night.

Behind Day, stationed on the *Resolution*, a door cracked like breaking bones.

He spun around. Peters emerged from the passenger deck, steam-shrouded, wearing a thick cream-colored jumper. The lantern-light illuminated a slice of his face, lingering on those cheekbones; Day could have sworn Peters had left England as an unremarkable-looking man.

"Where did you get that?" Day murmured, when they were shoulder to shoulder.

Peters shrugged. But there was something about that jumper: Stevens, Day realized, had worn one just like it. But he didn't know if it had left the ship with them, or had been dug back out of some moldering sea chest. Like digging through those stories Peters loved so much. Inserting himself into them.

A shiver.

Peters nodded at the other ship. "Are you sure they're the best men for the job?"

Carter and Holt patrolled her decks in the fine-blowing snow. Peters's lip curled. He'd wanted Carter put into sick bay after his return from that ghastly search party: *an attack of nerves.* Day didn't answer, glimpsing the two junior officers as stick figures, leaning into each other. They'd shared a cabin during Carter's convalescence, those Admiralty men; Day was sure that Holt had shared Carter's bunk long before that. The affection between them was very apparent.

He tried not to begrudge it.

A loud burst of laughter, too, came from the forecastle. There was something manic about the sound, an unpleasant edge; the crew, relieved of their duties, were driving back the dark as best they could.

"He might be long dead," Peters said quietly, candidly. "You know that. Long dead, or else he and his men would be here. We have to look out for ourselves now."

Day didn't answer. He could still feel Stevens's hands around his throat. He believed, utterly, that worse was to come.

He was sick of waiting. The night crawled on.

———

"Did you hear that?"

Peters shrugged. Day's skin tingled. It had sounded like a splash, far below.

The air seemed to coagulate.

Another splash. Then a knock, down where the hull met the ice.

Fear trickled down Day's spine. It sounded wet. Like someone beating their fists against an immovable object, in a vast and immeasurable—

Rage.

The second noise was higher, on the other side of the ship. The lantern at the mast swung slightly, and all shadows lengthened and distorted, as if they were being pulled towards whatever was climbing up.

"What was that?"

"Shh!"

A chill wind was blowing the snow like the sandstorms of the Sahara, and it burned his skin. A pause. A creak. The lanterns wavered.

Another wet thud, from a slightly different part of the ship. Day took a step back. If something was climbing, it couldn't be a man: it wasn't anywhere near a ladder. Slippery timber. No handholds.

And nothing could climb that fast.

"It's a bear," Peters said unsteadily.

For a moment Day wanted to clutch at him. Something had appeared at the top of the railings.

It was a bird, scratching its talons against the timber. It was a rat, sleek and gray.

It was a hand. Day stood very still.

A scrabbling. It was trying to gain purchase. But, in the half-light, he could see its skin sloughing off, nails long gone, the fingers sodden masses of flesh. The back of its hand was a mass of scraped channels, like a riverbed. Bony, tattered arms followed. Something pulled itself convulsively up.

A sharp inhalation. Peters's rifle barrel shook. "Do you see it?" he said softly. "Do you see—"

Day couldn't move.

The thing paused with both hands on the railings, and Day could see its flattened head. He could imagine someone taking a shovel to it: the wet sound, like a fruit overripe. Day had smashed a skull before, he knew the sensation. The way the blow reverberated up your arm, clear and sharp, before the *thud* registered a heartbeat later.

"No," he said, tasting bitterness.

No.

Stevens had first appeared hazy and glimmering, a trick of the Arctic light. But there was almost no light at all, dark of the moon, and this thing climbing up the side of their ship was solid. Utterly corporeal.

Judgment Day, he thought wildly. He'd been wrong, to think it wasn't about bodies. "Peters," he hissed. Didn't dare turn his head. Didn't dare move—

The gunshot startled both of them, and the shape disappeared back over the side.

"Come on!" Day yelled. "Come on!" And he launched himself over the railings in pursuit, half-climbing, half-jumping down onto the maze of ice boulders and ridges, the patchwork of a shifting landscape. He looked around madly, because the night was thick with blurry snow, and the few pockets of visibility were entirely empty. Turning, he stumbled through the drift towards their bow, and when he turned to look back—

A figure loomed.

Its face was a ruin; Day could see through its hollow cheeks to teeth. Tendons and sinews stood out in its ropey neck, and its scalp had come away from the skull in a slouch of skin. Hair like seaweed, bald patches glistening. Not so much *fouled*, he thought, as keelhauled.

This was a body that had been scraped under their hull, returned from the other side.

A flash of gold. The far-distant gleam of the ship's lanterns showed high aristocratic cheekbones laid bare. Flayed. Wet and suppurating. He'd been dragged behind them a very long time.

"It's Lee," Peters's voice was raw. He fell to his knees, the rifle dropping from his numb hands with a muffled thump.

"Shoot it," Day yelled, because the thing was perilously close. "Peters!"

And, oh yes—it *crawled*. With purpose and intent.

There was a terrified gleam in Peters's eyes as the wet hand made contact. Its fingers closed around his jaw, and Peters opened his mouth, gagging on the oozing gray flesh, as it started to drag him—

Day stumbled through the snow, the wind beating him back. He could smell putrescence. Something wet and blooming. Peters was disappearing into the darkness towards the other side of the ship. On hands and knees, Day scrabbled about in fine powder for the rifle.

"Captain!" Holt. "We heard gunshots!" Behind him, a red flare flew up from the *Reckoning*, bathing the scene in a crimson bloody light.

There was a crevasse in the ice ahead, wide and insinuating. Its sheer sides going down into dark water, endless dark water. The sea beneath the ship. Peters was being dragged into that hole, kicking so hard it made crackling, popping noises.

Holt strained, at the edge of the precipice, to reach an arm down towards him. The fear made Holt's face ghoulish, as if all protocol had failed him.

Here be monsters.

The crawling thing—*Lee*—was holding Peters suspended above that narrowing pit.

Day's fingers finally closed around the rifle. He fumbled—let off one shot into the air, panicky, as if to startle a wild animal.

Something erupted from that jagged darkness under the ice. Grabbed Holt by the throat. Dragged him down.

Peters hung on. Screaming.

But when Day made it to the crack—Carter shouting, "Evan, Evan!" like he could bring him back—all Day could see was dark water, like a vein standing out on the side of a neck. Something glittered blackly from the sides.

It was smeared with blood, Day realized.

Another officer who'd be keelhauled by the ice.

Sunlight spilled out. But some of the very worst things in Day's life had happened in Arctic sunshine, and he wasn't afraid of the dark.

The snow crunched under their feet. Up close, the distortions to the *Resolution*'s hull were painfully obvious; bent out of shape, like the ruined mass of Lee's face. The night before, the men had hacked to the bottom of that crevasse with axes, Carter howling like a wild animal; he'd had to be pulled away. But there was no sign of Holt. Whatever had taken him had been strong enough to drag a full-grown man through a tiny crack—too small—into the deep. Bones must have splintered. Flesh sloughed off. Day thought of Stevens, triumphantly pulling the skin off an Arctic hare in one clean motion.

Lee had never had that strength in life.

"Who saw it?" Avery's voice was hushed.

Day swallowed. "Me. Peters. Holt. And Carter, I think." He hardened his shoulders. "Why?"

"Oh no, I'm sure it was real," Avery replied, almost too quickly. His voice sounded thick. "Something attacked me, too. Once." A bob of his head—surely thinking of the black-masked Leviathan. "But people normally say they're at peace." He bent down, ran a shaky finger over the gouges in the snow. "The spirits. We're told they come to give us good tidings. But if the other world, the spirit world, is like that, it's a torment. No wonder they're so—"

Angry.

"Not all of them." Mrs. Stevens's voice was small. She held her own parasol, and the shadow it cast wavered across the ice. "I've never seen anything like this."

Avery scoffed, as if he knew exactly why.

Day looked at the smeared blood, dug his teeth into the soft flesh of his lip until the pain was a welcome distraction. "If they're angry— can you blame them?"

The dead weren't disembodied noises in a darkened room. Despite what he'd once told himself, leaning over a corpse hard and inanimate as cordwood, there was an imperfect separation between spirit and body. The flesh left behind wasn't just flesh. It still meant something.

It was still capable of being dragged along in their wake.

"We've always known it's easier to make contact," she said, very quietly. "If there's something connecting them to this earth. Or something—someone—on it."

Day blew out a gust of smoke. He couldn't see more than a hundred yards across the hazy ice, not even to the dark strip of land at the nearest islet. His world was white and blue and gray, as Holt's blood had dried unaccountably gray, as if all his vitality had been drained. But out there were things animated by hatred of William Day.

They might be a little farther than Lee. But they, too, would be coming home.

Someone would be held *responsible*.

"Why Lee, though?" Mrs. Stevens said at length. "It was an accident, wasn't it."

"Why would that make a difference?"

She shook her head. "Some come through easily. Others come through hard."

Lee's anger was the anger of entitlement, of dumb imperious arrogance. No doubt he, too, blamed Day for his death.

And what of those who were left in pieces, scattered across a tent circle? Or those who'd been consumed? Did some part of them live on, like Jonah in the belly of the whale? Present in every cell, capable of infinite division, no matter how minute or ragged. Chewed. Swallowed. Digested.

Sheppard. He hadn't deserved what happened to him. And for all his easy smiles, Sheppard hadn't been a saint. He'd just been a man, as capable of dark moods as any other.

Day pressed a fist to his chest. Something was stuck in his throat. He thought, irrationally, of something clawing its way out, something with fingers stained with lead and gunshot. Biding its time. Waiting to tear him apart in turn.

A dark shape, shrouded in sealskins, appeared around the ship's tilted bow. They all froze.

"Roderick."

He gave Day a faint nod in return; they were no longer pretending to be captain and ice-master, and Day found he liked it better that way. The old whaler frowned at the *Resolution*. Placed his hand for a moment on her hull. The shrug of his shoulders said it all.

In the boats they drank blood—

The ice gleamed, frost-smoke playing across its surface like little fires below. "There's something wrong with the other ship," Day said. He needed to make it clear. "You believe that death attracts death, don't you? At least your men do. Well, she's been attracting dead things for many, many years, and she doesn't lie easy. Last night something terrible attacked us."

"Aye. You would say that, wouldn't you." There was almost pity in Roderick's voice. "And who was there with you? . . . But more bad weather is on its way. We're about to run out of options."

He turned to leave, his coat playing out in the wind, all skin and bone; like the dark effigy Day had once found in the hold. "We'll need to open her up," he called over his shoulder. "Inspect for damage."

In the boats they—nearly—obeyed the rule of monsters. But stepped back from it. Delivered themselves from evil.

Day envied him that most of all.

The *Reckoning* was riding high, right up out of the ice, exposing her smooth copper-plated hull. She blotted out the pale daylight, sunbeams creating faint halos around her masts, reminding Day of marsh lights: false trails to lure travelers away from solid ground, towards something that would swallow them up entirely.

Dark figures gathered at the railings. "Do you see that," Day said softly.

But when he turned, no one was there.

Jonny Greenstreet looked down at him with an expression of distaste, mouth sagging and obscene, the bruised necklace of the noose all too visible. The next officer had hands half-formed, grayish stumps that called to mind the dreadful *plink* of his fingers being snipped off into the doctor's waiting bowl. He'd been frostbitten so badly—going after the deserters, because Talbot wouldn't let them die out there—that his digits had rotted before the rest of him. And finally, Day's immediate superior, who'd died of scurvy, babbling about open water on the horizon, a dreadful expanse of sea without end.

The awful contagious madness that had dogged the ship in her last days.

They thronged the railings: all the *Reckoning*'s crew of souls. They'd been dead before Day had finally given the order to abandon ship; had set out on the path that would strew the others across the ice. From God-Saves Harbor to Amelia's Pass, and the desperate confused push onwards to Cape Verdant. He'd left the dead in his wake—the things that now hooted, and gibbered, and crawled.

Mrs. Stevens had said she'd seen the man with the noose: Day had never told her of Greenstreet's death at his own hand. But she'd known nonetheless—perhaps because she was the wife of Jesse Stevens. There were many ways things could be connected; the lines of responsibility ran forwards and back. Quivering like ropes being pulled taut.

You thought you'd escaped, Jonny's face seemed to say. *You tried to leave.*

But they'll catch up soon enough.

The gaping mouth into the *Reckoning*'s belowdecks still smelled of rotting wood and tobacco smoke. Day had waited until nightfall, the sky darker than a coal mine, and it was snowing again, the faint pattering of snowflakes on canvas like someone quietly drumming their fingertips.

Day was going to see, once and for all, what was in her hold. He couldn't stop imagining Holt down there with all the dead, swaying, knee-deep in filthy water, looking up for a hatch to open; waiting for a spring that would never come.

Anyone might be next.

Day turned, shivering, away from the yawning corridor that led to her Great Cabin. His lantern gleamed off the frost sheeting the walls, the light scurrying ahead of him towards the galley, where the passage ended in a vast black void. Ropes hung from the ceiling, bristly with icicles.

A creak. He spun. The corridor was empty.

In the galley, signs of the disaster jostled at him. The sick bay behind the squat metal stove had been expanded, again and again, into a swaying maze of sheets hanging from the beams above, intended to give sick or dying men some privacy. "I can't work like this," Doctor Nye had said, pushing up his glasses, "with so *many*."

Behind those sheets was the aft hatch to the orlop deck. Day looked back, his lantern barely scratching the sides of the dark. For a moment he could see the crew all there, going about their nightly tasks, grumbling about the ceaseless cold outside: little John hopping along nimbly, carrying his book of lessons.

The sheets billowed and swayed. Cool air. The crunch of boots recently in fresh snow.

A gaunt face resolved itself.

"Valle?"

"William."

"What are you doing here?"

"I could ask you the same thing."

Valle kept his distance, holding up his own lantern. "My god, I'd almost forgotten," he said softly. "I hadn't had a single patient by the time we reached Baffin Bay. Not even the usual . . . indiscretions you'd expect among sailors. I'd almost started to expect a quiet voyage." His eyes were melancholy. "But this is how she ended up."

"Valle—"

"Well, then. Don't let me stop you." Suddenly brittle as old bones. "You're opening the hold, I suppose?"

"What—"

Valle gestured at the axe that Day was carrying, and heaved the hatch open with a single tug; he wasn't as weak as he seemed. "We're finally going to stop lying to ourselves, are we?"

"What do you mean?"

The air below was like plunging into icy water. "The ones you *abandoned*, William. When you left the ship."

Day stopped in his tracks. Valle took up all the room in the cramped passage.

"They're down there, aren't they?"

Day opened his mouth. No sound came out.

"You forget." A pause. "I knew Stevens. Leaving the ship—leaving the weakest to dwindle and die—oh, that has him written all over it. But someone had to give the order." Valle wheeled around, the sudden direct light making Day screw up his eyes. "And that someone had to be *you*."

"I didn't—"

"You can stop pretending. She could have been freed, if you'd only waited. She could have been sailed."

"She was about to be swallowed up!" Day said thickly. The ice outside was making a faint low moan, like someone waking to find they were in terrible pain, no help coming. "The ice—it had her. I swear. I'm as surprised as anyone."

It wasn't so much a lie as a prayer, that old prayer. Left unanswered.

"But she's here. Nonetheless. Whoever's down there—did they return to the ship, William? Or did you leave them here to die?"

Day staggered back.

"You were lucky not to face the consequences. Talbot shielded you from beyond the grave. You were so lucky no one else who got off that miserable rock would talk—" Valle made a small tight gesture. "Oh, not *him*, although he made a big show of it, didn't he? Saying he refused to dig it all up, despite his hints and insinuations. Playing out whatever role you'd agreed. But the others held their tongues. The other doctor—my assistant. He was an educated man, could have written his book, lived out the rest of his life in comfort."

But he hadn't. Nye had killed himself in a house so packed with food that the coroner had to break a window to let out the swarming black flies.

"And Jackson, the seminary, the fever—how convenient. Their silence saved you."

"Did it?" Day shouted. It echoed around the narrow orlop passageway. He could feel the crew crowding in where the lantern-light gave out. Listening with ears blackened and graying, wind-bitten, frost-bitten, *just bitten*—

"They were your responsibility—"

"Did you come here to accuse me?"

Day thought, with a wrench, of how glad he'd been that Henri de Valle had agreed to join the rescue expedition. He could have brought almost anyone else, but selfishly, Day had wanted a familiar face. He'd wanted someone who could shoulder part of it.

But no one could.

Valle laughed. "I saw my disheveled captain scrambling on board with an axe. I saw a man who stabbed one of his crew. The William Day I knew couldn't have wielded a knife, but you murdered him without a thought. Who's the *savage* now?"

He turned, the light receding. "And how many more will die from it?"

The provender store was at the end of the corridor, hollowed out: shelves missing, crates abandoned on the damp, rotting floor. That single grated hatch leading farther into the belly of the beast.

"I'm trying to—put him behind me." Day drew in an unsteady breath. "Valle, please. I've been trying to put this behind me."

"Have you," Valle hissed. "Your lack of insight is, as ever, *extraordinary*."

"I told you!" Day screamed, his cheeks burning as if he'd been slapped by flaming hands. Then, lower: "I told you. It wasn't—like that, between me and him."

Valle made a dismissive gesture. "I don't care. I care about—what's happened to you. What it's done to you." The shame coiled around Day's heart. "So you don't have to lie anymore. It's over."

Day stared at him.

"It's out of your hands. Entered into the ship's log this evening."

Day sucked in an unsteady breath. He should have known this day was coming. The day that Valle, in his crabby handwriting, declared him *unfit for command*.

No captain ever came back from that.

"You've become dangerous, William. Your madness has become contagious." Valle sighed. "I wanted to help you."

Contagious.

He swallowed. Tasted blood. "But if we don't find Stevens—"

Day was the only person who knew, who really knew, the danger faced by the innocent men of the *Fox*. Those poor souls. He'd been so careful to keep secrets, to protect Stevens, to protect himself. Because he was the only one who knew what was out there—

Monsters. Men made bestial by what had been done in the name of survival.

Those limbless, fleshless creatures.

And Stevens himself.

Inaction would be as good as a massacre.

"*Hang* Stevens!" Valle screamed. "Leave him to rot!"

It hadn't been so bad at all, killing Sinclair: it was just a matter of opening the door. Standing at the inky threshold, inviting it in. Stevens. The haunting. Whatever was dark on the other side.

Something is coming through.

Well, Day wouldn't be afraid of it.

And what was Valle, crouching like a beaked shadow in the dark, against the lives that might still be lost? What was one doctor, against all that was held in Day's outstretched hand?

There might be an accident. Any accident—the hold was deep, filled with freezing water. Day felt the weight of the axe. They hadn't had many tools at Cape Verdant; they'd had to make do with whatever came to hand. Chopping, bone splintering. *Thud.*

There was a certain freedom in that cleansing, bitter rage. Strengthening him beyond his wildest dreams. Letting it carry him away at last.

Day paused. He hadn't realized he'd raised the axe.

From below came the faint sound of rippling water.

"Are you going to kill me?" Valle laughed like he was choking. "Where's your *mask*, William?"

He could do it. A step forward. A swing of the axe. The hold would swallow up all of his mistakes. Out of sight—

"You should have done it already," Valle hissed.

"What—"

"Last night! It was you, wasn't it? I was lucky you didn't catch me sleeping. But I wasn't surprised to see you come." He gestured at his face, a gesture that described a long bulbous snout, a head bigger than a man's. "I suppose it's easier, isn't it, when you're someone or something else at the time."

"No." Day's mouth was so dry he had to swallow a few times to get the words out. "No, Valle, I swear, I didn't—"

Valle sneered at him. "Here we go. More lies."

Day dropped the axe with a clang. Valle, Henri de Valle, thought he was a murderer.

Or maybe Stevens had been there, as real and corporeal—with his killer-whale smile—as in Day's own bed. He'd done this; he'd sent Stevens after Valle, as he had after Avery.

The horror of it yawned in Day's calcified heart.

"I didn't try to kill you." An unhappy gulp. "There's something following us. Something connected to—me. And out on the ice, there are others—"

"Then why don't you spare the rest of us." Valle's lip curled. "And get on with it. That's what a *real* captain would do."

The lantern reflected off the icy walls, a mass of eyes in the darkness. Valle knelt at the hatch: "Here we are. Aren't you going to open it."

Another creak, this time from above. Up in the Great Cabin, where Talbot's chair sat forever empty; where the table was pitted from Stevens's knife; and the mirror glimmered in its eternal candlelight. Day looked.

Hanging through the hatch was Jonny Greenstreet.

The first lieutenant. They'd all thought he was getting better. They'd hoped, because Talbot was obviously going to die; or at least, it had seemed that way. Hobbled at the knees by scurvy, Greenstreet had crawled grimly around the deck in the doctor's madhouse parade, refusing to give up. But one day he'd paused, looked at the ice, pulled himself up, and taken one look over the side, into the yawning darkness of God-Saves Harbor, at the third coming winter, at the Northern Lights playing in the sky—and made his way down to officers' country and hung himself without another word.

Another thing Day had refused to put into the official records, where Greenstreet was marked, simply and tragically, as (scurv.)

The thin breeze of the *Reckoning*'s belowdecks swung Greenstreet's body in lazy circles. He was dripping a stream of water, as though he'd only recently been hauled aboard.

Valle was still kneeling. "Well?"

He looked up. Saw Day, his fixated gaze, the wavering lantern and the raised axe.

"No." Valle scrabbled back on his hands and haunches, like a spider.

"I told you," Day's mouth was numb. "I told you. The ship is—cursed." Because that was the word, wasn't it, for a haunting that did damage, a haunting that *stuck*?

"I'm cursed. I'm cursed—"

Their lanterns guttered. The creak of the rope. An exhalation from the shadows. A *tap tap tap* that could have been little John's peg leg. Valle's face was a rictus of horror as he continued crawling back, away from the hanging body, away from everything arrayed around Day, away from the awfulness of the *Reckoning*—

Suddenly he dropped.

Through the rotten decking. The condensation had eaten away at the timbers, leaving a gaping hole to darkness. Valle reached up—grabbed and clawed and clung on by his fingertips. Day was close enough to see his yellowing nails splinter.

"Take my hand!"

Valle was hanging over nothingness. The hold was a long way down, and the old man's bones were brittle. The sound of water was louder now, rushing, the crash of waves, and Day didn't think there was that much running water in the entire Arctic.

Day tried to pry Valle's hands from the edge, but the doctor wouldn't let go. A panicked gleam in his eyes. His face somehow askew.

"Valle!"

Something was behind him.

"Valle!"

Something was in the hold.

"No," Valle was saying, "no, no," and he wouldn't take Day's hand. He looked up—eyes widened in terrified recognition—and let go.

No splash. A wet *thud* sound that Day knew well. Silence.

Then Peters was on him, solid and strong. "No, he's already gone—"

Day's wordless scream echoed around the belowdecks. The crew listened with toothy smiles.

THEN

XXII
GOD-SAVES HARBOR, AUGUST 28, 1868

IT MAY BE THAT MY SONS HAVE SINNED, AND RENOUNCED GOD IN THEIR HEARTS.

From this angle, the *Reckoning*'s death is certain.

At least, that's what Day tells himself, though the only damage to speak of has been at her bow, when Jimmy Graham received shrapnel wounds from splintering Norwegian timber, pinioning him to the deck until he could be cut free, shrieking. She's been reinforced many, many times. But the ice is restless, a jumble of white boulders, sometimes spilling over the gunwales. Her hull is intact: but for how long?

The choice is impossible.

"Not even a bomb could breach her," the deck crew had said. "She'll stand fast."

Day can see Sheppard watching. He wasn't surprised: Sheppard is a good man, a prudent one. He sides with the men and their dead captain, knows the Arctic is about waiting for your time to come.

Day recalls how Stevens had screamed them down. "We need to leave the ship!" Pacing and spitting like a wild animal. "I'll hole her if I have to, I'll burn her to the ground!" Fisting his hands in Day's collar, drawing him within an inch of his desperate face. Eyes screwed up, cheeks red with rage, everyone looking anywhere but at them. "We can live out there. Here? We're doomed. I'll *make* you leave."

Day isn't perceptive enough to see how morbidly afraid his second-in-command is. He'll do anything to wrestle back some measure of autonomy, even if it means they all march to their deaths—

Day swallows. It lingers, the after-image of Stevens burned on the cold sky, as if he'd looked at a light source for too long.

The ship is now surrounded by a scrap heap of provisions and boats. He'd given the order too late, and the ice is restless: maybe she'll go down yet. It hasn't really been a summer. Day is the last one off, as is only proper, trying to hide the *rat-tat-tat* of his heart as he looks at the *Reckoning* for what will surely be the last time. The main hatch is shut fast to prevent snow drifting in. No one walks the companionways below, and the Great Cabin is cold and bare. The silence of the ship is terrifying.

Good-bye, old girl.

Day hears a slap ring out, and sighs. First Lieutenant Stevens, in his ragged coat, is beating the men again. Talbot would be turning in his grave.

Needs must.

"Will you stop that," he calls.

There's no reply, of course, and Day's shoulders slump. Stevens has refused to talk to him—cordially, with nothing that could be construed as rudeness or insubordination—since Day had refused to put their plan into action, abandon the men, *devil take the hindmost.* There were enough empty cabins by that point for them to sleep separately. Day hadn't expected, when he took command, that he'd be unable to sleep without the sound of Stevens's breathing.

And the silence is wearing away at him. Of all the things that have happened to Day, this might be the worst. Stevens's indifference.

Bill comes up to him, eyes bright inside his big fur hood. "We need to move," he says. "There are bears." Day knows perfectly well what his guide means—huge, implacable beasts, heavier than a ship's cannon, capable of killing a man with one swipe of their giant paws. "We can't stay on the ice."

"Yes, I'm aware, thank you," Day says stiffly. He doesn't want to look around, doesn't want to see the faces of his men, slumped over their sledges, expecting him to know what to do next. With the medicinal hunting of warmer days, they've been saved from scurvy, but only just: they're still weak. Easy prey.

He rolls his shoulders back. Thinks, with a pang of grief so sharp it surprises him, of Talbot, the way he would address the men. He wishes this hadn't fallen to him. To Stevens, maybe, hard-edged and fearless.

But something deep inside Day—even here, at God-Saves Harbor, a voice he never wishes to acknowledge—says quietly: *That would have been terrible, and you know it.*

They're divided up. Day wishes passionately that, like the Natives, they had dogs to share the load. White men aren't made for this work, he knows it for a fact, and there's a visible and shaming reluctance to be picked for Stevens's sledge. The men will need to be pushed hard, hard. The whaling season might have ended: no one is entirely sure when the fleet usually departs. If they don't make it south in time, they might as well be dead already.

Talbot would know what to say, he thinks.

"Let's get on with it," mutters Captain Day, acting commander of the *Reckoning* expedition, and the men take up harness to engage in the terrible grunt-work of dragging their boat-loaded sledges up onto the shore. It's just scree beyond, but better that than the jumbled deadly ice, sometimes slamming shut like a boulder rolled before a tomb, sometimes opening into terrifying yawning cracks in a matter of seconds. No one knows what the land will be like.

At least it's daylight. Perpetual daylight.

Bill puts a hand on Day's shoulder, very softly, and turns him around to face the ship.

Day thinks he's being asked, once again, to reconsider: he's ready to spit and swear as Stevens does, because the awful decision is *made*, they can't expect him to look back. He can see her masts sticking up at the sky, mutilated and forlorn, as if begging to be put out of her misery. He wishes they'd done something. They might have scuttled her, he thinks, as Stevens suggested. Taken an axe to her hold. Given her an end.

But Bill has more pressing concerns. "You see?"

Across the ice, where the sunlight sparkles like cut gemstones, there's something that doesn't reflect the light. It looks like a cloud sitting in the sky, an awful anticipation about its stillness.

The bears are huge, armored with fat and muscle, and the men know from experience it's hard to prevail against one when it charges. No matter how good a shot—the bears are capable of digging out bullets with their teeth, and any hit that isn't fatal will only enrage them.

This one's out of range, anyway.

"Stevens!" Day calls. "Take the rear. Keep a watch on the weakest."

Stevens gives him a mocking salute and trudges off onto the ice, unshouldering his rifle, eyes fixed on that lone distant bear.

Day thinks he sees, in his second's eyes, the gleam of a man who's been struck with an idea. He hesitates.

Then lets it go.

———————

The shore is harsh. There's not enough snow, and the ground is frozen pebbles, the very definition of barren. It tears at the sledge runners, and from time to time there's a horrible *screeeeee* as a piece of gravel gets caught under the weight, gets dragged along, has to be removed before they can go farther. A sound to put your teeth on edge.

If summer never comes, if the ice is this bad in the southern reaches of the channel, then pound for pound, the men will each have to haul the weight of a dead cart horse over a distance that seems ludicrous.

And that's just to Lancaster Sound—not to the whaling fleet, wherever it might be.

It's very obvious that most of the men simply don't have it in them. Day wishes, with a meanness that surprises him, that those individuals would do the decent thing.

Stevens, at the rear, says nothing, although the shore had been his idea. He doesn't beat his men. He just walks, rifle gleaming, under that constant numbing daylight. But Day can see him staring at the stragglers; some of their party must come up short under that pitiless gaze.

Stevens's plan had been to leave the *Reckoning* much earlier. To split the expedition, abandon the weakest. "Dead weight"—furious—"nothing but dead weight!" Day's heart aches. He can see how easy it would have been: they'd have been away like stevedores. Some of them might have lived.

Stevens was right, he thinks. *Stevens was right.*

The sensation grows, day by day, that they've left the real world behind. No wonder there are no birds. When Day asks Bill whether they might meet a hunting party—desperately hoping, because he knows the Natives mean the difference between meager survival and a white man's horrible death—Bill laughs out loud. "There's no game," he says, patiently, as if to a child. "There's no reason to be up here."

They've entered a sloping plain between the cliffs and the larger hills to the interior. A pass, silent as the grave, where the only sounds are their panting, the *scrape scrape scrape* of the sledges, snatches of conversation; sometimes the trickle of water, as thaws on the black rock create little creeks. It all seems calculated to break them.

"We'll head farther inland," Day calls. "Follow the water."

There's a general groaning. He stumps over to quell it, and Sheppard dares to take him slightly to one side.

Sheppard is no taller than Day, but he stands up straighter. Day remembers, with an ache, all those dead officers, yelling at him to *stop slouching*: the perpetual refrain of his chilly childhood, seamlessly transferred into shipboard bullying. "Let me go for water," Sheppard says. "The men are exhausted."

Day shades his eyes. The approach to the nearest stream is through rocky boulders, no doubt a rat race close up. A man could be lost from sight. Lose himself.

Day isn't quite sure where that idea comes from.

"Split up?"

"Look at them."

The men on Sheppard's sledge had been glad to be chosen; he was universally popular, and they'd sung marching songs, ragged and tuneless, voices echoing off the dome of the sky. Anything, as long as it helped. But they haven't enough meat for Jimmy Graham's shrapnel wounds to heal, and the bandages have to be changed with Jimmy biting down on a little piece of wood brought along for precisely that purpose. Diamond and Connor look like ghosts, waxy pale, their skin the color of milk frozen then thawed.

If this were a story for the history books, Day thinks, they'd have left of their own accord, gone off to die alone, not encumber the rest. They'd have stayed on the ship. But they don't. They want to live. They're scared.

Day has no more empathy left in him.

Looking back at Sheppard, he sees his hopeful gaze. That's the most damnable thing about Tom Sheppard: he expects you to be a better person. Day looks at Stevens in turn, clearly eavesdropping, pretending to sharpen his little hunting knife. Stevens shakes his head, saying something meaningful about the fact that Sheppard is armed, fully kitted, and leaving the group offers an opportunity to—what?

As if Sheppard would abandon them.

"All right," Day says in a rush, "I'll make a deal with you." He pitches his voice louder, so the men can hear. "We replenish water—send out a hunting party. We'll stop for a day, to allow them to get their strength back. And then we must continue."

"What of the ones who can't walk?" the doctor says peevishly.

"They will," Day snaps.

"This is a mistake," Stevens says quietly, but perfectly audibly, and Day bristles.

Vogel chooses that moment to collapse.

The daylight comes right in through the red canvas. Day turns over and over in his sleeping bag, trying not to hear the coughs and sighs and grunts from the men crammed into the sick-tent. The doctor is draining their wounds, but they'll have to keep moving on their ruined feet. They have to get south. Death awaits them.

Day thinks he sleeps, but isn't sure.

"You should know," Dr. Nye had said to him. "It'll be some time before they—" Then he wiped his forehead, smearing blood across it.

They won't do the decent thing and die quickly. The unspoken words ring around Day's head as he tries to sleep, pitiless as the sunlight and Stevens's glare: *You waited too long to leave the ship.*

Maybe if Talbot had died earlier, they might have had a chance.

Maybe Day wishes Talbot had died earlier.

Day thinks he dreams, but isn't sure.

Clawing his way to wakefulness, his eyes fly open, resting on Jackson's open mouth, snoring, and Sheppard's curved lips. He can't endure the crimson sunlight filtering through the tent walls. He crawls out, trying not to disturb anyone.

The deep silence of early morning. The sun hangs low in the sky, and the hilly ground casts a long wintergreen shadow across the huddle of tents. A small distance away, the light glinting off his rifle, Day can see Stevens watching over them.

He raises a hand. He's infinitely surprised when Stevens raises one back.

The creek they've camped beside makes a plaintive *drip*. Although it's full of those sharp, boot-shredding rocks, there's a narrow margin of pebbles, not quite frozen over. Day can see his own footprints. He waits to see if they fill up, with a sort of dazed curiosity. The daylight is getting to him: man isn't meant to live under these conditions.

Then he sees it.

A cough comes from the medical tent—a horrible *wet* cough—and Day can tell it's Vogel, suffering from pneumonia or tuberculosis or God knows what, really, it's not as if they have the ability to treat it.

Day kneels and looks at the paw print. It's bigger than both his palms put together.

Once again, Stevens raises his hand. The air feels empty, expectant.

By the time Day's trudged up the rise, he's as breathless as if they're far above sea level. "I thought you'd be sleeping," Stevens says, a quirk to his mouth, as if these aren't the first normal words they've exchanged in weeks.

"I can't."

Stevens's gaze is fixed on the campsite, which from here seems small and meaningless. "Uneasy lies the head that wears the crown," he murmurs. "He loved that one, didn't he."

Stevens isn't in any respect an educated man. He'd come into their backer's offices still smelling of the tundra, with a gun slung over his back and a *voyageur*'s air. No one really knew where he came from, this man who'd adapted himself to the cold places of the Earth. If Stevens has read any Shakespeare, rather than picking up portions that Talbot had so wryly quoted, Day can't imagine what lessons he's taken from it.

"The bear," Day says.

"She's been following since the ice. She padded around camp, getting the measure of us." He gives Day a penetrating look. "Waiting to pick off the weakest."

"You didn't shoot." Day's mouth is dry.

Stevens shrugs. "I might have missed."

They both know that's a lie.

"Thank you," Day says. "For conserving the ammunition."

But that's a lie, too, and he breathes out.

"I don't think I could have watched." He imagines seeing the terrible paws wading silently through the stream, inches from the vulnerable heads, the tender exposed throats, of the sleeping men. Inside his tent, Day had been trying to hide his face from the sunlight. A heartbeat away from those jaws.

Stevens says nothing.

"You said this was a mistake." Day sits on the black rock. "But they need to rest." He doesn't say: *they're not all like you.*

In Day's pocket he keeps a petition of sorts: scrawled on a page torn from one of their flimsy Bibles, in a careful though illiterate hand, it asks for permission to return to the ship. Asking Day to make that awful decision anew. *As if they'd survive the journey*, he thinks bitterly. He'd considered burning it. And then he'd realized—the thought coming sharp as bile—that he ought to keep it, in case it's needed later.

One day he might have to explain what happened to all those men.

"I know." Stevens's tone is softer than usual. "Vogel won't make it. Graham, too. He's too weak. And the others in that tent. They won't reach Lancaster Sound alive. Even if they do—"

"You're going to say we should have left them."

"No." Stevens sighs. "No, Will, I'm sorry. I shouldn't have asked that of you." He gives Day a sidelong glance, and his face is so open it hurts. "You don't have it in you."

It sounds, just a little, like love.

A cough rings out across the valley like a gunshot, and Day flinches, tries to quell his hammering heart. "You're exhausted," Stevens says, matter-of-factly. "You need to sleep. Come here."

Day stares at him. Like a beaten dog, he doesn't know whether to cringe away.

"Come here." Stevens smiles, and puts out his arm. "Lean on me."

Day rests his head, awkwardly, on Stevens's shoulder. It's hard to breathe.

"We haven't decided what to call this," Stevens says, as if they're surveying it all dispassionately from the deck of a ship, waves crashing, the world in its proper place. "I think even Talbot would have run dry by now." The name stabs through Day's heart. "We can't name another damn place for his wife," Stevens gives Day a little grin. "Let's not have the armchair cartographers think us simple."

Day laughs, a croaky sound. Through the thick padding of his fur jacket, Stevens smells of gunpowder. This is the Stevens he knows from the ship, from their cabin, reckless and humorous. Utterly his own person—the realest person Day knows, when he himself is patched together from bits and pieces.

"No sweetheart to name it after?" Stevens says. "No nice English girl waiting for William Day?"

Day swallows. "No," he says, feeling the weight of it on his tongue. "No sweetheart." He doesn't know, in this intimate moment, why they've never spoken of this before.

You know why.

Because they'd shared a cabin, sometimes a bunk, a blanket, wound their arms around each other to keep warm. Naming it, or other intimacies, would be stepping too close to the precipice. And they've never crossed that line, no matter what.

Emboldened, because he can't see Stevens, can only feel him: "You?"

"No one at all," Stevens replies. "A man alone."

A weight lifts off Day's shoulders: a weight he hadn't known was there. He wants to laugh. He knows it's entirely inappropriate, knows this is absurd, as they sit there and watch over their dying camp. Knows Stevens can hardly feel the same way as him.

"Amelia," he says. "I have a niece called Amelia."

"Of course you do." Stevens's tone is gently teasing. "Amelia's Pass, then, and we'll let them speculate, the mapmakers, who she was to you."

Day turns his head, hears his neck crack. His joints and ligaments are starting to show the strain; there's not enough meat in their diet, and soon everything will break down again.

"Oh, here—" Stevens says, and pulls Day's head, very tenderly, into his lap. "I'm not being unkind, when I say you don't have it in you. But things are going to get much worse."

Day snorts, seeing the plume of his breath. Stevens seems to run at a hundred degrees. "You mean we won't just—arrive in Lancaster Sound tomorrow? Paddle out in our boats? Flag down a whaler?"

Stevens laughs. It's a rich, totally unexpected sound. "Can you imagine."

Day closes his eyes for a moment. *England*, he thinks, in September, with the leaves just starting to fall. Where he wouldn't have to be in charge of anyone but himself.

"Back to civilization." Stevens shifts underneath him, and sighs. "I'm ill-made for it, Will, the coat's too tight. But maybe this time it'll stick: I'll buy a town house, throw lavish parties, scandalize the stuffy old guard with my profligacy, but they won't be able to say anything, because it'll all be *mine*. You'll be there, of course."

"Sorry?"

"There'd be plenty of room. You can keep me company."

Day swallows. Stevens's impossible dream is bright enough to burn him—

"Two Arctic heroes, they'll be falling over us; I'll find you a sweetheart, with those hazel eyes and mournful philosopher's looks. Only come home with me, at the end of the night, and we'll play chess by a roaring fire, stuffing ourselves with food and drink. There are *some* parts of that life I wouldn't mind."

Day's eyes prickle. "It sounds wonderful," he says indistinctly. "You hate chess."

Stevens laughs a little. Day doesn't think the gulf between them— the gulf between him and society, between him and what a man is supposed to want—is funny at all.

"But things will get worse." Stevens's voice shifts like the wind. "Much worse. Those men are begging to be left, Will, they'd rather die in their bags than drag their sorry bones across the rocks for nothing. They're not like you and me. We're *survivors*."

"Devil take the hindmost," Day mumbles, and Stevens laughs.

"Exactly."

Day can feel his jaw unclenching, the muscles relaxing under the faint but tangible heat of Stevens's body. He is tired, so tired. He doesn't need to open his eyes, as long as Stevens is here.

"But you don't have it in you. And that's why you need me." Stevens's voice is very quiet, now, just a whisper worming its way into Day's head. "You do need me, don't you? You know what I've done for you. What I'd be willing to do."

Day can feel himself slipping under the breakers of sleep. Just a little while. Stevens is here, and they're together, and though those fancy dreams are a lie, like everything else—

Stevens shakes him a little. "Will?"

"Yes," Day says, drowsily, shutting his eyes again. Despite what Talbot said. The devil driving. "I need you." Day can't lie to him. He can't, he won't, do all this alone.

"I've always needed . . ."

You know what I've done for you. He doesn't really think what Stevens must mean. There's a long silence, broken by coughing from the medical tent.

"You've made the right decision." Stevens's voice is like honey. "I won't let you down."

Day dreams the press of lips to his forehead.

———————

"Will," someone says in his ear.

"Will!"

Day wakes. Time has moved on. His conversation with Stevens, looking down over camp, is starting to fade. There's a hint of autumn in the air now, which smells metallic and crisp. The sun beats down on him through the tent fabric. He pieces it together, his splintered memories: the bear attack. Then the snowstorm, a darkening of the summer sky. The snow had come in needles and pins, like a punishment, and they'd scooped it up to clean the spattered blood off the remaining tents.

There are fewer of them, now. They have the bear to thank for that.

This is some days later.

"Will."

It's Stevens, putting his finger to those perfect lips. "Get up."

Day fears he's still dreaming, but he does as he's told.

They go to the west, where Day knows there's nothing but ice-crammed channels and the gyre of bergs farther out. He knows it with a dull hopelessness.

"Can you see it?" Stevens says quietly, insistent. He points.

It takes a moment. Day looks to Stevens, then back, and—

A rocky shore awaits, beside a silent sea.

Day presses his fists into his eyes, sure that he's gone snow-blind, or he's still asleep, or this is one of the illusions wrought by scurvy, and he's on the *Reckoning* still, strapped raving into a bunk as it consumes him from the inside out: one of the abandoned, and Stevens left him, too. *Stevens left him.*

But the beach in the distance is black granite, ponderous and unwelcoming, and the slopes fall away into water studded with icebergs like shrapnel. The waves ripple, dull and lifeless. There's no end, in any direction, to the wavering hushed ocean.

"You can see it, can't you?" Stevens says. If Day says *no*—

"I can . . . see it."

No birds wheel above it. Nothing breaks its surface. The silence is horrible. Day feels a wave of revulsion strong enough to make him shiver. "It's like—the Styx," he says, and the sound of his own voice startles him.

"It's the Open Polar Sea."

Day laughs. There's something not right about the whole situation. He turns to face Stevens; the specter of being left behind hangs in the air between them.

I need you, he thinks. *I can't survive without you.*

"You were dreaming of the ship," Stevens remarks. "I can see it on your face. Don't worry, Will. It's all taken care of. I told them I'd seen her sink. Going down so fast there was no chance of returning." He smiles. He's all teeth. "That's all they'll remember."

"You lied to them."

"Does it matter?"

Stevens flourishes something. It's that petition, creased and rumpled, begging Day to undo what he'd done.

"I wonder why you had it," Stevens says. "Could it have been—as leverage? But no, that's not a thought William Day would ever have." His tone is gently mocking. "If you had to account for the losses, you could say they disobeyed you, returned to the wreck of their own accord." Day's heart thuds. "Could it be you're *learning*, Will?"

"The men—" Day croaks. "We need to get the remaining men to safety."

Dead weight, a voice says in his head.

He looks at the Polar Sea, its endless silent waters. "We're so small," he says dazedly. Maybe he can wash off some of the blood, down there in the crimson darkness: wash off some of the wide horror in the men's eyes when they look at him.

"The world is so big," Stevens says softly, and smiles.

Neither of them mention the little knapsack stashed against the rocks, sitting in the periphery of their vision like a cannonball, like the ruination of all Day's hopes. The pack, and the rifle: everything Stevens needs to survive the Arctic. But Stevens won't abandon him, Day thinks. They're in this together. That's the pact they've made.

Dead weight. Let all the others be dead weight.

"Sheppard," Stevens says conversationally, "is becoming a problem for us."

NOW

XXIII: ECHOES
At anchor, October 15, 1882

our madness is contagious—

Day rolled in his bunk like the ship was pitching, adrift on a wide, open sea. Someone came in to give him medicine: the wrong height, the wrong accent, but he wept nonetheless, clasped the hand holding the needle and wept. They withdrew with a grimace of blackened teeth, and outside his cabin door Day heard hushed voices. Peters and Roderick, discussing the *Reckoning*'s beating heart. They would raise fire tomorrow. She was waiting for her crew.

Waiting for Day to finish what he'd started.

They'd been right to ask Valle to examine him regularly; had been right not to trust him, not here. Because who was to say that he hadn't worn that brittle black mask? Who was to say he hadn't crept aboard the *Reckoning* in the night, wearing a killer's face; making his way to the sick bay, deciding to neutralize any threat to his command. Who could prove a negative?

I'll take care of it, Will.

There was something very wrong with him.

Day saw, as through a dark tunnel, the moment he'd confronted the shrouded shape; the night Avery was attacked. Somehow—in a mirror image—he was looking at *himself* in that mask, disappearing down into the hold.

He'd learned so much from Stevens, hadn't he?

A day passed. Then another day, and another night. Whenever he tried to leave the bed, Stevens came to sit on Day's chest, completely nude, gripping Day's rib cage with his bare thighs. Stevens peeled an orange with his sharp little knife, and sneered with his too-wide mouth, the juice running down his slim fingers and wrists, sucking it off with such vigor his cheeks hollowed out, obscene and suggestive. He swallowed the segments down whole, without chewing, his long throat working like the gullet of a whale. All Day's most fevered fantasies centered around those plush, ever-perfect, ever-moist lips.

How many more will die from it.

Everyone else would go, one by one, until he was as alone and vulnerable as the day he'd met Jesse Stevens on the quayside. Their affinity had been a deadly one.

And still it—persisted.

That's what the curse was. The haunting.

Sometimes they fought, Stevens making horrible guttural noises, his fingers around Day's neck like the final squeeze of winter. Day smashed his mirror, his hands slick with blood, trying to stop him getting in. Too late.

Are you ready, Will?

But Day couldn't land the blow.

The door creaked open like an animal yawning. Stealthy footsteps. Stevens melted away into the furniture. Day found himself back in the real world.

"*You.*"

The two of them shared, if nothing else, an assessing quality to their gaze. Both had needed to grasp at what they were given with both hands; neither had had a Nicholas Talbot. But, pale under a cobwebby veil, Mrs. Stevens finally looked like she was mourning her husband, rather than imitating him.

She sat, delicately, on the chair beside his bunk. "Were you expecting someone else?"

He pushed himself up on his elbows. It felt like he'd slept a week. The shadows had darkened through the skylights, and something about the coolness of Mrs. Stevens's gaze made it possible to focus. A lens to see himself through.

Valle was gone.

And Day might as well have pushed him. Because the doctor, his oldest friend, had died thinking that Day had come in the night to murder him.

"Has Avery found it?"

"What?"

"That mask. The whalers' mask." Mrs. Stevens shook her head. Again, that assessing look. She appeared, for a moment, about to take Day's sweaty hand. "How long has it been?"

"Four days."

"So little." He swallowed. "Is Lars back yet?" One of the last things he remembered was sending their guide out into that wavery darkness, to see if he could find where the *Louisa* was or wasn't. He'd once learned to expend lives like tokens, hadn't he?

"No."

Day thought their guide might be very, very lucky to be away from the two ships.

"I came to say . . . I'm sorry." She drew her knees up to her chest, like a child.

"*You're* sorry?"

It was the very last thing he expected.

"You were right—I shouldn't be here. I should never have left America. But . . . I thought we'd find him, and I could say it was because of my gifts." A pause. "It would open up such opportunities . . . I wanted to understand him, too, maybe—he was my *husband*. But so many people have died. And we're not going to find him, are we?"

A quiver to her lip. "I don't think I can suffer it, Captain Day. To have him gone, really gone. To be alone."

Day swallowed. He felt the urge to put a hand on her small and bony arm.

"I've thrown it overboard, you know. My skull. His last gift to me." A twist to her mouth. "Never mind the whalers; I think Qila was very glad to see the back of it."

"Did you ever think where he might have dug it up?"

It came out harsher than Day intended. Because that was what explorers did—took shovels and picks to Native cemeteries, looted barrows, dealt unfair bargains. God had made the world in six days, and by the seventh, white men were fully in command, the project of empire being established.

None of this was worth it. The butcher's bill was enormous.

She shook her head. "I didn't ask. But, Captain Day, he might not . . ." Her mouth twisted again, and she drew back her veil, pressing pins into her wavy hair like she was trying to affix herself into place. "Look, it's just—bones. Cairns. Bodies. I've heard this story before." Her eyes were dark. "So they might have eaten their shipmates, in dire need. That doesn't mean he's—*unsalvageable*."

Does it?

Without the veil, the whites to her eyes were enormous. They were face-to-face, he realized, at last.

"I don't know about that," he replied, clenching his fists under the blankets until his nails drew blood. He felt sure that Stevens was about to step out of the shadows, with his Talbot-killing hands, *dead weight* on his lips. A third person in the room. Three points to a triangle.

"Eating someone, under grave duress—it doesn't make you a savage. Any more than not doing so guarantees you're civilized. You came back, didn't you? So could he."

He looked at her unhappily. It was true; some people did think that.

"You know," he said, because it seemed suddenly important to clarify this one thing, "I didn't leave men on the *Reckoning*. That's what they'll say about me, isn't it? Well, I took them all with me, at least at first. I tried. But something awful happened on the way."

He swallowed again. His throat was raw, like he'd been screaming.

Was he really any better than Stevens?

Yes. Yes. *He had to be.*

"You always knew we'd find her, didn't you?" he said.

"Of course." Unabashed. "Well, not so far south. That was a shock for me, too. But I kept your secret, didn't I? Believe me, I have no interest in raking up all those—old bones." She laughed. "I can see Jesse wanting to strike out on his own. And Avery always said we'd know when we encountered him—by the trail of bodies."

Day remembered how she'd looked so dispassionately on those bones. How Avery had promised a different kind of story for Day, one disentangled from Stevens. She looked down, fiddling with her necklace. Once he'd thought the bear claw was a kind of sign language, directed at him. A taunt, or a reminder.

It had taken a particular kind of hubris for Day to imagine himself so persistently surrounded by enemies.

Outside, he could hear Roderick's gruff voice. *In the boats they drank blood.* Because blood, after all, could be drunk—turn for turn—without killing the other person.

"Just after we left Greenland, Avery said my husband was a great man, but far from being a good one. And it's true that I held séances for his crew, and the spirits urged them onwards, no matter the cost. Dead relatives, those lost in the war—members of the fantastical tribe of free men, living in paradise, free from bloodshed . . ." Another gulp. "All the possibilities. It was very appealing to them. And Jesse said if he didn't return by the second summer, it meant he'd need me. That I should find you. And also . . ." She trailed off.

There was something she was unwilling to say aloud, even to Eat-Em-Fresh Day.

"I didn't ask what he'd need me for." She dabbed fiercely at her eyes with the back of her glove, unwilling to let even a single tear be visible.

"You should have," Day said, this time exactly as harsh as he intended.

She blinked at him. "Did you?" she said, very low. "I think you'd have done anything he asked of you."

"You still want him back."

She gave him a confronting look. *Don't you?*

"I know you and Avery think he's gone mad."

He laughed out loud.

The motion set off a burst of coughing, and the feeling of something rising in his throat. He heaved. Gulped for air. The ship was wallowing, turning sideways, and he recognized that somewhere out there the *Reckoning* was waiting, holding out her stumpy masts in an embrace.

Mrs. Stevens, practical as always, held the bucket.

He coughed and coughed, but nothing came out.

Day couldn't catch his breath, though. He couldn't speak. Because something was crawling—

Up.

The moment the thought entered his head, he recognized the sensation of fingers on the inside of his throat. He gestured, frantically, at Mrs. Stevens. *You should leave.*

She set her jaw. Shook her head.

Long, pale fingers, he knew, were testing his gag reflex. Coated with something slimy and viscous, like a skinned hare. Stevens was reaching out of him—

You could hurt her, he was saying. *Really hurt her.*

Don't you want to? A leer.

The first finger breached Day's lips, grayish white and wriggling.

Why should she get off so easily. Why should she come out of this unscarred.

Then—with a dizzying shift of perspective, like a kaleidoscope rotating—Stevens was on the bed beside him, three fingers shoved into Day's mouth, reaching down his throat to rupture his windpipe.

They didn't need words, the two of them.

And Stevens was perfectly visible. Bare, and bloated, like he'd been hauled off a beach at high tide, slippery and gelatinous as an eel. Fly-blown and waxy-skinned. A living dead man.

Mrs. Stevens screamed. There was no question she could see him now.

You could hurt her.

Stevens shoved in another finger.

But it wasn't a sign that Stevens was still alive, that he and Day were somehow connected. This was just something he'd brought back from the ice, something he'd let lodge itself in his heart. He'd chosen the shape it would take: a shape capable of growing until it destroyed him.

You make a god of the things you fear or love. What could be more natural than that?

Day lay alone again, his door locked from the outside.

He cleared his throat, spitting up blood like a scurvy patient.

Thought about the *Reckoning*'s crew of souls leaving the Arctic, slipping out through Lancaster Sound, whispering through the Middle Ice.

Day saw her passing up the Thames like a phantom. The thin haze of rain, London veiled in gauze like Cape Verdant. The heart of Western civilization, all stone and hard edges and brittle formality. That darkness, the *Reckoning*'s rage, with its thoughts of vengeance.

Where would it stop?

He saw billowing sooty gloom passing through the pillars of the Admiralty, creeping through a green door to strangle the Sea Lords at their determinations. Snaking up the steps of Buckingham Palace, turning the windows oily.

Day had no love for any of it anymore. Let it be useless.

But he couldn't allow more people to die.

Day thought, with a pang, about the first time he'd seen her. She'd loomed black-hulled and steaming with tar, smelling of gunpowder and flame, this proud and angry thing. She was the largest ship he'd ever seen, in size but also in temperament; he'd already felt responsible for her. Had meditated on whether he'd come to love her in time.

Why don't you spare the rest of us? Valle had asked.

He was—

He is—

So very tired.

He'll give her what she wants.

Day hopes it won't be too awful, but he's lived long enough to be suspicious of the concept of just deserts. Suffering doesn't make you noble, or any greater. It's impossible to measure one cup against another. It just means you've suffered.

Jesse Stevens intrudes into his memory, pulling him away from the ship, bright-eyed with Symmes fever. "A hole in the center of the Earth—imagine! Jungles and waterfalls, and men you've never seen. Imagine what they might be like, Will—like gods!"

Day will have heard this a hundred times, insistent and obsessive, by the time the two of them leave the *Reckoning*. He thinks being godlike would entail too much responsibility. Stevens, though—he believes in its absolute absence.

Revels in it.

Stevens grabs him by the hand, and Day looks down in surprise: no one has ever been so bold, and it feels utterly improper. Thrilling. No one has ever called him Will, either, but from Stevens the intimacy is so natural, makes promises Day has never even dreamed of. He's been chosen by this bright-eyed young American, as if there's absolutely no one else in the world who will do.

There must be something Stevens sees in him.

Day looks back at the *Reckoning*, which seems bigger than before. "Come and see," Stevens pleads. "There are such marvels. Don't you sometimes feel as though you could—eat the world?"

Day—with a creeping sense of horror, even within the dream— tries to shake himself free. Stevens laughs at him, the corners of his mouth creasing in a wild vulpine smile.

"Oh no, you don't," he says. "We've got a long way to go together, you and I."

The skylight in his cabin was open to the night outside, bitterly cold, so crammed with stars that they looked like sea spray. Tulloch, the night's appointed watchman, hauled Day up through it easily. He was becoming thinner, sharper: more like the William Day who'd knelt to divide his men's daily rations, civilization hanging by a thread.

"You should go—you'll be missed." The other whalers were all enjoying what would finally be their last night on the *Resolution*. The sound of a scraped violin wafted up from the mess hall.

Tulloch nodded. "I'm sorry," he said. "About the doctor."

"Is that all?" Day snapped.

Tulloch looked at him with a glint in his eye that said: *Don't push me.* Day had trespassed on his loyalty to Roderick enough, and the scar on his face—from Herridge's knife, from the boats, he knew that now—was silver under the moon. Day had never been so young or so confident.

"Be careful. Sir."

"Go."

Tulloch disappeared, and Day turned to survey his ship; he'd had time to grow fond of her endless stairs and winding passageways. The half-moon flickered above, and from the ice came the sound of a long, drawn-out death rattle. It was time to go; the *Reckoning* was familiar with suicide.

Day was going to give that ghost ship her captain.

A creak from midships. Day looked around, but there was no one else on deck, as if a plague had passed through and felled the crew entirely.

Her lanterns were swaying, though. A faint side-to-side movement. As he watched, something reached up over the side. Put its puffy, sloughing hands on the railings.

Day froze. *I'm too late.*

It raised its misshapen head, streaming with water.

Lee. Watching him through empty eye sockets, as if something under the ice had plucked them out.

"I'm sorry." Day put his hands up. "I'm sorry." It came out like a sob.

Lee just hung there in a mass of torn and ripped flesh and clothing. A tilt to his head, the ruined face jutting forwards, as if Lee were in the wardroom, demanding another glass of brandy, mocking his subordinates. Day knew his type: entitled, and impatient, and full of that proud rage.

No wonder he'd come back so quickly.

Day's skin crawled when he put Lee behind him, to continue down that endless empty deck. The wind shifted, and he gagged—the smell of rot, as if Lee had been hauled out of the water and left somewhere warm.

Did you ever see orange groves, William?

He half-turned.

Lee was gone.

Day crept across the ladder between the two ships. It wasn't far at all.

He was shaking, though, and everything around him was tall and gaunt against that splashed-star sky. He could go back, he thought. Get through the skylight and lie in his bunk and wait for the *Reckoning* to do its worst to them all, by inches, by degrees.

He didn't have to *face* it.

A sob.

He'd ceased to crawl. He remembered this feeling. Qila had been right; he'd let down everyone who trusted him, sooner or later. When everything broke down, and you could go no farther—when you needed someone else to shoulder your burdens—

Very faint, the sound of something breathing.

Day looked up.

Behind the ship's wheel, a large shadow crouched, breathing steadily in and out. The smell of blood in the air, metallic and sharp, was familiar and horribly alien all at once. So cold.

Day put his hand over his nose and mouth.

A low, quiet noise as the bear turned and regarded him with eyes like lumps of coal. The face of death.

He couldn't breathe.

A tall shape peeled itself out of the inky blackness and stood at the bear's side, one hand resting on the back of her leonine neck. Little smashed glasses.

It was Valle.

No, it was the other doctor—the *assistant* doctor, as Valle had always pointed out so sniffily. Doctor Nye had kept his silence, and gone back to France, and then—several years after their rescue, without much fanfare—taken a fatal dose of laudanum. Day hoped it had been quick, and untroubled. He suspected not. A long period of starvation leading to derangement of the mind, the coroner had said: Nye's face so lean and distorted that the polar bear scar barely figured at all.

It was very visible now, though—he'd been split in two, and had to stitch himself back together.

Day swallowed. There was a look of recognition in the doctor's eyes, a look of acknowledgment, and Day felt an unfamiliar warmth suffuse him.

It was possible to take a step forwards.

Then Valle was standing there. Valle, with Nye's wounds, all dripping with water, as if whatever was in the hold had taken a bite out of him, too.

Valle hadn't been *Reprieved from the Cannibal Crew*, as the papers had said. Not really. No one who came into contact with that story escaped its inexorable tidal pull.

The bear snaked its head forwards.

"All right," Day croaked. "I'm here now. I've come back."

Two sets of dark beady eyes watched him go.

———————

The Great Cabin shimmered into life around him.

The stern windows were rimed with thick layers of frost; but as Day watched, the ice receded and the moonlight flooded in, sending pools of silver across the floor, across the crimson Moorish rug Talbot had been so proud of. It should have been dusty, decaying: fourteen years in which the ship had been manned by no one but the dead.

The room seemed to flicker. The table shone with the gleam of spermaceti, no dust in sight, and Day ran his hand over the surface, marveling. The candles were lit, although he knew those candlesticks were now on the other ship.

Footsteps outside. The sound of men clattering up and down the ladderway, going about their work with a grumble and a sigh. Roderick's men, he thought in panic; he'd be discovered. But it was deep in the watches of the night, and the next sound was an unmistakable crack and swish of canvas from sails being taken in—sails that simply *weren't there*. The steady hum, one he'd long forgotten, of the ship's boiler. They couldn't possibly have got it working so soon.

But then again, she'd drifted hundreds of miles on her own accord. The *Reckoning* had come back for him.

Day caught his own eye in the mirror. Like everything that had been in the Arctic awhile, its surface was warped. He looked exhausted. He looked so determined, it startled him. An entirely different man.

He wouldn't have needed Stevens, he thought, if he hadn't been so afraid of dying. He could have been the captain they deserved.

Talbot's chair was empty, its whorls of carved wood glinting coffee-colored in the candlelight. Again, no dust. The floorboards squeaked as he pulled it back.

Don't give that man a command—

Day had spent more than a decade thinking that Talbot had been wrong, that the man's essential goodness had prevented him from seeing the truth: there could never have been a party of survivors led by William Day. Talbot had been kind, and upright, and had utterly overestimated his young protégé. Day had hauled himself from God-Saves Harbor to Cape Verdant in the certain knowledge that he was weak, needed Stevens like a starving man needs a knife.

But he'd been wrong, and Talbot had been right.

He could have done it without Stevens, if he hadn't been so afraid.

For a moment Day saw his younger self across the table, staring down at the chess set. Pondering the moves of black and white, night and day, *unclean* and clean alike. It clutched at his heart. He'd been so young. Desperate. In love. He'd wanted to live.

He could forgive himself that, at least.

"I'm here," Day said out loud. "I've come home."

———————

Day found that he wasn't afraid of it anymore: this reckoning he'd been running from his entire life. He placed his hands on the table, splaying out his fingers on the polished wood, accepting it as another one of her marvels. At least in this moment, the ship was just as he remembered, golden and beautiful. Maybe it wouldn't be so bad, the curse. He could take command, live a kind of life for a hundred years—Coleridge's bedraggled wedding guest—and she'd still be golden and beautiful.

Though not entirely.

There was a scratch on the table, a deep jagged scrape, and Day frowned at it. A series of circular pits, like the pockmarks left by pencil lead. Something about it nagged at him, and he pushed his fingers into those dimples—

Stevens.

A wave of revulsion hit him, and he could see, like looking through a telescope, Stevens sitting at the table, using his knife on it idly, glancing up now and then towards the empty captain's chair.

Day was sitting in it now. Exactly as Stevens had planned.

Go and get the doctor. I think his heart's given out.

Through the switchback corridor of officers' country, Day followed the knife. It had left a malignant channel in the paneling, continued over beams, over portraits, scratching through the canvas eyes of the *Reckoning*'s great and good. Someone had been here, and he didn't know how he hadn't seen it before: the hatch closed, the hatch open. Something very destructive had passed through, like a whale—capable of overturning a ship with its wild, thrashing, and not quite indiscriminate tail.

Stevens, jaw set, knife tearing and screeching like grit stuck beneath a sledge runner, dragging a man through those dark corridors. A mutineer or a deserter. Dragging him down to the hold.

Day's gathering fury propelled him onwards.

He paused outside his own cabin, where the sliding door was still marked in ornate capitals: *DAY, STEVENS.* It was open an inch; he could smell something burning. Peering in, the light from the illuminators was pure and sharp and impossible, as if this were a spring day, and not winter many years later. The twin bunks were still made up neatly with worsted blankets. A sandy-haired figure was sitting on the lower one, holding a sheaf of paper up to the light. Then using a long spill to set it on fire.

Jesse.

The figure looked up. It was Peters, sitting on Day's bunk, wearing Stevens's jumper; he even had one leg placed up beside him, in that loose insouciant way Day had once so admired, hips canted at an angle that emphasized his thigh muscles.

"Captain. You're up."

"What are you doing here?"

A shrug. Peters placed another sheaf of pages into the fire he'd made in the washstand basin. Watched them burn.

Day took a shallow breath. "We need to find Stevens. Immediately. And stop him."

Saying it out loud made him realize it to be imperative. Whatever responsibility he had to the *Reckoning*, and all she'd become—it started there.

How many more would die for the story they'd created?

And there was something hideous about the scene before him: Peters dressed as Stevens, sleeping in his bed, living out his most sincere fantasies. The smoke wafted around the cabin, and on the burning pages Day caught sight of Valle's furious hand. He'd seen it in those letters of complaint about the sick-bay situation, about the séances, the missed examinations. Now all the notes he'd made, every contrary and sullen account, were going up in smoke.

It made Day cough.

"It's gone," Peters said quickly. "Taken care of. The order relieving you of command never made it into the record."

Peters stared fixedly into the flames. The ship must be cold, Day realized. The ship must be deathly cold, although neither of them could feel it. The thought frightened him. A process of acclimatization.

Of contagion.

"If we return," Peters said softly, "they'll ask us questions. Why did Day do such-and-such? Was it for the best? Why did so many die? Now, and back then. They'll examine us down to our bones."

Peters's voice dropped further. "The officers deliver their journals to me for safekeeping. I've gathered up the rest. I'm guarding your legacy." A little breathless. "*Both* of your legacies."

The skin on the back of Day's neck prickled. "So you—what? Burn the bits you don't like?"

Peters shrugged. "The record isn't set in stone until we return. You've proved that, haven't you? People down there—they don't know what it's like up here." He raised his eyes to Day. Complicit.

"This wasn't in your orders."

"There are many things not encompassed by orders," Peters snapped, the first real sign of disquiet.

"And you should have seen some of the things he wrote about you. Valle. It was slander. A desperate man plagued by shame, his own sick desires. A liar and a murderer. The second murderer in high command—" A pause. "That was the moment he decided to ally with Roderick, to wrest control. Leaving you *nothing*."

Day swallowed.

"I hope I've proved myself to you now," Peters said. "I know you chose me." A curl of those lips. "Over Lee."

It was like a shadow flickering through the tiny room, crossing the bunks, reaching up to the shelf of abandoned books: of course, they hadn't planned to drag them. Stevens's books, from all those wild-eyed fanatics. Holes in the earth. Uncontacted tribes. The interior of a man's skull. The narcissism of it all; Stevens's terrible and boundless appetite. What would he do when there was nothing to check him, nothing at all?

Day remembered how Peters had frozen when Lee, streaming with water, had seemed to crawl straight towards him.

The vengeful dead.

"I know he was the Admiralty's choice. And I know I was yours." Peters's eyes were very clear and grateful in the firelight, glinting like meteor iron.

And there was something in the shadows under the bunk, something long and black, with wide teeth and a predatory smile. "I did this for you," Peters said, a thin note in his voice. Something desperate. Wanting to be seen. Waiting to be praised.

Maybe Day had once sounded the same.

THEN

XXIV
CAMP HOPE, AUGUST 31, 1869

SKIN FOR SKIN, YEA, ALL THAT A MAN HATH WILL HE GIVE FOR HIS LIFE.

I need to speak to you."

It's early morning on that fateful day—long before the trial, the execution, the meal—and the speaker is Christiansen, their half-Native bad bargain. He'd represented himself as an experienced hunter and interpreter: only one of those things proved to be true. He eats everything he can find, and Day has grown short-tempered: he'd come out here to get away from the men, and it would take very little for him to start beating them.

The other Arctic Highlanders had been good men, strong and competent; Day would gladly trade five Christiansens for one Bill. But Bill had been swallowed up by the ice.

"He disappeared without a splash," Stevens had said on that occasion. "I barely turned around and he was gone."

Day doesn't see how that could be possible. The ice creaks, groans, gnashes its teeth; Bill was a more than proficient ice-master, and at any rate would have surely shouted. The old Day would have told himself that Stevens has no reason to lie about this. This Day

just locks it down deep, because Bill is gone, either way, and he
needs—

"It's just—" Day had heard the tremble in his own voice, remembering Bill's fastidious care for his tools, his too-detailed stories about
his wife's various "talents," his low throaty chuckle. Day knows he
shouldn't show more emotion over losing one man than another. But
he'd liked Bill.

"He was a good hunter," Stevens had said, blandly. "There are
other hunters, Will."

Christiansen picks his gums with a broken needle, and in the harsh
morning light Day can see every crevice in his tanned-leather face.

"What are you doing outside?" Day had been quite clear: the risk
of bears is simply too great. Their off-white fur is invisible against the
ice—worse in poor weather, and terrible during the darker months—
and they have only one working rifle left. Day knows his regime has
fueled resentment. He doesn't care; he'd rather have the men hate him,
and stay alive.

Dead weight, he thinks meanly.

Christiansen gives a complicated shrug of his shoulders. Looks
around, warily. "It's the bodies," he says.

"The bodies?"

Frustrated, Christiansen waves a hand towards the grave-ridge, the
harsh slash of rock looming behind camp. "There are pieces missing,"
he mumbles.

Day just stares at him. Christiansen is tall enough to block out the
sun, and for an irrational moment Day thinks he looks like a murderer,
with his wild dark hair and foul-smelling breath. Well, if Christiansen
has been sent to kill him, Day isn't afraid of dying, only the suffering
that comes before. It's Sunday, and inside the hut, noon will be marked
with Bible readings. Ewing has appointed himself their spiritual pro-
tector, and bores the men with long theological discourses that sometimes lapse into Latin. They can't eat Latin, or God.

"The bodies," Christiansen says sharply. "*Sir*. Up on the ridge.
They are no longer whole."

Day sucks in a breath; the air is so cold his teeth are in immediate pain. He can't grasp, not at first, the immensity of what he's being told. "No one should be up there. That includes you, Christiansen." The man's pretty good at pretending not to understand English when it suits him.

"Go and see for yourself."

"You should be inside." Day's cheeks are flushed; he can feel his heart thudding in his chest. He wonders, distantly, whether this is the apoplexy that'll finish him off.

"You don't believe me, do you?"

Day shields his eyes against the merciless glare. The sky is white, as though they're on the inside of a bird's egg, fragile and luminous.

"No, I don't."

Christiansen scowls. "Because—I know why, very well." He says something incomprehensible in his Native tongue. There's no one left for him to converse with; he's even more cut off than the rest of them. Day doesn't know whether Christiansen is a Christian, or how he'd want to be buried when the time comes. "Your favorite—"

"I don't have favorites," Day says, which is manifestly untrue. He hears Christiansen's snort as he turns away.

Day refuses to give the impression he's eager to investigate. He's had to learn so much about command, in the horrible never-ending year since Talbot died. You can't let the men think there's anything you don't know, or that you regret. You have to make the hard decisions, and remake them endlessly; but you can't afford to look back.

You can never, ever, look back. Stevens has taught him this.

So he hasn't. He won't.

Day kneels to examine his reflection in the meltwater creek, and the frozen surface glints up at him. He runs a hand over his patchy beard, the flinty bones of his cheeks. There's nothing human about what he sees there. He's some animal, clinging to life by its claws.

Trapped forever in the eternal present.

Day had come out for a minute's peace. From all the muttered grievances; the sideways glances; the wide eyes following every movement he makes. The hunger is terrible. Their expectations are worse. Day squeezes a fist into his stomach, feeling the hollowness of it, an utterly delirious emptiness. All the body knows is hunger and its own base desires. Day's not above them. He knows he's failed. That impotent anger festers beneath the surface like an abscess.

They're all going to die. It's all your fault.

Day ducks straight back into camp to retrieve their rifle. Sheppard—still alive, still whole—hands it over immediately, offers to come with him.

Day trusts no one, and goes alone.

Climbing the ridge has him wheezing; his heart knocks in his rib cage, his breath comes in fits and starts. He'd once been strong. A promising young lieutenant. But that's all come to an end now: he's a captain now, and must do as captains do.

He turns in sudden fear, staring at the ice in the noonday sun, trying to see the bear he's certain must be stalking them. Perhaps it's come all the way from Amelia's Pass, more than a hundred miles away; perhaps it's the *same* bear, hungry for more of the expedition, thinking Day will feed the rest of them into that stinking maw.

Day has to sit as soon as he gains higher ground. His knees pop wetly with the strain. The wind is fitful, and the passage taunts him. The last party he sent out with boats could only get a few miles before the leads of glistening dark water vanished. The last with sledges and packs—the same, the ice breaking up contrarily into choppy tidal channels. It might have been possible to attempt the escape when they'd first arrived, when they were strong enough to carry the boats, portage them as needed. But Day's command had been hanging by a thread, after what had happened on Amelia's Pass, and he'd insisted they wait out the winter.

Day has thought recently about wading into the tarry water and letting nature take its course. Any end better than the grave-ridge.

He stands.

There are four shallow indentations in the gravel. The wind whistles in his ears, and for a moment he thinks he hears the sound of something padding towards him, snuffling, rooting, but it's just the breeze.

The first death was Williamson: anemia, they think—he'd had to be carried down to Camp Hope like a Viking king. The toes of his boots poke up through the gravel. Day had refused to contemplate stripping the dead for spare clothing or footwear; a decision he'd come to regret.

The second death was Connor: undetermined—they'll probably never know. He'd babbled, deliriously, about a sea, a great shining sea. Now his left shoulder is unburied, but there's none of the wild tearing or rummaging Day had feared. He almost thinks he should leave Connor undisturbed, out of respect for the dead. But respect is in very short supply here.

It takes Day some time to scrape away the rest of the dirt with his hands. The task is far easier than it should have been: here the ground freezes even as the sun burns. Connor ought to be like a fly preserved in amber.

Something has been digging up the bodies.

It can't be a bear, because it's too neat. Day wipes his face with filthy mittens, then gives a full-body shudder at what he's done. He doesn't want Connor, even the smallest piece, to cling to him.

Too late for that now.

The shoulder he's uncovered is bare. The jacket, Connor's green Army jacket, has been cut along the seams. Day can see the exposed scapula; the bone is grayish, bleached a little by the ominous sun, pockmarked like an orange rind. A jagged edge of skin has been peeled back.

A rising sense of horror. Day realizes his hunger is making itself felt; it's starting to stir his stomach, make him think how much the scraps look like beef jerky. The flesh of Connor's biceps and deltoid have been entirely cut away. It must have taken a very sharp knife.

To the right lie Blackman (wounds gone gangrenous) and Penn (starvation). Day knows, with a sudden convulsion of his empty stomach, that both will be in the same condition. Desecrated; part-covered.

Someone has crossed a line Day has long refused to think about.

Day doesn't know whether to scream or curse, but he does know that drawing attention to this will be the end of whatever leadership he's clung to. Their last days here threaten to be an every-man-for-himself situation straight out of the stories of savage lands: cannibal tribes, bones, skulls on spikes. Some of the men are strong enough to dig up the rest of the bodies. Some, despairing, might wheedle or take by force the means to die as comfortably as possible.

Some might do the unthinkable: kill for food. Murder.

Day knows he won't be able to stop him.

Them.

He screams, for a moment, into his mittened hands. It comes out like a croak. He thinks he might die, or go mad. He's not sure which.

"Will?"

The sky moves, and the blinding sunlight makes his second-in-command all gold and harsh white lines, nearly too bright to look at.

"You shouldn't be out here," Stevens says. "We can't have you getting carried off. The men need you."

Day comes abruptly back to himself. He feels the impulse to cover Connor up, as if hiding a Christmas present from an inquisitive child. Stevens smiles; he doesn't appear out of breath. He seems to have an inexhaustible supply of energy.

Day stops himself staring. He swallows hard. They have no secrets, the two of them. "I have something terrible to tell you."

Stevens makes a complicated shape with his mouth.

"Someone has been—" Day shows him the picked-at shoulder, the way Connor's clothing has been cut. It strikes him that someone carved it with beautiful economy. The light glimmers in Stevens's gray eyes, and he nods, slowly, as if Day is confirming what he's long suspected.

"Desperate men," he says softly.

"We should see how many of the bodies—"

Stevens shakes his head, puts a hand on Day's arm. "All of them," he says. "All of them, I should think. We mustn't let the others know."

Day bristles. It's no more than the decision he's already made, but it somehow sounds worse coming from Stevens. "It's not right," he says. "Someone should be held accountable."

"Oh, accountable to who?" Stevens says, a little too quickly.

Day's breath catches.

They stare at each other.

Day notes Stevens's perfect, untouched lips, the elegant hunter's strength in every inch of him. Stevens, in turn, must be taking in Day's own bruised eyes—the way he's coming apart.

There's a whole story, long-repressed and unthinkable, in those differences.

We're survivors, you and I.

"No one can find out," Stevens says, very low. "How did you—"

"Someone told me."

"Who?"

Day hesitates.

"Who?" Stevens asks again.

"Christiansen."

Stevens laughs a dismissive laugh. Pushes the toe of his boot against the part-frozen body. "That half-breed." For someone who believes the north hides an ascended race of men—who still believes in the Open Polar Sea, despite everything—Stevens is casually dismissive of those true northerners he has actually met, and Day understands why Christiansen would have hesitated to accuse him. Thinks, with a pang, of Bill and his laughter. Bill was a good man. Day won't see his like again.

Day stutters as he stands, the blood swimming from his head. He blinks his eyes hard against the light, the impression that the sky is swarming. He's desperate to move on past this moment.

Later, at the end of that interminable day, some men hold their noses as they eat. The smell puts Day uncannily in mind of pork tenderloin, and his stomach screams at him to pick up the spoon.

He should say something. Remind them that this was once a man. Was once *Sheppard*, with all his hopefulness and cheer and his undeniable good qualities, before the end. Before Sheppard had given in to hunger and despair, hatched his plot to take the rifle and leave them to die. But as Day looks around, he sees that everyone is already eating: the moment is lost. Lips smack; teeth chew; throats swallow.

Those other bodies had been exhausted, picked clean of their fleshy parts, and what's left on the grave-ridge is no longer wholesome. It must have been going on for some time. But Sheppard will feed them all for now, get their strength back up. Day can feel heat behind his eyes. It's gratitude. They've been brought back to life.

A prickle of discomfort.

Day coughs: let people assume he's choking on the food, rather than the sudden rush of misgiving that makes him beat his chest with grimy fist. Something about the timing strikes him the wrong way; it's a long time since William Day believed in providence.

He stands awkwardly, trudges through the twilight towards the tent. Few of the men even look up from their bowls.

The tent is just tall enough for the doctor to kneel upright, and the light filtering through the fabric is bloody. *A red tent.* Day squeezes his eyes shut. Amelia's Pass is many, many months ago—nearly as remote as the ship—but he can still hear the screaming.

"I don't think I can," Nye says without preamble. In any other time or place, he might be expressing doubts about operating on Campbell. Here at Cape Verdant, he's kneeling over Sheppard's body, the instrument bag lying beside him.

Day doesn't want to look, but it's impossible not to. The top of Sheppard's head has been obliterated. The left ridge of his skull is still jaggedly visible, and he lies on the ground cloth like a baby that hasn't yet learned to support its own neck. There's shockingly little blood. His trousers are missing, so Day can see that Stevens had started with the meat of Sheppard's calves, sliced from hamstring to ankle.

He tries to think of the body as meat, rather than Sheppard. It isn't working.

"We have to," he says to Nye, who's shakily polishing his glasses. Day pulls out the largest saw, which is bow-framed, double-handled. He thrusts it into Nye's hands, notices from a distance that his own aren't trembling anymore. "I should think this one."

"I'm not a—butcher," the doctor says faintly.

Day swallows; he wishes Stevens were there. But he needs Stevens to watch the men. It all hangs on a knife-edge, this fragile moment of timely salvation.

Things are slotting together. He wishes they weren't.

"We have enough for now," Day says, looking Nye in his one good eye. "For tomorrow, if we eke it out with lichen, or reboil it with the boot pieces. But that's one more meal. We need to think about what comes next."

Nye stares down at Sheppard's exposed thighs.

"You told me we would all die." Day thinks of the skeletons sitting around the fire, Campbell's sweaty stumps. "I'm giving you an order."

I'm making this easy for you.

"We need your knowledge of anatomy. Your skills with a knife. And we need to make the decision before this goes to waste."

It's freezing outside, the land coated in a nautical twilight the color of blueberry jam. But come morning, there'll be more dripping melt-water. Day thinks of the condition of the bodies on the grave-ridge, and bile rises in his throat.

Something in his expression must have persuaded, because Dr. Nye nods, making the muscles spike out from his lean neck, pull the scarred side of his face into a rictus. "I can remove the limbs," he says tentatively. "Then I have—ah—sharp blades, catlins, to cut off the flesh. We can dry it in the sunlight."

Day nods, not trusting himself to open his mouth.

"The rest I will strip. It can be boiled. The bones, the organs—later. We need to think about how this will last us longer." Nye looks reluctantly at Sheppard's ruined face. "The brains will deteriorate quickly, now they are exposed. They are nourishing."

Day swallows hard and looks at the ground for a few minutes. It feels like the silence goes on forever.

An urgent, claw-like hand grips his arm.

Day's heart stops. For a moment Sheppard isn't dead—has been lying there listening to his fate. He's grabbed Day to entreat him: *No, not that! Don't butcher me. Don't eat me!*

Don't murder me, whatever he says.

But Sheppard is already dead. His hands are still.

It's just the doctor. "Captain," he says. "You've made the right decision. We would all have died. I want you to know that. For now and—whatever comes. I'll support you."

Day meets his sunken eyes, and the hand is removed swiftly. "Ah," Day says, and can't think what comes next, because the feeling in his chest is so utterly unfamiliar: he thinks he's made the right decision, to eat Sheppard—now that he's dead.

He wants to scream, or laugh.

Nye nods, as if Day's made a sensible reply, and takes up the bone saw. "You don't need to stay. I'll do what's necessary."

Day thinks of Stevens, out on Amelia's Pass, watching over their sleeping camp with loaded gun. *You don't have it in you.* He backs out of the tent. His last impression of Sheppard is as a piece of timber, lying heavy and inarticulate in a sawmill, the blade glinting in red-tinged light. Sheppard's not a man anymore, he tells himself, he's—

Dead weight.

———

When Day returns from the doctor to the fire, Stevens is asking around again about Sheppard's missing diary. "If there are blank pages, we could use the kindling," he says casually, disingenuously. But short of ordering a complete search of the fetid camp, there's not much else he can do. "Wasteful."

Stevens catches Day's eye as he approaches, makes it his problem as well.

Neither of them knows what might be written in the diary about a polar bear attack. About a plot to leave the weakest to die on the ice-bound ship. No matter that their plan had never been followed through, and they'd taken all of the men from God-Saves Harbor, even the weakest. No matter that this had been Day's only sticking point. The very fact of the original scheme spoke to a dark and ruthless morality.

Complicity.

Something about the word *wasteful*, though, sticks in Day's head.

He thinks about the bodies on the grave-ridge: if Day had given the order earlier, if he'd grasped the weight of their situation earlier, they might have used them in similar fashion to Sheppard, treated them in common. That would have been better, somehow, than allowing one person to keep cannibal secrets between himself and the seething sky. Staying strong when the others grew weak. Waiting. Biding his time.

For—what?

Stevens is now wearing Sheppard's rifle, as if it had always belonged to him. He's accomplished at everything he does. A tracker, a marksman, a navigator. Day has puzzled over it; he'd asked Stevens, once, why he didn't leave.

Stevens had looked thoughtful. "I don't know why," he'd said.

It had sounded strangely naked.

Stevens picks a morsel out of his bowl with his wickedly sharp knife. He looks healthier, more vital, than most. Day watches him devour it with pink lips and white teeth. The missing diary. Everything Sheppard saw and heard. Jealousy. The rifle.

If this land is savage, Day thinks, it's because we brought our savagery with us.

5

NOW

XXV: WE DON'T LEAVE THE SHIP
AT ANCHOR, OCTOBER 20, 1882

Day stood on the *Reckoning*'s deck, arms wrapped around himself. While the mercury was blessedly above zero, soon it would be far too cold to be exposed to the elements unmoving. He remembered, with a pang, the stumble of the lieutenants as they took their noonday exercise, Dr. Nye's madhouse roundabout. The coaling hatch was open before him, a chute running into chilly darkness.

They were bringing up the bodies found below.

The boiler crew had finally climbed into the hold to reach Valle, his neck turned all the way around, a look of surprise on his face. A faint unsettling odor lingered, sweet and licorice, like a mouse left too long in a trap. Chipping away at the murky depths around the doctor had revealed others.

The ship had started to give up her secrets.

Avery closed his notebook with a snap. Day jumped.

"Are you sure they didn't find their way back, the sick men?"

Day had finally given Avery that interview. He'd told him about Talbot's sudden death, about Amelia's Pass, and how they'd dwindled and scraped, diminishing, so hopeless that the sick had *begged* to return to the ship while they still could. How they'd arrived at Cape Verdant on the brink of an inhuman mania, and never come back from it.

"They couldn't have," Day said bluntly. The pulley let out a long complaining screech.

"I was young, and healthier than most—I thought we could all make it out. Maybe if we'd left earlier, like *he* suggested . . . we might have." Day felt he couldn't stop talking, as if the speech had built up inside him over the years, and was now stuttering out. "That was what Sheppard knew. Stevens would have abandoned them all and saved himself."

And Day had been willing to go along with it.

"So Stevens had him killed," Avery said. "A neat solution to all your problems."

Day thought of Sheppard's family, their soft hands, softer voices. Back in Louisiana, they'd placed bougainvillea around Sheppard's daguerreotype, pride of place on the mantelpiece, their most favored son. Day couldn't imagine being anyone's most favored anything. The visit was meant to show his respects, and hadn't been required: he'd done it according to an unnamable impulse. But he could see, now, what had led him there. Sheppard's death. Campbell. The occupants of that sick-tent. The good doctor.

What followed him around was *Sheppard*—as much it was anyone else.

Day wished Avery would stop looking at him. The reporter reached out and, very solemnly, squeezed his shoulder through his thick officer's jacket. It had been a very long time since anyone had touched him.

Day thought he might die of the pity.

The darkness beneath the deck had started to disclose something being hauled up by its ankles, like cattle ready for butchering. Day swallowed. The bodies down there, the men had reported, had been neatly tied hand and foot. Wrapped in tarpaulin.

An abattoir.

"She wasn't always like this," Day said, wretched. "The ship."

The *Reckoning* still gleamed in the Arctic sunlight, as if she hadn't led to the deaths of so many men, her gilding deceptive. Day thought of El Dorado, fevers and delirium in the jungle, great snaking rivers and the splash of canoes, as Europeans went chasing something never theirs to begin with. Mosquitoes. Warm waters. Orange groves.

"She wasn't like this," he said again, his voice cracking. Once he'd dreamed of returning to her—returning home. But he had been right all along: it was truly *lost*.

Tulloch came over to receive the first body through the coaling hatch. Day wondered how long until it, too, raised its crab-like fingers.

"We can't stay here," he said. "We need to get word to the *Louisa* while we still can." It would be his ruin—begging for relief, for sanctuary. Abandoning his dying ship, and his post.

But a captain had to make decisions for the good of his men.

Avery looked at him gravely, as if remembering a time when Day had been haggard, desperate; when he had lunged through the New York crowd to seize a young reporter by his collar. The Arctic would do that to a man.

Maybe, Day thought, only to a white man. Someone unaccustomed to these harsh winds, hazy light, creaking ice. Someone who came here and tried to open a passage to whatever was judged of *value*: the northwest route, the balmy Open Polar Sea.

But in their hubris or greed, they'd let something else through entirely.

As Tulloch manhandled the first corpse onto deck and peeled back its covering, Day shook his head. The man was straw-haired and hollow-eyed, utterly unrecognizable. His skin was still intact. He seemed rather peaceful, if you looked at him right, apart from scratch marks on his face, four of them, running from his brow to his pursed lips.

There was no way he'd been down there for more than a decade.

"Not one of mine," Day said. The look of mingled relief and approval from Avery was enough to make him want to weep. He didn't deserve any credit for this.

"Stevens was here."

And the corollary: why leave a *resource* like this, if you didn't mean to return? The hold wasn't an abattoir. It was a cold store.

———

On the ice, a distorted cry. Someone was hailing the ship, in fits and bursts, halting, like language was coming hard to its speaker.

Day froze. "Can you hear that?"

Avery nodded, grim.

Day braced himself. His jaw suddenly convulsed, snapping tight on a meaty part of his cheek. Drawing blood.

"Captain—"

Something was approaching. The daylight had gone down, and the stars were burning relentless, the moon no match for the sweeping brilliance of the Northern Lights. Emerald waves rushed, wreaths of frost-smoke clinging to the ice. It was dark and light at the same time.

"Something's coming." Carter, his voice reedy.

Another shout. Day could now recognize it was Lars out there. That didn't engender any relief: the man was out of breath. Day could make out a blurry shape approaching, running as if the hounds of hell were on its heels.

Around it was a mass of misty forms.

Under the glimmering aurora, Day was sure he could see pelting figures, running alongside. They easily outpaced Lars, then fell back to deliquesce into the mist. Appearing. *Manifesting.* Then—gone. It was impossible to tell in the scudding, wraithy light what was real and what was not.

Day had thought they'd *crawl.* He'd thought they'd stumble. Everyone who'd died at Cape Verdant and Amelia's Pass: how could they not?

Then Peters was there, aiming the rifle—barrel wavering—towards the hurrying figure.

"Get away from the ship!" Peters shouted. "Get away—"

Panic sizzled through the air.

"Peters—"

A scrape. A scrabble. There was someone scrambling down over the side.

A bell rang above.

"Don't come any closer!"

"Don't shoot!" Qila was yelling, and she tackled Peters to the deck, knocking the rifle clean out of his hands. He *hissed* at her.

Suddenly Lars resolved himself into a stark living figure, panting towards the side of the ship. The shapes around him were drifting snow, animated by the aurora. Nothing more. Their guide thrust up three sallow-looking Arctic foxes into the lantern's glare. "Captain!" he yelled. "Captain!"

———————————

"The place of the foxes," Lars said, his dark eyes proud. He still had a sheen of ice on his eyebrows, snow on his boots, dripping loudly as they were thawed by the heat of the stove. On the galley table, those three animals lolled, one of them bearing a wide crimson smile. Qila had cut the collar off, holding her knife delicate as a pen, but something else had already nicked the fox's throat. She scrubbed her hands in the washbasin; the smell of an English garden lingered, incongruous, in the air.

The place of the foxes. Lars had built himself a small ice-shelter where the hunting was good, when the ship had been closer to those shores. He'd taken Qila there at least once: overnight, with an unmarried man, it should have been forbidden. By Mrs. Stevens, if not by Day himself.

But it was done. This was a different world.

Day turned the little metal disc from that fox collar around and around; it seemed faintly ridiculous that the tactics of the Franklin searchers would save them.

All is well.

The collar had carried a stamped piece of tin, bearing a code appointed long before they'd set sail, and Nathaniel had followed his orders to the letter. He was safe at the agreed location, a hundred miles south as the crow flew, that chain of caches waiting. Karl was searching for them.

There was something inside Day reluctant to trust this providence, and it leaned against the galley wall, blond hair plastered to its fox-like face in the steam.

Aren't you forgetting something? it said.

Peters scowled. "It changes nothing," he said. "We should send him back with a message, nothing more. We have supplies to last the winter, and we'll be safe on the *Reckoning*."

Lars frowned. He'd said Karl's name, his real name, several times, rich with concern, and Day thought with a pang about their separation, coming from a people that clustered together—no one marooned.

"Do I have this right?" Avery asked, quietening the room. With one finger in the spilled flour, he drew the shape of Talbot's Channel: a swan's neck facing west, with Day and the ships sitting at the rocky islets that formed its beak. A larger, curved patch of land made the outline of the swan's silky back; a round barren island its breast. Beechey, though, would be impossible to reach—that cheerless cairn-scattered shore was too far down on the swans-back side of the channel. They were indescribably lucky that the storm had forced Captain Nathaniel to overwinter on the west.

Avery made a large X at Cape Verdant, on the coast of the round island, the center of the swan's gullet. Day's skin prickled. He'd once said he'd rather die than return.

But there it was, and there the caches would lead them.

Carter's search party cast a long, mad shadow. The weather could turn any day, and a blizzard would stop them in their tracks. Fittingly, at the start of November—All Souls' Day—there would be no more daylight at all: just night, and the *Reckoning*, until breakup came in spring. They were less than two weeks from that deadline.

Day cracked his neck. "Could you lead a party to the *Louisa*?"

Lars narrowed his eyebrows. Nodded, slowly. "We'd need to go north first, cross the plains and hills. Stay on land as long as possible. The ice is too wild to cross immediately south. So we go north. Pick up the small boat and use the open water in the bay."

"We could do that?"

"The boat is already there," Qila said. "And it's not a hard journey. The only question is whether the water is open enough."

The only question. Day squeezed his fists at the sound of a laugh—choked, mocking—from the corner of the room.

"It's winter."

Tulloch flushed when they looked at him, but didn't take it back. He wasn't an officer, or a guide, or a passenger. Just some eighteen-year-old whaler who'd run onto the ice to help Lars the last few hundred yards, despite Roderick's prohibition on leaving the ships. Despite the risk of being shot. He was braver than Day had ever been.

"Exactly," Peters said, folding his arms. "And leaving the ship often proves costly."

"More than costly." Carter glared at the foxes as if they might turn into something else, snap at him with bared toothy jaws. Tulloch shivered, despite the room's heat.

Day found himself listening, holding up a hand for silence. They waited. But the only sounds coming from outside were the clangs of hammers, the whine of saws, the screech of winches.

Day took a deep breath. "We know . . . *he* was here. He left those men in the hold. Stevens was here, and means to return. We need to act now, if we're to have any chance of catching up with him before winter."

Tulloch glanced at Peters. "Why not wait for him to come to us?"

An approving look: while Day was incapacitated, Peters had clearly made good use of his time. He might have talked them all into staying.

"We need to rescue his men. Act now, to take Stevens into custody. We have reason to believe he's—hurting them."

A heartbeat. The stove knocked, and the fiddle-rail made its questioning clang. Like fish on a line, everyone found their gaze turning to Mrs. Stevens, who was sitting mute and dark at the table, cloak furled around her, as if conducting another séance.

She met Day's eye. Then shook herself, briskly and all over, as if trying to get rid of something clinging.

She nodded.

"Lars . . ." Day hesitated, wishing he knew how to address him by his real name. A familiar pain, because he wished he could mourn Bill by his real name; whether his death had been an accident, or whether he'd been fed into the ice by Stevens, dispassionate. "Could you take the passengers on to the *Louisa* without me?"

Lars blinked, and Day held his gaze. He knew some captains refused to let their guides leave when conditions grew bad. He'd heard stories. One man—one good, upstanding, Admiralty man, or so they said—had confiscated his guide's kayak until they were around Cape York, marooning him on the ship. Another had dragged a whole family back to London, to exhibit them before the queen. Living relics. As if they weren't people at all.

"And what about you?" Mrs. Stevens said hotly. "You *promised*—"

"Don't worry. We'll still be going after Stevens. Lars will keep you safe."

He thought he could see the faintest smile on Qila's face, hidden as she pretended to examine, again, the other two foxes. Her hair was escaping her scarf and topknot, and she'd omitted a smear of blood on the back of her bare left arm. But her gaze was warm. Approving.

"When?"

"As soon as possible. Before things get worse."

Another euphemism.

"Captain," Tulloch said. "What about those things on the ice?"

Stevens, leaning against the range, looked over at them with his face like a morning full of rain. A quirk of the lips, too wide at the corners; an inch of cheek omitted, showing wisdom teeth. *Yes, Will, what about them?*

At the same time, Avery said: "And what are you going to do if you find him?"

"Hold him responsible."

Responsible for what? The nonsense and half-truths you've been eking out? Stevens laughed. *They still don't know, do they?*

Peters was looking around, as if he could hear someone else in the room. Following Day's gaze to where dust motes swirled and Stevens leaned. For a moment they appeared to meet eye to eye. But Peters, Day knew, saw nothing.

"Enough. We need to go. The weather's holding, and every day counts."

He would have to meet whatever was on the ice. He was finished with waiting.

Tulloch hovered by the door as they all left. Day looked straight at him. "You're needed—even traveling light, they'll need another set of hands. If you can find it in yourself to help us, you'd be desperately welcome. I know Roderick won't send anyone else."

I wish you well, Roderick had said, and sighed. *I won't be part of it.*

"I'll come back for you," Day had promised, gripping Roderick's clean and weathered hand, and they'd both fallen silent.

Tulloch nodded, pursing his lips. Then slipped out into the night.

When he was alone, Day lowered his voice. "Enough from you, too." Anger, slow bubbling, because Stevens was flawless, still flawless, not a mark on him, just that unnecessarily toothy smile. "I'm done with you, *Jesse*."

Stevens took a step back, as if a favored dog had failed to heel— had chosen, instead, to growl at its master.

"Ah, William, we don't leave the ship."

Talbot had been very clear. "The ship is our world," he'd say. "Our mother and father. Womb and cradle and coffin. Without her we're nothing."

Day could see him in the Great Cabin, leaning over his plans. Talbot was a tall man, imposingly so, though his expression was usually one of boyish-eyed wonder. A look of openness that Day had never seen on the men in his family; his father glowered and peered like dissatisfaction itself. Talbot rubbed those eyes: scurvy had made them the color of egg yolks. In the assurance on his face, though, Day could see *the way things were done*, the assurance of a hundred Admiralty assaults on the ice. Others might go native. Others might innovate. Not Talbot, who, for all his amiability, was still held fast in the grip of a vast system, one that controlled the world.

Day had envied him that assurance.

"Yes, yes, I know," Talbot had said. "Some of the men are accustomed to surviving on land—that's what you're thinking, isn't it? The Native guides. Your bunkmate from the Yukon, if he's to be believed."

The mention of Stevens had made Day's throat seize up.

Talbot interlaced his swollen fingers. "When someone saves the life of"—and here he named the nephew of one of the expedition's backers, a bare-faced boy who'd been sent to survey railway routes in the wilderness—"you'll have to find a place for them, like it or not."

"It was bravely done, sir."

Talbot gave him a look that was very close to pity, and Day flushed, sure that his feelings were written all over his face. The nights spent in close-breathed proximity, staring at the bunk above him, thinking about the tale—the trapper's cabin amidst miles of silent trees, the inexorable snow, and the cries of animals out of reach in the winter-blanketed forest. They'd died in February, the cruelest month, until Jesse Stevens had stepped into that dark doorway and said, "Thirty days with no game? It's a marvel you're still alive."

"You have to wonder, don't you?" Talbot said, half to himself. The captain stabbed a caliper into the chart as if letting blood from an infected wound. He grasped the table, holding himself up, careful not to let the scurvy weakness show. "If he was watching the cabin all that time. If he knew they'd die without him."

Talbot looked at young William Day, and said—as if it were an observation in passing, and not slander, not the sort of thing that would make Stevens's eyes gleam hotly in the dark—"If he'd watched the cabin all those days, couldn't he have saved the others?"

———

It was nine o'clock in the morning when they said their final good-byes, and still only civil twilight. From the land, the *Resolution* was so obviously doomed there was no reason to talk about it.

Day looked back when they were crunching over the barren rocks, rocks that sidled upwards until they formed mean low-backed hills, scoured of snow, black and ocher. Lars was right: the ice immediately below the ship was too treacherous. The shore would be safer for now. The two of them had some experience of traveling in these latitudes.

He shuddered. It seemed to him that he could hear, again, the *screeee* of stone caught under sledge runners.

"This is a mistake," someone said by his shoulder. The pinched voice sounded so like Jesse Stevens—so like his peevish, sulky moods—that Day was almost surprised to see Peters standing there.

"Well?"

"You could have left me in command." He turned back. The *Reckoning* was a figure crouched on the ice. "I'd have taken good care of her."

"No," Day replied. "You're needed with me. We have to find Stevens. Imagine—being the one who found the lost captain of the *Fox*. Rescued his men. You'd come back a hero . . . you could prove Lee wrong about you," he added into the ensuing silence, dangling it in front of him like a worm on a hook.

Peters didn't take the bait.

After another few hundred scraping yards: "This is a mistake," he repeated coolly, looking at Day with clear eyes. "You don't know that the women will make it. They're *weak*. Not like us."

"They're our responsibility. We need to get them to safety."

He'd asked Qila: Did she think Mrs. Stevens could make it through several days' journey, on foot and in freezing temperatures? She'd nodded—then shrugged. "We don't have an alternative, do we," she'd said, shielding her eyes to look over at the *Reckoning*. And Day had shuddered to think of Stevens leaning naked over him—urging him to hurt his wife—threatening, gleeful, to do the same himself. *Why should she escape unscathed?*

She'd seen Jonny Greenstreet. It was all too close.

The crunch of snow. It was warm enough as long as they were moving. But if they got stuck, the wind would flay the flesh from their bones.

"We were perfectly safe! To abandon the ship, to look for someone who left *food*—"

Peters didn't finish the thought, but Day heard it, clear as a bell: *It's a waste.*

Day's skin crawled. He thought of all those nights Peters had spent in his old cabin, where Stevens had carved his name on the underside of the bunk for Day to look up and see, the last thing on sleeping, the first on waking.

"She's a haunted house," he snapped. "You saw what happened to Lee."

They both turned again. The ship's drowned-man figurehead had been restored to its rightful place, sticking out over the prow like a harpoon. But its face was now covered with a long thin mask, gleaming leather in the gloaming, a killer-whale smile and tiny beady black eyes. The whalers had finally chosen their mascot, to see them through the long winter, and it wasn't Roderick, the temperate man.

Leviathan.

Day thought he understood. Something dark had happened in those lifeboats, whether it was murder or the killer whales or the sheer hopelessness of the situation: and some men, in their desperation, had tried to propitiate the thing that destroyed.

Against the animal-headed men, they were still trying.

He thought he understood. Possibly he was the only person who did.

In the still, crisp air of the shore, they had to leave their faces uncovered, otherwise the fabric would freeze to skin, like the death masks of ancient kings, and there was new purpling at the side of Tulloch's jaw. Not scurvy; he'd been beaten. A punishment for his repeated breaches of loyalty—and now for leaving altogether.

It was understandable for his brothers to think they were owed something, for keeping him alive. The youngest and weakest was always vulnerable; families always demanded something in return. Day could almost see the anguish in Roderick's eyes, standing back to watch his mates landing the blows. He wouldn't have wanted this. Wouldn't have wanted any of this.

So what makes you think you're ready, something said inside him.

Qila crunched up past the sledge to pace beside him, briefly, as if her presence at his side was simply part of the ebb and flow of walking. The women wouldn't haul: they needed to keep up their strength. But she well knew the route from the ship to the hunting grounds.

"You're back," he said to her quietly.

She shrugged. "You're dangerous." Her voice was gentle. *A good man.* "I know."

Day's heart was pounding in his rib cage. He knew, somewhere deep within, there was Stevens's thrumming violence, just waiting to be unleashed. It was as much a part of him as anything else. Everyone was made up of their past, those seemingly disconnected choices leading to the truth of the whole.

And that anger had been rightfully his all along.

His eyes flicked to Avery, who kept turning, pencil clumsy in his gloved hands, to sketch for posterity the last-seen position of the two ships. Something about the sight, the sound of scribbling, gave Day a distant and foreign hope. That they'd find Stevens, stop it all from happening again. He could almost smell the promise of sunlight on the air, a faint scent of flowers in bloom.

XXVI: REFRACTION
LAND, OCTOBER 23, 1882

The shore was less harsh this time, like entering a bubble. No wind, no ice. No animals. Sometimes the sunlight made dazzling parhelia; sometimes the breeze brought bright glittering particles, forming around their heads like shimmering dust. The sun was pink with summer's last farewell, and now Mrs. Stevens, too, wore trousers tucked into boots, sweat beading her face.

"I've done the Nile," she said, only a little out of breath. "From

Cairo to Aswan. Jesse enjoyed the crocodile hunting." Her smile curdled, doubtless remembering Stevens backhanding, casually, the guides; the paraphernalia of disturbed graves. Day said nothing. Qila took her hand with a look of mingled pity and condescension.

They had two weeks, Lars estimated, before they'd be as far from Captain Nathaniel as they were from the moon. It was tight, but possible.

Day shaded his eyes, squinting north, where the clouds shattered sunlight into a hundred armor-piercing arrows. He kept thinking of that cairn Lars had found, and the word he'd used: *territory*. A little way along the coast, beside a ravine. It was a narrow margin to hang his hopes on—that he could strike out and find Stevens's camp in all this wilderness.

But the land was where it had started. That was where it would end.

The winds came back on the second day, just as they entered the lower ground to separate. "We make camp," Lars shouted. Day drew a circle in the snow with the toe of his boot, watched it blur. The sight filled him with unease.

"Did you hear that?" Qila called.

"What?"

"Gunshots." The wind shrieked in reply. Again, Day watched his footprints be erased; thought of a paw print, deep and ominous.

They awoke the next morning to find Tulloch missing.

The night's gale had blown out, the sky violet and dense, the temperature rising. None had slept peacefully; Day had clawed his way back into wakefulness to the taste of meat, and had scrambled outside to spit. Mrs. Stevens had heard someone say *Repent*, very loudly in her ear, startling her from sleep.

He needed men with the right set of ideas.

Qila had dreamed of her parents walking away. Leaving her in the snow. She now watched them all warily. As if they, too, might vanish in front of her.

Tulloch had been on watch; it took them longer than it should to realize that Carter was also missing, his sleeping bag no longer warm.

"Did anyone hear them leave?" Day asked.

"Did anyone hear them be *taken*," Avery said. "That's what you mean, isn't it?" He looked around with wide eyes. They were all thinking about those gunshots, far and elusive and impossible to gauge. "We're not alone out here."

"Maybe Tulloch heard game. Woke Carter, and they went out together." But Lars looked at Day and gave a single shake of the head.

It was entirely possible, though, that Tulloch had returned to the ship, begging his brothers to take him back. Supplication. Perhaps, even now, he was kneeling before the thing that would devour, because Tulloch was that cabin boy, wasn't he? Herridge's intended sacrifice. A death to draw off other deaths.

Day rubbed his neck, seeing Vogel on the rocks of Amelia's Pass, the bear crouching over him.

"You know Carter took it very badly," someone whispered. "When the navigator died."

It sounded like Peters, and the secretive tone set off alarm bells: something that couldn't quite be said out loud. Day flushed at the thought that the two men's relationship was well known, and the others were judging him for permitting it.

But he could still see the look on Carter's face as Holt vanished under the ice. And the spongy, waterlogged, seeping thing that Lee had become. The open-mouthed expression on Peters's face in turn.

As if Lee had come for him, and him alone.

Day dragged his second-in-command away from camp, marching him into the rocky defile like a condemned man. Dawn was a long way off.

"Captain." Peters moistened his lips with his little pink tongue. Something about the gesture, the fastidious neatness of it, made Day even angrier.

"Did you do it?"

Peters was wearing a battered black coat, buttons glinting at his collar, threatening to shatter in the cold. Stevens had run hot, and Day knew—a certainty deep as marrow—that if he opened that coat, he'd find the tear in the lining from when Jesse had torn it off in a panic, thrown it around Day, frozen and dripping and starting to turn blue, and hissed: "That was stupid. I can't afford—"

I can't afford to lose you.

"Do what?"

But Day had had enough of these games. "Where's the mask, Peters?"

Peters blinked. Whatever he'd expected to be asked, it wasn't that.

"I saw it. On the *Reckoning*. It's been you all along, hasn't it?"

Valle had teetered on the edge of the hold for a few moments, a splash echoing beneath him; Day had seen the fear in Valle's eyes, the overreaching, and had stretched out his hand too late.

He'd have to live with that tiny moment of hesitation for the rest of his life.

And Day had a confused impression of Peters lying him down on the rotten boards. A bundle of rags discarded in the shadows. A cloak. The gleam of a leathery mask, twin pinpricks of black eyes.

"Answer me!"

Day realized he was nearly choking Peters, the fabric bunched around his slender neck. There was still a small dent on his nose where his glasses had been.

"It's not here!" Peters panted, and Day let go. "I left it on the ship—in case they needed it." Day breathed out hard, and Peters gave him a quirk-lipped grin that made him want to scream. "Yes—I saved you. And the expedition. And Stevens. I came out here because . . . I needed to see it all for myself, what it was like. I knew I had to find myself *worthy*. If Lee had lived, he'd have ruined everything, wouldn't he."

Day made a strangled noise. "Drowning?"

"I needed to pick my moment. What better?" He looked up at Day with the beatific smile of someone who was sure he'd done nothing wrong. "You can't tell the others. You have to keep it a secret. You know why."

Unspoken: *You know what I'll tell them.* That Day had given him an order, an order too delicate to be entrusted to paper.

Peters understood the power of a well-placed lie.

"And Carter? Tulloch?"

"I didn't do anything to them!"

They scrambled two paces apart, staring at each other. The wind whistled down the culvert like it was trying to blow them off the rocky ground. Peters looked uneasy. A little bit afraid of him. A little titillated by that fact.

"I swear," Peters said, "I'll help you. I'll go this way." And he left, Day staring after him; that coat swishing and crackling into the very silhouette of Stevens.

Rocks gleamed like a jawbone against the twilight sky. The snow beneath was thin.

We should never have left the ship—

"Carter?" Day called. The wind whipped the name away like a jealous lover. In the distance, he thought he heard the scraps of a voice, low and urgent.

He looked around wildly.

"Stevens?"

The wind chuckled.

A crunch. A slide backwards. Day put out his hand, the horrible thought passing through his head, *I'll break my ankle—*

Dead weight—

The fall was only a few feet, but it knocked the air out of him nonetheless. He blinked, coughed. The shallow crevasse he'd fallen into was open to the peachy gray of the Arctic sky. A corridor led to the north, where Day could see pockets of shadow and light, the aurora prickling. Above, uneven boulders peered down like a row of judgmental observers.

He picked himself up, his heart pounding so hard it made his extremities tingle. He almost didn't see Carter, huddled against the rock face, but a wink of orange light above showed him the coppery color of his second lieutenant's hair.

Day exhaled with relief. "There you are."

Carter was facing away from him, curled into a ball, arms wrapped around his knees. He didn't turn around.

"Carter?" Day said cautiously. "Are you—"

The light shifted again, and the snow around Carter shimmered an unlikely shade of pale apricot. He still didn't turn. Just kept facing the wall.

"It's all my fault."

Day felt a slow crawling sensation moving up his spine.

"Carter." He gave it all the authority he could muster. "Turn around."

It wasn't the auroral light. The snow had settled unevenly, but around Carter it was a ghastly pinkish red, the color of meat hung up to bleed. The color of the Arctic sun shining through canvas, into a tent filled with dying men.

Day took another step closer.

Carter turned slowly, his neck moving by degrees, like a jam-jar lid being twisted off. His features looked haggard, the corners of his lips thinner than they had any right to be.

"Blood," he said numbly. "So much of it."

Day looked down. Carter's boot prints had broken through the crust, creating pits of burgundy.

Day exhaled a long, shaky breath of relief. "It's just red snow."

Carter shook his head. With a small start, he seemed to see where he was—the deep dark walls of the cave—and Day, crouched opposite. He shook his head again.

"It's just red snow," Day said again. "Some sort of plant life. Harmless." He offered his hand. "Come on. Why on earth did you leave camp?"

The wind whistled through the cave, rising, rising, until it made a plaintive shriek. Then silence.

"I couldn't sleep. I don't know how anyone can sleep out here." A half-laugh. "I'm not afraid to die—that's what I signed up for. But I should have saved Evan. And Tulloch—"

"What about Tulloch?"

Carter didn't answer.

Day's skin prickled.

Carter pressed his hand into the watermelon snow. "You should leave me. I'm full of scurvy, I know it. Debility. Raddled. Rotting from the inside. I'm no good. I should have saved him!"

"It's not your fault. You can't blame yourself for Evan."

Carter looked up when Day said Holt's Christian name, the whites of his eyes grayish. Something passed between them, something Day thought he'd never recognize in another living being, or have recognized in turn.

Carter's face was so open and honest it made Day afraid for him. This wasn't a world where some men could afford to want openly.

And if some of that secret had created Stevens—

"You loved him," Day said aloud. "And we're not going to leave you. Not while you live, I swear. Look, it's only—for God's sake, it's just—"

But any explanations died on his lips. Because Carter's right hand was covered in blood.

Real blood.

"Tulloch," Day said. It all came sharply into focus. "What did you do to Tulloch?"

Carter pointed to the other end of the gulley.

Day had to crawl on his hands and knees to get through. He looked back halfway, suddenly struck with a sense that Carter was coming after him, a rock clutched in his bloody hand.

But he hadn't moved. Just knelt there trembling.

When Day could straighten up again, he was struck dumb, unable even to shiver. Twilight was creeping up with a cold glow on the horizon, picking out more of that vermillion snow.

Tulloch.

He was hanging by his arms, stuck into a crevice, as if he'd been dragged up the rock face by an unseen force. Slit from his breastbone to his groin, his insides were pulled out until it was impossible to tell what was gore-soaked clothing and what was flesh. There was something ritualistic about it.

But also—something animal.

Tulloch's face was captured in a wide-eyed look of terror, jaw distended in a permanent scream. His teeth stained red. Day could imagine the confusion. The chaos. The smell of freshly spilled blood, meaty and abominable, iron-rich and vital, the special stink that only *life* gave. A smell so powerful that it drowned everything else out.

Reduced Day to his component parts.

Unmade him.

———

The hunger of Cape Verdant was like nothing he'd felt before or since. It made itself known on a base, deep, primal level. Every cell in his body screaming out for something, anything: anything to make the pain stop. This was why men ate boots, rope, the planks of their boat, then howled in agonies as their body tried to take sustenance from inedible things. People didn't talk about how excruciating hunger could be. It could drive you mad. A serpent endlessly devouring its own tail. You'd eat *yourself*, if you could. Corpses were found with bloody fingers stuffed into their own mouths.

Day hadn't been able to taste meat since. When he'd returned to London, he'd taken only fish, bread, and fruit. He'd always made sure no one could watch him eat: the ship's wardroom had been slow torture. He'd have rather gone hungry than have people see him putting things into his mouth.

Staring up at Tulloch, Day could feel that hunger again.

The blood had frozen glassy and shimmering. A horrible vitality was stirring in his bones. Something he'd carried with him for a very long time.

Hunger was only a few letters apart from anger.

Will, come back to me.

Tulloch's wrists were bent at unnatural angles. He'd clearly fought.

As Day stumbled closer, he could see that the rib cage had been cracked, the insides scooped out, the heart removed. As if someone had simply reached in, impatient for the feast.

———————

Day was screaming, "Why, why," into Carter's terrified face. There was a sort of high-pitched whine in the air, like the ringing after cannon fire.

Carter's mouth was bloody, and he spat out a tooth.

Scurvy, Day thought. He could see those teeth sinking into Tulloch's exploded rib cage, chewing at it, ripping fabric and skin, hoping that would save him. A ravenous consumption.

"I didn't!" Carter was on his back, struggling to raise himself up onto his elbows, and he shouldn't be so weak—

You can't let anyone see how weak you are.

Carter crying over Holt.

Day crying over Stevens.

He could hear his father: *Do you hear me, William, you can't ever show it. This is for your own good.*

The birch. The shame. The confused mass of feelings, dense and tender and awful, William Day had once felt for his bunkmate, and known he could confide to no one. There was no place for weakness out here. That high-pitched whine was filling him up: rage, all the rage he'd nursed and suppressed, for fear it made him a monster.

He saw himself pinning Carter to the ground, grabbing a rock.

Raising it.

Time slowing down . . .

Carter's face was gummy with frozen blood, and his shout echoed around the cave. "I came out here to die!"

Then—get on with it.

Day punched the rock into Carter's face. The blow had the texture of a hard-boiled egg, and a tiny spatter of blood flew up into Day's eyes. Like a blessing, or a curse. Like an anointing, and he was the chosen one, wasn't he?

The *Reckoning*'s captain.

Come home.

Day raised the rock again.

You'll die last.

It was harsh and unfair, but so was life.

———

A knife pressed to the nape of Day's neck. It made him freeze, brought him back into himself: he could suddenly hear the panting of his breath, the pulse hammering in his ears.

"You're here."

The mingled relief and horror made him weak at the knees.

Day put his hands up, very slowly, and struggled to stand, the knife allowing him up inch by inch. It was sharp, he knew, antler-hilted. The same knife Stevens had used to saw away at the frozen corpses.

He took a deep shuddering breath. "You're here again."

But it was Peters's voice that answered, very calmly: "What have you done?"

Day glanced at Tulloch's corpse—the approaching daylight made it seem to sway—then down.

Carter wasn't moving.

"Carter?" Day said, the chill air reaching every part of him at once. "Thom?"

Peters manhandled him until the two of them were face-to-face. "I knew it," he said, a little breathless. "William Day. It's you at last, isn't it? The butcher of Cape Verdant. I *knew*."

Day said nothing.

"You did him first." Peters nodded at Tulloch. "Then Carter must have come across you. And you crawled back to the tent and lay down beside us. Clever."

"It wasn't me."

"I don't *mind*." Peters moistened his lips. "I told you. I came because I needed to see it for myself."

"I didn't do it." The horror was rising. Carter still wasn't moving. "We need to get help."

"I didn't bring the mask." A sly smile. "But you didn't need it, did you? Of course not. You're William Day."

"It wasn't me!" Day screamed, and Peters snapped back: "Are you so sure?"

Silence.

The tail end of that rage. The hunger. It was submerging itself again, to unfathomable depths, like a great whale descending to avoid the hunt. Flicking its tail in the deep. Stirring up the surface. Keeping him from rest.

"Were you going to *eat* him?"

It was so dark that Peters looked like a skull floating in the gloom. Frost-smoke wreathed him as he breathed out, and disappointment bloomed on his face. "No. Oh. Well."

Peters nudged Carter with the toe of his boot. He moved, very faintly, spit and blood freezing in the corner of his mangled mouth.

Peters's own lips curled. "They'll think it was you, though," he said distantly. "For desertion. They'll think you went mad when you discovered them. Like you did with Sinclair. You have a reputation."

His face said: *It's so hard to escape your own reputation.*

"It wasn't me." Day dragged a hand across his mouth. He looked at Carter. "Not really."

"No." Peters's voice was matter-of-fact. "Of course I know that."

He still hadn't lowered the knife.

"But they'll think it all the same. They'll see this as a captain who lost control, then his mind—sending them out into winter with a couple of savages and a few tents." His eyes gleamed. "We'll go back. Get her boilers up and running. Make ready. We'll bring back the *Reckoning*. It's our chance for glory."

Day's skin crawled. "I should have executed you while I had the chance."

Peters looked at him calmly. "You won't have to do it," he said. "Captain her, I mean. I'll step in. It's my *turn*."

"I should have told everyone what you did. Murdering one of my officers—"

Peters swallowed. "I don't think you'd have done that," he said. "The thing about Lee was—I barely needed to hold him down. He never saw it coming."

Day remembered, horribly, how convenient it had all seemed. How seductive.

And if Peters had been seduced, who was to say whether it was obsession, or the great invisible pull of the *Reckoning* and her ghosts. The outcome was the same.

He looked at his own bloody hands, remembering the sense of inevitability that had come over him. *You'll die last.*

It would be the loneliest thing in the world.

Later, they told themselves, shivering, that it must have been wild animals. Or Roderick's black-lipped mates, punishing disloyalty with increasingly unhinged, Old Testament fury. *Are you not grateful.* Or perhaps the knocking had started up again on the *Reckoning*, a knocking fit to send them mad, the knocking of their dead and bloated captain, and they were trying to shut it up for a while. Gunshots. A ship under siege from the night.

Avery pointed out the way Tulloch had been hoisted up that rocky slope; the fact that someone must have held him down. No one person could have done it.

But Day thought of the terrible, unnatural strength he'd felt pouring through his veins. The sense that he was someone else—many different someones, roughly stitched together. He couldn't have been the culprit, because he'd been with the others when Tulloch had vanished; they'd seen him screwing up his face in his sleep, wan and troubled.

How do you escape a haunted house, when both the ghost—and the house—are you?

XXVII: THE RED TENT
LAND, OCTOBER 25, 1882

They came across the tent the next day, a scrap of crimson fabric just visible in the drift. Carter dug until his swollen hands were gray with the first signs of frostbite, Lars and Avery working grimly beside him. But the tent was old, and ragged, and empty. Each expedition was layered on the bodies of those who had come before. An accumulation of old bones.

This pass should have led down to the sea ice, but the gathering snow and dark made the depth of the ravine impossible to tell. They'd have to retrace their steps.

"Look."

Avery spread the tent out on the snow like a flayed body, blood-colored and vivid. The flaps were split at the front. There was a large, man-sized hole at the back. Day wrapped his arms around himself. He could almost hear the sound of ripping. Maybe those inside had cut their way out.

Or something else had torn its way in.

Carter straightened up. "It could be them—the men from the *Fox*," he said, his voice croaky. He looked sideways at Day—who was still, after all, the captain. He understood that, with all his training and upbringing and the Admiralty. He *understood*.

But then Avery sat down in the snow, rubbing his foot convulsively, as if all the determination had left him. His ankle was swollen to twice its size, red and angry, and Day knew they'd never get his boot back on. Avery had always had a particular way of walking, side to side, and must have been hiding the injury for some time.

Behind where the tent was buried, they could just make out the deep gouges of a sledge, overloaded, disappearing into the obscurity of mountains and passes and gorges.

Territory.

Daylight appeared and left within four hours.

The snow screamed, furious, outside. "It's bad," Avery's face was cadaverous with pain. "I'm sorry, but I don't think I can." He didn't need to complete the sentence.

A stronger gust of wind tugged at the tent ropes, made the fabric billow. Mrs. Stevens was fanning herself with her long-handled Spanish fan. It was stifling and cold at once, and Qila's hand kept going to her knife, like a newlywed checking that her ring was still there.

Day had thought they'd all get farther. Of course he had.

You don't leave the ship, Stevens said in his ear. *Haven't you learned?*

Shut up, Day snarled. *You always begged to leave.*

Horrified looks told him that he'd said it out loud; Day nearly laughed. He should be used to those looks by now. "That's enough," he snapped, his heart racing. It was hard to think over the perpetual din of blowing snow.

They'd had to camp almost on top of the abandoned tent. They weren't going to get any farther while it was like this. Hard decisions were coming. Avery was a cripple. Peters a murderer; a prisoner.

Dead weight.

This is why you don't leave the ship, Stevens said again, very close.

Mrs. Stevens's fan marked time. The snow thudded off canvas, and the sky was the darkness of the *Reckoning*'s hold.

"He can't go on," Qila said suddenly. "You know that."

The pressure continued to build.

"Could he go back?" Mrs. Stevens asked, and Avery shot her a wounded look. But they knew how far they were from the ships.

Day shook his head numbly. They were all looking at him. Someone had to make a decision, didn't they? And if the snow was impassable, if Avery couldn't walk . . .

He swallowed. They hadn't escaped the *Reckoning* at all. None of them had.

Qila's eyes flickered towards the entrance of the tent, as if she'd heard something.

A footstep.

Day held his breath.

No—a *large* footstep. Something indescribably heavy was walking around camp, impossibly audible over the sounds of the weather. The flap of canvas came like a gunshot, and he squeezed his eyes tightly shut.

Everyone in the tent was very still.

Another footfall. Whatever it was, it was behind them now.

"What is that?" Mrs. Stevens whispered, and Qila clapped her hand over the medium's mouth.

The thing outside seemed to pause, although there was no way it could have heard them.

Avery mouthed, eyes wide: "Bears."

Silence inside. Day felt something creeping around to the front of the tent, bit by bit; the suggestion of a shadow on canvas. But it was impossible. There was no light outside to cast that shadow, that large and menacing shape, moving quietly and stealthily on all fours, that sense of oppression—

"*It stalks you even now*," someone said in Day's ear, and he let out a harsh yell.

Stevens was crouched right beside him. His face a ruin, the features blurred as if he'd been underwater for a very long time. Stevens's skin was sloughing off, waxy and unreal, and he smelled of slowly blooming flesh. *The Open Polar Sea*, Day thought madly. The fruits of obsession. *This is what it does to you.*

He couldn't stand it. Qila grabbed his arm as he stumbled up, tearing the flaps open, to launch himself into the snow—

———————

Day blinked.

There was no sign at all of their other tent, the *Resolution*'s familiar brown canvas one, which should have been pitched directly opposite.

The snow had been blowing all day; the little *red* tent in front of him was dusted with it, benign as though snow had never killed anyone.

Something was behind him. Something awful. He could smell it on the breeze. He pressed his eyes shut and scrambled forwards—

He was inside that torn-up red tent, the one they'd just found. Three men, sleeping bags laced up tight, looked at him with sunken eyes. When one opened his mouth, silently screaming or begging, Day could see the severed roots of his tongue. The ground cloth was wet with blood, and the smoky remnants of a fire blackened the canvas from within.

That sense of *presence* outside.

A slow, deliberate ripping sound.

Day turned, slowly, to see the red fabric start to yawn like a mouth. A *bear*. An animal-headed man.

Sobbing to himself, he crawled blindly, shoving off the hands that wanted to pull him back—

And he was in another red tent. Redder than before. Red everywhere.

No. No, please, not this one. Not this.

Day could hear a creek outside, the chatter of water saying, *what'll you do, what'll you do.*

He was inside the sick-tent on Amelia's Pass at last.

It stank. The men inside had already been dying by inches.

"Water," Diamond was saying feebly, "water," not seeming to realize that everyone in the tent was too far gone to hear or care.

Outside, Day heard the sound of a sledge being dragged over scree, slow and determined. Leaving them behind. The sunlight shone relentless through the canvas, making everything *red red red*, a horrible cacophony. Rips and tears let in dazzling fingers of light, bright enough to make him shade his eyes. Someone was pulling at his feet, and he let out a tiny panicked scream.

It shouldn't be sunlight.

He shouldn't be here.

Diamond managed to lift himself up on his elbows. He looked

across at Day. "You," he said, very simply. "You." As if he'd always known who was the architect of this massacre.

Diamond's rib cage was cracked like something had burst out of it; Day felt the same hollow pressure in his own. Crawling to the tent flap, Day could see—in the distance, vanishing—the last dark shapes leaving. A tall golden-haired man was bringing up the rear, his sharp features turned to the sky. Then a crunch of rocks.

Then nothing, the sigh and silence of dying men.

The red tent. The worst thing he'd ever done. It haunted him.

———————

"It wasn't my idea," Day was sobbing. "I shouldn't have let him—"

Avery shook him. Wild, furious eyes, incandescent with righteous anger.

You don't leave the ship—

What was out on the ice had caught up with him at last.

Day had thought it would be crawling bodies, revenants, limbless men. But it was this.

"Stop lying to us," Avery said fiercely, and Day could see winter darkness all around, two perfectly normal brown-colored tents from the *Resolution*, the remnants of a fire; Lars watching them warily, ready to intervene.

Those ghostly red tents were gone, but this was still a grave. A haunted house.

He'd thought he could escape it, but it was built from his secrets.

And there was a monster in the attic.

THEN

On Amelia's Pass, all days are the same. Bright hazy sunlight; even squinting hurts. They travel at the rate of their invalids, Sheppard bringing up the rear. No one has ever crossed this part of the interior, and for all Day knows, this purgatory goes on forever. Talbot's Channel seems impossibly far south, as if they're hauling their boats over a distance that keeps increasing.

They make five miles a day. Then four. Then, finally—Fingal's feet rotting away in his boots—Day has to call a halt.

"They can't walk any farther." Dr. Nye takes off his spectacles, rubs his sharp beady eyes. "We'll have to carry them."

Day snorts. "Carry them? As if anyone has the strength."

They are bow-backed, now, close to the ground. Two indescribable winters of poor rations and ill use; they are stunted men, and the daylight won't make them any stronger. They just sit down wherever they stop. Jimmy Graham has been half-carried, surreptitiously, by some of Sheppard's favorite men.

They stop for the night, the eight hours of unwavering daylight only Day and the doctor know for sure to be nighttime. A little stream splashes and gurgles. Some of the men crawl to it, play their fingers listlessly in its chilly shallows.

They're not like you and me.

It's a flattering thought, but it keeps Day awake, worrying at it like a loose tooth. The petition is a way to divest themselves of dead weight; he carries it close to his breast.

They've started to pitch the sick-tent farther and farther downwind each night, distancing themselves from the smells and noises: Jimmy's sharp exclamations of pain as the sepsis gnaws at his bones; Vogel's wheeze. Ewing tries to lead them in prayer, and Day doesn't have the heart to tell him it's useless. They've started to warm their frostbitten fingers by stuffing them into their own mouths, and the sight disturbs him.

Day can hear someone walking outside. He smiles, a wide smile that hurts his cracked lips. *Stevens.* Keeping watch over them, as always. Day pulls on the rolled-up jumper that serves as his pillow, then quietly pushes his head and shoulders into the crisp midnight sun.

He's grabbed from behind.

He opens his mouth, but a hand comes over it. A very warm bare hand, pressing his lips shut; he struggles instinctively. Jackson pauses in his snoring.

"Don't move." A familiar voice in his ear. "Stay very, very quiet. Look."

The unforgiving sunlight makes distances into warm toffee—near or far, though, the sick-tent is hanging accusingly open.

There's a snuffling sound. Wet. Avid.

Her long neck entirely hidden inside the tent, the polar bear is making a low huffing noise like an oversized dog.

"Don't shout," Stevens says. "Stay still." He uncovers Day's mouth. The bear's massive hindquarters dwarf the tent, making it impossible to see the men inside. She has yellowish fur, must be old and determined. She's followed them there, hungry and intent, for a reckoning.

This is why, Day thinks hysterically, *you don't leave the ship—*

The muscles ripple in the bear's neck, and Day sees the same motion in Stevens. "Don't move," he whispers, crouched beside Day in the pale lemon sun.

The bear shakes herself. Lean and hungry-looking, she's investigating the sick-tent for an easy meal. The men inside might be awake. Might be lying utterly still, watching the beady black eyes inspect them, feeling the horrible warmth of the bear's breath. Or they might be asleep, nudged gently by a curious snout, like a dog trying to wake its master.

Day thinks about waving his arms, shouting, drawing attention. Stevens is holding a rifle: a distraction would allow him to shoot. But Day does nothing. He does as Stevens says, as if they're the only two men left on earth.

A cough from inside the sick-tent.

The bear sweeps to the side, and suddenly there's an explosion of scuffling. The tent bulges with panicked movement, shadowy figures appearing against the canvas. One paw lifts, and the bear plunges her entire torso inside.

A muffled scream. Day will think, later, how quiet it all was. The silence of Amelia's Pass hangs over them, the sun low and watchful, and there's a restrained . . . *patter* when a spurt of arterial blood paints the tent flap from the inside.

Day knows he should do something.

"No," Stevens hisses. "No. She'll take the weak, and move on."

Dead weight.

The bear makes a sinister sound of curiosity, and there's a frightened "Please—" in Jimmy's voice. The sound of timber snapping, a figure visible in silhouette, and then another voice, small, choked, that Day recognizes as the doctor's.

He feels Stevens tense. They both know they can't afford to lose the doctor.

"Trust me." It sounds a little like Stevens is trying to convince himself.

The bear roars, and Day hears men waking up.

"Oh, hell." Stevens shoves him onto the ground.

The bear starts to back out of the tent, her wide torso struggling to fit through, and Day can see something of the terrible scene within: the visibility is absolutely merciless. It's as though a spell has been broken. The men stop playing dead, and start screaming. Nye crawls out from under the ground cloth, rolls himself into the stream. The bear catches sight of him, and with two steps of her powerful legs she's on top of him, swiping at his face.

But then she leaves him. Goes back into the tent, drags Vogel out by the neck, and he's still alive, screaming, and trying to hold his hands to the gushing wound. Everyone behind Day is shouting. The bear turns and *roars* at them, a horrible primal sound, bouncing off the empty sky, coming from everywhere all at once.

As she drags Vogel she's coming closer. They're next.

"Captain—" Sheppard shouts.

"Will," Stevens says urgently.

Day nods.

Stevens's rifle rings out like the trumpets of Judgment Day. Blood sprays out of Vogel's chest. He falls limp. Another shot rings out. This one goes into the sick-tent, and there's a wet thump.

None of Stevens's bullets go anywhere near the polar bear.

She bares her teeth, raising herself up to her full height. Jumps, bouncing, onto Vogel's face. He is very still. She starts to drag him away.

"Nobody move!" Stevens hisses. Everyone obeys. Except Nye, who's whimpering, trying to crawl crab-like back into the tent, hands pressed over the ruin of his face.

They wait.

Sounds start to return: the trickle of the stream; Day's harsh breathing; Ewing muttering, "Oh my God." It's the first time Day's heard him blaspheme. The crunch of rocks as the polar bear drags Vogel's body, implacably, around the corner where the stream widens. It's the longest sound in the world.

The doctor is alive, and will live: his wounds have missed an eye. Jimmy Graham is dead; Stevens had used the opportunity to put one clean bullet in his forehead. Diamond is dying, his breath rattling through the inside-out chaos of his rib cage.

Three others have been badly mauled, and probably won't survive the next few days. Day feels it in his pocket, as if by mute condemnation: the petition. *Now we can leave them*, he thinks.

Finally.

Without the sick men, they have a better chance of making it to the channel, before it closes up for winter with them on the wrong side.

"We have to—" he says, looking around the circle of terrified faces. "There's blood everywhere. More will come."

Sheppard brandishes his rifle. "I'll go after the bear." There's a horrible bitterness in his voice. "That'll feed us for weeks. *Now.*"

"Don't be stupid," someone says. "You can't take down that thing alone," and Day clings to it, just for a second: this idea that Stevens couldn't have prevented the bear attack even if he'd wanted to.

He then discards it for the lie he knows it to be.

"Captain," Nye slurs through his ripped-up mouth. "The injured men?"

Day he can feel Stevens's gray eyes fixed on him. Something is starting to break inside.

We're survivors, you and I.

I   knew all along. That he was a monster. That he was a murderer. I lived with him on that ship for two years before he killed Talbot, and I wasn't *blind*."

Time begins anew.

There's no longer a William Day living in the perpetual present of God-Saves Harbor and Amelia's Pass and Cape Verdant, and another one, out in the real world, telling a story; trying to keep closed a cage that insists on rattling.

They're one and the same.

And the only time is—

Now.

Day coughs. It's raw, and the tears are making his eyes smart.

"But I was *desperate*."

A pause. No one rushes to fill it. He'd been so desperate that he'd looked at Jesse Stevens—the noble curves of his face in the failing light, his body golden and well made, the culmination of all Day's desires, and thought: *This is the only way.*

"I knew he was eating our dead. I knew he—I could have worked out what he meant to do with Sheppard. But I closed my eyes. Closed my eyes to all of it." Day gulps in an unsteady breath, almost a laugh. He can't look at Avery.

If William Day had turned out a monster, it was because he'd always had one at his side.

The disappearing *huff* of a polar bear on the wind, stalking away, its dread purpose fulfilled.

"I just didn't think—I didn't think he'd ever leave me. It was easier to tell myself I'd never known. It was easier than—to believe that."

———

The rock above them discloses the shape of Olive Emeline Stevens, silhouetted against the stars, wrapped in Qila's shawl. It's zero degrees, and the lack of wind is only scant comfort.

"I suppose I always knew he'd done something terrible," she says to Day as he sits down, feeling his bones creak. "In my heart. Although it didn't matter to me. Is that so bad? But—I don't think I could have abandoned or killed all those men. To let the others—*myself*—live."

"I think you could have," Day says, truthfully. She's hard-edged as anyone. "Desperation will do that to you."

She doesn't argue. There's a resignation to her gaze as she looks out over the swoop of granite hills, and he remembers that she comes from somewhere barren herself. The papers had sneered at her background, her number of unmarried sisters; at her loudmouthed father, his insistence that she was a servant of the devil; at the strap marks welted into the backs of her hands. Day has seen them once or twice, deep and parallel, like the lines that railway man's nephew would never build through the Yukon.

He understands why she wears gloves so often. Like him, she'd prefer to hide all traces of where she's come from.

"Well," she says at length. "Maybe."

The temperature is starting to drop.

"What will you do?" he asks. "Would you still go back to him?"

Her laugh is a rich, droll, drawing-room sort of sound. Something constructed, as carefully put together as the story of William Day.

"Are you making me an offer?"

Day shifts. She smiles, gentle. "I don't think you've got much interest in that kind of thing, though, have you," she says. "Women. I can understand why Jesse never spoke of you."

"We never," he says.

Her eyebrows are two perfect arches drawn on her face.

"We *never*," he insists, too loud and painful, although he doesn't know whether that's a shame or—when looked at carefully—the only thing that saved him.

"He never spoke of you," she repeats, slowly, and he finds his mouth twisting. Because Stevens places great significance in silence.

"We may not have," Day allows. "I won't say I didn't *want* to." He breathes out. "And you're right—I'm not interested in a wife. But I'm interested in you. Olive."

It feels wrong to keep calling her Mrs. Stevens, after their shared past.

"William." He feels her shiver through his shoulder, the place where they're connected. "I'll separate from him. I know some useful people. Reformists. Quakers." She was, in the end, a very different type of dreamer to her husband. "They might help me, if I can live apart from him, if I'm in a position to hold sittings again. And I think—after this—I will be."

A pause.

"I just couldn't sleep beside him." She speaks in a rush, as if saving Day the pain of picturing this. "Knowing what he really looks like . . . wondering whether he's dreaming. If he thinks about all this. Or if there's something missing. A hole where his conscience should be."

Day remembers lying in his bunk, hearing Stevens sleeping above. He doesn't believe Stevens dreams like a human. No, he probably falls into the oblivion of shapes and sounds experienced by animals.

"What will you do?"

"I'll tell the truth," she says fiercely. "About him. About all of this."

She's fighting back tears. He can imagine the stage, red flocked velvet curtains; the smell of smog, a city, the seat of civilization. No wide-open spaces. A true story of Arctic hubris: a good man gone bad.

"Qila will help. She's got the presence to her. She'll draw a crowd."

"You were a fraud," he says. "Before. Weren't you?"

She laughs. "I was a *good* one. I think that's what he liked about me. And—he let me continue my work, make money, be useful. So many wouldn't have granted me that liberty." A shiver. "Sometimes, it was possible to believe I really was gifted, that I knew things no one else did. And I used it to help him. To find men who'd believe a little too much." It's plain that the thought of those men still has the capacity to unnerve her.

"Some of the things I made up—it was wicked. Abominable. To play with their hearts like that. Some wept," she says, examining her gloves. "Some went—cold. Silent. Hard. Others didn't even blink. And once you have them in the palm of your hand . . ."

This, Day understands, was the help she was to render the expedition, if Stevens wasn't back by the second summer. If his authority needed shoring up. She was to cruise in as the emissary from another world, one who'd tell them exactly what Stevens wanted to hear.

"I was meant to bring more girls," she says, very faintly. "As many as I could. I don't know why I didn't try harder. And with Qila—I told myself she would probably run away before we met him, so it was all right."

They both sit with it a while, the horror.

Day looks at her sideways, unable to tell if she feels, as he does every day: the burning shame. The urge to hide.

"I didn't know," she says fiercely. "I didn't *know*. Don't look at me like that."

He looks down. Examines his grubby, bloody hands.

"I didn't know what you'd done!" She flings it at him like a missile. "I just wanted something better than what I had. Have I eaten anyone? Don't you dare say it's my fault! I won't. I won't!"

"Sometimes," Day says quietly, and shoves his hands back into his sleeves, "it takes a while."

Shame blossoms, he knows, like hoarfrost.

She looks up at the bitter sky. "Well. Has it helped you?"

It's too cold to be outside any longer. They're too far from the ships to return.

"If you need company, when you get back . . ." Day says at length, his voice thick.

She nods. A small hand worms its way into his. He's never liked her before this moment.

"You could tell me more about the Nile, and your other journeys," he says. "Maybe I'll visit New York, and we can sit by the fire. You can tell me about your adventures, where it's warm and there's no sea. No ice."

No Day. No Stevens.

That night, the moon is bright enough to shine through the tent like a searchlight, and Day holds up his hands to it, examining their bones. Anyone could see them now, he thinks. Anything on the ice.

Let them come, whether they be a bear or a man or a corpse. *Let them come.*

That thing he'd feared, his whole life—it's here and now.

Avery had spent the evening scribbling. Now he's taken something for the pain, is sleeping so deeply that Day can barely hear his breath. Day winds a blanket around his face to block out the light, like he's preparing himself for burial. He keeps Peters by his side; for now, Day uses bootlaces to tie his ankles and wrists together, carefully weighing the odds between escape and frostbite from obstructed circulation.

"You could just let me go," Peters whispers. "Let me leave. Who'd be any the wiser?"

But Peters is going to live, to face what's coming to him.

Day wakes to grunting. Snuffling.

There's something in the tent.

Something huge, pressing down on his chest with its stinking bulk, crushing the air from his lungs. He can't open his mouth.

It's found me, Day thinks. *After all that, it's found me.*

He can't move. He can't see. All he knows is that the bear has finally come to collect.

He scrabbles to get the blankets off his face. The moon casts a ghastly, cheesy color over everything, and the tent walls billow outwards. It's just him and—

Avery is on his back, making the horrible wet sounds Day associates with an animal attack. A gurgle. Avery's hands beat against that heaving dark shape, a silhouette that makes no sense against the ceaseless white noise of the moon. It's hunched and tall, bulky and angular, and when Avery's hand connects with its head—

It tips back a long pale throat.

Day can't move. He can hear people outside, but inside the tent it's so quiet, muffled. Like the scene is coming from far away, has taken a long time to get here.

The bear leans in to plant an open-jawed kiss. In the guttural moan that follows, Day realizes that he can see Avery's tongue through the wet ruin of his face—

Avery goes limp. Refuses to fight it. Day knows what that's like. He thinks, numb, that he could just stay still himself: wait for the danger to pass.

We're survivors, you and I—

But then Peters sits up and looks over at Day, and there's no bear at all. His mouth and lips are streaked with a vizard of blood.

Day's suddenly able to move, the weight gone from his legs. The light becomes fragmented, clouds passing over the surface of the moon, and Avery turns his head, groaning, blood bubbling through his jaw. Peters is still just looking at Day, and his broad shoulders— *Where did they come from?* Day thinks—seem hunched and bulky like the haunches of a bear.

He's still bound hand and foot; he'd used the only weapon left to him.

Peters grins. The creature had been mundane and real. No phantom bear. No ghouls out on the ice. The realization is so all-encompassing, Day can hardly endure it.

How thin and fragile, those walls separating each of them from a monster.

Peters opens his mouth, very deliberately, and spits something out. It's the tip of Avery's tongue. He says, wetly, "Speak no evil."

XXVIII: HAUNTED HOUSES

When Day leaves the next morning, Qila wants to go with him. He refuses: he doesn't put it past Peters to worm his way out of those restraints, disappear into the north to die. *He shouldn't get away that easily.* Qila gives Day a sideways look which clearly conveys, in any language, that she isn't sure about his ability to follow through.

She'd found faith in him—lost it again, in the way of all young people growing up.

The sky is still dark, and will be for hours. November is coming, and with it all the terrors of the cold season. Day doesn't know how far he'll have to go. But he'll go out alone—with his hunger, his anger, haunting, *curse*—and make an end to this.

"Promise me you'll find him," Olive whispers, raising her chin. A taut strength to her. "Free his men from . . . whatever hold he still has."

He clasps her hands, and nods.

"Tell them—about me. And promise me that, whatever he says . . ."

Day thinks of all the years she'd spent with Stevens, and before that: all the things an uneducated woman from a poor, religious family must have had to swallow to get where she is today. *I struggled.* They bend their heads close together; she still smells of rot, dead things being repurposed into life. "Get to safety," he says, very quietly. "I won't be blamed for killing you, too."

She laughs, that rich drawing-room chuckle. "Come back, William Day," she says. "I feel we've only just met each other, you and I."

He doesn't bother giving Lars any final instructions, just clasps his shoulder and squeezes. Lars is a far better tracker, hunter, and survivor, a far better man, than William Day: if anyone can lead them to Nathaniel, it's him.

"You must stay," Olive says. "*Please.*"

She's not talking to him, though: she's smoothing down Qila's sealskin jacket, wrapping a muffler around her neck, as though appearance is very important for the horrific journey ahead. Qila's impatient scowl dissolves into the reflection of a smile when she catches Day's eye: there are many different kinds of love, in a world that fundamentally lacks it, and whatever Day had felt for Stevens hadn't been wrong.

Except for the fact that it was Stevens.

Looking into the tent, Avery's jaw is bandaged in the cleanest rags they have, but he's lost a lot of blood, and his face is the color of whey. His life's work has eaten him up. Day doubts he'll ever wake.

The blood has dried on Peters's chin, gobbets of dark flesh in the

stubble, and he looks so wild and so handsome that Day can't get too
close. Carter gives him a kick, numb with horror: "Come on. Get up."

No one is getting left behind; Peters will haul if he wants to live.

Peters catches Day's eye and gives him a slow, insolent wink. His
pupils are huge, the iris the exact color of the *Reckoning*'s great shiny
bell.

What do you do with a haunted house? They've tried running. Day
doesn't think it can be destroyed. The only thing to do is to go after the
house's architect; prevent him from ever building another. Whoever
had left the tattered tent had gone inland, and so would Day.

He doesn't really expect to make it back alive.

The snow comes down so thick it's like a blanket pulled over a dead
man's face. The grayness swirls densely around him. Staring at the curves
of the terrain, half-glimpsed, Day expects to see an ursine head peering
back. The movement of moonlight on the ground ahead becomes the
swish of a giant paw.

The feeling of being followed is so powerful that he stops in the
ravine and waits. The snow whirls, stinging like a thousand tiny needles. It's madness to be out.

He thinks he hears the sound of pebbles falling. Impossible to see
anything.

To the north, Day can discern the faintest flicker of green lights.
The color makes him think of Hopkins, sitting in his velvet armchair
with ankle crossed neatly over knee, leaning forwards, gold-green eyes
burning: "We don't want another *Reckoning*."

When he first encounters the tracks, they seem to come from
nowhere. The snow is blowing underfoot, and there's no reasonable
way that it's packed hard enough for anything to leave a trace. But here
they are.

Day bends down, feeling every single pound of weight on his back,
his tent and india-rubber ground sheet becoming like iron chains around

his neck. His knees make a dull noise, and he puts a frozen glove over his mouth—well, an inch from his mouth, he isn't stupid—to try to stifle the sound that comes out. He knows these prints, huge and rounded.

The bear must be ahead of him. He's walking towards it, and all it represents, at last.

He feels the awful weight of a stare on his back. He's almost sure he sees something withdrawing into the shadow of the rocks.

"Who's there?" he calls. The snow swallows away his voice. He can't afford to stop walking to investigate; it's always warmer when it's snowing, and he doesn't want to risk traveling at night, when his spirit stove will be the difference between life and death.

The paw prints lead on.

The moon glimmers overhead for a second, and Day scrambles backwards at the sight of a hunched dark shape looming on the rocks above. Crouching. Watching. He can see its chest moving in and out. But then it vanishes, becomes just another part of the landscape, and the blood rushes back to his fingers and toes like they've been dipped in molten metal.

The tracks become blurred, dragging.

Like it dragged Vogel, Day thinks. Half-dead and dying. The bullet Stevens put in Vogel's chest was a mercy, wasn't it? Wasn't it?

He honestly doesn't know anymore.

So many people might have lived, if Day and Stevens had never met, and Day won't lie to tell himself otherwise.

Then it's not a paw print, but a footprint. Someone is walking ahead of him, and Day is following their tracks.

"God," he whispers.

He thinks he hears a laugh in the darkness. Of course, Stevens has always considered himself a sort of god.

"Eat the world," he calls into the void. "Isn't that what you always said?"

He doesn't think there was ever a bear. Like Stevens, it was something created from nothing. Something that had come to embody destruction.

"Is that what you did with your men? Is that why we can't find them?" There's a trickle of stones in the gulley behind him. A wavering figure ahead.

"What did you do with the *Fox*?"

Stevens pauses.

"Did you scuttle her, in the end?" Day's voice catches at the sheer waste of it. He chokes out a laugh. "Who do you think you are—"

The shape charges at him. Grabs him by the throat. Its fingers are blue and bony and bare despite the whistling Arctic sky. It's wearing a polar bear's head; from the bloody cavity of the throat, Stevens's white face stares out, his eyes burning cold and furious as the stars.

"*What* do you think I am, Will?" he hisses. No steam comes from those pursed lips. Day can see that Stevens is barefoot, leaving tracks in the snow somewhere between those of a man and a bear.

"You're my conscience," Day wheezes. "You're my—fear. My shame. All the things I tried to pin down, put in a box and hide. But the box rattled. Even in London, it rattled, and I couldn't get rid of you—" He almost laughed. "Not while I was there. So I brought you here. Some part of me must have craved freedom."

"I'd have liked to see London," Stevens says, and snaps his pearly teeth an inch from Day's throat. "To have met the old men at your Admiralty. The Arctic Council. Men who've seen the ice but missed the point." His lips twist. "They say it's for empire, but do they really admit—in their drawing rooms, over their port and cheese—what it's like up here, what it is they *really* like about it? When they've gnawed on raw meat, or fought over scraps, or been forced to choose who lives and who dies. To hold another life in the palm of your hand . . . to have a place where you can truly be free, without shackles or small-mindedness. Where nothing is sacred, and nothing is forbidden. It's the hypocrisy I can't stand, the lack of honesty about what this entails. And why men are drawn to pursue all the darkness and the glamour of it. Who doesn't long to be a *king*?

"I'd like very much, Will, to have met your Amelia. Wasn't that what you called this stretch of the savage lands?"

Stevens shrugs back his shoulders, like something spreading its wings at last, and Day knows he isn't talking to Stevens at all, not anymore. This is something they've made, bigger and far darker. The weight of ambition. Of greed.

Ready to—

"Eat the world," the manifestation finishes. "Come on. Let's get on with it. Or are you waiting for me to eat *you*?"

He takes a step closer until they're pressed together, as snug as those nights sharing body heat and a bunk. No one ever talks about it, because it's unavoidable: this shared intimacy, when the fires have gone out, and any touch of metal is capable of taking off flesh. To talk about it is to admit men like Day exist, with Day's desires. So no one ever speaks of how close Stevens's heartbeat had been to his own.

Stevens raises a hand, now, to the curve of Day's jawbone, where his teeth are clenched to snapping point. He presses his cold lips to it.

Day stays still, like an animal before a snake.

"I don't think you have the *stomach* for it," Stevens says conversationally, trailing one finger against Day's carotid artery.

"I'm not afraid of you. And I'm not ashamed!" Day shouts. He's starting to feel the lethargic numbness of cold creeping over him, the almost pleasurable pins and needles that tell him he needs to get moving immediately. But it all seems so hard, and there's so far to go.

Day almost doesn't hear the crunch of boots on rock—until the *thud* rings through his head like a bell.

Blinding pain makes him fall, reaching out to Stevens, hopelessly, as if somehow that'll still save him.

"William."

Someone is whispering in his ear. Low, warm, urgent. An accent of bougainvillea and warm places, bright petals and wind blowing hot against Day's cheek; he's been transported somewhere else entirely. The voice sounds like sunshine, the sort of perfumed sunshine never found in the Arctic.

Maybe I'm dead, Day thinks. He can almost see Talbot's orange groves: bright fruit like miniature suns, a trickling fountain in a court-yard where birds make chattering noises in the trees.

There's a dip, a bump, a stab of pain. The ground falls away.

"William, wake up!"

A horrible lurch of not-quite-recognition. He turns towards the voice, although he can't yet open his eyes. His head feels like someone has rammed a harpoon through it.

"William—"

Sheppard.

Day's shoulders stiffen, and he cracks one eye open with difficulty; all the moisture on his face has frozen, and a harsh wind is blowing.

William, the wind says, almost affectionate.

Tom Sheppard isn't there. Not in person, anyway.

Day comes back to himself.

He's being dragged, like a carcass, through blurry billowing white-ness, covered head to foot in smelly furs. The man pulling the sledge is too ragged to be one of Roderick's, and he's wearing a boxy animal-pelt helmet—when he turns, there's a white foxtail clamped between his teeth to protect his nose and mouth. His eyes are narrowed. Day can only make a croaking sound. The man turns away and resumes hauling.

Footsteps crunch, and he can see another man lumbering behind them, something slung over his shoulder, the flash of brightly striped trousers. Perhaps he imagines the colorful scarf falling away onto the snow, to be trampled and refrozen and forgotten.

No, he thinks, *no.*

Tensing his wrists, Day finds himself lashed to the sledge. He closes his eyes, still dizzy.

When he opens them again, they've stopped, and the men are con-ferring. Qila has been propped up beside him, and the weight of shock makes his tongue far too big for his mouth. He looks around desper-ately, but she's the only other captive. For a moment he thinks she's still unconscious, but then he sees the sliver of white as she flickers an eye in his direction: *stay quiet.*

Their captors aren't Natives—at least, not to the Arctic. They're wearing battered-looking but quite Western gloves, which when peeled off show pale skin at the man's wrist, white as if he'd crawled from under a rock. The man is missing his trigger finger and the one beside it. This strikes him as important, but his head is still ringing, and that previous sense of warm surety, of companionship, can't be grasped—at least, not consciously.

They continue all day and into the night, sometimes dragged, sometimes marched when it appears that immobility might endanger their health. Their captors appear utterly untiring, and Day has his suspicions about where they're getting that strength. On the second day, his lips crack and bleed from the cold, and when one of the men lumbers over, Day croaks: "Please. Water."

He's given it, but all his questions fall on deaf ears.

They've stopped on the shores of what must be a lake, where bamboo canes and scraps of red fabric mark a route through the dune-fields of frozen waves and rotten ice. He's unleashed from the sledge, the pain of standing making him stagger, and they're prodded unceremoniously upright, then half-dragged, half-marched, into the ridges.

They're taking us to kill us, Day thinks.

Qila stumbles, and she's yanked up immediately. She cries out, her eyes furious. Then hisses it away into watchfulness. Playing dead.

I'm sorry. You weren't meant to follow me.

They're on the northern shore, where Carter's search party had been plagued by disappearances. Day had thought it the *Reckoning*— its crawling crew of the dead and damned, recruiting by press gang. But something else has made this patch of land its hunting ground, and he recognizes, above all, the casual cruelty of it.

Raising his head, Day sees a sheer cliff wall of limestone; the whole thing is nestled in the range of dark hills that loom out of the haze in all directions. Well hidden. Silent and heavy as the grave.

As they approach, a cave takes shape. One side contains a building, walls sloping down to the rocks, giving it the appearance of an overturned boat, an impression echoed in the tarry blackness of its timbers. Day already knows those timbers, salt-saturated. This is what's become of the *Fox*.

Across the last few feet of frozen water, a wooden post faces them, standing tall and finger-like against the sky, a small round object at the top. It winks smooth, polished, and crimson in the disappearing sun.

Their captors separate them. Day finds his voice. "No! Let go of her!"

He's backhanded casually across the mouth. Qila shakes her head, lips pressed together, and Day flicks his eyes down to her boot—*Do you have your knife?*—because the camp must be full of men, living in desperation. The sort of men who'd follow Stevens to hell and back. His stomach lurches.

He's quite sure there will be no other women here.

Smoke wafts out of the cave into the darkening sky. There's a horrible restless energy to the scene. As Day is shoved forwards, he can see that the shadowy figures surrounding a smoldering fire are men, thin and shivering. He recoils at the clink of chains.

He looks back at his captors, with their fingerless hands, and can't quite grasp the horror of it all. Qila has been taken out of sight. When he turns back to the men, chained by the fire, one opens his mouth to plead—with missing tongue. Farther along the shore, in the dying light, there's another skinny wooden post. A body hangs; Day can almost hear the busy knives. There's a certain sound that skin makes when it's pulled away from bone.

This is Cape Verdant—a distorted reflection. What it could have been, if things had been otherwise.

Don't give that man a command.

The door to the longhouse yawns open, and it's like being swallowed down a dark and greasy throat. Day is pushed onto the floor. It takes a few moments for his eyes to adjust.

A voice is speaking. "Who shall say that, within the Arctic Circle, dwelling upon some of the islands or shores . . ."

It's a voice that demands to be heard. It's reading aloud, measured and a little belligerent, like its owner has just learned to read and wants—no, demands—to be applauded for it. That narcissism in everything he does.

"Some vestige of humanity—some fragment of our race, wafted thither by these mighty currents we have heard of . . ."

The structure inside is dim and cramped, and Day can make out a ring of upturned faces, wearing dressing gowns, uniforms, a mad assortment of clothing. One has a musk-ox head, slowly decaying, like a hobbyhorse gone terribly wrong. Day knows none of them will have their full complement of fingers.

"Amongst whom there may, at least—be found some of God's elect."

The speaker's eyes, when they meet Day's, are like the Open Polar Sea. They're dead eyes, and there's nothing in them at all.

Captain Jesse Stevens is sitting cross-legged on a carved wooden chair, like a monster crouching on old bones. He has lines on his face now, little grooves where he's scowled too often. The remnants of a bruise pool in one hollow eye socket, and Day wonders what happened to the person who'd dared to strike *one of God's elect*.

"Will. I knew you'd come."

His voice seizes at Day's heart, winds greedy grasping fingers round it. That familiar, self-assured drawl; Day had given up hope of ever hearing it again. He wants to crawl across the stinking floor and embrace Stevens.

He wants to punch him, and keep punching.

He wants to fall apart.

"Your men—"

It comes out as a croak. He's been living in the relative comfort of the *Resolution*, heated cabins and square meals daily, and Stevens has been out here for three lunatic years. But it sounds, awfully, like it's the other way around.

"Your men—" Day says again.

"Did you come to rescue me?"

In the vulpine quirk to Stevens's lips, Day sees killer-whale smiles, men with their tongues cut out. There's a thin shallow laugh from the man in the musk-ox helmet—then the others take it up, too, their shoulders shaking. He remembers what Olive said: men who'd believe a little too much. Fanatics. She wasn't scared of her husband, but she was of them.

Day thinks of Tulloch's wide-open eyes, so terrified the expression might have bubbled off them like steam.

"Well, here we are," Stevens says, and with a grace like nothing Day has seen on this earth, a lissome movement that makes him seem utterly boneless, he launches himself off his throne to kneel in front of Day.

Close up, he's not doing too well. There's a smell about him that Day associates with dying men, and his lips are cracked and bloodless. He puts a single white finger under Day's chin, tilts his face up to eye level. "These are my men, Will. Look at them! The crew of the *Fox*. As you can see, we're still very much alive and well." A secretive smile. "And coming into our own."

Stevens remains so handsome, even if it's rotted, curdled. Day wants so badly to believe him. *Alive and well.* But there's a difference between willful ignorance and outright lies.

"And the rest?"

Stevens shrugs.

There's a strange but familiar atmosphere: a smell seeping out of the timbers. Day's empty stomach turns over.

"We did what we had to. You'd have done the same."

A wheeze—was it laughter?—from the ragged men around them. They all know who he is.

Stevens sits back on his haunches. "We must talk," he says, as if they've simply met in a coffeehouse in London. "It's so good to see you again." He sounds utterly sincere, and his smile makes promises it can't possibly keep.

Day swallows, trying not to *taste* the air of this place.

There's a madness, too, in Stevens's eyes; an emptiness that Day has never before seen so clearly. But still it beckons him. It would be so easy, Day thinks, to follow this mirage, to run his ship aground on these impossible Croker Mountains. This is all he's wanted, for all the long miserable years without Stevens.

A homecoming.

XXIX: THE WHIPPING POST
FORT STEVENS, OCTOBER 28, 1882

WHERE IS THE HOUSE OF THE PRINCE?
AND WHERE ARE THE DWELLING
PLACES OF THE WICKED?

The whipping post is just a little taller than a man, stained and tarry from dried blood.

Day can't stop staring. He imagines himself pressed against it, his back bare to the frozen water, his face turned towards Stevens's mad eyes as he watches, avid, the lash.

Above him, the sky is unbroken, a thousand malevolent stars staring down. Day had been given a place in the sooty longhouse to sleep, strips of musk-ox jerky to eat, and had lain awake listening to the grunting and wheezing of men on the floor below. Outside, in these early hours of morning, the air is cold enough to make his teeth chatter. It's the end of October, he supposes, and back in England they'll be getting ready for All Souls' Day, commemorating the thinness of the line between the living and the dead. It makes him think of pale tea-colored, sightless eyes, and the horrible knowledge they're all still here, waiting.

Sheppard.

But that warm wind doesn't return.

"I see my conscience has finally caught up to me," Stevens remarks, when Day walks out to join him, and the men laugh. Stevens nudges Day with his elbow, sharp as a knife, and Day remembers to join in. The laughter hurts his throat, but the look Stevens gives him is buttery like sunshine, and makes the fine hairs rise up all over his body.

Just like old times, Stevens says quietly. He doesn't need to speak out loud.

They walk together through the rocks and gravel of that frozen shore, Stevens showing off his kingdom—Fort Stevens—with pride. Day sees dead things everywhere. It's typical of his tendency to excess.

The skull on top of the whipping post has been bound back together into a grisly overbite, as if its jaws had opened too wide and snapped back together like a bear trap. But the one at the apex of the longhouse is jawless, as are the three who watch from a ledge in the black cliffs, gleaming whitely in the moonlight. Beside those sentinels, a rocky track winds its way up into the hills, the only way out of this camp other than the lake's maze of rotten ice.

Day fixes this in his mind, although he tries to pretend he's examining the skulls instead. He can't tell whether they're natives or white men. He doesn't think it matters. Has ever mattered.

"Why?"

Stevens stops and looks at him. "Because I could," he says, very simply.

He laughs at the shock on Day's face. "Isn't that what I've always wanted, Will? A place where I could do what I would. A place that would be *mine*."

"My companion. Her name is Qila," Day says, trying to make Stevens see her as a person, someone real, not like the two of them. "What's happened to her?"

"Nothing." Stevens clasps his hands behind his back. "Believe me—I'm not in the business of hurting women. I've never needed to." A smug smile.

Day gives him a skeptical look.

"They won't touch her," Stevens hisses. "We're not like that here." A small hesitation. "Are there any others—with you?" He already knows the answer: there's disappointment on his face. "Pity."

Day thinks of Olive Emeline Stevens, crouching in a tent somewhere, determined and desperate: as perfect a counterpart to Stevens as he had once been himself. But they'd both come to learn pity, and horror.

It must have been a crashing disappointment, when Stevens found nothing up here but rocks and ice, no new tribe of men waiting. So he'd made his own—remade the world, or this small patch of it, in his own image.

Stevens examines Day's face, his ragged clothing. "The things I've had to do."

"I can believe it," Day says honestly.

Stevens shoots him a suspicious half-smile, hungry around the edges. He's fingering the collar of his robe with a fastidious gesture that seems utterly out of place here. He needs an audience. He wants, so badly, to know that Day is on his side.

"You saw her, didn't you? Our old ship."

Day swallows. "She's a wreck," he says carefully.

"Your crew—your ice-master—don't think so, do they?" Stevens says it with a casual diffidence that makes Day shiver. "They're planning to get her under way."

"You already know why I'm here," Day says.

He can't stop himself looking towards the charnel post, sheltered from the elements by that unyielding stone sky. He feels sure he knows which skeleton hangs on it: Thompson. A whaler who'd survived the small boats and their madness, Leviathan, signed up to do anything but whaling. A fresh start. Only to be dragged out of his tent by something far darker.

Canst thou draw out Leviathan with a fish hook. He feels sure Stevens would have drawn answers out of any captive.

The two of them stop walking when the shore peters out. Above, those three skulls are a mute audience. The camp is obscured by the smoldering fire, its soot sucked back into the depths of the cave. Day guesses the smoke will filter through the tunnels and the passageways for a great distance before exhaling with a sigh, making the camp hard for the uninitiated to find.

"What's back there?" Stevens says, very reasonable. "No, I mean it, Will. What's back there for you? Your Admiralty? Let me guess, they . . . buried you, didn't they? Because God forbid a man show a little initiative."

Stevens's face is all angles. His eyes are more sunken than Day remembers, flesh receding, as if it's started to fall off the bones. He's a grinning skull. *Perfected.* Day thinks about all his wild beliefs on evolution, how the north would adapt a soul. He's certainly done his best with the crew of the *Fox.*

"This was about clearing your name, wasn't it? Coming back with the lost Captain Stevens. Coming back a hero this time. Showing you were more than a—disgrace. A monster. Well, *I'm not coming back.* So you have a choice to make."

Day draws his coat tighter around himself.

"I never wanted to be rescued," Stevens says, very low. "Even back then. I couldn't stand it. And now—look at me."

"Look at you," Day echoes.

A laugh. "Sometimes I thought I saw you, you know? Watching me. You looked so disapproving . . . they were right, those armchair explorers, despite everything." The change of subject is jarring. Stevens opens his arms wide, and Day can see that his coat is hanging off him like a dressing gown. "The mistake was in supposing it would be a *new* tribe. An undiscovered people. The truth is far more straightforward. We all have the capacity to become—gods, of a kind."

He nods towards Thompson's corpse. "Don't you think that man spoke his last word thinking that I was a god? When I held the power to release him from his pain? When I could snuff him out like a candle?"

Day's mouth is dry. "That was one of my men."

Stevens shrugs. "And yet he died worshipping *me.* So why should the world down there offer you anything, Will?"

A pause. "I know you've tasted it."

He takes Day's hand. His voice is magnetic. "Here's what we'll do. I already know where to find your depots and supply ship. I'll take as I will. Just tell me where to find my wife—you won't have left her behind, she won't have allowed that." A harsh laugh. "I'll grant anyone who wants it safe passage through my lands. Even Olive—if that's what she wants."

Stevens's eyes gleam a little. He doesn't really expect her to turn him down—how could she, now he's become a king? Day sees the quirk of his lips that speaks of a compressed distaste: for women, for that particular woman, and how her rise had depended on him.

They'll need women at Fort Stevens, if they mean to build their *new world*. Maybe Stevens won't quite have grasped it—won't have thought that far ahead—but Day wagers his men have. He swallows bile. There's a lifetime's worth of horror in it for any women they get their hands on.

"I won't," he says faintly, and Stevens squeezes his hand so hard it grinds his bones. "It's not what you thought."

"I just want a place that's mine," Stevens says with a grin. "Haven't we all been promised that much? Well, I'll take what I can get."

Day shakes his head.

Stevens sighs. "Well then, how about this? You and I—we'll finish what we started. Go back to the *Reckoning*. Find that sea, and whatever lies beyond."

Day swallows. "Is that why you left bodies in her hold?"

Stevens shrugs again. "She's more than a ship, Will. She might already have met the Open Polar Sea. Even fur trappers on the shores of Siberia have their stories of a ghost ship. A ship with three masts, a drowned man at the helm: the windows of her Great Cabin, gleaming with frost."

A chill wind. Behind them, the lights of camp flicker and dance. "All the old men in your Admiralty—all those living-room explorers, urging us to consider the proof of the whale. There's a passage some-where up there, and you know, you saw—it's hardly possible that she left God-Saves Harbor to the south."

Stevens picks up a stone, weighs it in his hand, and tosses it up in the air. "She's the key."

He doesn't look to see where it comes down. Because that isn't the point, is it? This is all irrelevant, whether it's real or whether it's not. Stevens doesn't care where the *Reckoning* goes, where she's been. He'll make a charnel house out of wherever he ends up. Clinging to power by his dirty fingernails.

He grabs Day's shoulder. "Come back with me, Will."

Coming closer, he rests his forehead against Day's own with an audible click. He'd always been obsessed with bones, their measurements telling a man's character. Those three skulls grin down at them, and Day doesn't look towards camp, because he's suddenly terrified of it all, an unreasoning and bone-chilling terror. Madness pervades this place, and if it isn't supernatural, it's no less spiritually unclean.

"I was waiting for you," Stevens whispers, squeezing his shoulder harder, and Day hears the awful part unspoken: *this is all for you.*

The cold is making him dizzy. The greasy smoke spirals up, and the bones glimmer, and the skeleton on its rendering post is a mute accusation, all the things Day has done, the terrible *life* he gave to Jesse Stevens. He could have told the truth, he could always have told the murderous, cannibal truth, and damned both of them. But it never occurred to him to do so. Out of love.

And fear.

"You want us to return to the ship," he says finally.

"Just like old times."

"Who'll be in command?"

Stevens doesn't answer. He's never really had an answer.

The sky flickers. It would be easy, Day thinks. He could say that Stevens made him do it—whatever *it* turned out to be. And he'd live, wouldn't he? He'd be famous. He'd be immortal. Who else could guarantee that much?

The fire spits, and if there's sunrise coming, it's months off.

"It's what he would have wanted," Stevens says, in that smooth honey voice. "He always believed in the Open Polar Sea."

The blood crackles in Day's veins.

It's a mistake to mention Talbot, a terrible mistake, and they're close enough that the sweet rotten-fruit stink of Stevens's breath is—

Orange groves.

Stevens, coming out of Talbot's cabin, slinking away down the corridor in the sudden ghastly silence. The creak of timber and the scream of ice is the sound of a door opening, and Day doesn't want to see what's on the other side.

Day presses himself into the shadows, away from the light.

"His heart has given out," Stevens says in a hushed whisper, the faintest hint of excitement on his breath. The living man is a shabby ghost, a manifestation, something created from nothing. Because now, surely, with Talbot murdered and nowhere to turn, Day will keep his promises.

On the rocks of Fort Stevens, Day shoves him away. He wants to say something, but the words defeat him, and he has to trust his burning, prickling eyes to convey them.

The moonlight glimmers off Stevens's skull-face.

"Pity," he says softly. "I thought you'd *see*."

Day isn't tied up: he supposes this is Stevens being merciful. Or maybe it's Stevens knowing him too well—*I see my conscience has finally found me*—because Qila is nowhere to be seen, and he knows Day won't leave without her.

He listens, heart pounding, for the sound of screams. But there's nothing outside save Stevens's footsteps walking away. Day has been placed in a small flat-roofed construction, hidden away in the darkness before the cavern becomes a tunnel, and echoes are all around him.

Day thinks of his people huddling in a tent. How the Arctic can be so utterly and damningly silent: nothing but the soft hiss of snowfall, the ice creaking quietly in the distance, and your own heart pausing between beats to acknowledge that yes, this is the end.

Sudden hooting laughter echoes around the cave, coming from the longhouse, wild and unrecognizable as the screams of a fox in heat. An answering bone-weariness tells him how unlikely he is to ever leave this place.

The shape at the other end of the prison moves slightly, and Day has to clamp a hand to his mouth to quash his scream. As his eyes adjust to the near-darkness, he can see a mound of blankets moving, very faintly, up and down. Condensation drips down the back wall: the signs of someone breathing in a confined space.

"Hello?" Day whispers, and—knowing he'll scream again if he gets a response—prods the shape with the toe of his boot. "Are you alive?"

No answer.

Day crawls over on his knees and elbows, and the smell is enough to make anyone heave. He's back at Cape Verdant, and Captain Nathaniel is lifting him up, bearing him away from the madness and the destruction. His eyes are calm, a terrible pity. *The custom of the sea.* "You did what you could," Nathaniel says softly, and there's no judgment in it: but Day can see the judgment in his own men's eyes, the judgment to come from the Admiralty, from the press, the public.

He wants to scream: *You don't know what it's like to wield that knife.*

He's never spoken about the hammer, what he did to Campbell, has he.

Day pries off the blanket covering the man's face, and immediately looks away. A death's head mask grins back at him. Skin stretched over bone. Eyes horribly, unnaturally, wide. The man makes a whistling sound, but doesn't seem aware of his surroundings. His arms aren't bound, either—it looks like Stevens and his crew depend on isolation and helplessness.

"I'm here." Day doesn't know who he's saying it to anymore. "I'm here." The man doesn't reply.

Day pulls the sleeping bag down farther, and cringes back.

No surgeon had ever operated with such voracity. Both the man's legs are missing below the knee. It's a marvel he's even partially alive.

Just like Campbell, Day thinks, and he squeezes his eyes shut, relieved, almost relieved, to discover darkness, the terrible darkness of this place.

XXX: NOTHING SACRED

AND THE TENT OF THE WICKED SHALL
BE NO MORE.

D ay is given soup to eat in a bowl so shiny and round it might well be another skull. The man who shoves it through a crack in the door looks at Day warily; at the food, as though he covets it for himself. Day doesn't move, ignoring the growling of his stomach, the painful roiling inside.

"'S hot," his guard says briefly, nudging the bowl with his foot. When Day still doesn't move, he scowls. The message is clear: Day needs food, or he'll be carried off by *debility* as if the last thirteen years have been a dream.

But he doesn't eat.

The bowl takes on a nagging smell over the course of the next day. Sitting there as the sun takes its last peep through the cave entrance, lighting up the ice-sheeted walls, Day wonders, with slow-dawning horror, whether he should try to feed his companion. He looks from the food to that pitiful nest; it's possible the bowl contains the relevant cuts. A man halfway through the dread process of becoming meat.

Eat the world.

The animal-headed men come back much later, mob-handed. The door opens and a wickedly sharp spear is pushed through to skewer at Day, making him cower against the slimy walls. Their laughter is guttural, hoarse, like they've been chewing on stones. A man enters wearing a musk-ox head, its horns gleaming in the light. "Come on, Benny," he says, taking hold of the half-dead man by his spindly arms.

"No—" Day struggles to stand. He manages to dart towards his mute companion. But then there's a pain in Day's shoulder, and a throbbing warm bloom opens up beneath his armpit. He's been stabbed—no, not stabbed, *pricked*, like meat about to be marinated. The sleeping bag peels away in his hands like onion skin. He lets go.

Through the door, Day can see the spear wielder, who's little more than a boy, too young to grow a proper beard. He has the horrified eyes of someone who knows what he's doing. As they lock gazes, Day finds himself sinking to his knees. He questions how long the boy will have to regret his choices. Whether he'll grow up. Whether he'll dream.

The men open the door wider, with a loud grinding sound, to drag Benny out. Day catches a series of confused impressions, each burned into his eyes then replaced by a fresh horror: smoke billowing from a fire that blazes green as emerald mines. Its flames partially obscure the whipping post, which stands like a malevolent finger pointing at the sky.

Men wearing hoods, or animal heads. There's a fox, which makes Day's breath catch, but it's not Stevens: hunched, as if the man inside has been abused too often and now tries to make himself unnoticed. A mangy polar bear, the fur more yellow than white. Only one man remains unmasked, motionless before the fire. His resemblance to humanity makes him hideous, for it's as though someone has boiled all the fat off his face, then scraped and polished the bone.

The door is slammed, and Day is left alone. There's a thin sound, hollow and echoing, disappearing into the bowels of the cave, where the roof comes down in hoarfrost and the tunnel narrows into a mouth. He knows that must be where the butchery takes place. Distantly, he thinks it's interesting that even Stevens keeps it at some distance from the men.

Vanishing footsteps on rock. The crack of a whip.

Day's fellow prisoner is returned at dawn: the dressings are fresh, but Day doesn't dare peel them off to see the extent of the damage. He longs, with white-hot vehemence, for a doctor. He knows it's no good; that would only achieve cleaner and more efficient cuts.

"It's just another source of food," Stevens says, matter-of-fact, when Day eventually gets hungry enough to devour the contents of that bowl, chewing on the stringy fibers, running a grimy finger around the inside to lick up the last smears of fat. His eyes gleam like pirate silver. "We're beyond all those considerations—out here. There's nothing sacred about it, or profane."

"William."

Several more interminable, chilly nights have passed before Day is woken by a quiet insidious scraping.

He lies with his face buried in the rotting blankets, trying to blot it all out, and can't identify the noise, at first, as being anything that could possibly matter. Then he hears it again: the low precursor to the sound of the door's hinges. Someone is opening it with supreme care.

When he lifts his head, he can smell burning. He cringes from the entrance. He'd thought he'd learned the rhythms of Fort Stevens, but the king has clearly changed his mind, and Day is next for the cooking pot.

It makes a gruesome, recursive sort of sense: Stevens has been inside him for years, along with those less fortunate. Now it's his turn.

Day thinks about Sheppard's voice, waking him with its accents of sunshine.

He turns, with renewed hope—

It's Qila at the door, her eyes bottomless in the dark. "Are you hurt?" she whispers. He shakes his head.

When she comes closer, he catches hold of her wrists to examine her face, staring into it as if he's never seen another living human being. To her credit, she only flinches a little. "We have to go," she says. "Quickly." She has her knife in her hand; he's never been so grateful to see a blade. Its presence tells him they—unbelievably—didn't search her. She was left fully clothed and unmolested. Stevens was as good as his word. Day doesn't dare to think it means his other promises will hold water. Stevens is fickle as the wind.

The smell of burning is getting stronger.

"Are they outside?"

She pulls him to standing. "You have to leave him."

It takes Day longer than it should to appreciate that she's talking about the half-eaten man, Benny, huddled in the dark. He wants to hesitate, wants to be the sort of person who hesitates, but he doesn't.

Outside, there's a breeze blowing in across the lake, and white fog billows around their legs. They sidle around the cave wall farthest from the longhouse; Day can see something blocking its door.

"It's going to clear soon." Qila turns her face to the fog. "We need to get out of here. Split up. It'll be harder for them to follow."

Day realizes he can still smell burning.

"I won't let him have this place," she hisses.

There's a moment in which Day thinks about all the other men at Fort Stevens, some more or less innocent. Then he lets them go.

"It's not *his*."

Burn it to the ground, he says to her with a single nod. Put an end to the reign of Jesse Stevens, the Cannibal King. For a moment, the darkness of the cave makes him think of a ghost ship, bearing away, as if they've all just been dragged along in its wake.

"We need to go!" Qila shoves him, gently, towards the shore path. She's out onto the ice of the lake before he can say anything, although he doesn't know whether it would be thanks or a warning or an apology.

Day stumbles. His feet drag after days of disuse, and his toes are numb. It's bitterly cold. He reaches the crack where the three skulls look down. Starts to climb.

The route into the hills is less obvious than it had seemed from the shore, and sometimes he has to double back towards the cave. Someone shouts in the distance, high-pitched and furious, and Day flattens himself against the rocks, gasping for breath. He's very weak. The soup had been delicious, made with care and skill and human flesh, and he could have—should have—eaten much more of it.

As he gets higher, he can see the glittering blue-gray of the lake. There's a blur of movement that could be a girl running, or it could be just a swirl of smoke, a half-starved fox. Day doesn't have much hope he'll see any of the others again. Finding anyone out here takes skill and care, and impossible luck; he isn't Lars, isn't Stevens, or his lieutenants, or *anyone*.

The most he can hope for is that his end will be quick, when it comes.

He has to stop and rest, because he's losing the ability to balance. He clutches at the cliff face with filthy mittens, noting the little spade-shaped leaves growing from the cracks. He muses over whether they're edible.

Something insinuates itself out of the shadows behind him. Beneath, sparks fly, little pinpricks of light on the breeze.

"I thought you'd be back," Day says wearily.

A rush of cold air. He's taken to the ground with one hard *thump*, pinned to the rocks like a moth in the killing jar. Stevens smells of smoke and greasy meat. He clamps his hand over Day's mouth, and it's like the dressings on that half-dead man, sweet and unwholesome. Day retches against Stevens's bony fingers, feeling them about to wind their way between his desperate lips.

"We could have been—captains—together," Stevens snarls. The spittle flecking Day's face turns immediately to frost, and he knows this is no ghost. "Isn't that what you wanted?"

The fog is starting to clear. There's blue light in the sky across the hills; they're now too late in the year for true dawn. A hungrier, restless light flickers from the mouth of the cave; there's nothing that burns quite like an old sailing ship. Day thinks of Arctic foxes, changing their pelts to match the seasons.

Stevens shakes him. "Look at what you've *done*. I thought I was being merciful!"

Day realizes he's laughing, thin and quiet, shoulders heaving, because there's no quality to Stevens's mercy. And he'd only been left unbound and unguarded because Stevens had thought, after everything, *There's no way he's leaving me.*

His head is slammed back against the rocks; the base of his skull rings like a bell. A shrill scream comes from beneath them. Day scrapes his cheek across the ground to watch something pacing along the shore, limbs working steadily, trailing fire. From this angle, the man looks headless. But the screaming keeps coming, long and wavering, so he must still have a mouth—if not the need to draw breath.

Stevens punches him in the face again. Day moans, shocked at the sound of it.

"All of it—I was sure you'd want all of it. Back at Camp Hope—you wanted to live, didn't you? You wanted to survive, didn't you?"

Day scrabbles backwards on the rocks. The path they're on is no more than an indentation a few feet wide: the shore looms perilously below. For there to be a path at all, he thinks, Stevens must have been there for some time. He wipes his mouth, thinking of Stevens hefting that rifle, *Sheppard's* rifle, when he'd first been handed it; nodding as if things were finally falling into place.

"Why did you stay?" he asks.

An intake of breath. An opening. Day manages to struggle to his feet—spits, like a sailor—and takes two dragging steps away from Stevens and his burning camp. He won't show Stevens his back; that's how he gets you.

"I don't know," Stevens says wildly. "I don't know, I—"

Day's boots stutter, and Stevens lashes out an arm, fingers grasping, as if he's trying to stop him from—leaving? Falling?

"I stayed for you!"

Stevens's voice breaks, and he uses his free hand to scrub at his mouth, as if he wants to erase every single trace of weakness.

Once, Day would have clutched at this admission; would have made it his reason for everything. But if Stevens had loved him in return, it was the sort of love you give a dog.

He's not your friend, Valle had said. And he'd been right. For a moment, Day imagines that things had gone differently. That it had been Sheppard in his cabin, Sheppard to take him aside when Talbot was dying. Sheppard at his shoulder throughout.

That he'd never kept the company of monsters.

The next blow comes out of nowhere, and Day goes down on hands and knees. Something pops, and the pain in his hip bone makes him howl.

I'm just buying time, Day realizes, straining to look for the darting black shape of a girl running, sure-footed, through the labyrinth. He doesn't try to block the next blow, and it might have knocked him unconscious for a few moments, because when Day opens his puffy eyes again, raises his ringing head, Stevens is already speaking—

"Campbell, though—that wasn't me, was it? Tell yourself I'm a monster. But you were no better. Worse, because you believed it was wrong—all those high principles, noble ideas, and *you did it anyway*. You people—you're all the same. Hypocrites."

Stevens places a bony knee on his chest, and shakes Day like a dog shaking a bone. The ringing in Day's head threatens to white out and take him over.

"If Nathaniel hadn't come—"

Day chokes, a sound somewhere between a laugh and a wail. He's spent long enough thinking about it—telling himself he's never, *ever*, thought about it, those days that would have come after the end.

He knows the iconography. Casting lots, the bundle of sticks in a fist, one shorter than the others. Everyone should take a fair chance at being prey. That's how it should be done. Casting lots to be put on the fire, and none of the stories that make it back ever speak of those who were chosen and then *fought*: those who'd lost their nerve and had to be dragged to their deaths. The narrative of polar exploration is one of noble privation; they always leave out the pitiful desperation. How far you'll go to survive.

Day had wanted to live. He can't be blamed for that, he thinks. He'd wanted to live, and he'd loved, and despite the consequences, that had just made him *human.*

Day opens his mouth, but a rock is smashed against the side of his skull. White-hot. He rolls over onto his front, trying to crawl away, teetering on the narrow path like it's the boundary between heaven and hell—

Because he'd just gone down the sick list, hadn't he. Campbell first. Paver was next in line. Then Ewing, if they'd all lived that long. Good people, the righteous, had the luxury of casting lots, knowing they'd be exonerated for doing so. But Day had known that killing the strong to feed the sick would be a waste.

He'd chosen, and spared himself. And that's what made him every inch the monster people thought he was.

He refuses to be shamed for it.

"The only thing that makes sense," Stevens says, dispassionate, as if they're standing side by side on the *Reckoning*, "is that the strong survive. And the weak are to be pitied." He hefts that rock again, clearly liking the feel of it.

Day thinks Qila must be across the lake by now. It's enough.

He struggles up, sees a blur of movement, then there's a thud as Stevens's boot disappears into his ribs. He doubles over again, pressing his hands to his side, the pain going off like jagged fireworks. Stumbles to within an inch of the precipice. Rocks stare up at him, the harsh misty ground of Cape Verdant as seen from the grave-ridge. Breathing is agonizing. When he coughs, the blood comes red and stark and goes over the edge like the first patters of spring rain.

"Poor soul," Stevens says, looking down at him. "You've never been a match for me."

Day, though, has heard this before. And Stevens has come out to meet him alone, and unarmed: the sort of operatic hubris he lives by.

Day smiles through his gore-streaked teeth. That anger, that *righteous* anger, is a weapon in his hands at last. Sizzling. Warming. Strengthening. All the things that had been done to him by this man.

His one true friend.

Day's knees buckle as the fury pushes him up. He staggers a little at the top, vision going white for a moment, smoke filling his nostrils and mouth. He thinks he can taste human flesh. Hunger. *Anger.*

Stevens, single-minded as ever, hasn't noticed how close to the edge they really are. "Come on, then," he says, a grimace on his death's-head face. Day can't imagine finding him attractive, even for a moment.

When Stevens lunges, Day grabs him by the neck and holds him tight, tight, two skeletons locked together in a bony embrace. Stevens *hisses* at him, spits, tries to pull free, but Day has been here before: he's fought off Stevens almost every night. The struggle is silent save their grunting, splintered breaths.

They're more evenly matched than Stevens thinks.

Stevens's eyes are hollow. "I did it for you," he says, and there's nothing honeyed about his voice anymore. "I did it all for you—"

Day makes a noise like a wounded animal. Lets go, the rage stuttering and fizzling out for an instant, just enough for Stevens to pull free.

Day doesn't want it. He doesn't want any of it.

But then, inside Day: a slow true dawn. Not violent joy; not shame. It comes into his heart like a flower blooming, up here where there are none.

William.

Day clenches his fists. Stevens straightens up, gets out his knife at last. Day's ribs are a stabbing pain, every breath a wheeze. Maybe his lungs are already punctured, filling up. Maybe he's already drowning, here in the open air.

Stevens raises the knife, but Day won't go gently, and they're close enough to the edge that a little momentum will push them both over, clasped together like lovers.

"Come on, then," Day says, "you won't do for me as easily as you did for *him.*"

Stevens's eyes narrow at the mention of Sheppard.

Day feels, rather than sees, something moving behind the sky. The fog has all burned away, and the twilight is pale eggshell blue, the sort of blankness that entices the eye to pick out movement, shapes, looking for a way to make sense of it. The flutter of sails. Wings unfurling, beating, taking flight. The scribble of pencil on paper.

"You're all the same," Stevens says, distracted, and Day knows exactly what he means. Idealists. Good men. Anyone not adhering to the rule of Stevens, and the knife.

In his mind's eye, Sheppard, standing out on shore in a spring squall, laughs as Day struggles with Valle's fishing net and specimen bucket, the sun shimmering off his wet skin, lining his long eyelashes. They'd both been so young. Hair whips into Sheppard's face.

He beckons to Day, *come closer.*

Stevens turns.

He looks at something over Day's shoulder. His lips pull back, white, bloodless. The knife shakes.

"Who's that behind you?"

His voice is strained. There's shouting in the camp below, a bell ringing, the sound so clear and sharp it hurts Day's ears—

A split-second decision. The scent, distant and faint, of summer sun.

Day pushes.

Stevens goes quickly. He'd always been too near the edge. He doesn't even cry out, lips clamped together on the way down. A giddy moment of free fall before he hits the ground like a stone. He coughs. He twitches once, twice, convulsing like a man with lockjaw.

He goes still, and Day feels something inside himself *snap.*

Jesse Stevens is a crumpled shape lying on the shore of his own camp, gritty smoke drifting from the burning cave. Three skulls look down at him like a jawless jury.

The men look up to where Day is crouched on the edge, his hands balled into fists, his breath coming in wet-sounding gasps. He knows his ribs are broken. He'll have to crawl.

The men look up. Day doesn't know what they see. But there's an expression of reverence on some of those faces, under shaggy animal-head masks, in ravening orange light, as the fire *consumes*. He feels warm breath on the back of his neck, as if something man-sized—or bigger—crouches behind him. A sweetness that could be flowers or blood. An exhalation.

Day doesn't look around. He won't look back.

"Are you a man or a god?" someone shouts, voice hoarse from underuse.

XXXI: THE PROOF OF THE WHALE
THE *LOUISA*, NOVEMBER 24, 1882

WILL HE MAKE MANY SUPPLICATIONS UNTO THEE? OR WILL HE SPEAK SOFT WORDS UNTO THEE? WILL HE MAKE A COVENANT WITH THEE?

ike any group, they were divided into those who fitted in . . . and those who didn't."

Qila stood very straight, like a sentinel. Her own ragged clothes had been replaced, and her shiny-buttoned whaler's waistcoat gave her the look of a young sailor on his first expedition. Smart and fresh. You could give her any command, Day thought.

"Those who were close to Stevens, they were the ones inside the long-house. The ones granted a place by the throne. The ones who took guard duty, who went hunting. They wore animal heads. Musk oxen. Foxes. Anything they could find that was native to the Arctic." Her lip curled.

"They ate well, if they proved their worth, and didn't raise objections to the methods. One lieutenant called himself Symmes, and his love of the knife was notorious. These were the people trapped in the burning building."

The lantern light glimmered in the cabin windows. Day could almost hear, again, the screams.

"*I don't see why we have to listen,*" a voice hissed from the corner of the room.

"But the others," Qila continued, "those on the outside. They weren't really expected to live. They were chained—he couldn't afford any more deserters. And when the camp burned, those men managed to escape."

"Except for the one held with me," Day said quietly. "His name was Ben. Benjamin Carlisle. He wouldn't have made it out. I never learned what he did wrong."

Qila nodded, the anger flickering in her eyes like the embers of Fort Stevens. The Cannibal King had tried to build a new world, replicated all the cruelty of the old one, and done it somewhere that wasn't his to begin with.

"When the outsiders saw what was happening, they turned on the rest. Scores were settled."

Captain Nathaniel's dark skin gleamed as he steepled his long, capable fingers. There was a bitter *huff* of frustration and hurt pride from elsewhere in the captain's cabin.

"Stevens wasn't moving. The fight went out of his lieutenants, all except Symmes. He'd been set upon by some of the outsiders, and crawled out onto the frozen lake. He was injured, left a trail of blood behind that was easy to follow. But he went off the marked paths, lost his pursuers, and—disappeared. I searched for him for hours, and the ice was solid, unbroken. I gave up at nightfall, and never found his body. But the others sat down. Allowed themselves to be taken prisoner."

The account put Qila far from camp during the time that some of the worst acts of score-settling had taken place: the clean knife-wounds on some of the bodies were obviously attributable to those *outsiders*.

"By the time Karl arrived—the rest of your men—it was long over."

Day could see, in his mind's eye, the way the whipping and rendering post had been scorched, burned clean and black, erasing the bloodstains, crumbling the skeletons into nothingness. Destroying the evidence. An empire had fallen in a matter of hours, and Avery hadn't lived to see any of it. A flutter in Day's chest.

Who would report, now, what awful reign had prevailed?

Nathaniel folded his arms. Sat back in his chair. Qila gave him a nod that was almost a salute; Day expected to see her click her heels together. A look passed between them, from the black whaling captain to the Native girl, and Day could almost hear the subliminal *hiss* of displeasure from the cabin's other occupant.

The *Louisa* wasn't a large ship, and seemed almost unbearably gaudy to Day's dark-accustomed eyes. Her timbers were bleached gold, the walls decorated with embroidered Bible verses. Everyone knew that Nathaniel stitched them himself in the long winters-over, holding a pair of needlework scissors between pursed lips. None of the scripture, Day was glad to see, came from the book of Job.

"The men now in your mess—they were the ones who helped us restore control," Day said. "To keep it together until your men arrived. Those of lesser culpability."

But it was honestly hard to tell what that meant, measured against three years in the Arctic. One of Symmes's cronies had approached Day with cringing, fawning step: "We thought you was dead, Captain Day!"

Nathaniel nodded slowly. "The others will stay where they are." In the ship's hastily constructed brig, a compartment so cramped the men had to crouch. Some had held on to their musk-oxen masks, and it looked like an ark down there. Stank like one.

Nathaniel's eyes searched Day's face. "God, man. You know you look like hell."

Day swallowed.

We thought you was dead an' he was speaking to your ghost—

"Will."

A sigh.

"Will, are you going to let her *lie* about me like this?"

The other member of their party sat a little distance apart, on the couch; he needed the space for his splinted legs. His eyes were narrowed, the lines around them like spiders.

"You should have *left* me," hissed Jesse Stevens.

Then, addressing Nathaniel: "There's no time to waste. We can make it back up there before the winter sets in for good. Give me my men."

Day said: "Your legs are broken."

Stevens shook his head wildly, lips pressed so thin and tight Day might have counted his teeth—still white, still perfect—behind them. "You don't know what you've done."

He pulled himself up to standing, bracing himself against the table, giving Qila a dismissive look when she wouldn't move out of his way. The *Louisa* was trapped in the ice, frozen in like a stone, and although Stevens could balance well enough, Day could see that this show of strength was costing him.

"And you'll find I have powerful friends. You could be well rewarded. You'd have found the lost Captain Stevens. Offered him aid and assistance. Allowed him to prosecute his mission—"

"You should be the one *prosecuted*," Day snapped.

Sitting on Nathaniel's desk was the fat leather-bound wad of paper making up Avery's evidence. The sight of it made Day shut his eyes briefly.

This one will live, he'd once hoped. *This one will make it out.*

"Oh, Will," Stevens said with a sigh. He gave Nathaniel an apologetic look, as if to say, *I don't know how you put up with this.* "Look, there'll be plenty of time to point fingers later. And that girl doesn't know what she saw—"

"He's dangerous," Day said to Nathaniel.

"He's delusional," Stevens retorted. "He's always had it in for me . . ." He sank back onto the couch, as if suddenly overcome. "He tried to kill me!"

"Stop," Nathaniel said, very low, his hand on Avery's notebook. The captain of the *Louisa* wasn't a slow reader.

And there was a smile—just the hint of one—dawning on Qila's lips.

"I do remember you, Jesse Stevens. Last time. You were alone. You had some . . . story about what had happened to your companions. I think it suited you very much to be the last one left alive."

Nathaniel turned to Day. "He was howling like a damn animal. Screaming. Had to be restrained to be brought aboard. He nearly killed two of my crew. We persuaded him he could only make the open sea with men, and with ships. That seemed to calm him a while."

Day could picture it: the screaming emptiness. The howling of Stevens thwarted. Even now, with both legs broken, his animal energy was too big for this room. "You should have *left* me!" he was shouting, gripping the back of the couch with clawed and bony hands.

The door flew open.

"Confine him," Nathaniel said briefly. To Day and Qila: "We'll need to keep him separate. Something tells me he needs to be put where he can't speak to anyone."

Stevens struggled against the whalers. Flailing his stick-thin arms around, he was shouting about the Navy and Congress and his reputation with the press. He could lead them to the Open Polar Sea. He could give them the Arctic's famous ghost ship. *Such marvels.*

He spat at Day from the door. "You don't know what you've given up!"

Day, though, thought he did.

And if there was anyone who didn't deserve an easy death—who deserved to be *destroyed*—it was Stevens.

Then, from the corridor: "Oh, thank heavens! You poor woman! My wife! My beloved wife!"

Time was like treacle. Day staggered from the table to the open door, the smell of the clean cold air spilling over him like perfume. He could see over Stevens's bony shoulder, the world from his perspective: all furious shouting and struggle, gnashing teeth, golden hair. And the unveiled face of Olive Emeline Stevens, as she raised a gloved hand to smack her husband straight across the jaw.

Stevens's lips finally started to bleed.

EPILOGUE

*T*he *Louisa* had taken Stevens back to America with the remaining members of his crew. Those fingerless men. It had been a loyalty test: the midpoint of a process that had begun in Olive's candlelit salons, men believing themselves chosen for a great destiny in the north—the seekers after a new tribe, a new *world*—and ended with those same men chained in a cave, no ship, no supplies but those they killed or kidnapped themselves. Stevens had required them to give up their trigger fingers, so he could know they weren't plotting against him. It was the way his mind worked.

But he'd also run several purges, inquisitions, even after the unnecessary surgeries had been performed, and the men who'd eventually crawled out of Fort Stevens were those who'd been too evil or cunning or stupid to fall under suspicion. Day found he could lead them quite easily.

The only other person to have seen that madness in full swing was Qila.

She had departed the *Louisa* to head towards Cape York and her own distant people. *Arctic Highlanders.* He remembered how her eyes had shone on deck, the wind plucking at her hair: they'd been the first—and only—ship to give her a chance to escape the trap that Godhavn had become. As Valle had once predicted, she'd abandoned the white men, and all their agendas, to find a place for herself in the frozen north.

It's not his.

Day thought the doctor might have been sourly glad to be proven right.

Perhaps Qila had unwarranted faith in how believable the public might find Captain *Eat-Em-Fresh,* when he spoke of the reign of the Cannibal King. But Day wasn't one of those who kidnapped his own guides; he didn't begrudge her freedom, so doggedly won, and Stevens's famous wife would have to do her best alone.

Needs must. What would come out would inevitably be enough to damn Jesse Stevens; enough to damn both of them.

Day was very tired of waiting for the past to catch up to him.

He crossed and uncrossed his legs. His boot heels sounded hollow on civilization's polished wooden floor, and a small shiver passed over him. On the *Louisa,* the insistent tapping had dogged their nights, coming from everywhere at once. Leaving his cabin, heart pounding, had revealed to him the women floating in the darkness like a mad gothic fantasy, hair loose, holding up lanterns—knives—to track it down to the hold, where Stevens and Peters were held at separate ends.

Tap tap tap.

It wasn't the pipes echoing, or the timbers expanding. They were speaking, communicating somehow. Transmission. *Knock once for yes.*

But what was Day meant to do—cut off their hands?

———————

The Admiralty remained a hall of mirrors: ornate golden frames, swirling gleaming timbers like sunset sea in storm. A green door. A ticking grandfather clock. Beside it, a tall unsmiling marine captain was watching Day like a hawk, in case he chose to get up and make a run for it. He wasn't yet formally under arrest. He wasn't yet detained. But he was under no illusions about where he stood.

Across the glimmering hall, Lady Franklin stared down at him. She'd refused to be painted in black, because she'd refused to believe her husband was dead. It was the kind of stubbornness Day had once admired. He wondered whether she'd come to resent Franklin—for making her entire life, whatever she did, so inevitably and completely about him.

"They can't judge us," Peters whispered.

Peters had been dressed in his best uniform, but his attendants hadn't replaced those round clerk's glasses; his fists, in their cuffs, were clenched so tight that Day could see bone through bloodless knuckles.

"They can't *judge* us." Peters swallowed. The restraint collar, affixed around his neck like a leather moon, hid the bobbing of his throat.

Day supposed Peters was right: the judgment of others was only ever half the story.

On the other side, Carter looked ready to tackle Peters to the floor, ready for any excuse to knock him senseless: his forearm, under his own pressed uniform, was scored with bite marks. He met Day's eye, raised an eyebrow as if to say, *Can you believe what I've had to put up with?* and cracked a wan but warm smile.

Day found he liked Carter, this new Carter, very much.

They both glanced at that green door. Hopkins was out, someone else was in: the machinery of naval politics had ground on without them, and without his precious ship. Nathaniel had sent a search party in spring, more men and more weapons than necessary: "A spooked dog snaps," he'd said flatly to Day by way of explanation. But only the lonely spars of the *Resolution* remained. The *Reckoning* had vanished, and so had all the whalers.

Roderick had been good, a good man.

But even a good man couldn't stop the rot when it came to it.

Day knotted his fingers, cracked his knuckles. From behind the door, raised voices spilled out from time to time, and there were hurried footsteps, whispers, in the hall behind them. People listening. The sound of scandal. All this was familiar.

A chill crept through the corridor, making Day shiver, as if he was back in the Arctic. He'd spent a long time reliving the events on that cliff. *Who's that behind you?*

At first, he'd thought it was another dark double: a serpent devouring itself, the mirrors endlessly repeating, Day who created Stevens who created Day. Ouroboros.

Eat the world.

But then, with a knowledge that both warmed and burned, he'd known: what he carried inside him, that *haunting*, had just taken another form.

Sheppard.

————

"They can't judge us," Peters muttered again. It sounded like he was trying to convince himself.

"Quiet." Day knew how these things went. There'd be time to protest innocence soon enough.

A creak of floorboards. Was it Day's imagination, or did the marine captain look up—shoot an uneasy glance at thin air?

Quiet, Day said, with a sigh.

Stevens was pacing up and down, tapping his newly sharpened knife against one lean and muscular thigh. His boots were black as the night sky, no possibility of stars. His long hair was swept back into a neat knot, and he seemed to have picked up some sort of fur cape from the *Louisa*; had thrown it casually over his shoulders, as though he'd just come in from somewhere very cold.

He's right, you know.

Stevens stopped in front of Peters, and crouched on the squeaky floorboards to adjust his wide immobilizing madhouse collar. *Pity*, he remarked. *This one had promise.*

Peters shivered. Day knew the sensation well: like someone was walking over his grave. Perhaps one day, a long time from now, Peters might wake to hear Lee crawling up the walls of his asylum.

And back at Cape Verdant, without a proper grave, fragments of Sheppard's body might be becoming one with the black frozen soil, winding down to take root, still *there*. Part deliquesced into the elements, but still—perhaps—conscious. Part devoured, inside those unlucky survivors, anyone who had partaken in the sacrament. Chewed and digested and assimilated, he might be crawling on, even now.

An afterlife more terrible than could be possibly imagined.

Sheppard might one day slide his fingers up Day's throat to strangle him, now Day was no longer a tool for his vengeance. Day could hardly blame him.

We've got a long way to go, you and I.

Day had had a lifetime with Jesse Stevens, and it didn't surprise him that there was more to come.

He hoped Talbot was walking in orange groves.

He sighed. "Do you think it'll be much longer?" he said to the man in uniform. "We've been waiting a very long time."

ACKNOWLEDGMENTS

To everyone who asked me about the difficult second novel: yes, it was difficult.

Thank you to my agent, Oli Munson, for his immense patience and good humor. In an act of spectacular hubris, I took a print-out of my "second novel" along to our first meeting in 2020. Needless to say, this is not that novel. Not even close.

Thank you to my fabulous editor, Lara Jones, for your encouragement with this project (and for tolerating my constant DMing of memes captioned "William Day"): without your enthusiasm, I'd be lost. My thanks also go out to the entire team at Emily Bestler Books and Atria Books, particularly Chelsea McGuckin for the spectacular cover, Erika R. Genova for the gruesome interior design, and all the copyeditors and proofreaders who constantly have my back.

The support of other writers has played a huge part in keeping me sane this time around; very special thanks go to Emilia Hart and Lizzie Pook, talented novelists and amazing friends, for the Second Book Support Group (aka Ship Book Chat), many glasses of wine, and frequent howling.

As ever, I'm incredibly grateful to Sophie Wing and Lucy Apps for their beta reading and belief. Sophie, I hope Olive Emeline lives up to your expectations. Lucy, thank you for helping me, each time, with whatever medical terrors my characters face.

The brilliant Alix Penn from Casting Lots podcast (the only survival cannibalism podcast around) was kind enough to take an early look at the manuscript—thank you! They do, indeed, do the thing.

Immeasurable thanks also go to Kirstine Moller, my thoughtful sensitivity reader, for stepping up to assist with my portrayal of Qila.

To Robert Walton, literature's saddest, loneliest, and gayest Arctic explorer: I first met you when reading Mary Shelley's *Frankenstein* for English A Level, and have been obsessed ever since. I know you'd like William Day.

It's hard to write in a vacuum, and—when wrestling with séances and sawed bones—I was constantly blown away by the levels of support and affection shown to my first book. To the horror lit community, to the queer lit community, to every blurber, reviewer, podcaster, and bookseller: thank you.

Alex, you've been there every step of the way, with prosecco as needed. I couldn't ask for more.

My parents: thank you for never, ever, asking when I'm going to go back to a real job.

AUTHOR'S NOTE

here the Dead Wait, like my first novel, takes place in an imagined timeline of polar exploration. I have bent Arctic geography to create Talbot's Channel and its environs, which occupy a space roughly equivalent to Wellington Channel. I have also taken liberties, in the name of storytelling, with various naval hierarchies and protocols.

In the winter of 1850, while searching for Franklin's ill-fated expedition, Elisha Kent Kane was trapped aboard an ice-bound ship drifting in the region of Lancaster Sound. One popular theory of the time was that there was an open sea at the Pole, vulnerable to being penetrated by a lucky few. On his return from the Arctic, Kane reputedly embarked on a secret affair with Margaret Fox, of the famous Fox sisters—America's first "spirit rappers," who wielded unprecedented female power and spiritual authority. *Where the Dead Wait* is not about either of these people, but their stories provided the grit for the oyster, so to speak.

Survival cannibalism, on the other hand, has a long and storied history in Arctic exploration.

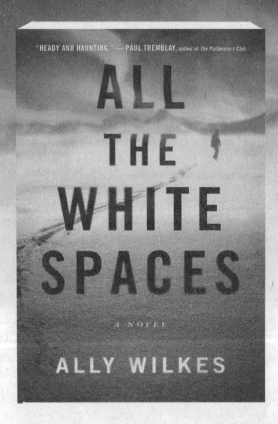